CRAIG RUSSELL

The Valkyrie Song

arrow books

Published by Arrow 2010

2 4 6 8 10 9 7 5 3 1

First published in Great Britain in 2008 by
Hutchinson
Random House, 20 Vauxhall Bridge Road,
London SW1V 2SA

www.rbooks.co.uk

Addresses for companies within The Random House Group Limited can be found at:
www.randomhouse.co.uk/offices.htm

The Random House Group Limited Reg. No. 954009

A CIP catalogue record for this book
is available from the British Library

ISBN 9780099522652
ISBN 9780099547945 (Export)

The Random House Group Limited supports The Forest Stewardship
Council (FSC), the leading international forest certification organisation. All our
titles that are printed on Greenpeace approved FSC certified paper carry the FSC logo.
Our paper procurement policy can be found at www.rbooks.co.uk/environment

Typeset by Palimpsest Book Production Limited,
Grangemouth, Stirlingshire
Printed and bound in Great Britain by CPI Bookmarque Ltd, Croydon, CR0 4TD

For Wendy

The heavens are stained with the blood of men,
As the Valkyries sing their song

Njál's Saga

The lots of life and death were distributed by the Valkyries, the handmaidens of Odin in the warrior hall of Valhalla.

It was the Valkyries, their terrible war cries filling the heavens, who swept across the battle-field, gathering up the souls of those to whom they had allocated death.

In Old Norse, *Valkyrja* means *chooser of the slain*.

Prologue

i.

Mecklenburg
1995

Sisters, she thought, are reflections of each other.

Ute sat and watched herself in younger reflection: Margarethe. Margarethe looked weary. And sad. It hurt Ute to see her like that: when they had been small, it had been as if the energy had been divided unequally between them – Margarethe had always been the livelier, cleverer, prettier sister. It also hurt Ute to see her sister in a place like this.

'Do you remember,' said Margarethe, gazing at the blue-tinged window glass, 'when we were little? Do you remember we went to the beach and looked out across the Schaalsee and you said that one day we would sail away across it? To the other part of Germany – or to Denmark or Sweden – and you told me that it wasn't allowed? Do you remember how angry I got?'

'Yes, Margarethe, I remember.'

'Can I tell you a secret, Ute?'

'Of course you can, Margarethe. That's what sisters are for. Just like when we were little. We always told each other secrets back then. At night, with the lights out; when it was safe to whisper, and Mamma and Papa couldn't hear us. You tell me your secret now.'

They sat at a table near the window, which looked out over the gardens. It was a bright, sunny day and the flower beds were in full bloom, but the view was tinged slightly cobalt blue by the thick glass of the window. It must be because it's special glass, thought Ute. The kind you can't break. At least it was better than looking through bars.

Margarethe eyed the other patients, visitors and staff suspiciously. She shut them out again, confining her universe to herself, her sister and the blue-tinged view. She leaned forward conspiratorially to speak to Ute. In that moment she became again the pretty little girl she had once been. The very pretty girl she had once been.

'It's a terrible secret.'

'We all have those,' said Ute and rested her hand on her sister's.

'It will take me a long time to tell you. Lots of visits. I've not told anyone but I have to tell someone now. Will you come back to see me and hear my story?'

'Of course I will.' Ute smiled sadly.

'You remember when they took Mamma and Papa away? Do you remember how we were split up and sent to different state care homes?'

'You know I do. How could I forget. But let's not talk about such things now . . .'

'They sent me to a special place, Ute.' Margarethe's voice was lowered now to a breathy whisper. 'They said I was different. That I was special. That I could do things for them that other girls couldn't. They told me I could become a hero. They taught me things. Terrible things. So bad that I've never told you about them. Never. That's why I'm here. That's what's wrong with me. All of these scary, horrible things in my head . . .' She frowned as if the weight of what was in her mind pained her. 'I wouldn't be in here now if I hadn't been taught to do such terrible things.'

'What things, Margarethe?'

'I'll tell you. I'll tell you now. But you have to promise me that after I tell you, you will make things right for me.'

'I promise, Margarethe. You're my sister. I promise I'll make things right.'

ii.

Hamburg
January 2008

She was waiting for him.

She had tracked him from the moment he first came into view on Erichstrasse, opposite the erotic museum. He was coming towards her but could not yet see her. She backed into the darkness of the small cobbled square. This was where it would be. The square had no light other than that which leached in from the streets at either end, and was shadowed further by the two naked-branched trees that erupted from the unpaved disc of earth at its centre.

She was waiting for him.

As he approached she recognised his face. She had never met him, never seen him in the flesh, but she recognised him. His was a face from beyond the real world. A face she knew from the television, from the press, from posters in shop windows. A familiar face, but familiar from a parallel universe.

She hesitated for a moment. Because of who he was, there would be others. Attendants. Bodyguards. She stepped back into the shadows. But as he drew closer she saw that he was truly alone. He hadn't seen her until he was almost upon her and she stepped out of the shadow.

'Hello,' she said in English. 'I know you.'

He stopped, startled for a moment. Unsure. Then he said: 'Sure you know me. Everybody knows me. You came here for me?'

She held open her coat and exposed her nakedness beneath

and his face broke into a grin. She looped her arm around him and drew him into the shadows. He placed his hands on her, inside the coat, her skin hot and soft in the cold winter night. Her breath too was hot as she put her mouth to his ear.

'I came here for you . . .' she said.

'I didn't come here for this,' he said, breathless, but he allowed himself to be pulled into the darkness.

'And I didn't come for your autograph . . .' Her hand slid down his belly and found him.

'How much?' he asked, his voice quiet but tight with excitement.

'How much?' She drew back, looked into his eyes and smiled. 'Why, honey, this is for free. This will stay with you for ever and you get it for nothing.'

She held his gaze but her hands moved fast and expertly. He felt his belt being loosened, his shirt being eased up; the cold night on naked skin.

He fell to the ground.

The cobbles were wet and cold beneath him and he gave a small startled laugh at his own clumsiness. He was slumped against the brick wall behind him, his legs splayed wide. Why had he fallen down? His legs felt as if they didn't belong to him and he stared at them, wondering why they had simply given way under him. Then he gazed up at her: she stood astride him and the fire in her eyes terrified him. He vomited without warning, without first feeling sick. A sudden, bone-penetrating chill spread through his body. He looked at the vomit that covered his chest and the cobbles around him. It glistened black-red in the dim light.

He looked up at her again, as if she could explain why he had fallen; why there was so much blood. Then he saw it: the sliver of steel that glinted in her gloved hand. He felt something warm and wet inside his clothes. His trembling fingers found his shirt front and he tore at it, buttons flying into the dark and bouncing off the cobbles. His belly was split and something bulged from the wound, grey and glistening and wet, red-streaked in the half-light. Steam fumed from his rent belly and into the winter night. Blood surged rhythmically from the wound, keeping time with the pounding of his pulse in his ears. He felt cold. And sleepy.

The woman leaned down and used the shoulder of his expensive coat to wipe his blood from the blade. Then, with the same expert speed and precision with which she had stabbed him, she went through his pockets. After she took his diary, wallet and cellphone, she leaned towards him again, and he once more felt the heat of her breath in his ear.

'Tell them who did this to you,' she whispered, still in English. Still seductively. 'Tell them it was the Angel who ripped you . . .' She stood up, slipping the knife into her coat pocket. 'Make sure to tell them that before you die . . .'

iii.

Twenty-four years before: Berlin-Lichtenberg, German Democratic Republic February 1984

'We're talking about children here. We *are* talking about children here, aren't we?' Major Georg Drescher's question hung in the smoke-laden air. Everyone remained silent while a young woman in a Felix Dzerzhinsky Watch Regiment uniform came in with a tray laden with a coffee pot and cups.

The Ministry for State Security – the MfS – of the German Democratic Republic, commonly and resentfully known by the population it purportedly served as the Stasi, occupied an entire city block in the Lichtenberg district of East Berlin. The huge room in which Major Georg Drescher sat was on the first floor of the main Headquarters building on Normannenstrasse. The impressive conference room was dressed in oak panelling with a large map of Germany – East and West – dominating one wall. Next to the map was a large mounted escutcheon of the Ministry seal, the motto of which promised that the Stasi was 'the sword and shield of the Party'. Like an aircraft carrier in a dry dock, a vast oak conference table dominated the centre of the room. A small bust of Lenin stood in the corner and, mounted on the opposite wall, portraits of General Secretary Erich Honecker and Minister of State Security Erich Mielke glowered disapprovingly at the assembly gathered around the table.

This was the Ministry's conference chamber: a room for talking, for deciding strategies and planning tactics. This was where the world's most successful secret police schemed against its enemies abroad. And against its own people.

The Stasi had other rooms. Rooms in this complex and, just a couple of kilometres to the north, at Hohenschönhausen. Rooms where things other than talking were going on. Storerooms were stacked high with underwear stolen from the homes of potential dissidents: names and numbers tagged to each item so that, if ever the need arose, the Stasi's specially trained tracker dogs would have a scent to follow. In other rooms, listening devices and special weapons were designed and constructed, poisons and serums developed and tested, while elsewhere countless hours of secretly taped conversations were transcribed, thousands of photographs developed, kilometres of clandestine film and videotape examined. Whole floors of the Stasi headquarters were devoted to the vast archive of files on citizens of the GDR. No state had ever amassed so much intelligence on its own people: information collected through the Stasi's network of ninety-one thousand operators and three hundred thousand ordinary people who 'informally cooperated' with the Ministry for the good of the State, for money or for promotion at work. Or simply to stay out of prison themselves. One in fifty of the East German population spied on neighbours, friends, family members.

And then, of course, there were the other rooms. The rooms with the thickly padded soundproofed walls. The rooms where pain was an instrument of the State.

But this was a room for talking.

Drescher knew the man who sat at the top of the table: Colonel Ulrich Adebach was in uniform, as was the boyish-looking lieutenant who sat to his left smoking, with an open red pack of Salem cigarettes in front of him. Adebach was a heavy-set man in his fifties, greying hair brushed severely back and sporting an inadvisably Walter Ulbricht-type goatee. His shoulder boards showed he carried the rank of colonel. Major Georg Drescher, on the other hand, wore a sports jacket and flannels with a polo-neck sweater, all of which looked of suspiciously non-domestic design and manufacture. But, there again, as an officer of the Stasi's HVA foreign-intelligence service, he enjoyed a level of contact with the West denied to almost all of his countrymen.

Drescher didn't know the male officer sitting to the left of the colonel nor the older woman dressed in civilian clothes and Adebach had made no effort to introduce them. Drescher guessed that the young lieutenant whose uniform collar hung loose around his thin neck was Adebach's adjutant. The air in the conference room was tinged blue with cigarette smoke and Drescher noticed that the young adjutant lit another Salem as soon as he had stubbed one out.

While everyone waited for the young female Watch Regiment officer to finish serving the coffee and leave the room, Drescher contemplated the lugubrious face of Minister of Security Erich Mielke as he scowled from his portrait. If General Secretary Honecker was East Germany's Tiberius, then Mielke was its Sejanus.

Drescher suppressed a smile. Humour and imagination were not attributes appreciated in a Stasi officer. And a sense of inner silent rebellion certainly wasn't. Drescher concealed all these aspects of his character whenever he was in the presence of his superiors. Whenever he was in the presence of anyone. But Drescher's unique way of rebelling consisted of composing in his head caricatures that he would never commit to paper: imagining his superiors naked and in humorously compromising situations.

The female Watch Regiment soldier finished serving the coffee and left the conference room.

'What are you saying? Are you telling me that you have moral objections to this operation?' Colonel Ulrich Adebach asked, shattering Drescher's mental picture of short, fat, joyless Erich Mielke naked except for a ballerina's tutu and giggling like a schoolgirl while being spanked by General Secretary Honecker.

'No, comrade colonel, not moral – practical. These girls all seem very young. We are talking about taking immature girls and setting them on an immutable course . . . sending them out on dangerous and complex assignments completely isolated from any form of direct command structure.' Drescher grinned bitterly. 'I have three nieces of my own. I know how difficult it can be to get them to tidy their rooms, far less carry out hazardous missions.'

'The age range is between thirteen and sixteen years of age.' Adebach didn't return Drescher's smile. 'And they will not be deployed in the field for several years yet. Maybe I should remind you, Major Drescher, that I was fighting fascists when I was exactly the same age as some of these young women.'

No, you don't have to remind me, thought Drescher, you've told me every time you've seen the slightest chance to lever it into the conversation.

'Fifteen,' continued Adebach. 'I was fifteen when I fought my way through the streets of Berlin with the Red Army.'

Drescher nodded, but wondered what it had been like to kill fellow Germans; to stand aside while countless German women were raped by your comrades-in-arms. Or maybe not stand aside. 'With respect, comrade colonel,' said Drescher, 'these are young girls. And we are not talking about combat. The heat of battle.'

'Have you read the file?'

'Of course.'

'Then you will know that we have very carefully selected these twelve girls. They all meet a consistent set of criteria. Each of these young women displays athletic or sporting ability, they are all of above-average intelligence and they all have, for one reason or another, displayed a certain disconnectedness in terms of their emotions.'

'Yes. I saw that in the file. But that disconnectedness, as you put it, has for the most part come about from some psychological trauma in their pasts. I have to say that one could describe them as, well . . . disturbed. These are problem children.'

'None of the girls is mentally disordered.' It was the older woman who responded this time. Drescher was not surprised to hear her speak German with a Russian accent. 'Nor are they truly sociopathic. But through experience or simply by nature they are emotionally less responsive than their peers.'

'I see . . .' said Drescher. 'But surely that on its own is hardly a qualification for what we expect of them. I mean . . . how can I put this . . . I know we live in the ideal society of gender equality and opportunity, but there is no doubt that the male . . . well, the male is more aggressive. Men are more inclined to violence. Killing comes more naturally.'

Adebach smiled wryly and rose to his feet. He walked around the table and stood behind the seated woman. 'Perhaps I should introduce you,' he said to Drescher. 'This is Major Doctor Ivana Lubimova. The major has been assigned to us by our Soviet comrades. I should tell you that Major Lubimova also served in the Great Patriotic War. She fought with the Seventieth Rifle Division. Special weapons training at Buzuluk.'

'Sniper?' asked Drescher.

'Thirty-three confirmed kills,' said Lubimova, blankly.

'And now you're an army doctor?' said Drescher, thinking of thirty-three dead Germans.

'Psychiatrist. And not for the army.'

'I see,' said Drescher, and he knew that the matronly Russian hadn't had far to come: just from Karlshorst, immediately to the south of Lichtenberg. KGB headquarters.

'I specialise in the psychology of combat,' continued the Russian. 'What you have said is actually true: women are much less inclined to kill in hot blood than men are. The vast majority of murders around the world are committed by men and are fuelled by rage, sexual jealousy or alcohol. Or any combination of these elements. And you are also right to say male soldiers perform more aggressively in front-line combat, particularly hand-to-hand. However, when it comes to *cold*-blooded killing – planned, premeditated homicide – then the pendulum swings the other way. Women who kill often kill in cold blood and for motives other than rage: motives that can be quite abstract. That was why so many of my female comrades made such excellent snipers. That is why these girls are perfect for what we have planned.'

'I don't know,' said Drescher. 'The killing is only a small part of it. These girls . . . women . . . will have to exist isolated from their controls.'

'That is where you come in, Major Drescher. You have a great deal of experience in Section A,' said Adebach, referring to the 'education' unit of the Stasi's HVA, responsible for training East Germany's spies. 'You will head up a team of instructors that will train these girls in the broadest spectrum of skills. The kind of skills they will need to infiltrate and maintain deep cover in the West.' Adebach took his seat again.

Drescher sipped his coffee and smiled: *Rondo Melange*. Drescher was a man who enjoyed good coffee. He had tasted the best around the world – in Copenhagen, in Vienna, in Paris, in London – but for Drescher nothing compared with Rondo. It was one of the few things that the GDR manufacturing monolith had managed to get right.

'What do you have in mind?' Drescher said.

Adebach nodded to his adjutant, who passed a file to Drescher. 'Are you familiar with the Japanese term *kunoichi*? The *kunoichi* was the female counterpart of the male ninja. Both *kunoichi* and ninja were trained as the ultimate assassins, but there was a recognition that gender had a role to play in how they went about their tasks. The *kunoichi* were expert in all forms of unarmed combat, but they were also trained in the art of seduction. They were experts on the human body, both on how to make it respond erotically and on where the weak spots were: how to kill swiftly and with the minimum of force and, whenever necessary, leaving little or no evidence of violence. They were also experts at concealment – disguising themselves as servants, prostitutes, peasants – and concealing weapons or improvising them from household objects. Added to this, the *kunoichi* were the ultimate poison-masters: they were trained in botany and could extemporise a deadly toxin from what they found growing around them. What we are aiming to achieve, Major Drescher, is to develop our own *kunoichi* force and bury it deep in the fabric of Western capitalism. These operatives will have all the skills of the *kunoichi* . . . but they will also be expert with every form of modern weapon.'

'Why?' asked Drescher. 'I mean, why specifically this type of operation? Why now? And why are the Stasi being asked to run it?'

'I'm sure the comrade major won't mind me saying this' – Adebach nodded in Lubimova's direction – 'but we have by far the best success rate in penetration of Western security services and organs of state. Of course, we enjoy an advantage that none of our allies in the Pact possesses – we speak the same language as our main opponent.' Adebach lit a *Sprachlos* cigarette and drew on it slowly.

'As to why we are launching this now . . .' Major Lubimova picked up Adebach's thread. 'We need new strategies to fight the West. We need to use a scalpel rather than a blunt instrument. As you know, we have just stood down from our greatest mobilisation. Late last year the West took us to the very brink of full-scale nuclear war. We now believe that NATO did not realise how close we came to launching a pre-emptive defensive attack. The so-called "Operation Able Archer Eighty-three" turned out, after all, simply to be a NATO exercise, but it was the biggest deployment of Western arms and forces since the end of the War. The capitalists were stupid enough to make it completely accurate, right down to the transmissions they sent between command structures. Transmissions which we intercepted. Added to which, our monitoring revealed that British Prime Minister Margaret Thatcher was in daily encrypted contact with President Reagan, often several times a day. What we didn't know then, but do now, is that this contact was about the Americans invading Grenada, and not preparations for a major war. It was simply two imperialists squabbling over who had the colonial rights to a scrap of land.'

'I can tell you, Major Drescher,' said Adebach, 'that the ordinary man and woman here or in the West will never know how close we came to cataclysm. The only thing that prevented all-out nuclear war was the collection and analysis of intelligence by the covert intelligence services – on both sides, it has to be said. Our agents only just managed to stop the Cold War turning hot. We have got to find new ways of striking at the enemy without escalation to war. Your department has achieved great things in infiltrating the West with intelligence gatherers. Our experience last year has emphasised just how impractical it is to use conventional military means against each other. If we have to take the fight to our enemy then we must do so on the "invisible front". We have several operations in planning, all of which aim to use intelligence, sabotage and subversion as they have never been used before. This is one of them. These young women will become our weapons deep inside enemy territory. They may sit there in the West and never be deployed, or they may be in continual use, depending on the prevailing political situation. The main thing is that, if the need arises, they can seriously impair the enemy's capabilities, or disrupt their plans.'

'By assassination?' Drescher refilled his coffee cup. 'I have to say, comrade colonel, that we already have the means and personnel to carry out eliminations in hostile territory.'

'We're not talking about Scandinavian journalists or the odd errant football star,' said Adebach, with a glance across at Mielke's portrait. 'I am talking about the ability to kill key personnel, even leaders, in the West. And, where the need arises, to do so without raising suspicion. For example, we have a plan to infiltrate a Valkyrie into one of the terrorist groups we sponsor in the West.'

'Valkyries?' Drescher suppressed a grin. Barely. He knew of Adebach's fondness for Wagner. 'Is that what we're going to call them? Isn't it all a bit, well . . . Wagnerian? It sounds like they could have been a special division of the Nazi League of German Girls.'

'That is the code name we've assigned to them,' said Adebach sternly. 'Your job, Major Drescher, is to head the team of instructors who will train these young women. Twelve girls, of whom only three will make final selection for deployment. And these final three . . . let me put it this way: there will never have been three assassins, three killing machines so perfect. Until then, you, comrade major, will be father, mother, confessor, teacher and keeper of these girls. It's all in there . . .' Adebach nodded to the file in Drescher's hands. 'Take that with you but make no copies. The status of each of these young women will be that of a UC, an Unofficial Cooperator like many of your free-lance operatives. At the end of the week I want the file returned. All personal files on your students will be destroyed on completion of the training. There is to be no surviving record of the preparation and deployment of these operatives.'

Drescher stood up. 'Very well, but surely that is unnecessary . . . no outsider is ever going to set eyes on the files of the Stasi . . .'

Off the coast of Jutland, Denmark
August 2002

Goran Vujačić watched the blonde girl stretch languidly on the steamer chair at the stern of the yacht. Her limbs were long and lithe but she didn't have the skinny, boyish narrowness across the hips that the other girl had. Vujačić liked his women to look like women. He sipped his beer, appreciating its chill on the hot day. And it *was* hot. Vujačić hadn't expected it to be just as warm as it was. He was no great lover of the northern European climate: he belonged in the humid Mediterranean heat of the Adriatic or under the baking sun of a Balkan summer. But today the weather was good, and he could watch the girls dive from the rear of the boat into the North Sea. He would have the blonde one. That would be part of the deal, a goodwill gesture of trade: that he would get to fuck the blonde one. After all, that was what women were for. That, and being deck ornaments.

'This little rowboat of yours must have cost you,' he said to Knudsen, running his hand over the red leather and varnished teak of the recessed deck sofa. Vujačić the Bosnian Serb spoke to Knudsen the Dane in English: the international language of business. And of organised crime.

'It's worth about five million euros. But I managed to get it cost,' said Knudsen wryly. 'I came to an agreement with the owner. Sure you don't want champagne?'

'I'm fine with the beer just now,' said Vujačić, glancing over his shoulder again at the girls. 'But maybe later . . .'

'Yes,' said Knudsen. 'Later you can let your hair down a little, huh, Goran? After everything is taken care of.'

Vujačić smiled. He felt relaxed. But not relaxed enough not to have brought Zlatko along with him. Zlatko stood mutely behind them, unsheltered from the sun and sweating menacingly into his Hawaiian shirt. It amused Vujačić to think that he now had a Croat watching his back. How times had changed.

Knudsen, a tall, tough-looking Dane, sat with Vujačić in a plush recessed area of the deck at the stern of the motor yacht. Uniformed crew members stood in the shade of the awning, far enough away not to hear the conversation, waiting to serve lunch. Vujačić breathed in deeply, as if inhaling the yacht's odour of wealth.

'You know, Peter,' he said, 'this is the beginning of a beautiful friendship. And do you know why? Because we complement each other. Supply and demand. What you need, I can deliver. This little operation of ours will become the main trading route for major drugs into Scandinavia and Northern Germany. You and I, my friend, are about to become very, very rich. Or in your case richer. Maybe I'll get a yacht like this – if you can find another one going at cost.' Vujačić grinned at the blonde girl. 'And maybe some of the fixtures too . . .'

'Tell me, Goran,' said Knudsen. 'Are you sure you've got everything tied up at your end? I mean on the distribution side. I heard that you had problems with some of your competitors.'

'Not any more. Any problems there had been were all dealt with before we first talked. I told you at our first meeting that I was totally in control of the distribution network. And I still am. I had to arrange for a few people to retire from the business. Permanently. Unfortunately I had to be more discreet than usual, so it all proved a little more expensive than expected.'

'You hired an outsider?' asked Knudsen.

Vujačić didn't answer for a moment. Instead he sipped his beer, keeping his gaze on the tall Dane as if weighing up how much he could trust him. Vujačić knew that Knudsen was rich. Well connected. Everything about him had checked out. But Vujačić had fought in war; often in wars where he had no place to be fighting. For the Serb, experience had taught him to divide men into two clear groups: fighting men and the others. Just like women were divided into the ones you'd fuck and old women. Knudsen bothered him: he was late forties, maybe early fifties, but there was no softening about him; none of the angles had been dulled by the good life. But there again, maybe that was just down to membership of an expensive gym.

'You know I have a partner . . . another partner,' Vujačić said at last, leaning forward and lowering his voice conspiratorially. This was clearly not even for Zlatko's ears.

'Yes, your other partner . . .' Knudsen frowned. 'I still don't like it, Goran. I mean, not knowing who this third party is.'

'But it doesn't affect you, my friend. My business with my other partner has nothing to do with what we're doing here. Just like you don't know anything about them, they don't know anything about you. Different businesses. I supply your pharmaceutical needs, while I'm a sort of recruitment consultant, you could say, for my other partner.' The Serb laughed at his own in-joke. 'And anyway, yours and mine is more of an equal partnership. Substantial as our little enterprise here is, it would be peanuts to my other associate. We're talking about a big fish. A really big fish. They play a much bigger game than you or I do, Peter. And for stakes beyond even your reach.'

'And what is their game?' asked Knudsen.

'Not drugs, if that's what's worrying you. Like I say, I

supply them with . . .' Vujačić ran his hand over the close-cropped bristle on his scalp while he considered the best description '. . . workers. And if I knew all of it, which I don't, I couldn't tell you about it. Anyway, as I was saying, I needed to sort out some difficulties with competitors. My other partner knows a contractor. The best in the business, apparently.'

'A hit man?'

'Yeah. Or maybe a hit woman, if the code name is anything to go by.' Vujačić leaned even closer; lowered his voice more. 'The Valkyrie. But what woman would be capable, huh, Peter? This so-called Valkyrie is based in Germany. Hamburg, apparently. He – or she – is supposed to be the best contract killer in the world.'

'Better than the Mexican?' asked Knudsen.

'Carlos Ramos? Last I heard he'd quit the business. But yes. At least as good, maybe better. I mean, I could take care of things myself. God knows I took care of a lot of things back home in the nineties . . .' Vujačić cast an eye over his shoulder as if to check that Zlatko could not hear him, then he turned back to the Dane. 'But this little exercise needed a little more finesse, if you know what I mean. So, this Valkyrie took care of all of the loose ends. Made most of them look like accidents or suicide. The cops are only looking into two of them. Really nice work. Tidy. Anyway, the important thing is that you don't need to worry about the distribution side.'

'Okay,' said Knudsen, 'if you say so, Goran. Are you ready?'

'I'm ready . . .' Vujačić turned and nodded to Zlatko. The huge Croatian bodyguard laid a computer case on the deck table in front of Vujačić, who took out a slim black laptop. The Serb tapped on the keyboard and the secure bank website opened up on the screen. 'Isn't Bluetooth wonderful?' He grinned.

Knudsen beckoned to the blonde girl. She folded a wrap around herself, came over to the men and handed Knudsen a cellphone. Knudsen made two calls: both brief.

'My contact has taken delivery of the merchandise,' he said and handed the phone back to the girl.

Vujačić closed the laptop. 'And the transfer of the funds has been confirmed.' He grinned at the blonde girl again, his eyes penetrating the diaphanous wrap and following the curves of her body beneath. 'Maybe now we should celebrate. Now we can party. You want to party, honey?'

'Ask the boss,' she said. 'It's his yacht.'

'You own everything around here?' Vujačić asked Knudsen.

Knudsen stood up and beckoned to the deck crew. 'You can serve it now.'

Vujačić didn't have time to react.

Suddenly the calm was shattered with a dozen voices shouting at him, commanding him to be still. The uniformed deck crew had drawn automatic weapons from where they had been hidden on the serving trolley. At the same time, the deck doors flew open and heavily armed figures in black uniforms and body armour burst out onto the deck. Vujačić heard Zlatko being wrestled to the deck behind him. There was nothing he could do. Instinct had moved his hand towards the Beretta tucked into his waistband and concealed under his loose shirt, but he checked the movement, knowing it could cost him his life.

'That's a good boy . . .' The blonde whispered into his ear in English, simultaneously jabbing the barrel of her service automatic painfully into the soft, stubble-covered flesh under his jaw. 'Wanted to fuck me, did you, Goran? I've got news for you, you piece of shit – you're the one who's fucked . . .'

Chapter One

Hamburg brickwork was unique. The very fabric of the city was woven in red brick. In fact, the saying went that the craftsmen who had constructed buildings like these hadn't built with brick, they had knitted with it.

Martina Schilmann looked up at the narrow-fronted red-brick face of Davidwache: the most famous police station in Germany. Davidwache stood right at the heart of the St Pauli red-light district of Hamburg and, as well as being a fully functioning police station, was a state-protected national landmark. Martina had been stationed here for six of her fifteen years in the Polizei Hamburg. Then she had moved on. Moved up. And, eventually, she had moved out.

Standing here in the cold damp night air, waiting for a B-list British celebrity to satisfy his prurient interest in the Reeperbahn, she wondered why. Martina had been a rising star in the Polizei Hamburg, but she had wanted more. Setting up her own company had been her way of getting what she wanted. And now, at forty, she had got it: money, prestige, success. But right now, looking up at the red-brick frontage of Davidwache, she thought back to those six years stationed there. Great times. A great team.

Martina pressed the earpiece of her concealed TETRA radio into her ear and squeezed the PTT transmit on her lapel mike. 'Where the hell is he?'

'I don't know, boss – I'm in Gerhardtstrasse,' Lorenz, Martina's subordinate, answered in his thick Saxon accent. 'He went into Herbertstrasse and hasn't come out yet.'

'Why in God's name didn't you go in with him? I told you to stick close.' Martina couldn't keep the frustration out of her voice. She walked briskly around to the side of Davidwache and crossed Davidstrasse to the entrance of Herbertstrasse. She could go no further: a baffle of metal walls obscured the view but allowed concealed access into the eighty-metre-long street. Or allowed access unless you were a woman or a male under eighteen. Eighty metres of Hamburg street was forbidden to the city's women except for the prostitutes who worked in Herbertstrasse, sitting illuminated behind hinged glass, like joints of meat in a butcher's window. Although the Hamburg government had paid for the erection of the metal baffles at either end, the prohibition against women entering was not imposed by the city but by the prostitutes themselves. Any woman who dared to encroach was likely to have water or beer – or even urine – thrown over them.

'He said he wanted me to wait for him . . .' Lorenz sounded plaintive over the radio link. 'That he wanted to have a look on his own. You know what these bloody celebrities are like – they think everything's a game.'

'Shit.' Martina looked at her watch. The British guy had been in Herbertstrasse for twenty minutes. That meant he'd probably gone with one of the girls. 'Lorenz, go in and see if you can find him.'

'But if he's . . .'

'Just do it.'

It was then that Martina heard the sound of a woman screaming. Somewhere in the distance, behind Herbertstrasse.

2.

Jan Fabel sat leaning forward on the leather armchair. On the edge. He still wore his raincoat and held his gloves in one hand. Everything about his posture spoke of imminent departure, even though he had only just arrived.

At one time, a long time ago, this suburban house in Hamburg-Borgfelde had been Fabel's home. He had been familiar with every room, every floorboard, every angle. It had been the focus in his life. His home. Of course, everything had changed since then: the furniture, the decor, the TV in the corner.

'You've got to talk to her.' Renate sat opposite Fabel, her legs crossed and her arms folded across her body in the same defensive pose that he remembered. Her hair was not the same shade of rich auburn it had been when he had first met her, when they had been married, and he suspected that she now coloured it. She was still a handsome woman, but the creases around her mouth had deepened and given her face a faint appearance of parsimony. God knows, thought Fabel, she's got nothing to feel bitter about.

'I'll talk to her,' he said. 'But I can't promise anything. Gabi is an intelligent girl. Her own person. She is more than capable of making up her own mind about her future.'

'Are you saying you approve of this? Support it?'

'I'll support anything Gabi chooses to do. But no, personally I'd rather she rethought her career. In the end, if it's what she wants to do . . .' Fabel shrugged resignedly. 'But let's not get ahead of ourselves. She has a long time to think it over. And you know what Gabi's like: if she thinks we're pushing her she'll dig her heels in.'

'It's your fault,' said Renate. 'If you weren't a policeman then it would never have occurred to her to join. Gabi hero-worships you. It's easy to be the hero when you're a part-time parent.'

'And whose choice was that?' Fabel fought back the anger surging up within him. 'It sure as hell wasn't mine. I was pushed out of her life. And as I remember you did the pushing.'

'And I was pushed out of *your* life by that bloody job of yours.'

'Right into Ludiger Behrens's bed, as I recall,' said Fabel and regretted it immediately. Renate was a petty woman; it had only been in the last stages of their marriage that he had seen just how petty. And she had always had the knack of reducing him to her level. 'Look, this isn't getting us anywhere. I think you're making too big a deal of the whole thing: Gabi has only started to talk about this. Let's just wait until she gets her Abitur results and take it from there. Like I said, it's a long time before she has to make up her mind about it. I'll talk to her and make sure she knows what she would be getting into. But I have to tell you, Renate, that if she is determined to become a police officer, then I will support her all the way.'

Renate's already dark expression darkened further. 'It's not right,' she said. 'It's no job for a woman.'

Fabel stared slack-jawed at Renate. 'I can't believe you said that. You of all people, Renate. What the hell do you mean, police work is no job for a woman? Just goes to show, all the time we were married I never had you down as a "Children, Kitchen, Church" type. Mind you, given your father's history . . .'

Fabel knew he was about to get burned by the fire that suddenly caught light in Renate's green eyes, and he was relieved to hear his cellphone ring just as she was about to launch something at him.

'Hi, *Chef*, it's Anna. You used to be into British pop in the seventies and eighties, right?'

'I take it that's rhetorical,' said Fabel, his voice laden with warning. 'What's going on?'

'Well, Jake Westland – you know, the lead singer from that

group in the seventies? – the thing is he's on tour in Germany at the moment and he's supposed to be doing an in-depth interview with NDR radio tomorrow.'

Fabel sighed into the phone. 'Anna . . . point?'

'Just that he won't be turning up for the interview. He's already spilled his guts – in the Reeperbahn. And *Chef*, he said it was a woman who cut him and then she told him to let us know who she was. She told him to say it was the Angel.'

'Shit.' Fabel used the English word and looked across at his ex-wife. The fire had been extinguished and she now wore the expression of hostile resignation that she had always had when work had called him away. 'I'll be right there.'

They had taken Westland across town to the emergency room at the hospital in St Georg. There was no point in Fabel going there: from what he had heard, Westland was in no condition for an interview. Instead he took the Ost-West Strasse into the Reeperbahn, Hamburg's Sinful Mile. Where ropers had once woven hawsers for sailing ships, giving the Reeperbahn its name, now strip clubs and sex shops, bars and theatres neon-sparkled in the icy night. By the time Fabel arrived at Davidwache he was already in a bad mood. The meeting with Renate had gone as ill-temperedly as expected and he had lost his MP3 player: whenever he felt stressed, he plugged it into his BMW's stereo system. No music, more stress.

The press had already gathered en masse outside the Davidwache station and three uniformed officers were holding them at bay. In addition to the media circus outside the station, there was some other separate commotion being created in Davidstrasse, to the side of the station. Young riot squad officers in their gear were struggling to load groups of resisting women into the large green police wagons. Some of the media had leached around into Davidstrasse to take pictures of the sideshow, but a fusillade of camera flashes saluted Fabel as he made his way from the car to Davidwache's double doors. A television news camera crew had jostled its way to the front; Fabel recognised the reporter as Sylvie Achtenhagen, who worked for one of the satellite channels. Great, he thought, as if the media limelight wasn't bad enough, he had that bitch on his case.

'Principal Detective Chief Commissar Fabel' – Achtenhagen emphasised his full rank for the camera – 'can you confirm that the victim of this attack was Jake Westland, the British singer?'

Fabel ignored her and walked on.

'And is it true that this is the work of the so-called Angel of St Pauli? The serial killer the Polizei Hamburg failed to catch in the nineteen-nineties?' Then, when he still did not respond: 'Are we to take it that your involvement, as head of this proposed so-called "Super Murder Commission", is significant? Are you being called in to clean up the mess the Polizei Hamburg made of the original investigation?'

Fabel pulled a mask of patience over his irritation and turned to the reporter. 'The Police Presidium's press and information department will make a full statement in due course. You should know the drill by now, Frau Achtenhagen.'

He turned his back on her and walked through the double doors and up the steps into Davidwache police station. The small reception area was crammed with personnel. He could hear shouting from through the back and to the left, from the custody area. Fabel was greeted by a bristle-scalped heavy-set man in his fifties and a pretty dark-haired woman wearing jeans and a biker jacket that was at least one size too big for her. Fabel smiled grimly at Senior Criminal Commissar Werner Meyer and Criminal Commissar Anna Wolff.

'How in God's name did Achtenhagen find out about the Angel claim?' asked Fabel.

'Money talks,' said Anna Wolff. 'That bitch isn't above bribing ambulance crew or hospital staff to get a scoop.'

'You're probably right. She's all we need. She practically built her career on the Angel case.' Fabel nodded in the direction of the commotion outside in Davidstrasse. 'What the hell is going on?'

'A case of perfect timing,' said Werner. 'A feminist group decided to pick tonight of all nights to stage a protest. They invaded Herbertstrasse. They object to a Hamburg street being closed off to women. They claim it's against their human rights or something.'

'They've got a point, to be honest,' said Fabel. He sighed. 'Okay . . . what have we got?'

'The victim is Jake Westland, fifty-three years old, British national,' Werner read from his notebook. 'And yes, he is that Jake Westland. From what we can gather he was having a little impromptu jaunt around the Reeperbahn – and not to recapture the spirit of the Beatles, if you catch my drift. Funny, though . . . I would have thought it would have been the gay bars he would have been interested in – him being English, that is . . .'

Fabel responded to Werner's joke with an impatient face.

'I don't know why they do it,' continued Werner. 'These celebrities, I mean. Anyway, Westland deliberately gave his bodyguards the slip and disappeared into Herbertstrasse. Next thing a working girl on her way into the Kiez finds him with his insides turned into his outsides. He tells her that his attacker told him that she was the Angel, then he passes out.'

'What's his condition?'

'He was still alive when they put him in the ambulance. Apparently the girl who found him knew a bit about first aid. But my guess is that his producers are already planning a memorial greatest-hits CD.'

'We've got the girl who found him through the back,' said Anna Wolff. She exchanged a look with Werner and her red-lipsticked mouth broke into a grin. 'And the bodyguards. I thought you'd like to interview them personally.'

'Okay, Anna,' Fabel said, with a sigh, 'what's the deal?'

'Westland was being looked after by Schilmann Security and Close Personal Protection.'

'Martina Schilmann?'

'You and she used to be close, I believe?'

'Martina Schilmann was an excellent police officer,' said Fabel.

'Then she must have been a better cop than she is a bodyguard,' said Werner.

A uniformed superintendent joined them. He was shorter than Fabel and had thick, dark, unruly hair.

'What I really want to know is,' he said sternly as he shook hands with Fabel, 'did anyone get his autograph?'

'Hello, Carstens,' said Fabel, with a grin. 'Still cracking tasteless jokes?'

'Comes with the territory.' Carstens Kaminski was in charge of the Davidwache team. Davidwache – Polizei Hamburg's Police Commissariat 15 – was the station that controlled the Kiez, Hamburg's 0.7 square kilometres of red-light district centred on the Reeperbahn. Every weekend the normal population of ten thousand residents would swell as over two hundred thousand visitors would pass through the Kiez, some of whom would be drunk, some of whom would be relieved of their wallets or valuables. And for some, their walk on the wild side would end in real disaster.

The uniformed officers who worked out of Davidwache had to have a particular skill: they had to be able to talk. The Kiez was an area populated by pimps, hookers, petty crooks and not so petty crooks; visited by young men from the suburbs who often drank too much, too quickly. Most of the situations that the Davidwache officers were faced with demanded sympathy and humour and more than one reveller had been talked into going home peacefully and out of a night in the cells. Carstens Kaminski had been born and grew up in St Pauli and no one was as in tune with the rhythm and changing mood of the Kiez. He also had the typically down-to-earth St Pauli sense of humour.

'What's the deal with the protest?' asked Fabel.

'It's a group called *Muliebritas*. Or more correctly it was organised by a feminist magazine called *Muliebritas*,' explained Kaminski. 'They stormed into Herbertstrasse and there was everything but all-out war with the hookers. God knows it would have been bad enough at the best of times, but with this Westland thing going on as well . . . We asked them to disperse, explaining that they were interfering with a crime scene and investigation, but the concept of consensual policing seems to have been lost on them.' There was another burst of shouting from the custody area, as if to underline his statement. 'Anyway, you're not here for them. By the way, did you know Martina's here?' Kaminski grinned.

'Yes,' said Fabel. 'Anna told me.'

'Didn't you and she . . .'

'Yes, Carstens,' said Fabel, with a sigh. 'We've already been through that. Do we have a description of the woman who attacked Westland?'

'All he said was she told him she was the Angel. And even that we've only got second-hand from the hooker who found him.'

'How do we know she's not the "Angel" herself?'

'From what we can gather she did her best to keep Westland alive until the ambulance arrived. And if this really is the work of the Angel, then the girl who found him would be too young for the original murders. Anyway, despite her trying to hide it behind a tough front she clearly was in shock. We suggested the quack should give her a mild sedative but she told him to stick it.'

'I want to talk to her anyway.'

'And Martina?' Kaminski grinned and cast a look across at Werner and Anna Wolff.

'And Martina. What about the new CCTV system we've installed in the Kiez? Will we have got anything on that?'

'No,' said Kaminski. 'Westland's attacker was either lucky or very clever – there are no cameras on that street or anywhere near the courtyard. As you know, the compromise we had to make on having cameras in the Kiez was that we had to be selective where we put them – none in a position that could reveal the honourable citizens of our fine city nipping into a peep-show or a sex shop. It means we've got a hell of a lot of black holes. But I've put a call into the ops room at the Presidium for the recordings from an hour before until an hour after the murder to be collected and analysed. We might get something from the surrounding streets . . . the attacker making their way to or from the scene. In the meantime, I'm flooding the streets with uniforms . . .' Kaminski nodded towards the assembled officers in the lobby. 'We'll question every hooker, pimp and club owner in the area. Business isn't exactly good in the Kiez these days and Westland was hardly an anonymous victim . . . Something like this is bad for business. Maybe we'll get lucky.'

'Thanks, Carstens.'

'Well, if you don't mind, Jan, I'll get back to briefing this lot.' Kaminski nodded towards the uniforms he had gathered. 'Unless you want to talk them through what we should be looking for?'

'No, Carstens, this is your patch,' said Fabel. He knew that no one knew the Kiez better than Kaminski.

Fabel hung his raincoat up in the station cloakroom, first of all patting his pockets.

'Lost something?' asked Anna.

'Bloody MP3 player . . .'

Fabel made his way with Werner and Anna through to the rear of the station. Until 2005 Davidwache had been an exclusively uniform-branch station: to keep pace with changing times a new extension had been built onto the rear of the protected architecture of the original station. It was in this newer part of the building that the detective branch was now based. Kaminski had put the conference room at their disposal for carrying out witness interviews. Fabel looked out of the window over Davidstrasse and part of Friedrichstrasse. He could see the green riot-police vans being driven down to the traffic lights, transporting back to the Police Presidium those protesters whom Davidwache's tiny cell block could not accommodate.

'Anna, I think you should lead the questioning of this witness,' he said. 'The girl who found Westland, I mean. It sounds like she might be in a pretty bad way.'

'Why me, *Chef*?' asked Anna. 'Because I'm a woman?'

'I just think she might respond better to you.' Anna had been on Fabel's team for five years, but he still found her difficult to handle. To understand. Anna Wolff was much younger-looking than her thirty-one years; she had shortish black hair, was no bigger than one-sixty-two centimetres, and strove for a punky look with her dark mascara, firetruck-red lipstick and oversized biker's jacket. And, despite Fabel doing his best not to notice, she was very attractive. But, most of all, Anna Wolff was by far the toughest, most aggressive member of his team. As well as the most insubordinate.

'Oh, I see,' said Anna with an expression of mock enlightenment. 'Obviously I'm going to be more understanding. Being female, that is. I'm sorry – I forgot that having a dick presents an insuperable obstacle to sympathy.'

'I'm not being sexist, Anna. I'm being practical, that's all.' Fabel sounded annoyed despite himself. 'Forget it. I'll talk to her myself.'

'I was just saying . . .'

'Yes, Anna. You're always "just saying". I'll conduct this interview.' He looked at his watch. It was two-thirty a.m. 'Werner, you sit in. Anna, you can go off duty.'

'Oh, come on . . . all I said . . .'

'I'll have a team briefing at two p.m. tomorrow. I want to see you in my office first, Anna. Be there at one,' said Fabel. Anna grabbed her leather jacket from the back of the chair and stormed out.

'You were a bit rough on her, Jan,' said Werner when she was gone.

'She goes too far, Werner. You know that. I'm fed up with every order being challenged or commented on. And I'm sick of complaints coming in about Anna.'

'We used to call it robust policing, Jan.'

'Those days are gone, Werner. Long gone. This is the twenty-first century.'

'You know she has a point, Jan.' Werner looked unsure of himself. 'I mean, about the male-female thing. You do tend to get Anna to do the female interviews.'

'What are you saying?'

'Just that, well, don't take this the wrong way, but you do tend to treat women like they're a different species.'

'How can you say that, Werner? My team has always been balanced. Well, maybe not now. Not since . . .'

Both men became quiet. The name Maria Klee hung unsaid in the air.

'Forget it, Jan,' said Werner a second too late. 'I just think you should go easy on Anna.'

Fabel's reply was cut off by a uniformed officer conducting a girl in dark jeans and a navy-blue quilted ski jacket into the room. She clutched a woollen hat and scarf in her hands. Fabel guessed that she was not a street girl: the hookers who worked the streets around Herbertstrasse dressed in bright colours and would stand in groups, holding pastel-coloured umbrellas above their heads whether it was raining or not as a sign to potential customers that they were available for business. Their contrived cheerfulness was so that their customers felt less sordid about the trade they plied.

Fabel kept his smile in place but noticed how young the

girl was: she looked to Fabel not much older than his own daughter, Gabi. He asked her to sit and tried to do what he could to put her at ease. Christa Eisel was pretty – very pretty – with shoulder-length fair hair. From the plainness of her outfit and her obvious attractiveness, Fabel worked out that she must have been a Herbertstrasse window girl who would have changed into a provocative outfit once she was at work. As they talked, Christa kneaded the hat and scarf on her lap, but there was something approaching defiance in her eyes.

'We'll need to take that, I'm afraid,' Fabel said, smiling. Christa looked down at the bloodstained jacket.

'It's no good to me now. I've left my gloves downstairs. They're finished too.' She slipped the jacket off and handed it to Fabel. Werner placed it into a large plastic forensics bag.

'How long have you been working the area, Christa?' asked Fabel.

'Six months. Just weekends. And not every weekend. I have a slot in one of the windows and I do some escort work occasionally.'

'Are you supporting a habit, Christa? Sorry, but I have to ask.'

The girl looked genuinely taken aback. 'No . . . no, of course not.'

'What do you do? I mean when you're not working here.'

'I'm a student. Uni Hamburg.'

'Oh really? That's where I went. I studied history. You?'

'Medicine.'

Fabel stared at Christa for a moment. 'Medicine? Then why . . . ?'

'Money. I want to earn extra money.'

'But this way?'

'Why not?' Again defiance glinted in Christa's eyes. 'A lot of students do it for extra cash.'

'You're clearly a bright, pretty girl with a lifetime of oppor-tunity ahead of you, Christa. I just don't understand why you would choose to do what you're doing. Is this what you think it means to be a woman?'

'Are you disappointed that I'm not some exploited junkie? You're right, I choose to do this. It's my body and I can do what I want with it. And anyway, it's relatively easy money. A few hours each weekend and I make more than most people do in a month. Trust me, it makes medical school a whole lot easier.'

'That's not the point, Christa. God knows in this job I know what the dark side of human nature is like. I just don't understand why someone like you would seek it out and immerse themselves in it. Believe me, maybe you think you can do this for a year or two and then get on with your life. You can't. It will stay with you for the rest of your life. Every relationship you have will be coloured by it. You'll find it impossible to see the good in people.'

'What's it to you, Herr Chief Commissar? You trying to save my soul?'

'This isn't about your moral well-being, Christa. It's about placing yourself in danger. You study medicine. Surely you know the risks. To your health, I mean.'

'And because I study medicine I know how to look after myself. Listen, Herr Fabel, I don't have to justify myself to you. Women have been exploited by men for centuries. I'm doing a little exploiting back.' Despite the defiance, Fabel could see that Christa had been badly shaken by what she'd gone through in the last hour or so. He didn't even know why he was getting into this with her. As she had said, it wasn't his business. He decided to drop it.

'It's your life, Christa . . .' Fabel sighed. He looked at the notes before him. 'Listen, I know this is very hard for you, but I need you to try to remember if there was anything else you saw or heard that you maybe haven't mentioned in your statement. You saw no one come out of the courtyard? I mean, as you made your way in?'

'No. No one. It's not that I've forgotten or didn't notice. I'm sure there was no one there. I use that alley if I'm in a hurry. It cuts across from Erichstrasse through the courtyard. You've always got to be on your toes for creeps, so I was paying attention. There was no one.'

'But that doesn't make sense. You must have got there moments after the attack.'

'I was, if the rate of his blood loss was anything to go by. But that doesn't change the fact that I saw no one come into or go out of the alley.'

'I heard that you carried out first aid. I take it your medical training kicked in?'

'For what it was worth, which wasn't much. He'll be dead by now. Whoever did that to him was very skilled. A single cut that eviscerated him. It was like the Japanese suicide cut – you know, the *seppuku*. Straight and very deep. From the amount of bleeding I reckon the abdominal aorta had been nicked. They won't be able to repair it before he bleeds out.' Fabel watched Christa's guileless youthful face as she spoke about a man's death: her description was clinical, but her voice shook as she spoke and her hands kneaded the woollen hat on her lap more vigorously.

'What did he say to you?'

'I've already told them. Before.'

'I'd like to hear it again, if you don't mind, Christa.'

'He was nearly unconscious when I got to him. Shivering. All he said was: "It was a woman. She said she was the Angel." He was speaking in English. It's funny, I didn't recognise him. I didn't know he was who he was until they told me. All I saw was . . . I suppose all I saw was a man dying.' She looked at Fabel earnestly. 'I've never seen anyone die before. I guess I'll have to get used to it.'

'You never do.'

When Fabel had no more questions and long after Christa had no more answers, he told her he would arrange for a

police car to take her home. She asked if she could be taken
to her parents' house in Barmbek.

'Can they drop me at the end of the street?' she asked.
'My parents . . . they don't know anything about what I
do . . .'

After Christa left, Martina Schilmann came into the conference room. She was wearing an expensive-looking dark blue
business suit and her blonde hair was gathered up behind her
head in a French plait. Looking at her now, for the first time
in three years, Fabel remembered why he had found her so
attractive. Martina was carrying two mugs of coffee. She
placed one in front of Fabel.

'At least I remember where the canteen is,' she said, and
smiled. 'Hello, Jan, how are you?'

'I'm fine.' He returned her smile weakly. 'And you?'

'You sure you're okay?'

'Yeah . . . sorry. Just thinking about doomed youth.'

'Oh God, I know . . . the "Happy Hooker". Did she try to
convince you that she was content in her work too? Kidding
herself. She is tough, though. I was the first on the scene after
her. She was doing a pretty good job of not going to pieces.
But it is depressing. She's just a kid. God knows I saw lots
just like her when I was working this beat. Anyway, it's good
to see you again. How have you been?'

'Fine. You look prosperous.'

'Business has been good.' Martina's expression darkened.
'Until now. I just can't believe that we've lost one. This could
be the end for me. I mean, that's the whole point of the
bloody exercise: to guard someone's body. Who's going to
want to hire us now?'

'From what I've heard, Martina, you've built Schilmann
Security into one of Europe's biggest personal-protection busi-
nesses. I would think this is a storm you could weather.
Actually, I was surprised when I heard you were personally

involved with Westland's protection. I would have thought you'd be on an ethereal executive level now, guiding lesser mortals from the clouds.'

'I'm a control freak. Hands-on. Too much hands-on, if I'm honest. We were short-staffed this weekend as well. I've got a big Russian tycoon coming in next month and I had to send half my team to liaise with his regular security people. God, I *hope* I've got a big Russian tycoon coming next month. When he gets wind of this he'll probably tell me to stick it. Anyway, never mind that: are you still involved with the beautiful Dr Eckhardt?'

'Yep,' said Fabel. 'Still involved.'

'Pity,' said Martina mischievously.

'What was the story with Westland?' asked Fabel. 'How come he gave you the slip?'

'What can I tell you? The usual rock-star megalomania. They pay us thousands of euros a day to keep them safe, then think it's all a game. Sometimes I think we're there for the cameras more than anything. Status symbols or shit like that. Westland was an arsehole. No big surprise there . . . He spent half the tour drunk and the other half chasing nineteen-year-old girls. The guy's in his fifties, for Christ's sake. To be honest, we saw him as a relatively low risk. Fending off drunks, persistent autograph hunters, paparazzi, that kind of thing. Anyway, we did a double-up on him, me and Lorenz. Lorenz is all bulk and no brains but he's good for visible presence, if you know what I mean, even if he is getting on a bit. And, like I said, not one of nature's great thinkers. He's a Saxon from Görlitz, bless him. Ex-Volkspolizei. Still calls a hamburger a *Grilletta* and probably jerks off to pictures of Katja Witt wearing a Free German Youth blouse.'

Fabel laughed. 'You're pretty scathing for someone from the East yourself.'

'I'm from Mecklenburg – a totally different proposition from the Valley of the Clueless,' said Martina with a smug grin, referring to the parts of the former East Germany which had not been able to pick up West German TV before the Wall came down. It was an affectionate jibe: it was exactly in the 'Valley of the Clueless' that the Monday Demonstrations had begun the peaceful mass protest movement that ultimately brought down the Communist regime.

'Anyway,' continued Martina, 'we were taking Westland back to the Hotel Vierjahrzeiten from a concert at the Sporthalle arena when he pipes up that he'd like to see the Reeperbahn, never been there, heard all about it, the Beatles, all that crap. I tell him it's not what it's cracked up to be and anyway it's not on the route to the hotel but he makes a fuss and we end up taking him on a brief guided tour.'

'I would have thought he would have been too tired after a concert,' said Fabel.

'Yeah, well . . . he seemed pretty lively. He was doing a lot of sniffing in the back of the car and I don't think he had a cold, if you catch my drift. No doubt it'll all come out in the autopsy. The funny thing was he had pissed off a few people by refusing to attend the post-concert party – tells them he's too tired and then badgers us to take him to the Reeperbahn. Anyway, we do the tour thing but all Westland is interested in is seeing Herbertstrasse and he starts giggling like a schoolgirl. So we take him. Of course, because it's Herbertstrasse and because I'm a woman, I can't go in so I drop him and Lorenz at one end and go and wait at the other. The Davidwache end. Naturally, Westland finds it easy to bewilder Lorenz and all the time I think he's with Westland he's actually just standing around like an idiot waiting for him at the far end. Next thing I know Westland's trying to repack his intestines and my business is down the tubes.'

'You say he was pretty insistent about going to Herbertstrasse. Specifically Herbertstrasse and not Grosse Freiheit. Do you think there's any chance it was prearranged? That maybe he had agreed to meet someone after losing you by cutting through Herbertstrasse?'

Martina furrowed her brow in thought for a moment. 'I doubt it. Could be, I suppose, but it all seemed pretty spontaneous to me.'

'It's just that it seems odd. If Westland was looking for a little bit of cheap excitement, then why go to the bother of giving you the slip where he did? I find it strange that he didn't just go with one of the window girls. You say he told you he had never been to Herbertstrasse before?'

'That's right.'

'So either he tore along Herbertstrasse and out the other end before you got there, or he cut through the side alley at number seven and out past the erotic-art museum. That looks pretty planned to me – like he knew where he was going.'

'He probably didn't. Like I say, I still think it was all spur-of-the-moment stuff.'

Martina went through the evening in detail: exact times, whom Westland had talked to, what he had talked about, how the concert had gone. Martina became, once more, the police officer and without prompting gave Fabel all the information he needed. Westland had made two calls before the concert: one to his wife, the second to his accountant regarding an investment or deal he was involved in.

'He spent some time alone in his dressing room before going on stage,' explained Martina. 'It's possible he took or made calls then, on his cellphone. There was no contact that I'm aware of after the performance, other than a brief call to the woman who was organising the concert. She was the one who wanted him to attend the post-concert party with Hamburg's good and great. I got the impression she – I mean the organiser – wasn't too chuffed when he cried off. After all, it was the whole point of the exercise: to raise awareness of the charity and after all that effort he couldn't be bothered doing a simple meet-and-greet afterwards. He was more interested in getting to the Reeperbahn.'

'We'll check his cellphone,' said Fabel.

'Oh, didn't you know? His mobile's been swiped. Wallet, too. And he had a diary – like a mini-organiser – that he always had with him. Whoever killed him nicked that as well.'

'So it could be a robbery?'

Martina gave a bitter laugh. 'No. But it could be the killer trying to disguise it as a robbery. The theft was amateur. The killing's the work of art.'

They talked for a while longer. Professional though her report was, there was nothing in what Martina had to say that offered any substantial leads.

'Not much help, is it?' Martina read his mind.

'Not much. But there again, this whole thing could simply be what it seems – a random senseless attack.'

'By the Angel?' Martina asked. 'You don't really think she's come back after ten years?'

'Who knows? According to the girl who found Westland, the wound inflicted on him was very professional. Single cut. One stroke.'

'Since when are hookers experts on knife wounds?'

'Since they started studying medicine at Hamburg Uni,' said Fabel flatly. 'If you remember, the Angel was a dab hand with a blade.'

'I'm not likely to forget,' said Martina. 'I was stationed here when the second last murder took place. I won't forget that crime scene in a hurry. We found him dead in his car in Seilerstrasse. Minus genitalia. The last one was dumped in a corner of Heligen-Geist-Feld. Also minus working parts. That's why I don't think this is the Angel. No castration, the fatal knife wound was in the belly, not the throat . . . and there's a gap of nearly ten years. The other thing is that the Angel never stole from her victims. Other than their love tackle, that is. And anyway, like I said, I've seen the Angel's work. If that girl hadn't told me what Westland had said, I wouldn't have made the connection.'

'Maybe she misheard him. He was speaking in English.'

They were interrupted by Carstens Kaminski, the Davidwache commander, who stuck his head around the conference-room door.

'Okay, Jan, whether the attacker was the Angel or not, this one is now officially all yours. I just got the call from St Georg. Westland's dead.'

It was a dry night but bitterly cold, the kind of cold you felt in your lungs when you breathed in the night air. Fabel took Werner with him. They left through the rear exit to Davidwache and walked to the murder scene. They headed up Davidstrasse and passed the end of Herbertstrasse with its red-painted metal baffles.

As they approached, Fabel saw a tall grey-haired man wearing a long dark blue overcoat slip through the baffle screens. Everything about the man spoke of him being well-off, respectable. Fabel imagined the life of this stranger: an unsuspecting wife at home, children. Grandchildren probably. He was maybe even a respected figure. Someone whom others looked up to. There was something about the man's furtive sidestep into sleaze that thoroughly depressed Fabel.

They walked along Erichstrasse, passing the occasional illuminated window and ignoring the tapping on the glass and beckoning gestures of the prostitutes.

'Ah . . .' Werner sighed sarcastically. 'The siren call of a two-minute knee-trembler . . . I mean, would you ever consider . . . ?' He jerked a thumb in the direction of the last window they had passed.

'You're joking, right?' said Fabel.

'Some men – a lot of men – go in for it. Complication-free sex, I suppose.'

'Unless you consider picking up a disease a complication. I hate the way the Reeperbahn is painted as "naughty but nice". A tourist attraction. The truth is it's cheap and nasty and sordid.'

'Granted. But it's here. And here to stay.'

'Everybody keeps telling me that,' said Fabel. 'But I'm not so sure, Werner.'

When they reached the crime scene they found that there were still two uniforms on duty and a single forensic technician in a white bunny suit was still working the site. Fabel held up his Polizei Hamburg ID and one of the uniforms lifted the tape.

'Is there anywhere you don't want us to walk?' Fabel called over to the technician.

The technician stood up and Fabel saw it was Astrid Bremer. Astrid had replaced Frank Grueber to become Holger Brauner's deputy two years ago. She had the hood of her forensic suit pulled up over her hair and its elasticated edge turned the oval of her face into a pretty, almost childlike mask.

'Nope . . .' she said. 'You're okay. We finished processing the scene an hour ago.'

'So why are you still here?' asked Werner.

Astrid shrugged. 'My mother always said I was a stubborn child. I just thought we were missing something. It was winding me up.'

'And were you missing something?' asked Fabel.

'The killer knew what she was doing,' said Astrid, 'but it's difficult for any human being not to leave some trace somewhere of their presence. I reckon she stepped back into the shadows over there by the tree. We didn't quite get a footprint, but the heel of her boot sank into the earth at the bottom of the tree. From that we might be able to get a rough indication of her weight. That started me thinking about her height. There's only one hundred and forty-two centimetres of clearance between the bottom of the tree and the first branches. Unless she was a midget, she would have had to duck in to keep concealed without getting tangled in the branches.' Astrid grinned and held out a plastic evidence bag.

The bag looked empty to Fabel until he stepped out into the street and held it up against the street light.

'A single strand,' said Astrid. 'It's maybe not connected to the killing, but given where I found it I think that's very unlikely. I would say your killer is a blonde. And we have her DNA.'

3.

The Altona Balkon – the 'Altona Balcony' – is a plateau of parkland elevated thirty metres above the River Elbe and fringed with a bench-lined boulevard. The Balcony affords one of the finest views of Hamburg, all along the Elbe to the Kohlbrandbrücke, making it a favourite spot not just for the people of Altona but for those from all over Hamburg.

A still-handsome man of about sixty, his coat collar turned up against the cold, sat on a bench at the edge of the snow-dusted Balkon and watched the distant activity of the ships and tugs, loaders and cranes in the container harbours. Above him the sky was a pale winter blue and behind him the low sun sparkled gold through the naked branches of the trees. It was a peaceful moment: a moment in which he realised how little peace he had enjoyed over the last twenty years.

A woman with a dog walked past, followed by three teenage boys on skateboards thundering along the rock-salted foot-path, their breath fuming in the cold air. Then peace again.

'Hello, Uncle Georg.' A young woman in her thirties, expen-sively dressed and tastefully made-up, sat down beside him and kissed him on the cheek. She laid her handbag and a copy of *Muliebritas* magazine across her lap and placed a carrier bag on the bench beside her.

'You know, it wasn't all bad,' he said as if she had been beside him all the while. 'Back home. Back then, I mean.'

'No, Uncle Georg, I suppose it wasn't.'

'I mean, I did believe in what we stood for. What we did. There were things that were better then. People cared for each other more. We had a sense of community. Of society. Whatever dreadful things we had to do, we did them for the greater good of the people, of the world.'

She rested a gloved hand on his arm. 'I know you did. What's wrong, uncle?'

'And sometimes . . . well, sometimes I look at the way we live now and think we maybe had it more right than everybody says we did. It wasn't what we believed in that forced us to do these things. It was a war. A cold war, maybe, but it was still a war.' He stopped and smiled at her. 'I'm sorry, my dear. Just an old man ranting.'

'Are you sure that's all that's wrong?'

'I thought . . .' He frowned, his gaze out across the Elbe river. 'It's nothing. It was just I got the feeling that I was being watched or followed. Instinct. More like paranoia.'

'Are you sure there wasn't more to it? Maybe you *were* being followed,' she asked.

He shook his head. 'No one's that good. I used all the old tricks and checks. Like I said, paranoia.'

'I got you a present,' she said and handed him the carrier bag.

He looked into it and smiled. '*Rondo Melange* . . .'

She smiled too. 'They started making it again. Like you say, not everything from back then was bad.'

'But I suppose they make it for a profit now. Everything that was done then for the good of the people is now done for a profit. Like us. Like the way we've turned what we do into a business. All for money now.' He laughed bitterly. 'I'm an entrepreneur.'

'To be honest, Uncle Georg, most of my life has been since,

not before. Almost all of my meetings have taken place since the Wall came down. And we've done well out of them, haven't we?'

'Yes, my child.' He turned to her and smiled sadly. 'But the things I taught you and your sisters. All those terrible things.'

'It's our business, uncle. It's what we do. What we are.'

He nodded. 'Did you see the media coverage of the St Pauli killing?'

'Yes . . . they're talking about it being the Angel again.'

'What about the forthcoming meetings – is everything going to plan?'

'Yes, uncle. Everything is going well.'

'Will the Hamburg one look like an accident?'

'Suicide. The meeting will be as the brief required.'

'What about the big one? You clear on everything?'

'Not a problem. It will actually be easier. No need to disguise it. I'm going to use the Sako TRG-21.'

'Is it okay over that distance?'

'Perfect. And anyway, I'm comfortable with it. And that new suppressor works well. It doesn't just muffle, it distorts any report and sends scanners looking in the wrong direction for the shooter. But in a remote location like that, it won't be an issue anyway. If the intel is correct, he'll be alone.'

'You'll have to get out quick. Back across the border, I mean.'

'I always do, Uncle Georg.'

'That suppressor is the last new bit of kit I can get you. It increases our exposure risk every time I acquire new equipment. Our client sourced it for me and I don't like getting them involved. I've got no control over the supply chain and we could be lumbered with traceable gear.'

'I understand. Do you have the details for the other meetings?'

He handed her a data stick. 'I can't get used to this technology. I feel like I'm living in the future and I don't belong in it. All that information, stored on something so insignificant. If we'd had these back then we'd have been able to destroy all our files before the rabble got their hands on them.' He sighed. 'You never ask. Why do you never ask?'

'Ask what?'

'Why they have to die. Are you never curious?'

'You taught us not to be. It's none of my concern. My job is to complete the meeting. Sure, sometimes when I'm preparing . . . watching them . . . it's like seeing into their lives and I sometimes wonder why this person has to be ended. But not much. I just do my job.' She ran her hand through his grey hair. 'You worry too much, Uncle Georg. Remember how you taught us to take every moment of pleasure we could? To enjoy the time in between meetings?'

'Yes. I do remember. Do you enjoy your life?'

'I enjoy everything this life gives me. I've got you to thank for that.'

'But the killing . . .'

She smiled, but looked over his shoulder to make sure no one was within earshot.

'We all die. I learned that from you. We all die alone and many of us die in pain and fear. Terrifying diseases. Horrific injuries. Lingering deaths. All my meetings are ended quickly and the target has little idea what's happening to them. Sometimes no idea: not even an instant of fear or pain. And, for all you or I know, I could be saving them from great future agony and anguish. That's the way you trained me. I don't feel bad about what I do; you told me not to feel bad about it.'

'Even though we're doing it for money now?'

'The fact that we're doing this for ourselves instead of for the state isn't our fault. They changed the world around us. We are what we are, you and I. Just like everybody else who was cut adrift when the Wall came down. Try not to worry so much.' She placed the data stick in her handbag and kissed him on the cheek again. 'Goodbye, Uncle Georg.'

'There's one more thing,' he said, halting her as she rose from the seat. 'We may have to arrange another meeting. Not for a client.'

'Oh?' she said. 'We've never done a non-paying job before.'

'This is a self-protection thing. Someone is beginning to ask too many questions in the right places. A policeman. And he's maybe getting a little too close to home. We may need to deal with it. Discreetly.'

'When?'

'I'll let you know. It may come to nothing. Goodbye, my child.'

'Goodbye, Uncle Georg.'

After she left, he remained on the bench, fists rammed into his coat pockets, his collar turned up against the cold, and tried to recapture that moment of peace. But he couldn't.

4.

Fabel drove into the Police Presidium in Hamburg-Alsterdorf at ten-thirty a.m. He had only managed to get five hours' sleep and felt leaden and dull. He spent the rest of the morning preparing for the team briefing. His weariness suddenly intensified when he was intercepted in the lift by Criminal Director Horst van Heiden.

'A word, Jan . . .' Van Heiden pressed the button for the fifth storey, the top-brass floor, signalling that the word was formal.

Fabel followed van Heiden into his office and sat down. When van Heiden sat down on the executive leather chair behind his desk, he straightened his tie and adjusted a notebook and pen on his desk. When the order of his bureaucratic universe was once more restored, he began.

'I just wanted to catch up with a couple of things. Are you okay for this conference on violence against women? I've had the organiser on the phone again. I think she's worried that we'll send someone junior.'

'It may come to that, if I'm honest.'

'This murder last night?' asked van Heiden.

'I take it that was one of the things you wanted to talk to me about . . .' Fabel failed to keep the weariness from his voice.

'It's all over the media,' said van Heiden. 'And there are some elements who blame us for not catching the Angel the first time round. If that is indeed who we're dealing with.'

'That I don't know, Horst. I actually think it's very unlikely. The modus is totally different. But I'm digging out all the old files. Obviously, it wasn't my case the first time around.'

'Mmm . . .' Van Heiden again nudged the silver pen a fraction of a degree. 'That's the thing . . . I'll be quite frank about this, Jan, we are getting a lot of funding from the BKA for you to set up this Super Murder Commission.' The BKA was the Bundeskriminalamt, the Federal Crime Bureau. 'It's quite an accolade for the Polizei Hamburg to have a unit that will have a republic-wide brief. Within legal restraints, I mean,' van Heiden continued. 'As I've said to you before, it is an opportunity for us to establish ourselves as the centre of excellence in investigating complex and multiple murders in much the same way as the Institute for Judicial Medicine at Eppendorf is seen as the centre of excellence in forensic science.'

'But . . . ?' Fabel raised an eyebrow. Van Heiden was beginning to sound like a commercial. And he always did a commercial before he hit you with the punchline.

'But I do not delude myself that the reputation that has won us this accolade is a collective one. It's yours, Jan. You're the one everyone thinks of as Germany's leading expert on complex and multiple murder cases.'

'Thanks for the compliment.' There was a resigned scepticism in Fabel's smile. They both knew that van Heiden was getting pats on the back for Fabel's achievement. 'But let me guess: I inherit the Angel of St Pauli case that no one could solve in the nineties and, if I don't get a result, suddenly my reputation takes a knock.'

'Something like that.'

'Well, for what it's worth, I really don't think this is the work of the Angel. But I'm not ready to go on record with that yet.' Fabel stood up.

'Oh . . .' Van Heiden reached into a drawer and took out a letter. 'There was something else. We've received a request for an interview from the Danish police.'

'What about?' Fabel leaned over his desk and took the letter from him.

'It doesn't say. As you know, the Danish police have a liaison officer here, but this has come direct from a *Politidirektør* Vestergaard. One of his officers, Jens Jespersen, is flying in from Copenhagen, specifically to speak to you. There are no other details. It would appear that your reputation is becoming truly international.'

After checking all his drawers, without success, to see if he had left his MP3 player in the office, Fabel had a coffee and a cheese roll at his desk before taking a few minutes to prepare himself for his meeting with Anna Wolff. He knew it was going to be a difficult one. So did Anna, if her expression was anything to go by when she walked into his office, as always without knocking.

'Sit down Anna,' said Fabel.

'What is this?' she said, still standing. 'Am I getting the sack?'

Fabel sighed deeply. 'Yes, Anna. Effectively you are.'

For the first time since he had known her, Anna looked truly taken aback. She dropped down into the chair and gazed at Fabel blankly.

'I'm sorry, Anna. I'm going to request that you be re-assigned. I've warned you more times than I can remember about your attitude.'

'What? Is this because of the crack I made last night?'

'Not exclusively, Anna, but I've got to tell you it didn't help. I need officers who will respect the decisions I make and follow the orders I give. Most of all, I need a team that pulls together. I need people I can rely on.'

'Are you saying you can't rely on me? When have I ever let you down?' Anna did what she could to restore her composure.

'Listen, Anna, it's a constant struggle trying to build and maintain an efficient Murder Commission team. Added to that I now have this added responsibility that the BKA have asked me to take on. Over the last four years we have seen Paul Lindemann killed and Maria Klee . . . well, Maria is going to need care for a long, long time.'

'You don't need to tell me about Paul Lindemann,' said Anna, once more defiant. 'He was my partner, after all. And Maria was my friend.'

'And they were both my responsibility.' Fabel paused. 'I know you were close to them both, Anna. But Paul's death and what happened to Maria have made it very clear to me that we have to tighten up our procedures. We need to operate as a fully disciplined unit. The discipline we need is a discipline that you seem to lack.'

There was silence for a moment. Anna looked at Fabel as if trying to read his face; to measure what room for negotiation there might be. Something like resignation settled into her expression.

'I thought you put us together as a team because we were all different. Because we each had something to offer.'

'I did,' said Fabel. 'But I need this Murder Commission to work cohesively. No loose cannons or personal agendas.'

'Oh, wait a minute . . . This is all about Maria, isn't it?

Because she took off on a personal crusade you decide to crack down on . . . on *individuality*.'

'I'm not talking about you expressing your individuality, Anna. I'm talking about you totally ignoring the fact that you're part of a team.' Fabel realised he had raised his voice. He took a breath, then, in a measured tone, said: 'I can't have a renegade on my team, Anna.'

'I'll bet.' Anna's expression was close to a sneer. 'That would screw up your chances of becoming Germany's Crime Fighter Number One. What is it, Jan – are you afraid I'll embarrass you?' This time it was Anna who paused. 'I'm sorry. This is where I want to work. If you transfer me, I'll quit.'

'That's your decision, Anna. And believe me, I wanted things to work out differently. I wanted to move you up to become joint deputy with Werner. But I can't recommend you for a Senior Commissarship because of your attitude.'

'Have you put the papers in yet?' asked Anna. 'For my transfer, I mean.'

'Not yet. I've got to get this new Angel case rolling. The other thing is I wanted to give you the chance to put in for a transfer yourself. It would look better on your CV.'

'Give me to the end of this case, *Chef*. Then I'll go quietly.'

'Okay.' Fabel hesitated for a moment. 'I'm short-staffed as it is. But while you're still part of this unit, I need you to rein in that independence a little.'

After Anna left, Fabel sat looking out of his window over the snow-frosted treetops of Winterhude Park. The expression on Anna's face lingered in his mind. He recalled too the eager if prickly Anna he had recruited five years before. It had been Anna's edge, her drive that had convinced him she would be an asset to the team. Somehow, somewhere during those five years he had lost his way with her.

But the thing that churned in his gut was that he was still not convinced he was handling it right.

Fabel's thoughts were interrupted by the phone ringing. It was Ulrich Wagner, from the BKA Federal Crime Bureau. Fabel liked Wagner, but could have done without the interruption: he was keen to prepare for his team briefing. After the usual chit-chat, Wagner got down to business.

'There's a Federal Republic-wide alert gone out – I don't know, maybe you've seen it – about Margarethe Paulus.'

'Sorry, I haven't,' said Fabel. 'I'm up to my eyes with this St Pauli murder. The alleged return of the so-called "Angel of St Pauli".'

'Well, in a way that's why I'm calling. Margarethe Paulus was confined to the state mental hospital in Mecklenburg, which isn't too far away from you. She's been in there for thirteen years. Three weeks ago she decided to discharge herself. Unofficially. There's not been a trace of her since. Margarethe Paulus is considered to be a highly dangerous individual. Before she was committed there was a spate of armed robberies, all very efficiently executed and all carried out by a lone woman. It was all very cool and organised. Each time it was a woman of completely different appearance, hitting a different type of target – a bank, then a store, then a security van. But always for cash. Never jewellery or any other loot that would have had to be fenced. And that meant no need to involve any third party.'

'So how did they get her?' asked Fabel.

'They didn't. The Mecklenburg police were never able to put together enough evidence to identify the woman, far less to nail Margarethe Paulus. But she started to think bigger. Look for accomplices. Or at least that's what we think was going on. She got involved with a biker gang. The story she told is that she met up with them to discuss potential co-operation. But they weren't interested and things turned nasty. Three of the gang attempted to rape her.'

'Attempted?'

'I've seen the crime-scene photographs, Jan. It's almost

impossible to believe that a woman, alone against three hard-ened villains, could have done all that. But forensics proved that she did.'

'She killed all three?'

'More than that. She castrated them. From what the Mecklenburg forensics people could ascertain, she killed two instantly, and castrated them post-mortem. But the third, the ringleader . . . she kept him alive and conscious throughout the whole process. It was his screaming that alerted people in the neighbourhood who then called the police.'

'God . . .' Fabel considered what Wagner had told him. 'That fits with the original Angel murders.'

'It does. But they couldn't have been committed by her. She was incarcerated in the State Mental Hospital at the time. However, when I saw the report on the latest killings . . .'

'I get your point,' said Fabel. 'But this time there's no castration. Evisceration, yes, but balls intact. Can you email me the relevant stuff on her, including the most up-to-date images?'

'I've already arranged it.'

'The Mecklenburg police will have a record of her DNA: could you arrange for that to be sent too? This time our killer may have left a trace of herself behind. A hair.'

'Not a problem,' said Wagner. 'So you maybe have a break this time.'

'Maybe. But I'm not counting on it.'

Fabel held his team briefing in the Murder Commission's inci-dent room. In addition to his now depleted core team of Werner, Anna and Anna's partner Henk Hermann, there were other detectives who had been drafted in by Fabel to beef up the team. Thomas Glasmacher was a large, burly blond who, at the moment, was sniffing and sneezing into his handker-chief, struggling, as he had been for the last week, to fight off a winter cold. Dirk Hechtner was smaller and dark-haired.

Fabel had borrowed Hechtner from a Police Direction in Hamburg-Harburg. In their brief careers to date, both Glasmacher and Hechtner had shown a great deal of promise as well as an ability to think unconventionally when needed. Neither was aware of the fact that Fabel was considering recruiting them both permanently. In total, Fabel had to find four new investigators for his unit: five once Anna was gone. In addition, he was going to push for specialists to be attached to the Commission.

There were three photographs of Jake Westland on the incident board: an enlargement of his passport photograph, a publicity photograph and the last photograph that would ever be taken of him, lying bleached of colour on a slab in Eppendorf's mortuary. On the other side of the board were smaller pictures of five other men and some cuttings from newspapers. Fabel walked over to the board and wrote four words in red marker: MOTIVATED, STALKER, ANGEL and COPYCAT.

'Okay, you've all read through the case file as we have it so far. The only direct witness to the murder was Westland himself – and his account only comes to us second-hand. As far as I can see, these four categories are the options which present best at the moment.' He pointed to the word MOTI-VATED. 'Everything seems to point to Westland being in the wrong place at the wrong time. Westland's actions last night after the concert seemed all to be spur-of-the-moment. But if for a moment we assume that someone knew he would be at the back of Herbertstrasse and when he would be there, then we could be looking at a premeditated, motivated murder. Westland's wallet, diary and cellphone are missing, so we could be looking at theft as a motive, although I feel that's highly unlikely. He had a few minutes alone and undisturbed in his dressing room earlier in the evening. It could be that his phone and diary were taken to hide details of a planned meeting, though God knows why he would pre-arrange to meet anyone in a sleazy Kiez backstreet. I've been in touch with the British police and asked them to provide us with his cellphone records. In the meantime, I want us to do all the usual investigations into Westland's background, his marriage, his business affairs – all the usual checks.'

Fabel jabbed a finger at the word STALKER.

'Jake Westland was a singer, a celebrity. A late seventies, early eighties pin-up. He was also a multimillionaire. He was exactly the kind of figure who attracts the wrong kind of attention from obsessives. I've emailed the police in England to see if I can get any information about stalkers, persistent fans, threatening fan mail, that kind of thing. In the meantime, I've been able to talk with Westland's bodyguards . . .' Fabel ignored Werner's knowing smirk. 'And they confirm that there wasn't anything out of the ordinary that took place either before or after his concert. They've actually been with him during his whole tour, and they say there's been nothing unusual or that caused them concern since he arrived in Germany. They are also pretty certain that Westland suggested visiting the Kiez as a spur-of-the-moment thing. In short, I think either of these options is unlikely. And that brings us to . . .'

Fabel circled the word ANGEL.

'Between nineteen ninety-six and nineteen ninety-nine, five men were murdered in the Kiez district. Their ages ranged from thirty-five to fifty-seven. All the victims were repeat visitors to the Reeperbahn area and all were frequent users of prostitutes. Every victim met his end the same way – throat cut with a single lateral slice. The entry wound was always on the right side of the neck, straight through behind the trachea and out. Death would have been pretty swift and, because the windpipe had been severed, silent. The bodies were found in different parts of the Kiez, more often than not in their own cars. Forensic evidence pointed to them being attacked from the front passenger seat of their own cars.

Absolutely no forensic traces – fingerprints, DNA, fibre samples – were ever found. But maybe our killer has slipped up this time – we've retrieved a single blonde hair from the scene. If it really does belong to the killer, it's yet one more difference from the original killings. The other difference is that the original killer certainly never left his or her victims alive long enough to tell us that it was the "Angel" who killed them. The last in the original series, a forty-nine-year-old ship engineer, was found in November 'ninety-nine. Then nothing.'

'Until now . . .' said Werner.

'So how did she get the name "the Angel"?' asked Dirk Hechtner.

'There was massive media interest in the case at the time, as I'm sure everybody remembers,' said Fabel. 'When I turned up at Davidwache last night I was greeted by Sylvie Achtenhagen and her camera crew. As you know, Frau Achtenhagen has become quite the celebrity herself, with her own news-magazine show on HanSat. But ten years ago no one had heard of Sylvie Achtenhagen. At that time she was a young and very ambitious new reporter for one of the public broadcasters. She built her reputation on her coverage of the murders and she ended up getting to do an hour-long special on the case. I have to admit she handled the whole thing very cleverly, even if she was way off with her conclusions. Basically, Achtenhagen gave the whole thing a feminist twist. Her take on it was that almost exactly one hundred years after Jack the Ripper, a female Ripper was doing pretty much the same thing in Hamburg. We've all heard the saying that Hamburg is the most easterly suburb of London . . . anyway, Achtenhagen exaggerated the similarities between the two cities. She also drew parallels between the cases: both involved the use of a surgically sharp blade, mutilation of the bodies and the removal of trophies. In the case of Jack the Ripper those trophies were sometimes the genitals; in the case of the

Angel they were exclusively the genitals. Both series of murders took place in red-light districts: Whitechapel in London, the Kiez in Hamburg. And, of course, both series of murders seemed to be within the context of prostitute and client.'

'The Angel was – is – definitely a prostitute?' asked Werner.

'It looks likely. Or pretending to be one. Anyway, Sylvie Achtenhagen turned this idea on its head; there was a hint that while Jack the Ripper represented the age-old repression and abuse of women, the Angel represented their liberation. Total crap, of course, but it captured the imagination. It came close to making the Angel a feminist icon. Achtenhagen managed to imply – very subtly, mind – that it was the victims who were the aggressors.'

'And Sylvie Achtenhagen's documentary was the first to describe the killer as "the Angel"?' asked Anna.

'Achtenhagen planned to make a name for herself with her hour-long TV special. She succeeded. But she also made a name for the killer. The "Angel of St Pauli" caught the public's imagination and it stuck.' Fabel threw the marker down onto the conference table. 'What I resented about what Achtenhagen did is that it cemented the idea of a female avenging angel stalking the streets of Hamburg looking for male victims. While that is maybe the case, the truth is we have only one witness account of one of the victims being seen in the company of a youngish blonde prostitute shortly before the supposed time of death. Apart from that, for all we know the killer could have been a man. And the precision and method of the throat cut could suggest a military or even special-forces background. But Achtenhagen succeeded in closing the public's eyes to anything other than an iconic female vigilante.'

'I don't know . . .' Werner winced. 'The castration thing. To kill another guy is one thing . . . but to slice off his todger. My money's on it having been a woman . . .'

'All right, settle down,' Fabel said to suppress the laughter that broke out. 'Like I said, I think it's more likely that the Angel was a prostitute. From what I've gleaned from the original case files, the Angel was suspected to be an Aileen Wuornos-type serial killer. A woman, abused as a child, who turned to prostitution and carrying out revenge killings against clients. But whether male or female and whatever her motives, the so-called Angel was very, very careful not to leave forensic evidence or to give any clue to his or her identity. And that makes me very doubtful about the Angel disclosing her identity to Westland as an announcement that she is rising from the ashes. Which brings me to what I think is our most likely prospect . . .' Fabel slapped his hand onto the board next to the word COPYCAT.

'The Angel of St Pauli exists as a concept, if perhaps not as a reality. A powerful concept that has maybe caught more than the general public's imagination. I think it's entirely possible that Westland's murder is the work of the Angel by inspiration rather than execution. There are fundamental differences between his murder and the original killings: the killer didn't carry out a post-mortem castration or take a trophy . . .'

'That could simply be because she was disturbed,' said Werner. 'Christa Eisel found Westland still alive and bleeding out fast. If she hadn't applied pressure he wouldn't have made it to the ambulance. Maybe the killer heard Christa coming.'

'Maybe so, but a panicked escape doesn't fit with the fact that no one was seen leaving the scene. Carstens Kaminski's Davidwache team have spoken to almost every girl working the Kiez that night – and bear in mind that most of them sit watching the streets from their windows. Normally *any* unknown woman passing through the street would stand out. The problem we have is that it was an exceptional night in the Kiez, given this near-riot feminist protest. But, prior to the protesters' invasion of Herbertstrasse, no one noticed a woman who didn't belong wandering around. Also, Christa

Eisel swears no one passed her coming out of the square. But let's say the killer *was* disturbed – it still doesn't alter the fact that she eviscerated Westland instead of cutting his throat. What's more, Westland was on foot, where all of the original victims were in their cars. And let's remember we are nearly a full decade on from the last Angel murder. There are, however, specific similarities – particularly the expert use of a blade. For the moment my money stays on this being the work of a copycat.' Fabel slipped a large printout from the folder on his desk. He stuck it up on the incident board. A woman of about thirty stared blankly out from the photograph. She was wearing no make-up and her blonde hair had been brushed back severely from her face. The image had the bleached, stark lighting of an official photograph.

'This is Margarethe Paulus,' explained Fabel. 'I've just been sent her details by the BKA. Three nights ago, she escaped from a secure mental hospital in Mecklenburg-Vorpommern. I haven't had a lot of time to go through all the details, but the main thing you should know is that she is a highly dangerous individual. She killed and castrated three men in nineteen ninety-four and would have been a prime suspect for the original Angel killings had she not already been locked up. And we have to bear in mind that her murders were spree, rather than serial. She is familiar with Hamburg, apparently, and was brought up in Zarrentin, in north-west Mecklenburg. Although it was in the former East, it's only seventy kilometres from Hamburg. It's highly unlikely, given that she only escaped three days ago, that she's involved with these latest killings, but we have to keep an open mind. She would certainly be a candidate for a copycat killer. At the very least we need to be on the lookout for her.'

'How did she manage to escape?'

'Walked out of the main gate, apparently. She had complained of feeling unwell and an orderly and a nurse were escorting her to see a doctor. She broke the male orderly's arm before knocking him out, then stole the nurse's uniform, electronic door key and identity card before locking her in a storage room, bound and gagged. It's clear that Paulus is a highly organised type. Somehow she had managed to collect make-up and hair dye over God knows how long so that she could make herself look like this nurse.'

'So she had targeted the nurse, rather than just grabbing an opportunity to escape?' asked Dirk Hechtner.

'Probably months in advance.'

Fabel spent the rest of the briefing going through what they had in the way of statements and the initial forensic evidence. He then allocated investigative tasks to each team member. After he had wound the meeting up, Werner loitered until the others were gone.

'Let's have it, Werner,' said Fabel, gathering up his papers. 'What's on your mind?'

'Anna told me about your chat.'

'My God, it didn't take her long to find a shoulder to cry on.'

'It's not like that, Jan. I asked her how it had gone. She's in shock, I think. So am I, truth be told.'

'You think I'm making a mistake?' Fabel asked.

'I think you would have handled it differently if Anna had been a man, to be frank, Jan.'

'Not that again, Werner. I don't let gender influence how I deal with my officers.'

'Well, whatever the reason, I think you should give Anna another chance. She's put her neck on the line more than once for the sake of catching a killer.'

'But don't you see that's the point? Anna has put her neck on the line. She nearly got herself killed twice doing exactly that. This isn't the Wild West, Werner. I mean, I thought you would understand. If anything it's you that's kept me from screwing up because you always make sure we follow procedure. There have been times when Anna has all but rendered evidence inadmissible because she hasn't followed the State Prosecutor's guidelines.'

Werner sighed and rubbed a shovel of a hand over the grey stubble on his scalp. Fabel always thought Werner looked like a retired boxer or hardened sailor: his broken nose, picked up early in his career as a street policeman, his Hamburg Low-German way of speaking combined with his faintly scruffy way of dressing and his powerful build made him look like someone who was probably inclined to use muscle rather than brain. But no one had the eye for detail that Werner had. A tiny discrepancy in someone's statement, some event that didn't quite fit into the chronology of a crime, a forgotten scrap of evidence that changed the whole picture: these were the things that Werner caught when everyone else, including Fabel, had missed them. The truth was that Fabel relied heavily on Werner's counsel, and it troubled him that his friend thought he was making a mistake over Anna.

'Listen,' said Werner, 'I know you've been looking for a replacement for Maria Klee to partner me with. Team me up with Anna in the meantime. You could put Henk together with Dirk for a while. I think Anna and I could work well together. A good balance. Give it a go for a month or two. Then, if you still think she should go, fair enough.'

'Have you talked to her about this idea of yours?' Fabel asked suspiciously.

'No. I promise. It's just that she's desperate to stay in the Commission, Jan. And Anna really would be a loss to the team. Another loss. She's a good officer, Jan. She just needs to be brought into line. Let me have a crack at it.'

'Okay, let me think about it,' said Fabel.

'Hard day?'

'I thought you were asleep,' said Fabel to the shadow in the bed.

'I was. I asked if you'd had a hard day . . .'

'The usual. Murder. Mayhem. Paperwork. You?'

'The usual. I heard you have another celebrity murder on your hands. Are you sure you're not doing them yourself, just to advance your career?'

'Our career. I can see I'm going to have to bring you into this one,' said Fabel. 'That's the deal: I'll keep killing them to keep us both in work.' He slid between the sheets. They were cool and clean on his skin. 'By the way, have you seen my MP3 player lying around?'

'No. You've already asked me. How did it go with Renate?'

Fabel sighed. 'How does it ever go with Renate? She was as bitter as hell, as always. I don't know how the hell she has managed to turn the whole situation around so that she's the injured party. It was Behrens who dumped her. Not me.'

'It's a woman thing.' Susanne still had her back to him. 'If you can't find *the* man to blame, find *a* man to blame. I hold you responsible for Hans Zimmerman not choosing me as his partner for our kindergarten parade.'

'I knew there was something,' said Fabel. 'Anyway, Gabi is thinking about joining the police. Renate blames me and wants me to talk her out of it.'

'Will you?'

'No. Not talk her out of it. Give her an informed picture, yes. Talk her out of it, no.'

'We'll talk about it tomorrow.' Susanne's voice was thick with sleep, but Fabel slid close to her, put his arms around her, cupped her breast in his hand.

'I'd like to make up for the kindergarten parade . . .' he said.

Jespersen had been relieved that the seat next to him on the plane was unoccupied. Jespersen liked to use travel time to sort things out in his head: to review, to do a bit of broader thinking. The Scandinavian Airlines flight to Hamburg's Fuhlsbüttel Airport from Copenhagen had only taken a little over fifty minutes but, during that time, Jens Jespersen had been able to study the information he had obtained through Europol on *Erster Kriminalhauptkommissar* Jan Fabel.

Most of the information related to the consultative role Fabel was adopting for cases outside the Polizei Hamburg's jurisdiction. He was being touted by Europol as a major expert in complex murder investigations. The 'go-to guy' as the Americans would call him. Jespersen didn't like Americans much. He liked Germans less.

As the seat-belt lights came on and Jespersen put the file back in his case, he reluctantly admitted to himself that the German was probably the best person to talk to. Talk to about what? It suddenly struck Jespersen that he had come a long way to meet with the German and he didn't really have that much to discuss. All he had was a remark made by a drug trafficker during a sting operation; a couple of potentially connected events that may be nothing more than so many coincidences; and a legend: a vague and most likely exaggerated spook-story from the dark ages of the Cold War.

After touchdown at Hamburg Fuhlsbüttel, Jespersen called the Politigård headquarters in Copenhagen and was put through to his office. He spoke to Harald Tolstrup, his deputy. Tolstrup confirmed that Jespersen was booked into a hotel on the Alter Wall, in Hamburg's city centre. Tolstrup also said that Jespersen's boss, *Politidirektør* Vestergaard, wanted to speak with him as soon as possible and hadn't sounded happy. After Jespersen hung up from his call to the Politigård, he phoned the Hamburg Police Presidium and asked in English to speak to Jan Fabel. He was told that Fabel was in a meeting: Jespersen gave his cellphone number and asked that Fabel call him back.

After Jespersen checked into the hotel he took a walk around the city centre. It was cold but bright and he looked up at the pale blue of the sky. It was the same sky as in Copenhagen. As in Stockholm or Oslo. Hamburg's light was a Nordic light and Jespersen found it strange to be in a foreign country amongst people he disliked and yet to see the same sky, the same light, the same architecture, the same faces in the street. He knew that the illusion would have been dispelled if he had travelled even a little further south. But here, in Hamburg, and totally despite himself, Jespersen felt at home. He walked along Grosse Bleichen and found himself in front of an impressive red-brick building which announced itself with a plaque as the Hanseviertel. Jespersen went in, partly motivated by curiosity: he had come across the word 'Hanseviertel' once before, when he had visited Bergen in Norway. Bergen had been part of the Hanseatic League and there had been a part of the city where German traders had settled in the Middle Ages called *Tyskebryggen*, the German Wharf: Bergen's own Hanseviertel. This Hanseviertel in Hamburg, however, was something completely different: behind the red brick lay connecting avenues and galleries of shops, all now covered over by glass. It looked like the ideal place to get some lunch and, while he was at it, he would pick up a small gift for his twelve-year-old niece. Everywhere he went he would find some small soft toy for Mette, his younger brother's daughter. She was beginning to pretend she was too old for such nonsense, but he could tell she liked it. He found a small shop in the arcade selling gifts that were a little more upmarket and unusual than the usual tourist stuff. He bought a small stuffed bear for Mette: it was dressed in a blue jacket with 'Hamburg' embroidered on the back and was wearing a Prinz Heinrich fisherman's hat. Jespersen found a pleasant-looking café and ordered a light lunch. He sat eating slowly and watching Germans go by.

Germans. Jens Jespersen had been a police officer for twenty-three years. His father had been a police officer before him. And his grandfather before him. It was a tradition he was immensely proud of. And in that tradition lay the roots of his dislike of Germans. But now was not the time to think of such things.

A female voice asked him something in German. Jespersen looked up: the woman was in her thirties with light blonde hair, pale skin over high cheekbones and bright blue eyes.

'I'm sorry?' he said in English.

'May I sit here?' she repeated in English.

He nodded, moving his coat to allow her to sit. She was about to say something when Jespersen's cellphone rang. He answered it without excusing himself.

'Herr Jespersen? This is Principal Chief Commissar Fabel, Polizei Hamburg Murder Commission. I got your message. I'm sorry I couldn't get back to you earlier but I was kind of tied up with something. We've just had a major case kick off – I'm sure you know the drill. Anyway, I believe you would like to arrange a meeting.'

Jespersen, whose English was excellent, was surprised to hear the German speak in perfect and, to Jespersen's ears, unaccented English.

'Yes, Herr Fabel. I have a few things to check out so I'll be in Hamburg for a few days, but I'd like to talk to you as soon as possible. Would you be able to see me tomorrow?'

'Tomorrow might be difficult. Like I say, we've just launched a major inquiry. Give me a moment . . .' There was a short silence. 'How about four-thirty at the Presidium?'

'I'll be there,' said Jespersen.

'I hope you don't mind me asking, Herr Jespersen, but when you say you have a few things to check out, does that mean you are conducting part of an investigation here in Hamburg?'

'I see what you're getting at . . .' Jespersen managed to get just the right element of irritation into his voice. 'If I were conducting an investigation, I would have gone through the appropriate channels. No, Mr Fabel, your toes are not being trodden on. I'll see you tomorrow at four-thirty.' He snapped his cellphone shut. Bloody Germans: was there one who wasn't a born bureaucrat?

'Are you English?' the woman sitting next to him asked after he had pocketed his phone.

'No.' He smiled wearily, not really trying to conceal his disappointment at having to make small talk. 'I'm Danish.'

'No! I'm half Danish,' she said fluently and enthusiastically in his native tongue, but with a heavy German accent. 'My mother is from Fåborg – you know, on Fyn – but I was brought up here. My father is from Hamburg.'

'You don't say,' Jespersen said. The woman was clearly delighted at the happenstance that she should sit next to a Dane; Jespersen despaired at it. He liked to have time to think things through. But, there again, she was an attractive woman.

'Are you here on holiday?' she asked.

'No. Business,' said Jespersen. He looked at the young woman more closely. She certainly had the colouring of a Dane. Something about her reminded him of Karin. Her almost white blonde hair had been gathered up by a band but protested in a torrent of kinks and curls. Jespersen smiled, this time not wearily.

She really was very attractive.

7.

Carstens Kaminski called Fabel at his office in the Presidium first thing.

'We've got someone you should talk to,' he explained. 'It's probably nothing, but I think you should hear what he has to say.'

'In custody?'

'No. A witness. Of sorts.'

'I'll come over,' said Fabel.

'No, it's okay. I'll send him over to the Presidium. He'll be there in twenty minutes.'

Even after all of these years, after all of the things he had seen, Fabel still found it difficult to understand why some people got involved in the things they did. Despite his experience, Fabel still sometimes found himself fooled by people's appearances. Jürgen Mann, who now sat opposite Fabel in the interview room, did not look like someone who should have inside information on hookers. Mann was thirty-five years old, tall and slim, dressed trendily but tastefully in a grey jacket and trousers and a black sweater. He had a wide, strong jaw forested with the kind of designer stubble that actually took a lot of maintenance to look so casual. Like the grey-haired man Fabel had seen ducking into Herbertstrasse, the fact that someone so outwardly normal, so unexpected, could be a regular user of street prostitutes depressed him.

Because of the 'sensitivity' of the interview, Fabel conducted it alone.

'What is it you do?' asked Fabel. 'For a living, I mean?'

'I'm a designer. Packaging, signage, that kind of thing.'

That would explain the stubble, thought Fabel. 'Are you married?'

'Yes. I don't see—'

'Children?' Fabel cut Mann off.

'One. An eight-year-old. Girl.'

'And you visit the Reeperbahn regularly?'

'Now and again. Listen, do you want to hear what I've got to say or not?' Mann asked defiantly.

'I need to know how you came by such information. I need to know about you. How often is "now and again"?'

'Once every couple of weeks or so, I'd say. Sometimes more, sometimes less.'

'And is it always street prostitutes you use?'

'Yes.'

Fabel regarded the young man. He thought of his wife and eight-year-old daughter. 'And this prostitute you told Herr Kaminski about: do you use her frequently?'

'No. It was just the once. And I didn't get to . . . well, there was no contact.'

'Have you seen her before?'

'No. That was the first time. And she approached me. Just sort of came out of the shadows and asked if I wanted to go with her. She told me how much and it was cheaper than usual, so I said yes.'

'Then what happened?'

'Like I told them at Davidwache, she led me into this court-yard. It looked like she planned that we do it there but I said I wanted to go to her room. It was then that she pulled the knife. She had me cornered and said that if I didn't hand over my wallet she would cut me up the same way as she had sliced up that English singer.'

'You believed her?'

'If you had seen her eyes . . . I knew if I didn't do what she said – and maybe even if I did – she would have a go at me with the knife.'

'What kind of knife was it?'

'I don't know. A bloody big one. Maybe a filleting knife or something. Like a butcher knife but thinner.'

'And you gave her your wallet?'

'Yes. I threw it to her and when she caught it, I shoved her as hard as I could and ran for it.'

'And this happened last night?'

'Yes. I knew what she was talking about because I saw this thing on the news about the Angel being back.'

'Yet you still went to the Kiez and wandered into an empty courtyard with a prostitute.'

'I suppose I did. Anyway, it cost me my wallet.'

'So why did you wait until this morning to go to Davidwache and tell them about the robbery?'

'I was going to leave it . . . notify my credit card companies that I'd lost my wallet and have the cards stopped and forget all about it. But then I thought about the fact that she said she was the Angel. I thought I ought to let you know.'

'Very public-spirited of you.'

'Listen, I didn't have to—'

'What did this prostitute look like?'

'She was older than the usual girls. Thirties. Maybe older. She had blonde hair . . . looked dyed. She was quite tall, about one-seventy-five. Slim. She was attractive, but looked – I don't know – hardened, I suppose you could say. She was wearing a dark coat and black leather boots.'

'Okay, I'll need you to go and talk to one of our police artists here. We need to get a good picture of her. Then I'd like you to go through some mugshots for us, on the off chance that you might recognise someone we already know about.'

'I need to get back to work.'

'Fine,' said Fabel. 'I'll send someone over to your home this evening to go through them with you. I take it your wife knows about all of this?'

'Okay . . .' said Mann. 'I'll do it here.'

Fabel got up to leave the room.

'There's one other thing,' said Mann.

'What?'

'Her eyes. If you had seen her eyes. They were so full of hate and anger. That's why I ran. I knew that if I hadn't, she would have killed me for sure. She was the Angel. I know she was the Angel.'

* * *

Carstens Kaminski was in the Murder Commission when Fabel returned. Kaminski was half-sitting on the edge of Anna Wolff's desk, smiling and chatting. He was small and dark and had something about him that was relaxed and confident. A charmer. Fabel heard that he had been quite the ladies' man at one time. If the smile on Anna's face was anything to go by, he probably still was.

'Come on through,' Fabel said to Kaminski and led him into his office.

'Pretty girl,' said Kaminski, with a lazy grin. 'I heard she's looking for a transfer. I'd sure like to accommodate her.'

Fabel stared at Kaminski incredulously. 'My God, it doesn't take long for word to get around, does it?'

'What did you think of Mann's story?' asked Kaminski. 'Nice office you've got, by the way.' He craned his neck. 'Can you see the Winterhude Planetarium from here?'

'Mann's a creep,' said Fabel. 'But I have no doubt that he believes he's had a real brush with death. Or that he truly believes it was the Angel who mugged him.'

'But you don't think it was. Me neither,' said Kaminski. 'But the way she approached him suggests to me that she was keeping out of sight of the other girls. That and the way she was dressed makes me think she wasn't a regular working girl. And she lured him into an isolated courtyard . . . she may not be the original Angel, but she certainly fits with the killer the other night.'

'That's what I thought. Hopefully Mann will be able to give us a good enough artist's impression or pick her out from the mugs. Having said that, like you say I don't think she's a regular in the Kiez. Your guys pick anything else up?'

'We talked to all the window girls in Herbertstrasse that night. Two of them remember seeing a man they thought was Jake Westland. He came in the Gerhardtstrasse end and made his way straight along the street without looking right or left and out onto Davidstrasse.'

'That sounds planned,' said Fabel.

'I don't know, Jan,' said Kaminski, fiddling with the desk calendar on Fabel's desk. 'It could simply be that he was trying to give Martina Schilmann and her guy the slip. Just acting on an impulse. If Mann's hooker is our killer, she certainly didn't arrange to meet him.'

'No . . . but maybe he had arranged to meet someone else and simply ran into the killer. It's just that it seems so . . . purposeful, I suppose. The way he rushed along Herbertstrasse and out the other end, knowing he had only minutes before Martina would start looking for him coming out onto Davidstrasse. But whatever Westland's intentions, I reckon we've got an Angel copycat on our hands. I also reckon Jürgen Mann is probably very lucky that he wasn't her second victim. Brace yourself, Carstens,' said Fabel. 'My thinking is that we're just at the start of a whole new series of killings.'

8.

He looked at his watch: four-fifty. Nothing irritated Fabel more than people being late.

He was the first to admit that he was too obsessive about punctuality. Ever since he had been a boy, the idea of being too late for something had tied knots in Fabel's gut. It was one of those things, like his inability to get drunk, to push himself that one carefree drink too far, that characterised him. That made Jan Fabel who he was.

But this time, as he sat at his desk fuming, Fabel felt justified in his irritation: he had impressed on Jespersen that he was in the middle of launching a major murder inquiry. To be twenty minutes late was more than a lack of courtesy: it was unprofessional. Fabel picked up his phone and called the number he'd been given for Jespersen's cellphone. It rang for a while and then switched to voicemail. Fabel left a message for Jespersen to call him as soon as possible.

Fabel's desk phone rang almost instantly he hung up and he answered expecting it to be Jespersen. It wasn't.

'Hi, *Chef*,' said Anna Wolff. 'I've got something you've got to see.'

'Where are you?'

'I'm up in Butenfeld.' Butenfeld was police shorthand for the morgue at the Institute for Judicial Medicine which was based on the Eppendorf street of that name. 'You're really going to want to see this.'

Fabel looked at his watch and thought about the Dane's infuriating lack of punctuality. 'Okay, I'll come right up.'

9.

'How long has the apartment been vacant?' Ute Cranz turned and smiled at the younger woman. They had spent half an hour viewing the attic apartment and the young female estate agent had done her best to project a maturity and experience that she was clearly years from possessing. She was dressed in a mannish dark blue trouser suit. Why was it, thought Ute, that so many women in business think that to compete with men they have to dress like them?

'It's only just become available for rental. We haven't even advertised it – in fact, we were surprised when you enquired about it. How did you know it was vacant?'

'I've been looking for a flat in this area. I heard that the previous tenant was moving out.'

'I see,' said the estate agent, although she didn't sound entirely convinced. 'You were right to move quickly. Properties of this quality in Altona don't tend to hang around. We've just completed a full renovation of an apartment building around the corner in Schillerstrasse. We had the apartments filled before we had finished the work.'

'How much?' Ute Cranz walked across the lounge to the window, her high heels clicking on the hardwood floor.

'Well, this is nearly two hundred square metres. And it has a balcony with views out across to Palmaille. The monthly rent is two thousand nine hundred euros. Excluding utilities. That's pretty standard for this area.'

Ute looked out of the window at the street below. She saw a man approach the front door of the apartment building. He had grey-white hair but had broad shoulders and moved like a younger man. He was dressed in what she would have described as an 'English-style' heavy tweed jacket and corded trousers.

'Is this one of the neighbours?' she asked the estate agent, who came across to the window and looked down.

'Yes – yes, it is,' she said. 'That's Herr Gerdes. He has the apartment above. A very quiet neighbour, as are the rest of the people in the building. A nice class of resident, as it were.'

'I'll take it.' Ute turned back to the agent and smiled. 'But I'd like to see the kitchen again . . .'

10.

'What have you got?' asked Fabel. Anna had been waiting for him at the reception of the Eppendorf mortuary.

'Well, from the look of it, a middle-aged man and a heart attack,' said Anna as she led him into the mortuary's body store.

Fabel stopped in the hall. 'A heart attack? So what's that got to do with us?'

'Not what,' said Anna. 'Who. The victim was found dead in his hotel bedroom this morning. On the face of it, the cause of death doesn't seem suspicious: all the signs are that it was a heart attack but he'll be given the full treatment, of course. But the victim is a Jens Jespersen, a Danish national.'

'Shit,' said Fabel. 'The Danish police officer. I was supposed to be meeting with him.' He looked at his watch. 'Half an hour ago.'

'Well, you better not keep him waiting any longer,' said Anna, with a grin.

A mortuary attendant wheeled a trolley into the centre of the morgue and removed the covering sheet. The man on the trolley was tall; his short-cropped hair was blond and looked a sickly yellow against the grey pallor of his skin. His lips had a bluish tinge. The Danish passport Anna handed Fabel told him that Jens Jespersen was fifty-four years old, but the man on the trolley had the physique of a much younger man and Fabel guessed he was looking at someone who had been serious about keeping fit.

'He doesn't look like the usual heart-attack candidate,' said Anna as if she'd been reading his mind. Fabel took the plastic bag containing the rest of Jespersen's smaller personal belongings. The watch was a heavy-duty military type. Jespersen's Danish National Police ID card identified him as a *Chefpolitiinspektør*, which Fabel guessed would be somewhere equivalent to his own rank. There was a notebook with general reminder notes scribbled in it, including the Hamburg Police Presidium number, but Fabel could see that this was a personal notebook, not one used for police work. On one page of the notebook was the name OLAF, written in block capitals and double underlined. He slipped the notebook back into the plastic evidence holder.

'Is this it?' He held up the bag and its contents.

'That's it,' said Anna. 'Oh, except he didn't like to sleep alone.' Anna arced an eyebrow and tossed a second evidence bag to Fabel. This one held a souvenir teddy-bear toy, dressed in nautical gear with a Prinz Heinrich peaked cap. Fabel took the bag from Anna and stared absently at the stuffed teddy.

'Doesn't it strike you that something's missing?'

'He doesn't have *Moin! Moin!* embroidered on his little jumper?' Anna smirked. 'I know what you mean. Something is missing. Jespersen was here to talk to you about something, yet there's no sign of his official notebook, no notes of any kind, no paperwork, except for his travel documents. And take a look at this . . .'

She tossed Fabel Jespersen's cellphone. Fabel had to reach quickly to catch it and he scowled at Anna. Flipping the phone open, he searched through its memory.

'Nothing.'

'No recorded incoming or outgoing calls,' said Anna. 'No stored numbers. No registered service. My guess is someone's switched SIM cards on him thinking that no one would think to examine his phone.'

'Damn it,' said Fabel. 'Has forensics looked at any of this?'

'No. The emergency-service doctor who came out to the hotel treated it as a heart attack. Obviously, as a sudden death, the body was sent up here and Möller and his team will have a look at it. I've suggested to Möller that he has a good look at it.'

'What did he say?'

'You know Möller. Top pathologist but world-leading asshole. He told me not to tell him his job, but you know he'll give this one the full works. I've also told the hotel to seal off the room and alerted Holger Brauner that we may need his forensics boys over there, but I wanted to wait till you saw this. I didn't want to overstep my authority . . .'

Fabel fired a warning look at Anna. She stared back, her face empty of expression. It was a trick she had.

'Anyway,' she continued, 'the scene has been trodden on by God knows how many by now. I don't know, *Chef*, this could be innocent enough and there's no evidence of it being anything other than natural causes . . .'

'No, Anna – you were right. Something stinks here.'

'If this isn't kosher,' said Anna, 'then we've got trouble. If this is a deliberate killing then it's been a professional job. A very professional job.'

In his office with its view out across Hamburg's Altstadt, Peter Claasens frowned and thought about the questions he had just been asked. He had put the receiver down but sat with his hand resting on the phone, for once oblivious to the rhythmic thumping and clanging that resounded through the building.

He had been reworking a draft of the letter that Emily had asked him to write when the phone had rung. Maybe it was because he had been concentrating on the letter that the journalist's questions had caught him completely off guard.

The Norwegian hadn't actually alleged anything, and his questions had been carefully put; yet Claasens could see what he was trying to find out. No one else would have drawn such a clear conclusion from the Norwegian's questions but they had struck a chord with Claasens. Claasens knew better than to confirm or deny anything to a member of the press: he was scrupulously discreet, maybe even overcautious in his professional life, if not in his private life.

Why had the Norwegian specifically asked about Norivon and shipments to China? It had been that specific question that had struck a nerve and Claasens was worried he had let it show in his voice. It had been two months ago that Claasens had noticed the anomaly: an inconsistency between two shipments and the legally required paperwork. Both shipments had been to China. Claasens had queried them, naturally. Lensch, his contact at Norivon, had sounded equally confused at first. Then, within twenty-four hours, Lensch had come back to him with a reasonable explanation and the paperwork to back it up. Reasonable – but not entirely convincing.

Claasens punched up the account file on his computer and buzzed through for the hard-file paperwork to be brought to him. It was Minna who came in, laid the binder on his desk and walked out again. Sulkily. Claasens cursed himself for having broken his 'not on my own doorstep' rule. He had banged Minna for a month or two, tired of her and had then expected everything to go back to business as usual. It hadn't worked out that way. Minna had been a bitch ever since, and he couldn't think of a way to get rid of her without making even more trouble for himself.

He suddenly became aware of the reverberating thudding of the workmen again. Peter Claasens's office was on the top floor of a building in Hamburg's Altstadt, a block to the north of Willy-Brandt-Strasse and next to the Kontorhaus Quarter. It was a brand-new building, but with a view out over the Speicherstadt and sitting so close to brick-built icons such as the Chilehaus and the Sprinkenhof that it had been designed to be a modern but sympathetic interpretation of a traditional Kontorhaus, with a huge central atrium open to the sky. Claasens had moved his offices there on the scheduled completion date only to find there were dozens of things still to be finished off by the builders. One of them had been the balustrade on his floor around the central atrium, which had meant he had been forbidden to move staff into his offices for a further week. Even now there was a gap in the railings that was blocked off, meaning that staff often had to walk around the entire circumference of the building to reach adjoining offices.

Claasens snapped off the band that held the binder closed. He had slipped Lensch's paperwork in there along with the original documentation showing the shipment discrepancy. He had tagged the relevant sections with yellow Post-it notes.

Claasens looked at his watch. It was five p.m. The rest of the staff would go and Emily would phone soon, just to check the coast was clear. Emily made everything go away: all the stress, all the hassle. When he was with her he became someone else. Someone better. He smiled, thinking of her phoning; of the cutely ungrammatical German she spoke with her sweet English accent. Then she would come up to his office and they would be alone. But first he had to double-check those figures. Just in case the Norwegian had had a point.

It was exactly like when you lost your keys and kept going back to where you thought you had left them.

Claasens stared at the page as if his concentrated attention on the words and figures would restore them to what he had seen before. And he had seen the error before. Except it wasn't there now. No paperwork from Lensch. No yellow Post-it notes. This was mad. He flipped the thick binder over and checked inside its back cover, just in case the paperwork was there. Of course, that didn't make any sense, but what he'd been looking at had made even less sense.

He tried to shut out the sound of the workmen and focused on the file. He felt he was going mad. Everything tallied. No discrepancies.

What the hell was going on?

His cellphone rang and he knew it would be Emily.

Chapter Two

'Anna . . .' Werner asked tentatively. 'I hope you don't mind me asking, but have you just farted?' He hit the button and the side window of the Polo slid down. They were parked in the Kiez, at the far end of Silbersackstrasse, facing towards the Reeperbahn. Here the street was narrow and dark.

'Close the window, Grandad,' said Anna. 'It's freezing out there.'

'I'd rather take my chances with the cold.'

'Anyway, who smelt it dealt it.' Anna smiled innocently.

'Sometimes you're less than ladylike.' Werner closed the window but left a small gap at the top.

'Well, you make up for me. You remind me of my Auntie Rachael. Except you've got less facial hair, of course. What's the time?'

'Twenty past midnight.'

'I'm bored. I am really, really, really, seriously bloody bored.'

'It's part of the job. I thought you would be used to it by now.'

'How come I'm teamed up with you, all of a sudden?' asked Anna. 'Is this *Lord Gentleman*'s idea of keeping me on a tight rein until he can dump me on someone else?'

'*Lord Gentleman*?' Werner turned to her.

'You know – Fabel . . . the *English Commissar*. Where the

hell does all that Anglophilia come from? I mean, he's a Frisian, for fuck's sake.'

'His mother is Scottish,' said Werner. 'You knew that. And he went to school there for a while. You know, you could be more ladylike in the way you speak as well.'

'Half Scottish, half Frisian – no wonder I've never seen him get a round in. Anyway, I take it this was his idea?'

'As a matter of fact it wasn't. It was mine.'

'What? Oh, I see . . . so now you think I'm the problem child of the family too.'

'Anna, sometimes – and don't take offence – but just sometimes you are the most insufferable pain in the arse. I used to wonder why you always wear that heavy-duty leather jacket: it's to stop the chafing from all those chips you carry around on your shoulders. I suggested he team you up with me because I thought we could work well together. To be honest, I'm trying to keep you as part of the team. I think Jan really wants that too.'

'Oh, I know,' said Anna with sarcastic earnestness. 'He really showed me that by giving me the sack.'

'You know, Anna, a little less attitude would suit you a whole lot better. And you're not sacked. Yet.'

'So you thought we would work well together . . .' Anna grinned.

'That was before I knew about the farting.'

'Look . . . over there . . .' Anna rested her hand on Werner's forearm and nodded towards the corner of the street. A tall woman with blonde hair, tied back into a ponytail, wearing a long black or dark blue coat, moved quickly along the street, keeping to the shadows as much as possible. She passed the bar on the corner and kept heading towards Silbersacktwiete. 'This looks promising.'

There were six unmarked cars dotted around the Kiez, as there had been every night for the last week since Westland's murder, all watching over unlit courtyards or, like Werner and Anna, the occasional piece of open ground, shadowy and dense with bushes and trees. The woman slowed her pace, looked up and down the street, then disappeared into the large triangle of waste ground.

'I think we're on,' said Anna. She switched the interior light to the off position, so that the car would not light up when Werner got out.

'I'll head in the other direction, then cut back,' he said, getting out of the Polo and easing the door closed behind him. In the dark, Anna unholstered her SIG-Sauer service automatic, checked the magazine and pushed back the safety with her thumb.

Werner passed the car on the far side of the street. He maintained an even pace and kept his gaze straight ahead, not giving away that he had seen the woman move, a shadow within a shadow, up ahead and off to the left. He was now only thirty metres away from where the woman had concealed herself. He guessed that Anna was now out of the car and shadowing him on the other side, crouching to keep concealed behind the other parked vehicles. He kept his shoulders hunched and his hands rammed into the pockets of his thick woollen pea coat, as if shunning the cold night, but his hand was closed around the automatic he had stuffed into his right pocket. Without indicating he knew where she was, Werner angled his course out from the wall that would soon give way to bushes and trees, and walked on the cobbled street. There was no one else around. If this was their woman, she would make her move soon.

He feigned surprise when she stepped out in front of him.

'Hello,' she said. Werner heard tension, almost nervousness, in her voice. 'Are you looking for fun?' The woman was tall, blonde and heavily made up. At first Werner thought she was in her early thirties, but when he took a step closer he could see that the make-up was thick to hide skin that had seen a lot of summers.

'That depends,' he said. 'How much?'

'I'm not greedy,' she said. 'I'm not supposed to be working here. I'll make it cheap, but we have to do it in here, behind the tree.' She began walking backwards into the shadows, crimson lips smiling.

'Okay . . .' Werner followed her without looking up or down the street, keeping her eyes held with his, in case she spotted Anna moving in.

'How much?' he asked again, making it look as if he were reaching for his wallet while using both hands to start easing his automatic from his coat pocket.

'We'll talk about that later,' she said and held out her hand. 'Come on.'

'I thought you girls always like your money up front,' said Werner. This was it.

She reached inside her coat.

Werner drew his automatic and aimed at her face. 'Polizei Hamburg! Put both hands on your head! Do it. Now!'

He was aware of Anna moving in behind the prostitute. He didn't know how, but she had managed to manoeuvre around to the back of the scruffy triangle of waste ground. The hooker stared at Werner, confused. Anna grabbed her by the coat collar.

'On your knees. Now!'

The woman complied and Anna snapped a set of cuffs onto one wrist, pulled it down behind her back, then the other. Werner radioed in for a custody vehicle.

Further down Silbersackstrasse a group of young men came out of a bar. They were heading towards Hans-Albers-Platz, but the activity on the waste ground caught the eye of one, who called the others. The knot of men moved up the street, craning their necks to see what was going on.

'Is everything all right?' said one, with slurred suspicion as they drew near. 'What the fuck y'doin' to her?'

Anna held up her bronze oval Criminal Service disc. 'Police. Nothing for you to worry yourself about.'

'What the fuck's going on?' asked one of his friends. 'What the fuck's she done?'

'Nothing,' she said pleadingly, 'I've done nothing. I'm just a working girl and they've arrested me.'

'That's not right,' said the first drunk, shaking his head sombrely. 'That's just not fuckin' right.'

'Yeah – fucking pigs,' one of his friends contributed.

'Okay – take it easy,' said Werner. He moved the hand-cuffed woman to place himself between her and the group of men, keeping hold of her elbow. He did a quick head count. Five. They were drunk and slurry but their casual clothes looked expensive. Rich boys out slumming it in St Pauli. Nevertheless, Werner wondered how long it would take for the uniformed unit to arrive. 'This isn't any of your concern.'

'It's just not fuckin' right,' repeated the other. They moved forward as a group.

'Please don't cause any trouble.' Anna took a step towards them, placing herself in their way.

'Or fuckin' what?' The first man pushed his sneering face into hers.

'Or this,' she said calmly. The drunk doubled up like a jackknife and keeled over onto the cobbles, clutching the testicles Anna had rammed her knee into. She snapped her service automatic out at arm's length and scanned the group of youths with it, but at groin height.

'Next one who gives me trouble gets their dick blown off,' she said, smiling. 'And trust me, I'm an expert shot, no matter how fucking small the target.'

They backed away, leaving their companion to moan and roll around on the slushy cobbles. At that moment, a silver and blue Polizei Hamburg personnel carrier pulled up and three uniformed officers jumped out. They took the hand-cuffed prostitute and placed her in the back.

'What's the story here?' the uniformed commissar asked, pointing to the youth dragging himself to his feet, still clutching his bruised groin.

'Nothing to report,' said Werner. 'Can you take her directly to the Presidium?'

'All right. You sure he's okay?'

'I think his pride's been hurt,' said Anna and smiled sweetly at Werner. 'I'll get the car.'

2.

Sylvie Achtenhagen took a break from the chaos of press cuttings and files that seemed to have exploded across the polished wood floor of her living room. She went to the French window and opened it, stepping out onto the balcony. The night air was ice-knife sharp and she welcomed its bite: she had been bent over the files for an hour and a half and her brain felt fogged and slow. Sylvie's apartment was on the third floor of a block on Edgar-Ross-Strasse in Hamburg-Eppendorf. It was elegant and spacious, with its own balcony and set in a pastel-coloured apartment building with a fancy Art Deco façade. She had moved into the apartment when her career – and her income – had started to kick off seriously. She had originally had her eye on one of the Jugendstil villas on Nissenstrasse, one street back. But they had been too expensive. And they would stay too expensive if she didn't deliver the goods for the station soon.

HanSat TV was jointly owned by the NeuHansa Group and Andreas Knabbe, who ran the station. Knabbe was a thirty-year-old who looked about twelve and had spent so much time in the US that he seemed more American than German; his management style was *definitely* more American than German. Knabbe had the habit of calling all his staff by their first names and frequently used the informal *du* form of address, even to the older and more respected members of staff. It was all meant to be shirtsleeves-informal and friendly and family atmosphere and crap like that. Truth was, though, that if Knabbe thought you weren't worth your salary, or if you didn't fit with his business model, then you were history. And Knabbe had often talked about Sylvie's success with the Angel case back in the nineties: increasingly he talked about her career in the past tense.

Sylvie began to feel at the mercy of events: that she was just being pulled along by the forces around her, just like everybody else. That was the problem. She had become reactive. Lazy. Back then, she hadn't waited for things to happen: she'd made them happen.

Sylvie hugged herself against the cold, pulling her thick woollen cardigan tight around her, and went back into her living room, closing the windows against the chill night. She poured herself another glass of red wine and sat cross-legged on the floor, letting her eyes range over the scattered material around her. Somewhere in there was a starting place. Somewhere there was some detail, some forgotten remark or photograph or piece of information that would point her in the direction of this killer. The Angel killings in St Pauli had launched her career: she had put so much into the case and had reaped the rewards. If she wasn't first to deliver the scoop on these latest killings, they could equally easily end her career.

She sipped again at her wine. She could be pretty certain that she would get no help from that pompous arse Fabel. The Polizei Hamburg were no great fans of her after her groundbreaking documentary on the case ten years ago. Cops have long memories. And anyway, there was something about Fabel she disliked intensely, and she got the idea that the feeling was mutual.

Sylvie knew that there was only one way forward for her:

she had to find out who murdered Jake Westland before the police did. She didn't have their resources, but she also didn't work under the same kind of restrictions they did. And, she knew, she was a whole lot smarter. But her main advantage was that she was pretty sure the cops were looking in the wrong direction. They were probably trying to establish links between the current murders and the Angel killings ten years ago.

And this wasn't the Angel. These latest killings were the work of a copycat. Sylvie just knew it.

3.

Armin Lensch wasn't sure what hurt most: his bruised testicles or the laughing and taunting from his mates. He had staggered after them as they had made their way to a pub near Hans-Albers-Platz, they had found a table and Armin had squeezed into the corner, sipping tentatively at his beer, hoping the nausea would subside.

'Police brutality – that's what it was. Police brutality . . .' he said in earnest and was greeted with howls of laughter.

'No, it wasn't,' said Karl, leaning in close. 'That wasn't police brutality – that was you having your ass kicked by a girl. Did you see the fucking size of her? You got your ass kicked by a little girl.'

'She caught me unawares,' muttered Armin.

'No, she didn't, she caught you in the balls!' More laughter.

'Fuck you,' said Armin, shoving past them and wincing at the surge of pain in his groin. 'Fuck the lot of you.'

He staggered out into the cold night air. The nausea followed him out of the pub and collided with him. He voided his gut onto the pavement. A couple of passers-by cursed at him.

'Fuck the lot of you,' he said again, under his breath. He would make the bastards pay. Who did they think they were? Armin and his friends all worked in the Neustadt-Nord part of Hamburg. They all worked there but Armin was the star. He was the one who was going to the top. And he would get all the help he needed: now that he had found out what he had found out. He started to walk back in the direction of the Spielbudenplatz and Reeperbahn. He would get a taxi there. He thought about the cop who had kneed him in the groin. He wasn't going to let her get away with that. Here, now, he was just like everybody else with too much drink in them. But outside the Kiez, in his normal life, he was somebody. He was connected. He would make the bitch pay. But the thought of her made him want to cry: to be beaten up by a fucking woman. For Armin, women were good for only one thing. He had seen them at work. Getting promotions over him. He knew how they managed that, the whores. He had had a lot of girlfriends, but nothing that had lasted too long. Normally they would get out of line and Armin would give them a slap and they'd get all hysterical on him. Fuck them. Fuck them all.

Armin walked on, his internal rage and the ache from his groin making him blind to all around him. He stopped. Where the fuck was he? He had thought he knew his way around the Kiez well enough, but he must have taken a wrong turning. He took a moment to reorient himself and took the next right. He saw the Reeperbahn ahead of him but he was further up than Spielbudenplatz. Still, it wouldn't be difficult to find a taxi. At that moment he caught sight of a beige Mercedes and his hand went up. An automatic reaction: in Germany, all taxis were beige; all beige cars were taxis. He eased himself with a moan into the back seat.

'Eppendorf . . .' he said between his teeth.

'Are you okay?' asked the driver. 'You don't look well.'

Fucking great, thought Armin. A female taxi driver.

'Just take me to Eppendorf,' he said. The woman driver shrugged, started the car and took a left into the Reeperbahn. It was only after she took the wrong turning at the end of

the Reeperbahn and he realised that they were down by the
river that Armin noticed that there was no meter in the front
of the taxi; nor was there a certificate on display with the
driver's name, photograph and City of Hamburg licence.

By which time it was too late.

4.

Fabel felt exhausted. It had been a much more gruelling experience than he had expected. Susanne had come along too and
he had been grateful for her presence.

'That was very worthwhile,' said a tall, thin woman of
about fifty as she approached Fabel. She had a name badge
that informed him she was Hille Deicher, representing
Muliebritas. 'I hope you can take something useful away from
our workshop.'

Fabel smiled. He could never understand why business
people, self-help gurus and others insisted on calling confer-
ences 'workshops'. No one made anything. None of the people
who attended these things worked with their hands.

'It was interesting,' said Fabel. 'But I hope I made it clear
that the Polizei Hamburg needs no prompting to deal with
the issue of domestic violence, or violence against women in
general. We are very . . .' He struggled for the word.

'Proactive,' interjected Susanne helpfully.

'Quite,' said Fabel. 'We've been running an anti-violence
programme for several years now. We do, I assure you, have
a zero-tolerance attitude when it comes to violence against
women or children. And we have one of the most successful
records in Europe in dealing with the issue. But I have to say
that we are committed to protecting all of Hamburg's citizens, regardless of gender. Or ethnicity.'

'I'm afraid that crime isn't as gender-blind,' said Deicher.
'You said yourself in your presentation that the vast majority
of murders are men killing women, and the vast majority of

those are within the domestic environment. Add to that the countless assaults on women in their own homes.'

'All that is true.' Fabel shot a pleading glance at Susanne. 'And we have, as I said, made it a priority area.'

'Maybe that's why this woman in St Pauli is committing these murders.' Deicher smiled without warmth. 'Maybe she's motivated to redress the balance of male-on-female violence. After all, I can't think of a better place for her to go about it. It is a farce that there is a street in Hamburg to which women are forbidden entry.'

'Listen, Frau Deicher,' Fabel felt himself suddenly angry. 'It isn't the police or the state that—'

'What does *Muliebritas* mean?' Susanne interrupted Fabel, directing her question, and her smile, at Deicher.

'It is the Latin form of "muliebrity". You know, the quality of being female. It is the name of the magazine I work for. And the charity we support.' She looked pointedly back at Fabel. 'We organise emergency accommodation for women subject to domestic violence.'

'That's an interesting name,' said Susanne, still smiling. 'Is that where the Spanish *mujer* comes from?'

Somehow, Susanne managed to steer the conversation into calmer waters and, after a while, Deicher drifted off to mingle with other delegates.

'Thanks for that,' said Fabel when Deicher was gone. 'That woman was really beginning to wind me up. I don't know why they insisted on sending me to this.'

'Because you're the head of Hamburg's Murder Commission, and, like it or not, what Frau Deicher was saying is true: we still live in a society where women are victimised by violence. Anyway, I thought you did really well.' Susanne smiled and straightened his tie, as if she were about to send him off to school. 'Especially because women get you all flustered.'

'What do you mean?' asked Fabel indignantly.

'Well, you do. It's pretty clear you think we're from a

completely different planet. But don't worry about it, most men are the same.'

Fabel was about to respond when his cellphone buzzed. He checked the call screener. It was the Murder Commission.

'Sorry,' he said with a shrug as he lifted the phone to his ear. 'Probably another murder.'

'If it is,' said Susanne, 'even with all of these Angel killings at the moment, I'll bet the victim is female . . .'

5.

Fabel met Anna and Werner in the hallway outside the interview room. Both officers wore an expression that was less than triumphant.

'Tell me this is our killer . . .' said Fabel.

'She looked good for it, Jan,' said Werner. 'She looked really good. She lured me onto waste ground and out of sight. She didn't seem to know the drill for a hooker and when she reached inside her coat we took her down.'

'But?'

'Her name is Viola Dahlke,' explained Anna. 'She's forty-five and has no previous convictions. She's a housewife from Billstedt.'

'That doesn't mean she's not our killer. Did you get a knife?'

'No,' said Anna. 'When she reached inside her coat Werner and I both thought that she was going for a knife, but it turned out to be a packet of condoms.'

'Condoms?'

'Nothing else,' said Anna. 'Don't ask me what a forty-five-year-old housewife from Billstedt was doing in the red-light district offering to ring Werner's bell.'

'All right,' said Fabel, 'I won't. I'll go and ask her myself . . .'

Arrest is a deprivation of choice. You are removed to a place not of your choosing and your freedom to leave that place is taken from you. Career criminals accept arrest as a natural element of their lives, even the ones who fight and struggle every centimetre to the cells. For everyone else, the experience of arrest is traumatic. At the very least surreal.

Fabel could tell at first glance that Viola Dahlke had never been in custody before. There was a good chance she'd never even set foot inside a police station before, far less the Police Presidium. Dahlke looked startled, confused. Afraid. Her face was pale behind her overdone make-up and the stark lighting of the interview room seemed to jaundice her pallor and deepen the shadows under her cheekbones. Her hair was the dull putty-blonde that many North German women dyed their hair when it started to lose its natural colour and pulled up into a ponytail. The make-up and the hairstyle looked all wrong on her, like an outfit that didn't fit right.

'Frau Dahlke, I take it it has been explained to you that under the terms of Article One-Three-Six of the Criminal Procedure Code you have the right to remain silent. You also have the right to a legal representative. Do you understand these rights?'

Viola Dahlke nodded. She looked as if she was carrying the world on her shoulders and was resigned to the burden. 'I don't want a lawyer. I want to go home. I'm sorry. If I've broken the law I'll pay the fine. I didn't mean any harm. I'm not really . . . I'm not really one of those women.'

'Frau Dahlke, I don't think you understand. We're not interested in whether you are a prostitute, full-time, part-time or not at all. I am Principal Detective Chief Commissar Fabel of the Murder Commission. The officers who arrested you were murder detectives.'

'Murder?' Dahlke raised eyelids heavy with mascara. Genuine shock. Her fear cranked up a ratchet. 'What have I got to do with murder?'

'You've heard about what happened last week? Let's face

it, Frau Dahlke, you can't have missed it, it's been all over the press and TV. Jake Westland, the British pop singer.'

Realisation began to dawn on Dahlke's face. A terrified realisation. She searched Fabel's face for something. Reassurance, maybe. He withheld it.

'I've got nothing to do with that . . .' Her voice was tremulous. 'I swear I've got nothing to do with that.'

'Frau Dahlke, you are a middle-aged housewife masquerading as a prostitute and you tried to lure one of my male officers into a dark corner. Last week, less than two hundred metres from where you were arrested, Jake Westland was lured into a dark corner and murdered by someone pretending to be a prostitute.'

Dahlke stared at Fabel as if lost for words. Or just lost.

'I take it you can see the seriousness of your position.'

'I didn't . . . I wouldn't . . . I didn't mean anyone any harm.'

'Where were you between eleven p.m. on Saturday the twenty-sixth and one a.m. on Sunday the twenty-seventh?'

'I was at home. In bed.'

'Who can confirm that?'

'My husband.' Again Dahlke's expression revealed that her fear had suddenly been ratcheted up a couple of notches. 'Oh please, no . . . please don't speak to my husband.'

'Frau Dahlke, you still don't seem to understand the seriousness of your position. If we cannot establish your whereabouts for the time of the murder you will be held here for further questioning and we will carry out full forensic searches of your home. If you were at home with your husband then we must have him verify the fact.'

'But I didn't do anything wrong!' she sobbed. 'I didn't hurt anyone. I swear.'

'Do you work, Frau Dahlke?'

'I work in the local library. Part-time.'

'And is your husband in employment?'

'Yes – he's an engineer.'

'So why do you work as a prostitute?'

'I don't. I . . .' Again she looked at Fabel with eyes desperate for some kind of understanding. Then the desperation was gone: her head bowed and her gaze became fixed on the table in front of her. 'I've only done it three times,' she said, her voice now leaden and dull once more. 'I don't do it for the money.'

'Then why? Why on earth would you put yourself or your health at risk?'

She looked up again. Her eyes were glossy with tears that tumbled down her cheeks, streaking them with mascara. 'I'm ordinary. I've always been ordinary. Dull. I have a dull life with a dull husband and dull kids. I'd never been with another man before I got married. I went into the Kiez one night. Just to look. I don't know why. I wanted to see what happened. The type of people who go there. I don't know why I did it, but I went into a bar and this man . . . I did it with him.'

'Where?'

'In his car.' The sobs were now silent convulsions between statements.

'I still don't understand why,' said Fabel. 'Why would you want to do that?'

'You wouldn't understand. No man would understand. I did it for the excitement. To be wanted. Desired.'

'Did you get all that?' asked Fabel when he met Anna and Werner in the hall. They had been watching the interview on the closed-circuit video monitor in the next room.

'Yep,' said Werner. 'Weird. Do you believe her?'

'There's absolutely no way she could have dumped the knife before you arrested her?' asked Fabel.

'None,' said Anna. 'She was in Werner's sight all the time and we searched her thoroughly immediately after she was arrested. Nothing. And nothing dropped or dumped, either.'

Fabel shook his head. 'I give up sometimes. Keep her in

and check out her alibi for last week with her husband. And try to be – I don't know – *diplomatic*.'

'Oh yeah,' said Anna. 'Maybe I should ask him if he's ever seen Catherine Deneuve in *Belle de Jour*. I'm not being funny, *Chef*, but there's no diplomatic way of telling some guy that his wife's been moonlighting as a hooker. "And, oh, by the way, don't feel too bad about it: it's not that she's struggling on what you give her for housekeeping – she's doing it for the love of dick."'

'Anna's got a point, Jan,' said Werner. 'There's no sugaring this pill.'

'Simply keep to the fact that she's a suspect in a serious crime, and that you need to establish her whereabouts on the night in question. Leave the explaining to her.'

'Okay, *Chef*.'

Fabel made his way to his office. He checked his email. There was an internal note from van Heiden to remind him that *Politidirektør* Vestergaard, the boss of the dead Danish cop, Jespersen, was flying down to see them in a couple of days. Van Heiden helpfully provided the flight's arrival time.

'I've got nothing better to do,' muttered Fabel. He really wanted to talk to Jespersen's boss but he had thought, given that he was up to his neck in a major murder inquiry, that van Heiden could at least have arranged the pick-up.

He looked at his watch. Two a.m. He'd go home, catch four or five hours' sleep and head back into the Presidium. He yawned. He was really getting too old for this. He thought of Viola Dahlke and the fact that she would be lying, wide awake and afraid, considering every thread as the fabric of her life unravelled. What the hell had she thought she was doing? She had been right: he didn't understand; just as he hadn't understood why so many of the people he had encountered in his career had done the things they had done. Human sexuality was a perplexing thing. A lot of the murders he had investigated had had bizarre sexual elements to them and Fabel had been forced to navigate some dark and stormy seas over the years. Sometimes it was as if women remained an unknown continent for him.

He took his English tweed jacket from the back of his chair and unhooked his raincoat from the rack. As he made for the door he almost expected the phone to ring.

It did.

6.

It was strange, given the very nature of his job, that the one thing that Fabel had never fully come to terms with was the sudden extinction of life.

He had heard that astronauts, once they are truly in space, look back at the Earth and tend to become, in that instant, either entirely atheistic or totally convinced of the existence of a god. No middle ground. Whether in reality it was as absolute as that, Fabel could understand the experience. He had a similar feeling every time he looked at the dead. A corpse has no humanity: it doesn't look like someone sleeping, it becomes nothing more than a human-like object. An empty shell. And in Fabel's case, most of the dead he looked upon had been forcibly evicted from that shell.

Where some would have seen the vessel abandoned by the departing soul, Fabel saw only emptiness. The final shutting down of an interdependence of biological systems. The ending of a universe seen from a never-to-be-repeated viewpoint.

However Armin Lensch had seen the world, he wasn't seeing it now.

His body lay on a scrubby patch of grass and rubble down near the shore of the River Elbe, close to Hafenstrasse. A few empty beer bottles and the wheel of some long-discarded child's toy served as his pillow, and the grass on which he lay was framed by broken red bricks from whatever dock building had stood there at one time. The rain had turned to sleet, then to snow so the technicians had erected a white forensics tent to protect the crime scene and had illuminated it with lights on telescopic stands. Like Westland, Lensch had been sliced across the belly and his viscera, spilling sideways from the mouth-like gape of the wound, glistened in the harsh light of the arc lamps the forensic team had erected. A nauseating stench from his sliced-open abdomen lingered in the air of the forensics tent.

A man almost completely concealed in white hooded coveralls, blue latex gloves and a surgical mask came over to Fabel.

'Hello, Jan.' Holger Brauner, the forensics chief, slipped the mask from his face and smiled. 'It's a nippy one tonight . . .'

Fabel returned the smile. Brauner was almost invariably cheerful, despite the nature of his work. Or maybe because of it. 'Hi, Holger. What's the story?'

'From my estimation, we're talking about a male, twenty-nine years old, one-seventy-nine centimetres tall, white-collar job – finance sector – blood group O rhesus negative, suffers from a nut allergy and lives in Eppendorf.'

'Very impressive, Sherlock,' said Fabel. 'You found his wallet, didn't you?'

'No, of course not. I established it all with DNA and the arcane skills of the forensic wizard. Do you never watch *CSI*?' Brauner grinned and held up a plastic evidence bag containing a black leather wallet and a state identity card. 'It's all in there,' he said. 'All his credit cards and cash too, as far as I can see. Cellphone as well. Robbery doesn't seem to have been the motive.'

'Leave the detective work to us, lab rat,' said Fabel, with a grin. Someone entered the tent behind him and he turned to see Anna and Werner. It had been Werner who had called Fabel. Werner rolled his eyes as he and Anna stepped back into the enclosed scene of crime. Fabel read his meaning: Anna's make-up was thrown out in stark contrast to the pallor of her skin. It was the same effect he had seen on Viola Dahlke; in Anna's case it was Armin Lensch's mutilated belly, which she worked so hard not to look at, that was the cause of her lack of colour. Tough little Anna's Achilles heel and another reason for her to consider a transfer.

'You all right?' Fabel asked.

'I'm fine,' said Anna defensively, but she still avoided looking at Lensch. 'So we've got number two. Looks like we're at the start of another series.'

'I need you two to get on to finding out when he was last seen, who he was with . . . Werner, what is it?' Fabel noticed Werner leaning close to the body, staring at the dead man's face intently.

'Anna, come here and look.'

'Yeah . . . very funny.'

'No, Anna, I mean it. Look at him – isn't he the guy from earlier? When we were arresting Dahlke?'

Anna moved closer, holding the back of her hand to her nose. 'Shit . . . you're right.'

'Okay,' said Fabel. 'Let's have it.'

'Just a coincidence, *Chef*,' said Anna. 'I *think* it's a coincidence. Remember we told you there was a bit of trouble when we arrested Dahlke – the drunks . . .'

'I remember.'

'He was the ringleader,' said Werner.

Fabel looked down at Lensch. The dead man's lips gaped slightly as if to speak and his eyes were still half open, as if a camera had caught him mid-blink. His hair was cut short and had been styled with some form of gel. The shirt looked as if it had been expensive, but the lower half was now sodden with blood. Lensch's trousers were unfastened and his fly half unzipped. The slice across his belly again spoke of a single, purposeful stroke. Whoever had killed him had known what they were doing. Had done this before.

'So why wasn't he arrested?' asked Fabel. 'Did he go quietly?'

'He moaned a bit,' said Anna and Fabel caught Werner firing a look at her.

'Don't tell me, Anna . . .' Fabel said, exasperated.

'Listen, *Chef*, things were starting to turn ugly. We were waiting for back-up and Sonny Boy here started to give us gyp. It is regulations that if someone acts aggressively and they've been warned to stay one and a half metres away, if they step closer we can knock them to the ground.'

'Is that what happened? Did you give him a formal warning?'

'We told him to back off,' said Werner. 'It was this guy who was stirring it up. Anna acted properly, Jan.'

'Did you draw your firearm?'

'Yes,' said Anna.

'So why haven't you submitted a report? Did you strike him?'

'Well, yes – kind of.' A sigh. 'I kneed him in the groin.'

'Marvellous! Bloody marvellous, Anna. You realise you're going to have to make a full report to that effect? Any swelling you caused will probably be noted in the autopsy. For Christ's sake, Anna. And you, Werner – I thought you'd have the sense to keep her on a short chain.'

'A short *what*?' Anna glowered at Fabel.

'Okay, Anna, leave it . . .' said Werner. 'Jan – when this guy here started to kick up, we thought there was a good chance we had the Angel in custody. Or at least Jake Westland's murderer. And like Anna said, we were outnumbered. I think you should let this one go.'

'Oh, you do, do you?' Fabel sighed. 'Anna, make sure you have a complete report on my desk tomorrow.' He looked at the ID Brauner had handed him in the polythene evidence bag. 'Armin Lensch . . . Did you see where he went after you had dealt with him?'

'He followed on after his mates,' said Anna. 'They went in the direction of Hans-Albers-Platz.'

'Then I suggest you get enlargements of this . . .' He tossed her the evidence bag with Lensch's identity card. 'And start going around the bars to see if you can find where he was and when. Werner, check out next of kin. Speaking of which, have you seen Dahlke's husband?'

'Not yet. We were on our way when we got this shout.'

'Okay, leave Anna to get started on the bars – I'll arrange a uniform to chaperone her – and you head out to get the story from Dahlke's husband.'

'Okay, Jan,' said Werner. 'But it's a bit redundant now, isn't it? I mean, she can't have done this guy. She's been in custody since we last saw him alive.'

'We still need to confirm her alibi for Westland.'

Fabel made his way down the steep embankment to St Pauli Hafenstrasse, where his car was parked next to the silver and blue police cruisers. He felt tired and irritated and, for a moment, he nearly headed off in the direction of the city centre and Pöseldorf, where he had had his attic flat for five years. Instead he turned west towards Altona: his new home. His shared home.

Hamburg is a city where gentility and prurience rub shoulders uncomfortably: the deliberate vulgarity of St Pauli sits directly next to the restrained gentility of one of the grander parts of Altona. Back in the days when Altona was Danish, St Pauli was the marshy no-man's-land between it and German Hamburg. Both Altona and Hamburg were resolutely Lutheran. Catholics seeking freedom to worship had to find it outside the boundaries of both cities: hence the street called Grosse Freiheit, the Great Freedom. But St Pauli had also become a dumping ground: a place known in the late Middle Ages for its unsavoury inhabitants, its poorhouses and its pestilence hospitals.

Yet, as Fabel headed along Breitestrasse, it took only a couple of minutes for the crude glamour of St Pauli to give way to the wide tree-lined boulevard of Palmaille, with its grand villas on either side. It had started to snow and the naked branches of the trees sparkled in the lamplight.

Fabel suddenly had an idea. He pulled over to the kerb and reached down between his legs and under the driver's seat. His fingertips brushed against something small and metallic.

'Got you, you little swine.' After a little scrabbling he retrieved his MP3 player and put it into the plastic tray behind the handbrake. He replaced his seat belt, pulled out into the road and resumed his journey. As he did so, his smile faded. At the next junction he made a left into Behnstrasse. Then another left into Struenseestrasse. Left again and he was back on Palmaille.

It was still there.

Fabel had first noticed it as he had driven off after finding his MP3 player. Headlights about sixty metres behind him, pulling out maybe thirty seconds after he had. The last three manoeuvres had made no sense and the car behind had followed. What bothered Fabel was that he had only just picked up on it. Whoever was following him knew what they were doing. God knew how long they had been on his tail: at least from the murder scene, and maybe before that. Fabel was not far from the apartment he shared with Susanne, but he was not going to drive there. He had no idea who was on his tail, or how dangerous they were. He swung across Palmaille and headed straight on towards Neumühlen and Övelgönne. As he drove, he flipped open his cellphone.

'Principal Chief Commissar Fabel here,' he said to the operations room officer who answered his call. 'I'm in Altona, on Palmaille heading west. I've just passed the fishing museum. Where's your nearest traffic camera?'

'There's one at the junction with Max-Brauer-Allee.'

'I'm in a dark blue BMW 3-series, old shape. There's very little on the road but there's a car behind me. When I turn north into Max-Brauer-Allee, could you get his index number and check it out?'

'Yes, Chief Commissar. Do you need assistance? I could send an area car.'

'It's probably nothing, but if there's one available, send it to the Max-Brauer-Allee. Call me back on this number when you have a make on the car.'

Fabel turned into Max-Brauer-Allee at the intersection. As he drove north he checked that his tail was still there. The white baroque edifice of Altona City Hall slid by on his left and as he passed the road end at Platz-der-Republik, he saw the silver and blue police cruiser waiting at the junction. His cellphone rang.

'Chief Commissar Fabel, Presidium Ops Room here – we got the index plate. The car behind you is a Mercedes CLK cabriolet, registered to a Sylvie Achtenhagen, Edgar-Ross-Strasse, Altona. Isn't that . . . ?'

'Yes, it is. Thanks. Tell the patrol car to pull her over.'

Fabel drew into the kerb once he had seen in his rear-view mirror that the Mercedes had been pulled over. He got out and approached Achtenhagen, who was out of her car and remonstrating with the two uniformed officers.

'Thanks, I'll take it from here,' he said to the uniforms.

'This looks like harassment,' said Achtenhagen in half-hearted indignation. 'Pulling over members of the press for no good reason. Other than, that is, the fact that I'm embarrassing you by pointing out your incompetence to the public.'

'Are you quite finished?' asked Fabel, with a sigh. 'I want to know why you were following me.'

'I wasn't. I live in Altona.'

'Cut the crap, Frau Achtenhagen. It's nearly three-thirty in the morning and I have a home to go to. You trailed me in a complete circle. You've been on my tail since I left the murder scene.'

'There's been another murder?' asked Achtenhagen. Her shock was about as genuine as her earlier indignation. Fabel folded his arms across his body, signalling his impatience for Achtenhagen to stop the pretence.

'Okay . . .' she sighed. 'But I've got every right to drive where I want and follow who I want. You and your department have been less than helpful. I decided I would keep tabs on you. It sure as hell paid dividends tonight. Who was the victim?'

Fabel remained silent.

'Listen, Herr Fabel. You and I haven't got off to a good start.'

'We haven't got off to any kind of start. It's not my job to deal with the media. I told you that. And, let's face it, Frau Achtenhagen, satellite television isn't exactly the home of in-depth quality news analysis. I've heard your theories about how broadcasters should make the news, not just report it. All you want is sensationalism. Gory details and a cartoon-character villain to scare the public with. I deal in the real world.'

'We can be of help to each other,' said Achtenhagen.

'No, we can't. Or at least you can't help me. This isn't one of your cheap Saturday-night dramas. Catching and convicting a murderer means using professional policing and forensic skills, plus modern technology, and collating legally obtained evidence. It's not about some satellite-TV Nancy Drew putting it all together for us.'

'That's not what I'm talking about!' Achtenhagen's voice was raised now. 'Whatever you think of what I do, there are things I can find out that you can't, people I can talk to who would run a mile rather than speak to a cop. I know all about Carstens Kaminski, man-of-the-people boss of Davidwache. You think he has his finger on the Reeperbahn pulse. He doesn't know the half of what's going on. He's still a cop. People don't like cops. People like the television. They like me. They talk to me.'

'As I told you—'

'Listen.' Achtenhagen cut him off. 'I'm not saying that I can deliver the killer. I'm not even saying that I can offer hard evidence. But there's a chance, a real chance, that I can point you in the right direction.'

'That's very public-spirited of you.' Fabel made no attempt to suppress his sneer. 'You'll come to us before you spout your theories on HanSat, I suppose.'

'As a matter of fact I will. On one condition.'

'And that is?'

'If I deliver something which leads you to the killer, then you give me an exclusive on the arrest. Five . . . no, ten hours before you release the details to the rest of the press.'

'Even if I were remotely interested in such an offer, I'm not in a position to agree to it. Our press department has got really good relationships with the local media. It wouldn't have for long if we cut them out of breaking news.'

'Your press people would get over it. And you'd have your killer.' Achtenhagen tugged at the collar of her coat. 'Listen, it's freezing here. My apartment isn't far. Why don't I make you a coffee and we can talk about it in comfort?'

'I'm going home, Frau Achtenhagen,' said Fabel, his voice suddenly cold and hard.

'Well, at least think about what I've said.'

'Goodnight, Frau Achtenhagen.'

Fabel got into his car. He watched Achtenhagen in his rear-view mirror until she had driven off. He sat for a moment, his mind going over his exchange with the television journalist, before he put the BMW in gear and headed towards Othmarschen.

7.

Fabel parked outside the Psychiatric Centre of the University Clinic Hamburg-Eppendorf and, with a nod to the security man on the desk, headed up the stairs to the first floor. He knocked on the door displaying the nameplate: 'Dr Eckhardt: Forensic Psychology'.

'Hello, stranger . . .' The woman behind the desk was in her late thirties with dense, dark hair gathered up in a French plait. She spoke in a soft Bavarian accent. Fabel smiled.

'Hi . . . I hope I didn't wake you when I came in last night.'

'You know me,' said Susanne. 'When I'm out, I'm out. When did you get in?'

'About four. I had a lie-in this morning, though.' He yawned loudly.

'It didn't do you much good. You won't be working late tonight, will you?'

'Not if I can help it,' said Fabel. 'Anyway, I can't stop. You were on my way. I called in to give you this . . .' He dropped a heavy buff file on Susanne's desk. 'I couldn't email it all.'

'This to do with the Angel case?'

'The Angel Copycat case, if my instincts are right. Could you have a look through it? I'll raise the appropriate paperwork to cover your time.'

Fabel made for the door, but checked himself, frowning. 'Do you want to know something strange? About last night, I mean.'

'What?'

'Sylvie Achtenhagen – you know, the TV presenter and reporter, the one on HanSat – well, she was following me. I had a silver-and-blue pull her over. She started to offer me help on this case. Nonsense, I know, but the strange thing is . . .' He stopped mid-sentence, laughed and shook his head. 'No, I must have been too tired.'

'No, go on.'

'Well, she was really trying to persuade me to help her get the scoop on the Angel case. I could have sworn she was offering to have sex with me . . .'

'You're kidding!'

'No – she said I should come to her place so we could discuss it in comfort.'

'She must be really desperate for a story.' Susanne arched an eyebrow.

'Thanks for that. But yes, I rather think she is. God knows she did more harm than good with the original Angel case. It's almost as if she has to find out who the killer is.'

Susanne leaned back in her chair, rattling a pencil between perfect porcelain-white teeth. 'As I remember, Sylvie Achtenhagen is a rather attractive woman.'

'Her charms are completely wasted on me, then,' said Fabel. 'Can't stand the woman.'

'On your way where?' asked Susanne.

'What?' Fabel frowned.

'You said I was on your way.'

'Oh, I've got to pick up this Danish cop from the airport.' He looked at his watch. 'Shit, I'd better go. Have a look at that when you get a chance and I'll talk to you later.'

8.

Standing in the arrivals hall of Hamburg-Fuhlsbüttel airport and holding up a clipboard with the name 'VESTERGAARD' on it in large block capitals written with a felt-tip marker, Fabel felt faintly ridiculous. He stood alongside others doing exactly the same thing, some with names, others with company logos; all the others, however, were professional drivers sent to pick up business travellers flying into Hamburg.

Fabel could simply have sent a patrol car with a uniformed officer to pick up the Danish cop, but he had thought it more diplomatic to collect him himself. There seemed to be a protocol, an etiquette to these things that Fabel always seemed to get wrong. He had decided it was best for him to make a personal appearance: it appeared that Vestergaard was a high-ranking officer and, after all, one of his men had died while in Hamburg. But, standing there with his clipboard, Fabel felt less like a diplomat, more like a chauffeur and a lot like an idiot.

The arrivals board announced the landing of the Copenhagen flight and after a few minutes a wave of business suits swelled through the arrivals gate. Fabel played the game of scanning the emerging figures, making a bet with himself that he would be able pick out Vestergaard before he made himself known to Fabel. He was momentarily distracted by a very attractive blonde woman wearing an expensive suit and a deep blue coat. She caught his eye for a moment and he looked away, partly in embarrassment at having been caught watching her and partly in annoyance that he had been distracted from his challenge.

Then he saw him: a tall, light-blond man of about fifty whose business suit did nothing to disguise the bulk of his shoulders or take the edge off his tough look. He had cop written all over him and Fabel imagined that Jespersen, in life, had looked a little like that. The man nodded in Fabel's direction and headed his way. Fabel smiled and was about to offer his hand when the man walked straight past him and handed his bags to the chauffeur who had been standing next to Fabel, holding up a board with the IBM logo on it. To add insult to the injury Fabel's deductive powers had suffered, the 'Dane' proceeded to give instructions to the driver in a broad Bavarian accent.

'I guess I wasn't what you were expecting . . .' a female voice said in English. Fabel turned in the direction of the voice. The attractive young woman he had noticed earlier was now standing directly in front of him. She arched an eyebrow.

'*Politidirektør* Vestergaard?' he asked feebly.

'Yes, I'm Karin Vestergaard. I'm sorry – I know it's *so*

confusing.' She sighed and rolled her eyes. 'I got promoted because I'm so damned good at making coffee and they sent me here because all the men were too busy solving really complicated cases.'

Fabel gave a half-laugh at the joke, then let his smile die when he saw the cold glint in Vestergaard's ice-blue eyes. Not a good start. 'My car is parked outside,' he said weakly.

It wasn't a cosy journey. After Fabel asked Karin Vestergaard how her flight had been, and what the weather was like in Copenhagen, he struggled to make small-talk as they walked to his parked BMW. *Politidirektør* Vestergaard was obviously not the small-talk type. They drove in silence down the Alsterkrugchausee towards the city centre.

'We have an election coming up in a few months,' he said eventually, with artificial cheer. 'For Principal Mayor. Effectively that's Prime Minister for the State of Hamburg. Anyway, one of the candidates is actually a Dane. Well, she's a German-Dane – you know, from the Danish-speaking minority in Schleswig-Holstein.'

Karin Vestergaard turned to Fabel and gave him a weak smile of uninterested indulgence. There was something about her face that troubled him, but he couldn't work out what it was. They passed the sign informing them that they were entering the city quarter of Eppendorf.

'Isn't this where your Institute for Judicial Medicine is based?' she asked.

'Yes,' said Fabel. 'Indeed it is. You know Hamburg?'

'No. I checked before I came down. Is that where Jens is?'

'That's where the morgue is, yes.'

'I'd like to see Jens. Now.'

'You want to go now? I thought I'd take you to your hotel first before going into the Presidium. I know that—'

'I don't understand.' Karin Vestergaard interrupted him, her voice cold and hard. 'I don't see the problem if we're passing through Eppendorf. I want to see Jens's body. Can we go or not?'

Fabel shrugged and turned off into Geschwister-Scholl-Strasse.

The University Clinic Hamburg-Eppendorf was a huge complex of buildings, almost like a small town in itself, sitting between Geschwister-Scholl-Strasse to the north and Martinistrasse to the south. The University Clinic even had its own park to the south of Martinistrasse and, as Fabel passed along its northern boundary towards Butenfeld, huge cranes towered above the complex.

'The hospital here is a teaching one,' explained Fabel. 'They're building a new campus. It's all going to be very high-tech.'

If Vestergaard was impressed, she hid it well; instead she stared grimly ahead, as if her mind was already ahead of them and in the morgue with her dead colleague. Fabel found a parking space outside the Institute for Judicial Medicine and led Vestergaard in through the glass double doors to the waiting area. It took Fabel a couple of minutes to arrange a viewing of Jespersen's body, during which time Vestergaard sat impassively in the reception area.

'We can go in now,' he explained and she followed him into the morgue.

Fabel didn't know what to expect in the mortuary. Despite having shared the journey from the airport with her, the Danish policewoman remained a complete stranger to him. He didn't know anything about her professional relationship with Jespersen, or what kind of personal relationship they might have had. Fabel watched her face when the sheet was pulled back from Jespersen's body. Again he found himself distracted by her appearance. There really was something about the way she looked that perplexed him . . . Then he realised what it was: her features were perfect. Her face possessed an absolute symmetry and every feature was in classic proportion. The effect was strange: it gave her beauty; true archetypal beauty. But it was also a forgettable beauty.

Fabel watched the bland beauty of Karin Vestergaard's face as her subordinate's dead body was revealed to her. There was a flicker of something in the expression and then it was gone in the same instant. But Fabel had recognised it: anger. She was angry with Jespersen for having died.

'I'm very sorry,' said Fabel. 'Had you worked together long?'

'When is the autopsy scheduled?'

'Tomorrow,' said Fabel. 'Two p.m.'

Vestergaard leaned forward and examined Jespersen's face more closely. Then she pulled the sheet completely clear of his body.

'What are you looking for?' asked Fabel, no longer hiding his irritation with her uncommunicativeness.

'Who'll be doing the autopsy?'

'Herr Doctor Möller. He's our Chief Pathologist. He's really—'

'Tell him to look for puncture wounds. Needle marks. Particularly in hidden areas: under hair, skin folds, around the anus . . .'

'Look, said Fabel. 'I think this has gone on long—'

'Do you believe this is a natural death?' Vestergaard turned to him. More cold fire in her eyes.

Fabel sighed. 'It looks very much like a heart attack.'

'Do you believe this was a natural death?' she repeated.

'No. Or at least I have my doubts. It was Anna Wolff, one of my officers, who brought me into this. She thinks there's something fishy going on too.'

Vestergaard straightened up but continued to gaze at the face of her dead colleague. After a moment she turned to Fabel again. 'We need to talk . . .'

*　*　*

Fabel took Vestergaard to her hotel on the Alter Wall. Somehow it didn't surprise him that she had booked into the same hotel where Jespersen had died. It didn't surprise him but he thought it ill-advised. He arranged for coffee to be served in a quiet seating area off the bar while Vestergaard took her bags to her room.

'I thought we'd have a coffee and then head up to the Police Presidium and talk about Jespersen.'

'Let's talk here,' she said. 'There's no one around. Neutral territory. Then we can head up to the Presidium.'

'Neutral territory?' said Fabel. 'We're supposed to be cooperating. I didn't think that colleagues needed "neutral territory".'

'Just an expression,' said Vestergaard, sipping her coffee and leaving a trace of pink on the rim of the cup. 'Maybe it's just that my English isn't as good as yours. I notice you don't speak English with a German accent.'

'I learned it when I was young,' he said, annoyed at the distraction technique. He knew what she was doing, and she knew he knew. They were both police officers; both inter-rogators. 'I am half-Scottish. I grew up bilingual.'

'I see.' Another sip. 'It's unusual to hear a German speak without an accent. In Denmark we subtitle all English-language films and TV. You dub them. Germans don't have the true exposure to the language we do. Like a cultural condom. That's why we Danes and the Dutch speak better English. With less of an accent, I mean. But I noticed your lack of accent when you picked me up at the airport. It would have made things easier for Jens. You didn't meet him, you say?'

'We spoke on the phone. Once.' Fabel laughed without warmth. 'Is this an interrogation, Frau Vestergaard? If so, I'd remind you that I am the police officer here. And if there is anything suspicious about Jespersen's death then it is my case, not yours. This is my jurisdiction.'

'Jens didn't like Germans,' she said, still cool. Cold. 'Did you know that?'

'No,' Fabel sighed. 'Any particular reason?'

'The usual. The war. Like me, Jens was very proud to be a Danish police officer. It's a noble heritage to have. Do you know one of our proudest moments?'

'I imagine you're going to tell me.'

'During the war, unlike the police in other occupied countries, the Danish police wouldn't collaborate. They barely cooperated. Basically they just tried to get on with the job they were supposed to do. Being policemen. Then, when you Germans told them they had to guard installations against attack by the Danish resistance, they told you to shove it. So do you know what happened?'

Fabel shrugged.

'You sent them to Buchenwald concentration camp.'

'Listen, Frau Vestergaard, I didn't send anyone to concentration camps. I wasn't alive then. And even if I had been, I wouldn't have been a Nazi.' Fabel was annoyed that he had let his irritation show. She was deliberately baiting him.

'Really?' she said as if vaguely surprised. 'Anyway, dozens of Danish police officers died in Buchenwald. It was only after they were transferred and their status changed to that of prisoners of war that the death rate slowed down. But they still wouldn't do what you . . . I mean the Germans . . . I mean the Nazis . . . sorry, I get confused who it was who was supposed to have violated Denmark . . . wanted them to do.'

'And that's why Jespersen hated Germans? To be frank, I get the feeling you share his prejudice.'

'Jens was from a long family tradition of police service. His grandfather was a policeman during the war and his father, who was only twenty-one back then, was also a police officer. They were both transported to Buchenwald. Jens's grandfather was one of the ones who died. His father barely survived.'

'I see. I understand. But what's your point?'

'That Jens would not have set foot in Germany unless he had a damned good reason to do so.'

'And you don't know why he was here?'

'I have an idea. But that's all. Jens was . . .' For the first time since he had met her, Vestergaard looked lost for the right word. 'Jens could be difficult. He had a tendency to go off and do his own thing. Follow a hunch.'

'There's nothing wrong in following a hunch.'

'No, not if you keep your colleagues – your superior – informed of where you are and what you are doing.'

'But we got an official request from you yourself to assist Jespersen. You knew he was coming here.'

'He told me some of what he had going on, but not all. Things were difficult with Jens. He was old-school and I started out under his command. He found it difficult to accept that he was now accountable to me. Added to which he had a habit of going off on his own little crusades.'

Vestergaard must have picked up on the subtle change in Fabel's expression. 'It looks like I've struck a chord,' she said.

'Long story,' said Fabel. 'I have . . . I *had* an officer who did the same thing. It cost her her sanity.'

'I see. Well, I think Jespersen's last crusade might have cost him his life. Have you heard of the Sirius Patrol?'

Fabel shook his head.

'The Sirius Patrol is a special-forces unit of the Danish Navy. It is responsible for patrolling the extreme north-east of Greenland, just in case our Russian friends ever come to call. These guys are the toughest you're likely to come across. They cover nearly twenty thousand kilometres of coastline, travelling mainly by dogsled in temperatures that can hit minus thirty. And, of course, in winter they do it all in perpetual night.'

'Jespersen?'

'A two-year tour. After that, when he joined the Danish National Police, he was accepted for the *Politiets Aktionsstyrke* or AKS. It's our police special forces. A national SWAT team used for major incidents, drug busts, et cetera. I take it you can see where I'm going with this?'

'That Jespersen was a tough son of a bitch?'

'That, and the fact that he was extremely fit. He kept himself in the same kind of shape he'd been in as a Sirius soldier.'

'Not a heart-attack candidate . . .'

'Not a normal heart-attack candidate, let's say. Of course it's possible and it would be the most straightforward of explanations, but I just don't see it unless the autopsy reveals some congenital cardiac weakness.' Vestergaard drained her cup and shook her head when Fabel went to refill it. 'Too much coffee makes me nervy.'

Fabel tried to picture a nervy Karin Vestergaard but it was beyond his powers of imagination. 'So what's all this about looking for puncture wounds? Do you have some kind of idea who's behind Jespersen's death?'

'All I have, Chief Commissar, is a bundle of unconnected facts. And I suspect that's all Jens had, but he somehow saw a bigger picture. I am willing to share everything I know, but I expect a little quid pro quo . . . I was assured of your full cooperation by Herr van Heiden. I would appreciate it if that cooperation extended to keeping me fully informed of your progress. I suspect that this case extends across our common border. Maybe beyond. And if my . . . if *our* suspicions are right, then we are talking about the assassination in Hamburg of a senior Danish police officer. No small matter.'

Fabel looked at Vestergaard for a moment. She had freshened up her make-up when she had gone up to her room. A different shade. It had changed her look subtly. Maybe having perfectly regular features allowed you to alter your look more easily than other people. Despite her beauty, Fabel imagined that Karin Vestergaard could even make herself look plain and uninteresting.

'I take it you're staying in Hamburg for some time?'

'I've left my booking open.'

'Maybe we should think about a different hotel – this was the murder scene, if Jespersen's death was murder.'

'Then it might help to be close to it.' Vestergaard's expression still gave nothing away of the emotions that might be behind it.

'As you wish,' said Fabel. 'But I'm going to assign an officer to you. Just to keep an eye on things.'

'That's not necessary,' said Vestergaard. 'I told you that Jens Jespersen had once been my superior, rather than the other way around. Well, that was when we were both in the *Politiets Aktionsstyrke*. Trust me, Mr Fabel, I'm more than capable of looking after myself.'

'So was Jespersen,' said Fabel.

9.

It was comforting to be back. In Norway. In Oslo. In this light. Strange but comforting.

The clouds had dispersed from the sky and the ever-optimistic Oslo café owners had placed aluminium tables and chairs, and the occasional strategically placed patio heater, outside on the streets.

Birta Henningsen sat at a pavement café, drinking her coffee and watching, from behind her sunglasses, the ice-blue *Oslotrikken* tramcars passing up and down the street under a matching ice-blue sky lightly streaked with wisps of white cloud. The February sun that shone on Oslo did so brightly if without any real warmth. But that suited Birta perfectly: she belonged in this climate, in this light, this clean, cool air; in this environment. Birta had, of course, spent time in the

Mediterranean and other beautiful parts of the world, mainly through her work, but there she had always felt conspicuous: foreign. And Birta did not like to feel conspicuous.

It was here, in the North, that she felt at home.

Birta had eaten a light meal and now the coffee restored some of her energy. It had been a long drive from Stockholm – seven hours – and the day before she had driven all the way from Copenhagen, crossing the Öresund Bridge. She would drive back to Stockholm afterwards. She found her thoughts drifting to the meeting arranged for later in the day. It was an important one. One of the most important of her career. She had prepared well for it: she found that she performed better, was less nervous, if she had concluded all her research and preparation well in advance and simply relaxed immediately before.

There was a mother with two children three tables away. Birta watched them. The mother would have been roughly the same age, shared Birta's colouring and was dressed in typical Oslo chic. Expensive but restrained. And warm. But, unlike Birta, there was something not entirely contained about the young mother: a vague sense of chaos. Birta recognised it as the consequence of motherhood; that a substantial fraction of the woman's life was no longer hers to control and Birta wondered what that must feel like.

She turned back to watch the trams and the passers-by. She had never had children. She had never divided herself. And she never would. She had chosen career and herself above all else. And now she sat under the pale Norwegian sky, watching the trams pass and glancing over at the woman and her two children and felt a vague ache in her chest.

This was futile. Sentimental wandering. She was annoyed with her own self-indulgence since she'd arrived. Like the trip to Holmenkollen.

Birta had not planned to visit Holmenkollen, but she had felt the need as soon as she had approached Oslo.

She had driven overnight and had approached the city along the Mosseveien highway that ran along the shore, as the day had broken painfully beautiful in deep red and purple-blue silk over the Oslofjord. She had parked in a municipal car park on the outskirts of the city and had taken the T-Bane train to Holmenkollen and mingled with the handful of off-season tourists at the ski centre. Like the tourists, she had looked out over the city from the top of the ski jump. But it had been the circuit around the centre, the one used for the biathlon, that she had come to see. One more time. It had been a pointless exercise and so unlike her. And now she sat in the centre of Oslo surrendering to pangs of jealousy as she watched a woman fuss over her children.

This was not what she was here for. She was in Oslo on business, not to sightsee or for indulgent self-reflection. She paid in cash for her coffee and left without another glance at the woman and her children.

The sun was already low and the long Nordic winter night would come soon. It would be dark. Time for her meeting.

10.

'Okay,' said Fabel. 'It's a deal. We share information. But I have to say that for the moment it's going to be very much a one-way trade. You're the one with the background info. All I've got at the moment is something that looks like a death from natural causes.'

'Like I told you,' said Vestergaard, 'Jens Jespersen was my commanding officer when we were both in the *Politiets Aktionsstyrke*. I learned a hell of a lot from him during that time. I don't think I'd be where I am today if it hadn't been for him.'

Fabel watched Vestergaard closely for signs of thaw in the ice maiden. If they were there, they were too small for him to detect. She spoke of Jespersen with respect, even a hint of affection, but there was no warmth in her voice.

'There was a major drugs bust, six years ago. We set up an elaborate sting – or more correctly Jens set up an elaborate sting and we landed Goran Vujačić. You know, the Bosnian Serb warlord turned drug smuggler.'

'I remember,' said Fabel. 'It's funny how people like Vujačić start off with some kind of ethnic or political agenda and then embrace the criminal free market with enthusiasm. He was a bad bastard from all accounts. He's dead, isn't he?'

'I'll get to that, but yes, he died four years ago. Vujačić was as slimy as he was a vicious piece of work. He had been a member of a Bosnian Serb police unit and was directly involved in some of the atrocities that went on during the Bosnian War. He was never tried at the Hague. Not enough evidence. But the bastard was there at the massacres and the rape camps. Anyway, Jens Jespersen set up a sting and we took Vujačić down. A few months before we had managed to trip up a Danish businessman called Peter Knudsen who had been dabbling in drug exporting. Jens did a deal with him and Knudsen collaborated with us in setting up Vujačić. We used Knudsen's yacht and Jens played the part of Knudsen. We staged three meetings on the yacht and one in Copenhagen. Vujačić went along with it all. The last meeting on the yacht was where the money changed hands, electronically. It was a very expensive op for us to put on but it seemed very successful.'

'So how come Vujačić went free?' asked Fabel.

'Unfortunately, Jens hadn't dotted all the i's or crossed all the t's and Vujačić's legal team started to argue entrapment. It wouldn't have got him off, but his legal team managed to get him bailed between hearings. His passport was impounded, though, and he was restricted from travelling outside Denmark. It was all a bit of a mess and, to be frank, it wasn't just that my career overtook Jens's, it was the fact that his came to a standstill. He was blamed for leaving open a potential loophole through which Goran Vujačić could walk free. Anyway, it was when Vujačić was on bail pending trial that someone decided to relieve the state of the burden of court proceedings. We found him in Tivoli Gardens just sitting in the rain on a bench. Someone had used a small, thin file or knife to stab him in the heart. It was a truly professional job: there was hardly any blood and it took us ages to find the entry wound beneath his sternum.'

'I guess you make a lot of enemies in his line of business.'

'And some strange partners,' said Vestergaard. She paused while a waiter came in and took their cups away. 'You see, that was the start of Jens's obsession with the Valkyrie.'

'The Valkyrie?'

Vestergaard held up her hand as if to slow Fabel down. 'We had set up this luxury yacht for the sting. Fitted it out with bugs and hidden cameras to record the whole operation. One of the things we got on tape was Vujačić talking about the third partner in the deal. A sleeping partner who had financed the whole drug deal and was looking for the lion's share of the profit. It was this anonymous third partner we had really wanted to uncover.'

'So you think it was this partner that had Vujačić killed?'

'Almost definitely. Vujačić was nothing if he wasn't a negotiator. All through his questioning he had kept shtum about the identity of the moneyman. He knew that if his defence of entrapment didn't work, he could do a deal by giving up the name of his backer. But anyway, if we go back to the conversation we recorded on the boat . . . Vujačić had mentioned that the moneyman had a contract killer who was the best in the business. Vujačić claimed that this contract killer had cleaned up the competition for him at the behest of this sleeping partner. He also claimed this killer went by the name of the Valkyrie, that she was a woman. And he claimed that if the circumstances called for it, this killer was an expert at making the deaths look like accidents or natural causes. Oh, and by the way, the crooked businessman we used to set Vujačić up also died prematurely.'

'So that's why you want our pathologist to check closely for puncture marks or anything unusual . . .'

'Exactly. But Vujačić had more to say about the Valkyrie. And this is where it gets really interesting for you: he claimed that she was based here. In Hamburg.'

Fabel leaned back in the leather sofa and gazed out across the empty lounge and through the vast plate-glass windows to the Alsterfleet beyond. 'You believe this?'

'Jens did. But, like I said, he didn't share information the way he should have. And from what I've seen of your report, his laptop and notebooks have disappeared as well.'

'I thought he was travelling surprisingly light. And we were pretty sure his cellphone was wiped. But we didn't know for sure that stuff had been taken. I'll get someone to start questioning the staff.'

Vestergaard shook her head. 'No point. His stuff wasn't filched by immigrant cleaners. Whoever murdered Jens took them.'

'If he *was* murdered. But, from what you say, if his death is foul play then everything would seem to point to this Valkyrie,' said Fabel. He found his thoughts wandering: as head of the Hamburg Murder Commission, it was no small thing for Fabel to be told that an internationally active contract killer was based in his city.

'It would be a natural assumption. Of course, you do know that this Valkyrie may not even exist. And if he or she does, then it's by no means certain that he or she is based in Hamburg. It could simply be that communication is channelled through here somehow.'

'Jespersen wasn't killed by a communication channel,' said Fabel. 'What else have you got?'

'I checked what I could of Jens's paperwork in Copenhagen. Also his Internet history, et cetera. He had piles – and I mean piles – of research material on the former East German police and security apparatus, he had detailed lists of former officers of the Volkspolizei, as I think you called it, and, of course, masses of stuff on the Stasi.'

'And you think that this is connected somehow with this supposed Hamburg hit woman?'

'I don't know. Maybe there's no connection. But Jens was very focused on this investigation. Officially he was looking for Vujačić's killer, but his attitude towards the case was bordering on the obsessive. Anyway, there were a few names – of former Stasi people, I mean – which he seemed to take a very special interest in. One above all others, a Major Georg Drescher, seemed to be the main focus of his attentions. Interestingly, from what I can see, Drescher simply vanished into thin air as soon as the Wall came down. Drescher worked for the HVA department of the Stasi. The espionage wing. My guess is that as soon as Drescher sensed the wind changing direction in eighty-nine, he used his Stasi resources to set up under a new identity. Maybe even here in West Germany. But why Jens was so interested in Drescher, I don't know for sure. Having read through the notes, I reckon that Drescher would appear to have been a major figure in the recruitment and training of agents for deployment in the West.'

'So you think this "Valkyrie" is an ex-Stasi agent?'

'It would make sense.'

Fabel frowned. He did the arithmetic and somehow the idea of a now middle-aged woman carrying out such efficient assassinations didn't add up. 'Let's not get ahead of ourselves. We'll see what the autopsy reveals and then explore all possibilities. Anything else?'

'A few other names. Notes on Vujačić's contacts, that kind of thing. A couple of strange things as well . . . you've heard of Gennady Frolov?'

'The Russian oligarch?'

'That's the one. Personal wealth valued at twelve and a half billion. Jens had made a whole lot of notes about him. Just general stuff and not a dossier.'

'Vujačić's moneyman?'

'I doubt it,' said Vestergaard. 'I did a bit of digging and compared with most of the other oligarchs Frolov is Snow White. But it is all a bit odd. As well as Frolov, Jens had tons of information and corporate literature on Vantage North, the ship designers and builders in Flensburg. They designed and built Frolov's luxury yacht, the *Snow Queen*.'

'And you're sure that Frolov couldn't be the moneyman behind Vujačić?'

'It doesn't make sense. The supply of narcotics to Scandinavia and Northern Germany is a multimillion-dollar business – but that's still peanuts to the likes of Frolov. The risk of conviction would vastly outweigh any benefit.'

Fabel leaned back for a moment and rubbed his chin as he thought. 'Who is Olaf?'

'Olaf?'

'In Jespersen's notebook – he wrote the name Olaf. Do you know who that could be?'

Vestergaard frowned. 'I know a hell of a lot of Olafs, and so did Jens. But I can't think of anyone in particular.'

'Was there anything else in Jespersen's notes that could be useful?'

'No. Not really.' Karin Vestergaard reached into her attaché case and pulled out a file. 'But maybe you'll see some relevance in something I've missed. I've got a copy of everything in here.'

Fabel reached out to take the file from Vestergaard but she held it firm for a moment. 'I've shared all I have, Mr Fabel. I take it you intend to live up to your part of the bargain?'

'I told you I would give you my fullest cooperation.'

The irritation was evident in Fabel's tone. 'I will keep you informed of everything as it happens.'

'Then I'm sure we'll get along fine,' said Vestergaard, with a smile devoid of warmth, and let go of the file.

Chapter Three

1.

After Birta picked up the hire car from the municipal car park and drove out of Oslo, she tossed the ticket out of the window as she cleared the city limits. When she returned the car there would be no evidence that she had ever been in Oslo or even in Norway. She had programmed several false destinations around Stockholm into the car's satnav system, the sum of which would account for the kilometres accrued on the odometer. Throughout her trip she had observed every speed limit, every traffic regulation. And because she hadn't stopped over in a hotel and had paid for all fuel with cash, there was no evidence that she had crossed the border.

Birta switched on the music system and Wolfgang Haffner filled the car. The German jazz and the Norwegian winter landscape fitted together perfectly and she eased back into her seat. But she found she couldn't stop thinking back to the café and the woman with her children.

Birta's client's place was to the north of Drøbak, set deep into the forest on the shore of a small lake. She knew he worked from home and this had been the ideal location for a meeting. She had even identified the ideal window in his schedule.

She parked in a car park in Drøbak: she had established in her reconnaissance that it was unmetered and not over-looked by CCTV cameras. She changed in the back of the car, pulling on three layers of thick woollen socks, partly to keep out the cold but mainly to allow the heavy oversized men's boots she then put on to fit her: carrying out a meeting in snow was a blessing and a curse at the same time. She would leave the tracks she wanted, where she wanted. But she'd have to take care not to leave unintentional signs of her passing.

Birta slipped into her dark parka and tucked her blonde hair under the black woollen beanie hat, making sure every strand was secure and out of sight. She put on her rucksack and slung the rifle case by its strap over one shoulder, then made her way on foot from the car park and out through the back of the town, keeping out of sight of the houses.

It took her half an hour to reach where the forest opened up around the lake. At the north end the lights of a house reflected on the water. Three rooms were illuminated, but she knew he would be alone. His wife and children were visiting family in Frederikstad and wouldn't be back until lunchtime tomorrow. He was staying at home to pack and prepare for his trip to China in two days' time.

Birta made her way through the trees and around to where the long drive swept round to the front of the house. The drive had been cleared, the snow pushed into metre-high banks on either side. Birta edged along backwards, sweeping her footprints away as she moved, until she found a thinner stretch of piled snow. She jumped over it and onto the drive. From here on there would be no tracks to find. Before moving closer to the house, she unslung the rifle from her shoulder, unrolled the canvas sheet and laid out the parts for assembly.

'What the hell are you doing?' A male voice came from behind her.

Everything happened in one movement: she stood, turned, unfastened the sheath, and arced the knife up and into his chest, under his sternum. She thrust it with calculated extra force to penetrate the man's heavy parka and the layers beneath. The man didn't react: he would not have seen the knife, its non-reflective black polycarbide surface and the speed of her strike making it invisible in the dark. Still in the same continuous movement, Birta twisted the knife. The man's eyes and mouth gaped at her as if in outrage or confusion, then he sank to his knees. Birta stood to one side and let him tilt forward and crash onto his face. She turned him over and established two facts within a second: he was dead; he was not her client. The dead man was in his late forties. It was difficult to tell through the layers of clothes, but he looked heavy-set. She opened up his parka and felt the warmth of a body that would no longer generate its own temperature. She checked him for a weapon. None. Not a bodyguard or cop. He had been carrying a large snow shovel and Birta guessed he must have been some kind of handyman. Why hadn't he come up in her reconnaissance? She cursed to herself and wiped the blade of her knife clean on the shoulder of his coat, at the same time scanning the length of the driveway and the forest on its fringes. She resheathed the knife, unzipped her parka and unholstered her silenced automatic. No sign of anyone else.

Scanning the forest and the snowbank edge of the drive, Birta chose a spot and dragged the dead man across to it, through the snow and into the woods.

Back on the drive she picked up the unattached telescopic sight and used it to study the big bright squares of window on the house. She knew where the client's study was and that he should be there working until about nine. The blinds had been left open and she could see the whole study. No client. She checked the other illuminated rooms. Nothing.

This was not good. Birta felt a vague panic in her chest and used her will to force it from her, as she'd been taught to do. When you were afraid, when you became stressed, that was when things went wrong. That was when you slipped up with the meeting; that was when people noticed you as you made your departure. Calm. Stay calm.

Birta again checked the driveway. Nothing. She stood motionless, holding her breath, absorbing the sounds of the night and the forest. She cursed again. She was going to have to close the forensic distance. It was a simple rule: the greater the forensic distance, the less the chance of detection and interception. The long-range sniper rifle was the perfect example: the bullet, which might have endured the trauma of passing through wood or glass, then flesh and bone before becoming impacted into brick or deformed by stone, was the only forensic link between you and the dead client. You had a forensic distance from point and moment of death, meaning you had a greater chance of getting away unseen.

But if she couldn't see the client, she couldn't use the rifle. He could, of course, simply be in the kitchen making himself a sandwich, but the fact that she had had to take care of a secondary meant she didn't have the luxury of time. If she hadn't been discovered by the handyman, then she would have sat it out, maybe an hour, maybe more, waiting for the client to reappear. She would have to get close. Maybe even go into the house. And that meant she was no longer forensically distant from the meeting.

Birta repacked the rifle in its case, again unholstered her handgun, and made her way towards the house.

2.

Anna Wolff had spent three nights retracing the drunken footsteps of Armin Lensch. She had also spent the time thinking about the situation she had got herself into. She had been involved in seventeen murder cases since Fabel had selected her for his team. Seventeen different killings for motives as banal as drunken rage or sexual jealousy.

And a few, like these latest ones, had been for motives so twisted and abstract that she knew that no matter how long she served in the Murder Commission, she would never get the measure of the minds behind them. Fabel did, though. It was in itself a creepy thought: that he understood these people. Maybe he was right after all: maybe she wasn't suited to being a Murder Commission officer.

Anna still couldn't wrap her mind around the fact that the guy she'd kneed in the groin was now dead. For some abstract reason she couldn't understand, she felt she had contributed to his death. Maybe it wasn't that abstract. From what she could gather from his friends, they had teased him about his encounter with her and he had gone off on his own into the night. And then someone had murdered him. The final element in a sequence of events that she could have been said to have set in motion.

It was too close for comfort.

'Where do you want to go now, Commissar?' Theo asked her. She turned to him. Theo Wangler was the Davidwache uniform who had been assigned to accompany her as she did the rounds of the bars and clubs. And the uniform hung well on him: Wangler was two metres tall and obviously worked out. Weights, Anna reckoned. He had a broad, strong jaw and when he had taken his hat off to brush back his hair with his fingers she had noticed it was thick, dark and wavy. People as good-looking as he was were usually assholes. She had decided in that instant of first meeting that she disliked him, but would not rule out a bit of a tumble with him. As it turned out, her first impressions had been wrong: Wangler was a quiet type, almost shy. But as they had gone from one bar to the other, she had seen he had a quiet assertiveness about him that kept the unruly in their place yet was un-aggressive enough for him to be able to talk reason into all but the most drunk or the most cop-hating. It was, she realised, an ideal temperament for a police officer. A temperament she knew she didn't possess. Anna decided to dislike Wangler all over again.

The Reeperbahn was long and wide and straight, ideal for weaving the *reep*, as rope was called in Low German, from which the former ropewalk street had got its name. By day it looked dreary and tawdry, by night it became one of the most illuminated streets in Germany. But, as they made their way along the Reeperbahn, there was something about its ten-thirty neon sparkle that was deeply depressing. A forced, manic jollity. Anna and Wangler had visited one sleazy bar after another, getting nothing from the bar staff. They had done most of their talking to the security men on the doors of the clubs and bars, most of whom, like the bartenders and hostesses, greeted Wangler with a warm handshake or at least a nod of acknowledgement.

'I've worked here for four years,' explained Wangler, as they made their way along the sinful mile, passing a sex shop with a window full of improbably proportioned sex aids. 'You get to know people.'

'Do you like working this beat?' asked Anna.

'It's okay . . . people have the wrong idea about the Kiez. An old idea, I suppose. Even Superintendent Kaminski. He was on the beat here in the old days and I sometimes think he's of the opinion that it's all going to the dogs because the brothels are shutting up shop and the trendy bars, musical theatres and luxury flats are moving in. There's even an advertising agency setting up its offices here.'

'That's all good, isn't it?'

'Well, there's the other side to it. The Reeperbahn used to sell cheap sex. Now it sells cheap booze. The Kiez has become infected with the British Disease – binge drinking, particularly in the clubs. It's changed the kind of street crime we deal with. Less thievery, more violence.'

'Isn't the ban working?' Anna referred to the recent injunction against the carrying of any weapons in the Reeperbahn and the Kiez. A designated weapon-free zone had been set up, with yellow signs standing at the perimeter.

'A little. But your Angel seems to be contravening it . . .'

Anna laughed. They broke off their conversation as they came to the doorway of another club. Two bull-necked Neanderthals stood with their hands folded in front of them in the traditional stance of security staff.

'Why do they always stand like that?' Anna asked Wangler. 'You know, as if they're protecting their balls?'

'Maybe they've heard about you . . .' Wangler laughed.

'You know about that?'

'Everybody knows about that.' Wangler turned to the first doorman. 'Hi, Heiner.'

'Hi, Theo.' The huge doorman spoke with a remarkably soft voice. A little high-pitched. 'How's it going?'

'The usual. Listen, Heiner, this is Criminal Commissar Wolff of the Murder Commission. She'd like to ask you a couple of questions.'

'She can ask me anything, any time . . .' The doorman smiled at Anna. His mate joined in but Anna reckoned it was a reflex action. The other doorman did not look sufficiently evolved to be capable of independent thought. Anna returned the smile with a weary one of her own. She handed the doorman a photograph of Armin Lensch.

'I don't suppose you've seen this guy?' asked Anna.

The doorman glanced at the photograph. He shrugged colossal shoulders and handed it back to Anna. Then he checked himself. 'Wait a minute. Let me see it again . . .' Anna handed the photograph back to him. 'Yeah . . . yeah, I seen him. I seen him on Friday . . . no, Saturday night. Over there.' He pointed across the wide roadway. 'I seen him get into a taxi.'

'You remember everyone you see getting into a taxi?' asked Anna.

'No. But I remember this guy because I didn't think it was a taxi. Or a taxi on duty, anyway. It looked dodgy.'

'What do you mean?'

'Well, it was the right model – a Merc E-class, and it was the right colour, ivory-beige – but it didn't have a roof sign. The reason I paid attention was 'cause I noticed the car came up from behind him. I don't think he realised it wasn't a taxi. You've got to watch for shit like that – you know, pervs pretending to be taxi drivers and picking up girls and stuff. Or drunken guys being picked up and rolled for their cash. It don't happen much because nobody's got a car the same colour as a taxi.'

'And you would identify this man as the one who got into the taxi? Or fake taxi?' Anna tapped the photograph.

'Yeah, he was in here earlier in the night with a bunch of other guys. Mouthy little prick. I recognised him when I saw him over the road.'

'You said you watch out for guys being rolled – why didn't you report seeing him get into the car or do something to stop it?' asked Wangler.

'It could have been a genuine taxi. Whether it was or not, I didn't think at the time that he was in danger.'

'Why?' asked Anna.

'Well.' Heiner the Neanderthal shrugged his massive shoulders. 'I reckoned he was safe. With it being a woman driver and all . . .'

3.

Birta drew close to the house, keeping to the edge of the shields of yellow light cast out onto the snow by the uncurtained windows. It was, she reflected, something you would never think about: drawing your blinds or curtains when you lived in a place like this. The forest was your shutter against the world. No one else to see you.

She could see no one in the lit rooms: she scanned the blank, dark windows too. Nothing. She made her way around the side of the house. There was a door halfway along. Locked. She went around to the back, keeping tight against the wall. There was another door at the back. She turned the handle and was rewarded with the door easing open. It led into the kitchen of the house: a large pine-clad room with expensive-looking fittings and a clutch of unmatched leather and upholstered chairs in one corner. The large fridge was bedecked with children's drawings, scribbled notes, fridge magnets. Birta eased the door closed behind her and stood perfectly still, diverting all of her attention to any sounds from inside the house. Nothing. Shit, maybe he wasn't here. That would normally not be a problem: she could replan, reschedule. But Birta had left her mark on this location: there was a middle-aged man with a ripped heart lying out in the woods.

She edged out into the hall. Still no sounds of life. Birta made her way along towards the study. She was about halfway along, checking every room as she passed, when the door to the left immediately ahead opened and the sound of a refilling toilet cistern filled the hall. The client stepped out into the hall and gave a start when he saw Birta standing there. She snapped the pistol up and aimed at his head.

'I've been expecting you,' he said, and smiled falteringly.

'Me?' Birta said.

'Well, not you specifically, but someone like you.' He looked past her along the hall. 'I suppose I expected it to be a man.'

'I'm not a man,' said Birta. No point in looking behind me, she thought. Your handyman is not coming. No nasty surprise for me. No reprieve for you.

'I can see that . . . listen, you don't have to . . .' The client didn't finish the sentence. Birta's bullet hit him in the centre of his forehead and he toppled backward, his body rigid, like a felled tree. She walked over to where he lay. Birta knew he was already dead: there were sounds from his body

– post-mortem sounds – his pale trousers were stained with urine and she thought she could smell excreta. Violent death, she knew, was seldom clean. Or odourless. Dark red, almost black blood oozed from a nostril and his left ear. Nevertheless, she crouched down at his feet, aimed along his fallen body at the underside of his jaw and fired a second shot. The client's head twitched as if he was shaking his head in protest, but Birta knew it was the low-velocity hollow-point doing its work inside the confines of his skull, destroying his brain.

She stood up and marked in her head where she was in the hall and how she had got there. Measuring the forensic distance.

Meeting concluded.

She drove back through the night. There were flurries of snow but the highways had been cleared. She settled back into the comfort of the driver's seat and switched on her music, making sure she was relaxed but not so much that she would make a mistake that would draw attention to her. She again crossed the Swedish border on a road without a customs point and headed towards Stockholm. Birta returned the car to Stockholm-Bromma airport the next morning and then made her way to the airport car park where her Danish-registered car was parked. As she did so Birta Hennigsen, who had existed as an identity for only a little more than thirty-six hours, began to fade from being.

4.

Fabel headed into the Police Presidium early, driving through Winterhude just as the sun was coming up. The sky was clear and the lying snow had been crisped by the overnight frost. Fabel loved it when it was like this. Since he was a boy, he had been a winter person.

When he arrived at his office he checked the internal email and found there was a reminder from van Heiden about the conference on violence against women. Another reminder. Fabel typed in a brief response explaining he needed a meeting with van Heiden urgently. He also left messages for Anna and Werner that he wanted to see them as soon as they came in.

Fabel opened his desk drawer and took out the sketch pad, laid it on his desktop and flipped it open. He stared at the empty, clean expanse of white paper and sighed. It always started this way. Fabel had used these sketch pads for fifteen years of murder investigations. Singles, multiples, serials. No one except Fabel ever saw these pads. For Fabel, this was a completely different exercise from the plotting of an investigation on an incident board. This exercise had nothing to do with a team effort: it was the externalisation of his thought processes. These clean pages would fill with names, times, places: all connected by a web of lines. Alongside them would be phrases, press cuttings, quotes from statements. And ideas: foul, dark ideas. Fabel remembered how once, when investigating a serial-murder case, he had come across the notebook of the killer: obsessively neat but tangled threads connecting; words underlined, scored out, circled, triple question-marked. It had chilled Fabel to the bone to see how similar the insane methodology of the killer was to his own.

Fabel took a marker and at the top of the page wrote in block capitals the name ANGEL, followed by three question marks. Then he noted, on opposite sides of the page, the names of the two St Pauli victims. Then, referring to the case files and his notebook, be began plotting out the key elements of the case. But as he did so, another case kept shouldering itself into his way: that of the dead Danish policeman. He tried to shake it clear of his mind: it wasn't even a case yet, although Möller, the forensic pathologist at Butenfeld, had grudgingly promised that the autopsy results would be available about lunchtime. He thought back to Karin Vestergaard and remembered that she had been beautiful, yet somehow he could not picture her face.

His reflections were interrupted by the arrival of Anna Wolff and Werner Meyer in his office. He closed over the sketch pad and put it back into his desk drawer, asking Anna and Werner to sit as he did so.

'Okay,' he said. 'Where are we?'

'I went to see Viola Dahlke's husband,' said Werner. 'That was tough. Nice guy, ordinary family. Had no idea his wife had a secret life.'

'I take it you didn't enlighten him about the nature of that life?'

Werner frowned. 'Give me some credit. But she sure has a lot of explaining to do. Anyway, her husband confirms that she was at home the night Westland was killed. I take it we can let her go.'

'A spousal alibi isn't enough in itself,' said Fabel. 'But we don't have enough to go for an extension of detention. And anyway, I'm convinced both St Pauli killings are the work of the same person and we know for a fact that Viola Dahlke did not commit the second one.'

'I've checked all the taxi drivers working St Pauli the night Lensch was killed – three of whom were women. None of them picked him up or remember him at a rank or trying to flag a taxi. So it looks like it was our woman.'

'Almost like she was targeting Lensch or someone like him,' said Fabel.

'But that doesn't make sense,' said Anna. 'Her choice of victims so far has been pretty diverse. Westland was a celebrity, a foreigner and in his fifties. Lensch was a nobody, a German national and in his early thirties. The only thing that I can see they shared was that they were both male and they both happened to be in the Kiez.'

'Maybe that's all she needed. But the whole thing with the taxi is odd. No one has a car that colour, especially an E-class Merc, unless they're in the taxi business. This is a highly organised killer. Why go to all of that trouble and then pick a victim at random?' Fabel sighed. 'What about CCTV – anything?'

'Not so far. I've got that rather hunky uniform from Davidwache going through it.'

'Why?' asked Fabel. 'Shouldn't you do that yourself?'

'Listen, I'm not dodging out of anything. It's just that Wangler has been on that beat for four years. He knows every inch of it, including where each camera is. That Mercedes must have been picked up somewhere on the way in or out. If anyone can find it and find it quickly, then it's Wangler.'

'Okay, okay.' Fabel held up his hands defensively. 'Did you check out Jürgen Mann?' he asked, referring to the witness who had approached Carstens Kaminski.

'Yep,' said Anna. 'He checks out. One conviction for cannabis possession; nothing else. He's a dying breed, apparently.'

'What do you mean?'

'According to Wangler—'

'Your new best chum,' interrupted Werner.

'I wish . . .' Anna sighed. 'Anyway, according to Wangler, there are fewer and fewer creeps like Mann in the Kiez these days. With all the CCTV in the Reeperbahn, even if it is supposed to be strategically sited, no one wants to be seen going into or coming out of a brothel these days. It's all call girls, online escort agencies, that kind of stuff. Wangler says that, compared to the past, street girls are struggling for custom these days. Added to which there is a steady supply of trafficked women being brought into the unregulated prostitution business elsewhere in the city.'

'Against their will, for the most part,' said Fabel.

'Maybe so, but when you're a sleazeball paying for sex,' said Anna, 'you're not the kind of person who cares if your chicken is free-range or battery, if you know what I mean. Anyway, there are fewer punters on the street. Nowadays the Kiez is full of the Armin Lensches of this world, getting pissed and getting into trouble. For what it's worth, I think Mann was on the level. I think he genuinely believes he came face to face with the Angel. But again we've got no CCTV to back up his claim.'

'Okay . . . ' Fabel paused and leaned back in his chair. 'Listen, we have a guest. A colleague from Denmark. I've asked her to come into the Presidium this afternoon. I'd like you to talk to her, Anna. You too, Werner.'

'A PR job?' asked Anna. 'Of course I will. After all, we all know that I'm a natural diplomat.'

'That's not why I'm asking you to talk to her, Anna. Her name is Karin Vestergaard and she's a senior officer in the Danish National Police. More senior in rank than me.'

'Is this to do with the Dane who died from a heart attack?' asked Werner.

Anna exchanged a knowing glance with Fabel. '*Supposed* to have died from a heart attack,' she said.

'*Politidirektør* Vestergaard has exactly the same kind of suspicions that you did, Anna. And she has some evidence to base them on. I'd like you to talk to her because you picked up on the Jespersen death.'

'So it was murder?' asked Werner.

'We'll know by lunchtime, hopefully. If Möller does his job.'

'Möller may be a wanker,' said Werner. 'But he's one of the best pathologists I've ever worked with.'

'Well, Frau Vestergaard was able to point us in a couple of specific directions. Listen, I don't want to get into it all now but there's all kinds of serious stuff going on in Jespersen's background. And if the autopsy comes back with anything suspicious, then Jespersen's death becomes an active case. If he was murdered, then it's a major investigation with all kinds of implications. The main thing is, Anna, it was your catch – a good catch.'

'So what's she like?' asked Werner. 'This Danish cop, I mean?'

'Wear your gloves when you shake hands with her,' said Fabel. 'Otherwise you'll get frostbite . . .'

5.

'You're from the telly?' The old woman smiled as she asked the question and Sylvie Achtenhagen wished that she hadn't. Her ruined teeth looked as if they needed the attention of an archaeologist, rather than a dentist. 'Is that what you said? You're from the telly?'

'That's right . . . HanSat.' Sylvie smiled sweetly, the way she'd learned to smile when she wanted information from someone. She cast her gaze beyond the broken-fence-edged square of waste ground. They were down by the harbour, on the southern edge of St Pauli. Across the Elbe, vast machines were hoisting containers from an armada of freight ships. The cold air rang with the rhythmic beeping of reversing cranes.

'Never heard of it. Don't have a telly.' The old woman made a sweeping gesture with her arm – as sweeping a gesture as her countless layers of clothing would allow – taking in the broken paving, the smear of scrubby grass, the discarded bottles, a used condom. 'I find it would ruin the ambience I've built up here.' She chuckled at her own joke. 'So you doin' sommat about the Kiez? About them murders? This is where they found the last fella, y'know.'

'Something like that. And yes, I know the latest victim was found here. That's why I came to talk to you. Is this your usual spot?'

'Coppers've asked me 'bout it already. They got a bee up their arses 'bout this 'un.'

'Is this your usual spot?' Sylvie repeated the question. Be patient. Smile. Offer money. 'Listen, I can pay for information. Only if it's good information, though. Is this your usual spot?'

'This is my abode,' the old woman announced grandly. 'How much?'

'That all depends. Do you sleep in a hostel?'

'Sometimes. When it's too cold. Sometimes I sleep here.'

'There are better places than this, surely. I mean the State Social Office would help find you a place.'

'Oh, I know . . .' Another broken-toothed chuckle. 'They offered me a villa in Blankenese, but I said it was too down-market for someone of my breeding.'

Sylvie shrugged. 'Okay, you said the police talked to you. What did they want to know?'

'They asked me if I saw anything the other night, when that fella was killed. I said I didn't. It was too cold so I dossed down in the Red Cross hostel. But I was here drinking until about eleven. But didn't see nothing. Then they asked me if I seen a taxi in the area. Driven by a woman.'

'A taxi?'

'Yeah. They said it might not've had a sign on it, though.'

'Did they say why they were looking for a taxi?'

'Yeah – the police always tell me them kind of things. Discuss cases. I'm like a special consultant.'

'Listen, you can get smart or you can get money. Not both.'

The down-and-out shrugged her padded shoulders. 'Just jokin'. No . . . they didn't say why.'

'Anything else?'

'They showed me this picture. I suppose it was the guy what got killed. I never seen him before and I told them so.'

'Did they give you a name for the dead man?'

'No – they did say he was about thirty and not too tall.'

'Anyone else doss down around here?'

'No, it's too far out for them. I sleep here 'cause I'm a woman. It ain't safe elsewhere.'

Sylvie looked at the woman. She looked eighty but might only have been forty. A couple of years older than her. She wondered how a woman could end up in a situation like that; she imagined that the tramp had seen all kinds – experienced all kinds – of horrors. Sylvie handed the tramp a fifty-euro note.

'Thanks . . .' The tramp looked delighted with her bounty. Suddenly eager. 'Listen, you come by tomorrow. I'll ask some of the others if they've seen something.'

'That would be good.' Sylvie smiled. 'You do that.'

Sylvie drove back into the Reeperbahn and parked near the taxi rank at Spielbudenplatz. Unlike the female down-and-out, the drivers waiting for fares or taking a break at the snack stand knew exactly who Sylvie was. They were keen to help, especially when she hinted that if she got anything worthwhile she'd return with a camera crew to get their statements on tape. The fact was, however, that they had nothing much to offer, although one or two had been very open about what the police had said to them.

From the scraps she had gathered, Sylvie was able to piece together that the guy who had been murdered had been picked up by an ivory-beige Mercedes E-class, but the police thought that it had probably been a fake taxi. That kind of planning, she thought to herself, was bordering on the professional. The drivers told her that they were all now looking out for the phoney cab and driver.

While she was at Spielbudenplatz, Sylvie thought it was worthwhile calling into Davidwache. When she asked the uniformed female officer behind the counter if she could speak to Herr Kaminski, she was told he was unavailable. All day.

Sylvie tried to wheedle some information from the desk officer but got nowhere.

When she got back to her car, her cellphone rang. It was Ivonne, her assistant, calling to tell her that the police had released an identity for the latest victim: Armin Lensch, twenty-nine, had worked for the NeuHansa Group.

'God – that's a bit close to home,' said Sylvie. The NeuHansa Group was the company owned by Gina Brønsted, the Hamburg senator who was running for First Mayor. Through NeuHansa, Gina Brønsted had a finger in every pie in Hamburg worth having your finger in. One of those pies was HanSat TV, Sylvie's employer. The rumour was that Brønsted had financed Andreas Knabbe's start-up of HanSat.

'Yep,' said Ivonne. 'Apparently Lensch worked for a subsidiary, Norivon. It's NeuHansa's environmental technologies division.'

'Now that's interesting . . .' Sylvie sat in the car staring out through the windscreen but seeing nothing; instead her mind raced through a dozen possible connections. As well as being a successful politician, Gina Brønsted was a million-airess several times over. She was running for the office of Hamburg's Principal Mayor, basically on the platform that she could run the city like a business. Having an employee of one of her companies linked to these murders, even as a victim, was not the kind of publicity she would want. 'Ivonne, get me everything you can on the NeuHansa Group and Gina Brønsted. Get me a few names inside the company and find out if the dead guy was of any importance in the group. Have whatever you can lay your hands on emailed to my personal address or couriered over to my flat tonight. I'll be back home from about eight.'

'I'm on it. By the way, Herr Knabbe has been looking for you.'

Sylvie smiled to herself: Ivonne was a great assistant.

More importantly, she hated their mutual boss as much as Sylvie did. Ivonne's little rebellion was to reject his Americanised informality and never address or refer to him as Andreas.

'What did you tell him?' she asked.

'That you were following up a hot lead. I also told him that the battery on your cellphone was low and you'd temporarily switched it off and I couldn't reach you.'

'Ivonne, you're a star.'

'So they tell me. Oh, there was another call for you. Some guy phoned saying he had to talk to you urgently but he wouldn't leave a name. He said he would call back. He sounded a bit creepy, if you ask me.'

Sylvie told Ivonne to let Knabbe know she'd be back in the office first thing tomorrow morning and not to worry about the anonymous caller. Probably some crank. She hung up, pulled out into the traffic on the Reeperbahn and headed back into the city.

6.

Fabel got a phone call from Renate just as he was about to go up with Anna and Werner to the Presidium's fifth floor to meet with van Heiden.

'Have you spoken to Gabi yet?' Renate asked without preliminaries.

'Not yet. You know I haven't. Why are you phoning me at work to ask me something you already know the answer to? I'm seeing Gabi on Thursday. I'll talk to her then.'

'You could have phoned her.'

'This isn't something I want to discuss with her over the phone. I choose the right time and place. You should try it, Renate. Anyway, Gabi's choice of career is hardly pressing: she hasn't even sat her Abitur yet.'

'Trouble?' asked Werner when Fabel came off the phone.

Anna and Werner had been standing awkwardly during the exchange.

'The worst kind. Renate. Gabi is thinking about a career in the police. I'm a bad influence, according to Renate.'

'I wouldn't have wanted one of my daughters doing this job,' said Werner.

'Oh yeah? So what if you had a son?' asked Anna.

'You know I don't have a son, so I don't know. It's got nothing to do with gender politics, Anna.'

Fabel took a deep breath. 'Ready? Then let's go and walk amongst the exalted . . .'

They stood waiting outside van Heiden's office for five minutes. But they weren't invited in; instead van Heiden emerged from his office, putting on his suit jacket as he did so.

'Follow me.' As he spoke, van Heiden cast a disapproving eye over Anna's jeans and T-shirt.

Hamburg's Police Presidium had been built in the form of a giant Police Star, the symbol of police forces throughout Germany. The entire Presidium was built around a central circular atrium open to the sky: all office suites, including the Murder Commission, radiated out as the arms of the star from its circular hallways. Fabel, Werner and Anna followed van Heiden along the sweep of the fifth-floor corridor until they came to doors of the Presidial Department. This was where Hugo Steinbach – Hamburg's Police President – and his deputies had their offices.

'Police President Steinbach has asked to be involved in this meeting,' explained van Heiden. He paused for a moment and turned to Fabel. 'Listen, Jan, I don't like being caught on the back foot. What have you told Herr Steinbach?'

'Nothing,' said Fabel. 'I thought you—'

Van Heiden shook his head. 'Looks like we're both on the back foot. I suppose we'd better find out.'

When they arrived at the Presidial Department, they weren't directed to Steinbach's office but were told to go straight into the conference room. When they entered, Fabel was surprised to see Karin Vestergaard sitting at the conference table next to Hugo Steinbach. The Police President stood up and shook hands with van Heiden and then with Fabel. Steinbach was the opposite of van Heiden in many ways. Van Heiden could be nothing other than a policeman and somehow managed to wear his smartly tailored Hugo Boss suits as if they were uniforms. In complete contrast, Hugo Steinbach was softly spoken and had an avuncular, easygoing appearance. To look at Hamburg's Police President, one would have taken him for a schoolteacher or some rural family doctor. The truth was Steinbach was highly unusual for an officer of his rank in Germany. He had not entered the police at senior level but had started out as a uniformed beat Polizeimeister and had worked his way up through every rank. Fabel knew that part of that journey had involved being head of the Polizei Berlin's murder squad. Fabel respected Steinbach as an officer, but he also liked him as a person.

'I know you wanted to talk to Criminal Director van Heiden about what Frau Vestergaard discussed with you yesterday, but I thought we should all have a chat about it. If you don't mind, Jan.'

'Hello, Frau Vestergaard,' said Fabel in English. 'I thought we were meeting later to discuss this. I had hoped to brief Herr van Heiden, as Herr Steinbach has suggested.'

'I'm afraid events have moved on a little from then,' said Vestergaard without a hint of apology. 'New information has come to light and I felt it would be appropriate to discuss it with Mr Steinbach.'

'Why don't we all sit down?' said Steinbach in a clear attempt to ease the tension between Fabel and Vestergaard. 'And perhaps you should update Herr van Heiden on what this is all about.'

Once they were seated, Fabel outlined Vestergaard's theory about the Hamburg-based contract killer and Jespersen's death not being natural. Vestergaard sat silently throughout Fabel's commentary in German, her expression as impossible to read as it had been the day before.

'How sure are we that this so-called Valkyrie is based in Hamburg?' asked Steinbach when Fabel was finished.

'With the greatest respect to Frau Vestergaard and her deceased colleague, there is absolutely no proof that the Valkyrie even exists.' Fabel looked again at the Danish police-woman. There was no sign that she understood what he was saying in German. But there again, he thought, she wouldn't show it even if she did. 'To be frank, Herr President, I feel that our foreign colleague here is not being as communicative as she might be.'

'You think there's more to this?' asked Steinbach.

'I don't know. In fact, there may be less to her story than meets the eye. And I have to be honest, with this supposed resurrection of the Angel of St Pauli, I can well do without some wild-goose chase. But we'll get the autopsy report on Jespersen this afternoon.'

'I see,' said Steinbach. 'What do you think, Horst?'

'I think we can't afford to ignore the possibility. There are those in the international security community who feel we dropped the ball in not nailing the so-called "Hamburg Cell" before they launched the attack on the World Trade Center. It could be embarrassing if we were seen to have had advance warning of this assassin operating from Hamburg and then for something to happen. A political assassination abroad, for example.' Van Heiden turned to Fabel. 'Sorry, Jan . . . I understand you're under pressure with this Angel case, but we have to treat this seriously.'

'I agree. Especially if the autopsy throws up something.'

Vestergaard cleared her throat.

'I'm sorry . . .' Fabel said in English. Then, to the others:

'Maybe we should all speak in English from now on, for Frau Vestergaard's sake.'

'Natural,' said van Heiden in heavily accented English. 'We will, of course, you bet.'

The look Vestergaard fired at Fabel eloquently communicated an 'I-told-you-so' reminder of their conversation about the difference between how Danes and Germans spoke English.

'I think Frau Vestergaard has something you should hear,' said Police President Steinbach. 'Please, Frau Vestergaard.'

'My office in Copenhagen has been in touch with me,' she said. 'They in turn were notified by the Norwegian National Criminal Investigation Department of an incident in Drøbak, near Oslo. This incident, which involved the murder of two men, took place yesterday evening.'

Vestergaard paused while she took her notebook from her bag.

'Jørgen Halvorsen is – was – a leading investigative journalist for newspapers and magazines throughout Scandinavia,' she said, referring to the notebook. 'He was a Norwegian by birth but worked in Copenhagen for a great many years. He moved back to Norway about five years ago. For the sake of his health, you could say. He made some heavyweight enemies in Denmark and Sweden. You see, Halvorsen had two specific areas of interest, areas that were not always mutually exclusive: the extreme right in Europe, and corporate and political corruption. He was assassinated yesterday evening in his home in Drøbak. His family were away overnight, so the timing suggests surveillance of the house. Also, Halvorsen was planning a trip abroad. The Far East. Where exactly in the Far East and for what reason we don't know. But it suggests the killer knew Halvorsen's schedule and everything points to a timed, planned killing – except that Halvorsen's gardener obviously happened along at the wrong moment. He was the other victim. Single knife wound to the heart.'

'And you think this is the work of the alleged Hamburg Valkyrie?' asked Fabel.

'It could be . . .' Vestergaard shrugged. 'It was a highly professional job. The other thing is that the Norwegian police had been keeping an on-off eye on Halvorsen's house.'

'Why?' asked Fabel.

'About two weeks ago someone broke in and stole Halvorsen's laptop and selective files, including back-ups of his computer data. And this is where it gets creepy . . . Halvorsen, being a security-minded man, also backed up to an online source. Someone used his access code and passwords to wipe that too. Again, the work of real professionals.'

'What was it that he was working on?' asked van Heiden.

'We don't have details yet. You see, the Norwegian National Police isn't the only agency with an interest in Halvorsen: PST, the Norwegian security agency, and Økokrim, the economic and environmental crime bureau, were very much interested in what Halvorsen was into. They had both been cooperating with Halvorsen – basically because they knew he would turn over what he found to them.'

'Your Norwegian colleagues seem to have been very open with you,' said van Heiden.

'That's the way it is in Scandinavia . . .' Vestergaard shrugged. 'The Nordic Police Agreement has been in force since nineteen sixty-six and was expanded in two thousand and one. We enjoy much more freedom to cooperate without formality across our borders. Anyway, organised crime, right-wing extremism, that kind of thing – it all tends to spread wider than one constituent country.'

'So do we know what Halvorsen was working on?' asked Fabel.

'Without his files or back-ups, no. Over the years Halvorsen has exposed quite a few major figures. Powerful figures. He had learned to play his cards very close to his chest. But we do have a few theories. One is that it may have had something to do with the trafficking of women. Norway, as you probably know, is currently the chair of Interpol's Working Party against Trafficking in Women, and it's possible that Halvorsen was tying a story in to coincide. A couple of my colleagues believe that he might have been about to expose a major environmental crime by some corporation or other, or maybe by a government. We're compiling a list of the information he asked for from Økokrim. One thing we are pretty certain about is that whatever it was he was investigating, it involves Denmark. He made several trips to Copenhagen. He seems to have had a particular interest in the Øresund Region: we do know he did research at Copenhagen University on the region as a politico-economic identity.'

'I'm sorry,' interrupted Steinbach, with a frown. 'Maybe my English . . .'

'The Øresund Region is partly in Denmark, partly in Sweden,' explained Vestergaard, speaking more slowly. 'It's where the new bridge between Denmark and Sweden is. Historically, that part of Sweden was Danish. Same way we used to own Schleswig-Holstein.'

'Why was Halvorsen interested in this region particularly?' asked van Heiden.

'No idea. It's maybe not significant in itself. Halvorsen was known to have an interest in Euroregions. You know, groupings within the new EU that tend not to conform to national boundaries. The part of Sweden that is included in the Øresund Region is open to a lot of social and linguistic debate: the majority of linguists say the Scanians speak in an East Danish dialect, while others maintain it is a South Swedish dialect. The point is, there is a sense of Europe dividing into self-identified units rather than traditional national units. You could argue, for example, that Hamburg has more in common with Denmark in terms of identity and culture than it does with Bavaria.'

'I don't see a big story for Halvorsen in whether a bunch of Swedes speak with a Danish or a Swedish accent,' said Fabel.

'Nor do I,' said Vestergaard dismissively. 'And his visits to Copenhagen and visits to the region may have nothing to do with his death. But remember Halvorsen's special interest was neo-fascism. Scanian identity isn't just about being Danish or Swedish. There are several extreme-right groups who want autonomy for the region and to expel all Muslims to "Sweden".'

Vestergaard was interrupted by the ringing of the phone. Steinbach answered it.

'It's for you,' he said to Fabel, holding out the receiver.

'Fabel, Möller here. I'm about to send the autopsy results on Jespersen to your office, but I thought you'd want the main points.'

'I appreciate that, Herr Doctor. I take it our suspicions were justified?'

'Just like your less than charming Danish colleague suggested . . . By the way, do you know she got in touch with me directly and started to harangue me, telling me what I should be looking for?'

'No, I didn't,' said Fabel, firing a look across the conference table at Vestergaard. 'My apologies.'

'Well, anyway,' continued Möller. 'Turns out she was right. I found a hypodermic puncture wound. What looks to me like a deliberately concealed hypodermic puncture wound. In his groin. I would have missed it if I hadn't been looking for it specifically.'

'So what was injected?'

'We'll have to wait for the full toxicology report, but on a hunch I tested a blood sample myself. I was looking for and found signs of hyperkalaemia.'

'Which is?'

'Elevated potassium levels. Whatever was injected pumped up the level of potassium in his system. That would cause hyperkalaemia, which, in turn, would cause arrhythmia and ultimately cardiac arrest. It could be a number of agents that caused this, or a combination of agents, but I've included tox screens for potassium chloride and suxamethonium chloride.'

'Well, we can stop speculating,' said Fabel after he had hung up the phone. 'It looks like we are now cooperating on a murder enquiry, Frau Vestergaard.'

7.

Ute Cranz examined herself in the mirror. It was like looking at a stranger.

She was tall and slim. Beneath the expensive clothes her body was lithe and sleek. She had spent a great many hours working on her body. Making it strong, supple, graceful. But she felt disconnected from it. Dislocated from the person who stared back at her, cold and blankly, from the glass.

As a little girl, Ute, like her sister, had excelled as a gymnast. She could have gone far – international competition – but her parents had not approved of what they saw as the abuse of her body. Enjoy your sport for what it is, her father had once told her, but don't let them abuse your body, damage your health, for the sake of a falsehood. She hadn't understood then, but she did now. She had seen what they had done to her sister. Margarethe had told her what they had done. Each visiting time a little more, a new horror.

They had stolen Margarethe's life. What they had done to her was like rape. No, it was worse. They had destroyed her, taken away her humanity. Then, when it became clear to them that she wasn't up to what they wanted, they cast her away.

Ute turned from the mirror and crossed the lounge to the window that looked down onto the street. No sign yet. She looked at her watch. A few more minutes. Crossing back to the mirror, she applied a little more make-up and pushed at her hair with her hands.

She had planned her costume carefully: it was dressy without looking too much for this time of afternoon on a Wednesday. And it was exactly at this time of afternoon on a Wednesday that Herr Gerdes came home. He lived in the top-floor apartment – the one with the roof terrace. Ute had established that Herr Gerdes lived alone, although she had no idea if he was divorced, a widower or a confirmed bachelor. He really was a quiet neighbour: the only sound she had ever heard issuing from his apartment was the music he listened to – Brahms and some Bruch, she thought – and she had only heard that occasionally when making her way up to her own apartment.

Ute laid her hand on the brass snib, eased the door open and listened. After a moment she heard the outer door downstairs slam shut and the sound of footsteps on the stairs. She stepped out onto the landing just as Herr Gerdes reached it.

'Oh, hello, Frau Cranz,' he said, and smiled. He was wearing a chunky polo-neck jumper under an expensive-looking tweed coat. He carried pale pigskin gloves in one hand. 'It's a cold one today. Are you going out?'

'I'm glad I caught you, Herr Gerdes,' she said formally and ignoring his question. 'As you know I've not long moved into the apartment and I have a problem with the lease. I wondered if you could explain it to me.'

'Well,' he said, frowning. 'I would love to, but at the moment . . .'

'Oh no – not right now.' She gestured an apology. 'I wouldn't impose on you at such short notice. I was thinking . . . well . . . I wondered if you would join me for a meal on Saturday evening.' There was a short silence and she rushed to fill it. 'You see, I don't get the chance to cook for anyone any more and I've got these fillets . . .'

He silenced her by taking a step towards her, his smile broadening. 'Frau Cranz, I would be delighted.'

8.

It had been a tiring day. Partly because he had had to spend so much of it with Karin Vestergaard. Fabel would never have imagined that spending time with a beautiful woman could be so tedious. She *was* beautiful, wasn't she? He still found that if he were out of her presence for any length of time her face was almost impossible to recall. And Fabel was good at remembering faces: after all, he had made a career of it. He phoned Susanne from his office before he left, explaining that he had felt obliged to volunteer to pick up Vestergaard at eight and take her for a meal.

'Please, please come along,' he pleaded. 'This woman is incredibly hard work and I need your support.'

'I couldn't possibly burden the taxpayer. You'll be putting this all on expenses, I take it?'

'You're involved in the St Pauli investigation. It's a legitimate expense. Vestergaard would be interested in how you work with the Commission. I'll even pay myself.'

'God, she must be hard work.'

'I'm booking a table at the fish restaurant in Neumühlen – your favourite.'

'I don't think . . .'

'Did I tell you that this particular Nordic ice maiden is also particularly beautiful? And there'll just be the two of us if you don't come . . .'

'Okay – I'll come and protect your honour. Pick me up at the apartment.'

* * *

Fabel was aware that he had become an object of envy. Every man in the restaurant turned in their direction as he, Susanne and Karin Vestergaard entered. The truth was, he got a kick out of being seen in the company of two such beautiful women. Seeing them together, Fabel was struck by how different they were: Susanne's hair was raven black, her eyes a rich hazel and her skin, even in the middle of a Hamburg winter, had a hint of summer gold to it; in complete contrast, Karin Vestergaard's hair was almost ash-blonde, her complexion light and her eyes a striking pale blue. The southern Celt and the Viking maiden.

Again Karin Vestergaard had done something different with her make-up and it had totally changed her look. Softened it. Susanne and Vestergaard chatted warmly as they sat at the table by the window. The restaurant deliberately kept its lighting subdued to allow diners to watch the silent ballet of vast container ships and other vessels drift past the huge picture windows that looked out over the Elbe. It was odd for Fabel to hear Susanne talk in English – he had only heard her say a few words in the language during their whole relationship. He noticed that even though Susanne could speak it well, her Bavarian accent was even more noticeable in this second language.

Susanne and Karin Vestergaard had hit it off as soon as they'd met and Fabel had felt a vague confusion at the way Vestergaard's personality seemed to have changed totally. Not for the first time he felt completely lost when faced with the complexity of the female mind. He had seen this kind of thing before: women interacting with each other in a completely different way than they did with him. He had *seen* it before, but had never understood it: sitting there, it was as if he had been allowed admission to an exclusive club, only to find out he had been handed a limited day pass.

'So you've been stuck with Jan for most of the day,' said

Susanne. 'You must need a drink.' She beckoned the waiter over and they ordered a bottle of white wine.

'He's not so bad,' said Vestergaard. She smiled at Fabel and he realised it was the first time she had done so. 'Just takes a bit of getting used to.'

'Tell me about it.' Susanne arched an eyebrow and grinned knowingly. 'How do you like Hamburg?'

'I like it fine,' Vestergaard said. 'It's odd, but it doesn't feel that foreign. Like it's a little bit Danish.'

'You said yourself, earlier today,' said Fabel, 'when you were talking about Euroregions, that Hamburg had a Nordic element. Well, where we're sitting right now is in Altona. Altona was a city in its own right until the nineteen-thirties when it became part of Hamburg under the Greater Hamburg Act. All of this was Danish soil for more than two hundred years. And Hamburg itself was jammed right up against the Danish border for most of its history.'

'God, don't get him started,' Susanne said to Vestergaard. 'Everything turns into a bloody history lesson. I know what you mean, Karin. I'm from the south. Bavaria. When I first came to Hamburg I felt it was very Scandinavian. Although they're always banging on here about how English they all are. By the way, do you know what Jan's nickname is?'

'Oh, not that old chestnut,' said Fabel. 'Some people call me *der Englishe Kommissar*, because I'm half-British. Scottish, actually.'

Susanne laughed. 'No, not that. I bet you don't even know this one: Lord Gentleman.'

'Who calls me that?' Fabel looked accusingly at Susanne.

'See?' she said to Vestergaard. 'Now he's all offended. Do you know he buys all his stuff in the English shops in Hamburg? I used to think Harris Tweed was a romantic novelist until I met this one.'

Vestergaard laughed. 'Actually, it's funny,' she said to

Fabel, 'when I first met you I thought you looked like a Dane. But so do a lot of people here.'

'Aha.' Fabel pointed his fork in her direction. 'You've got it all wrong. I get my blond hair from the Scottish side of the family.'

'I thought they were all red-haired with big bushy beards and drunk half the time.'

'That's only the women,' said Fabel.

'I'll tell your mother you said that . . .' Susanne smiled.

'How did you two get together?' asked Vestergaard. 'If you don't mind me asking. Was it through work?'

'We worked together on a case about four years ago. He pursued me more relentlessly than he did the killer.'

'As I remember, you didn't try very hard to escape.' Fabel grinned and took a sip of his wine.

'Doesn't work get in the way? I mean, having a personal and a professional relationship?' asked Vestergaard.

'We try not to let it,' said Fabel. 'We used to have this rule that we didn't talk shop outside work. We still pretty much keep to that. But, of course, there are times when you can't help it. The other thing is that Susanne is only involved in a small percentage of the cases I investigate. Ones like this killer we've got on the loose in St Pauli.'

'I think that's what went wrong with Jens and me.' Vestergaard stared blankly at the table as she spoke.

'You and Jespersen?' Fabel put his wine glass down. 'You were involved? Oh God, I'm sorry. I had no idea.'

She smiled weakly. 'We split up about four years ago. Like I said, Jens found it difficult to accept that my career had overtaken his. Everyone knows that Denmark is a very liberal country. Along with Sweden and Finland we score the highest in the world for gender equality. But statistics don't take the Danish character into account. Jens was a Jutlander and a very old-fashioned Dane. Sometimes I think it just stung too much that I was a woman promoted over him.'

'Didn't that make working together awkward?' asked Susanne. 'I mean after the split?'

'We were in separate divisions for a while. It was only last year that we started working together again. And yes, it was difficult. But that had more to do with the way Jens went about his job and his general attitude to authority.'

'Jespersen seems to have been a little like Maria Klee,' Fabel explained to Susanne.

'Maria Klee?' Vestergaard raised her eyebrows.

'The officer I told you about,' said Fabel. 'The one who had a complete breakdown after going off on a personal crusade.'

There was a silence for a moment, only broken when the waiter arrived with their orders.

'I'm sorry,' said Vestergaard. 'I've killed the mood somewhat.' She raised her glass and forced a smile. 'No more shop talk. Agreed?'

'Agreed,' said Susanne.

The conversation slowly found its way back to shallower waters and the inconsequentialities that people who don't know each other that well tend to discuss. But, as they chatted, Fabel watched Karin Vestergaard. He thought back to the anger she had shown when she saw Jespersen's body at the mortuary. Anger directed at her dead colleague. Her dead ex-lover. He was beginning to understand the Danish detective a little better. So why did it give him a bad feeling?

9.

There were things Fabel enjoyed about his job. And there were things he hated.

Leading a Murder Commission was a management task, bureaucratic and demanding a certain meticulousness: Fabel was not a natural bureaucrat nor naturally meticulous, or at least not when it came to paperwork. He had started the day off by getting Werner into his office. Werner's heavy build and tough-looking appearance seemed at odds with what Fabel often thought of as a watchmaker's mind within. Over the years, Fabel had learned to rely on Werner's attention to detail and whenever he was thinking about allocating tasks to the team he called on his deputy's counsel. Fabel had asked for, and got, extra resources to investigate the St Pauli killings while running an inquiry into Jespersen's death. Technically, Fabel was supposed to manage the inquiries in parallel: assigning a team to run each while he directed them remotely. Oversight or overview or whatever the hell they liked to call it. Fabel didn't like working that way. He believed a senior investigating officer should do just that: investigate. But the Polizei Hamburg, as Sylvie Achtenhagen was wont to point out any time someone aimed a TV camera at her, had screwed up the original Angel investigation. It was his job to make sure that there was a cross on every 't'; a dot above every 'i'.

'Put me and Anna on the St Pauli case,' said Werner, taking clumsy care not to use the word 'Angel' and spark his boss off. Fabel was famous for despising the cartoon-character tags that the media liked to attach to multiple killers. 'And team up Dirk Hechtner and Henk Hermann on this Danish thing. At least we've got enough other bodies drafted in. For once we seem covered.'

'It's amazing what the wrong kind of publicity can do for you,' added Fabel grimly.

'Cynicism doesn't suit you, *Chef*,' said Werner. 'We've all come to love you for your shining wit and cheery disposition.'

'Speaking of your overwhelming respect for me, do I have a nickname around here?' asked Fabel.

Werner shrugged.

'Do you know,' said Fabel, 'that some people have apparently been calling me "Lord Gentleman"? Making a big joke about me being half-British?'

'Probably more to do with your wardrobe,' said Werner, who moved on quickly. 'News to me.'

By the time Werner had left they had worked out a comprehensive investigative plan for both inquiries. The St Pauli inquiry was already well under way, but the Jespersen case was still amorphous: ideas and conjecture rather than any kind of evidence. Another blank page in Fabel's sketchbook.

On the St Pauli killings, Fabel had decided he would look into Jake Westland. The file told Fabel that Westland was British, born 1953, presumably illegitimately because he had been put up for adoption immediately after his birth, and had been brought up by middle-class adoptive parents in Hampshire. Studied music in London; first band formed 1972, second '78, went solo 1981. Two gold discs, one platinum. Married three times. Four children by two of those marriages.

Fabel knew he needed to get beyond the naked facts. But the last thing he needed right now was to have to make a trip to England to talk to Westland's family and friends. Hopefully, if she was not too distressed, he would get a chance to talk to the pop singer's wife in a few days when she came over to claim the body.

In addition to the formally acquired information in the file, Fabel did an Internet search for Westland on his office computer. Putting together the pieces, Fabel started to build a picture of a man he did not like. Westland was, by all accounts, arrogant, opinionated and egocentric. No surprises there: to be a successful performer you needed an ego that could fill a stadium. But the truth was that Westland was no longer filling stadiums. His promoters had scaled down the size of the venues he played in. A strategy which ensured that he could still claim the odd ticket sell-out. With the information Fabel found, he could mentally plot a bell curve of fame for the British singer, reaching its peak in the mid 1980s.

After that, his popularity, if not his wealth, had gone into rapid decline. Jake Westland was, clearly, fast becoming yesterday's man. Until he left the stage permanently and spectacularly in a Kiez back alley, Westland had been struggling to make any headlines. There had been an abortive attempt at acting, but the press had been derisive. The only time he returned to public attention was when his sordid sex life excited the British tabloids. His decreasing publicity clout did not, however, prevent him from pontificating on a range of social issues to anyone who would listen.

Fabel scanned through the background material that Anna had gathered on the event at the Sporthalle. The charity benefiting from the concert was called the Sabine Charity: Declaring War on War Rape. Looking through Anna's report, Fabel saw that the charity was devoted to assisting the victims of military or genocidal rape from Bosnia to Rwanda. The concert organiser was a woman called Petra Meissner. The name rang a bell with Fabel. He flicked back through his Internet search history and found a photograph of Westland with Petra Meissner which had appeared in one of the British tabloids. Meissner was an attractive woman in her mid forties, with dark hair cut short. The photograph was innocent enough – Westland and Meissner were together to attend an event in aid of Meissner's charity in Berlin – but the English headline demanded *Who's the HUN-ney, Jake?* And, of course, the text went on to make much of the fact that Westland's escort was a German woman; lots of tasteless jokes about the war. The usual brainless stuff. Fabel loved all things British: except their press. And the fact that, as a nation, the British seemed permanently stuck in the past.

There was little else of note about Westland that Fabel could see, other than the Englishman's obvious business acumen. He might have been a mediocre singer and an even worse actor, but he had been an astute investor. Westland's back catalogue of music and his more recent CDs assured him a reasonable income from his established fan base, but the real income had come from his portfolio of investments. And, from what Fabel read, it appeared that it wasn't his accountants or advisers who had guided this success but Westland himself, who seemed to have an eye for the up-and-coming business concept or the unusual opportunity that other investors would be wary of.

It had been snowing again and, although the roads were clear, the pavements around the city were white-blanketed. Fabel drove through the city and through the Elbe tunnel into Hamburg-Harburg.

The Sabine Charity had its offices in an older building on the corner of two busy Harburg streets. There was a certain art-deco grandness about the building but this had been diminished by copious graffiti on the walls. The charity's offices comprised a handful of rooms on the ground floor. Fabel had phoned ahead to make an appointment, but when he walked into the offices he could find no defined reception area. For some reason he had expected this informality. There were four women and two men working at various desks, most of whom were engaged in phone conversations when Fabel entered. A tall, handsome woman with short dark hair, whom he recognised from her photographs as Petra Meissner, stood up and came over to him.

'I got your message, Herr Chief Commissar.' She extended her hand and smiled. Without warmth, thought Fabel. 'It's a bit chaotic here. There's a café around the corner – would you mind?'

'Not at all,' said Fabel, and stood aside to allow her to show him the way.

*   *   *

'I take it this is about Jake's death,' said Meissner. 'I've been expecting somebody to get in touch. Especially after that awful woman from the television was here.'

'Let me guess. Sylvie Achtenhagen?'

'Your paths have crossed?'

'You could say that. Frau Achtenhagen can be persistent.'

'Well, her persistence did her no good with me.' The hardening of Meissner's expression suggested to Fabel that she was not a woman to cross. 'I sent her packing. The whole thing with the way Jake died . . . it's tragic. And sordid. I'm afraid the charity can do without that kind of publicity.'

'I'm sure his wife and children could do without it, too.'

'Of course.' Meissner stirred her latte macchiato and licked the froth from her spoon.

'How well did you know Herr Westland?'

Meissner gave a cynical laugh. 'I didn't think you really asked questions like that. I thought that was only in the movies. If you are trying to ask me if I was having or ever had an intimate relationship with Jake, then why don't you just ask me outright?'

'Okay. Did you?'

'No. Despite what the gutter press in Britain alleged. Jake wasn't interested in me that way. And I can assure you that Jake Westland was definitely not my type. I take it you have found out a bit about him?'

'Naturally.'

'Then you'll know that most people thought he was a phoney, arrogant asshole. Well, most people were right. But I'll tell you this: he was totally committed to the Sabine Charity. There was nothing phoney about *that*.'

'So why your charity in particular?'

'That I don't know. And I didn't ask. The Sabine Charity isn't like others. We're not involved in famine relief, or disaster support in the conventional sense. These are issues that people can talk about; feel good about supporting.

There's something about the work we do, the things we talk about, that takes people to a place they don't want to go. But some people have a good reason to go there. I'm sure there was a very good reason for Jake to be so committed to the Sabine Charity. Maybe it was just genuine outrage, maybe he encountered a victim of war rape. Whatever the reason, it was not something I felt I could question. I was grateful for the support. Jake Westland was as high-profile as we've managed so far.'

'Did you see him on the night of the charity concert?'

'Of course. We had a pre-event reception with a few city-state and national political types. The federal government sent the Minister for Women and the Hamburg Senate sent Mieke Brün, the Senator for City Development and Environment. Schleswig-Holstein sent along a couple of representatives too. And Gina Brønsted, who's running for Principal Mayor – she was there as well. To be honest, she rather monopolised Jake. Must have been a fan.'

'That was it?'

'Unfortunately, yes. We had planned an informal after-concert party, but Jake said he was too tired and not feeling too well. He just wanted to get back to his hotel and sleep. As it turned out, that was clearly a lot of crap. We went ahead with the party anyway. It worked out okay, actually. Without the star to distract them, I was able to collar a few of the politicians. Not Brønsted, though. She left straight after the concert too.'

'Okay . . .' Fabel paused for a moment. 'What is it your charity does?' asked Fabel. 'I mean, I know what it's about, but what specifically does it *do*?'

'We have three goals. Our first priority is to identify conflicts and regions where rape is currently being used systematically as a weapon of war. We then campaign for international action to protect women in those zones. We lobby politicians here in Germany and throughout the EU. Sometimes beyond.

And, where possible, we put people on the ground in the trouble spots.'

'Isn't that risky?'

'It can be. Very. But we have a team of volunteers, doctors, nurses and psychologists who are very committed to the task. Herr Fabel, when you encounter the victims of war rape, you never forget it. You become very motivated. Anyway, our second objective is to raise awareness of war rape as a crime against humanity generally, and historically. Thirdly, we provide evidence to back up the arrest and prosecution of commanders and individual soldiers involved in rape campaigns. We have to be very careful with this, because, as I said, we often have people on the ground in these zones and we don't want to put them in added danger. The military and paramilitary groups behind these atrocities wouldn't think twice about shooting a potential future witness against them. But we have contributed to successful prosecutions against war rapists in Bosnia, Somalia and Rwanda.'

'And you get all your support from here, in Germany?'

'We are an international charity, with registered offices in a number of EU nations, but yes, we are headquartered here and our funds come predominantly from German donations. A disproportionate amount, given its economic woes, comes from the former East Germany. That makes sense, when you think about it.'

'I suppose it does,' said Fabel. At the end of the Second World War more than a million, maybe as many as two million East German women had been raped by the invading Soviet troops, many of them repeatedly. In some towns and villages, every female between the ages of ten and eighty had been raped, often in front of their families. Since the Wall had come down, it had become well known that the Soviet War Memorial in East Berlin had been known for decades as "The Tomb of the Unknown Rapist".

'It's possible to argue that the former East Germany was

a child of rape,' said Meissner. 'While it existed, the GDR was a nation haunted by the violation of its women. I know what I am talking about: I was born in Dresden. Both my mother and grandmother were victims. My mother was twelve at the time. So there you have it, Herr Fabel – my reason for fighting against war rape.'

'I see.' There was an awkward silence. Fabel found he didn't know what to say to Meissner about her violated mother and grandmother, just as he would have struggled to respond to Jespersen if they had met and he had told Fabel first-hand about the fate of his father and grandfather. 'Have you ever heard of a Bosnian called Vujačić?' Fabel said eventually and scrabbled in his pocket for his notebook to check the first name.

'Goran Vujačić?' Meissner beat him to it. 'Of course I have. He was lucky to slime his way out of prosecution. The dodgiest defence of alibi I've ever come across. Vujačić was a particularly sadistic son of a bitch. And son of a bitch is right: he led a paramilitary gang who called themselves *Psoglav*. It means "Doghead" in Serbian, but it's got some deep cultural meaning amongst Bosnian Serbs, apparently. In any different context, in a peacetime European city, the crimes he committed would have him condemned as a sex criminal and paedophile. But for some reason, in a war situation, some men behave in a way they maybe wouldn't otherwise believe themselves capable.'

'Not all men.'

'No . . . not all. Perhaps. But in a military context it seems there is a new set of values, a different morality. War rape is an act of cultural humiliation and sometimes, as in Bosnia, of genocide: a deliberate attempt to destroy the enemy's genetic pool by forcing pregnancy and birth on the female population. In Bosnia it was so clearly a military strategy that the UN declared it a crime against humanity. But there is research that suggests that there is another side to it: that participation in mass rape is a bonding mechanism for men within a military community. There was evidence – not hard evidence, more rumour and hearsay – that Vujačić used it in exactly that way. That's what made him worse. Vujačić rationalised it and used it as a tool. But, like I said, we never got to prove it in a court of law.'

'Well, he might have wriggled his way out of prosecution, but somebody certainly caught up with him in Copenhagen.'

'I know. It was too quick a death. From what I read about it, anyway. What's Vujačić got to do with Jake?'

'Nothing,' said Fabel and smiled. 'Nothing at all, in fact. It was just that his name came up in connection with something else. I knew he'd been involved in the Bosnian War and had been implicated in the rape camps.'

'Unfortunately, the case on Vujačić is closed. Like I said, a quick death with a knife in the heart is no just punishment for all the crimes he committed. Although I do understand why it was done.'

'Actually, it was probably unconnected. More to do with rivalry between organised-crime bosses.' Fabel drained his cup and stood up. 'Thanks for your time, Frau Meissner. If anything else comes to you that you think is relevant, even if you don't think it's that important, please give me a ring.'

He handed her his Polizei Hamburg business card with the Murder Commission number on it.

Meissner smiled. 'I'll do that.'

10.

Hamburg was a low-rise city. With the exception of the Fernsehturm TV tower, the five spires of its Protestant churches, the single Catholic cathedral and the Rathaus had been allowed to retain their dominance of the city-centre skyline. Over the years, the city planners had ensured that almost nothing in the heart of the city exceeded the height of the established Kontorhaus buildings.

There had, however, been the occasional glaring slip-up and the odd monolithic hotel glowered over Hamburg from the fringe of the city centre. But, unlike Frankfurt or London, there would be no attempt to ape an American skyline: there was to be no Canary Wharf for Hamburg. Instead, architects met the creative challenge of developing striking buildings that sat well with the character and history of the city. The HanSat building was not one of them. Sitting in the Neustadt quarter of the city, the satellite TV station's gleaming glass and steel headquarters was the type of restrained corporate tower one found in Hamburg. This building had had its skyscraper ambitions cut short, literally. Sylvie Achtenhagen's office was on the third of ten floors. She had just returned to her office after filming her piece for that night's show when the door opened and Andreas Knabbe walked in without knocking.

'How are you?' Knabbe asked in his usual manner that suggested he did not really give a damn how the hell she or anyone else was. He sat down on the edge of her desk.

'What can I do for you, Herr Knabbe?' Sylvie smiled with the same level of sincerity.

'I've just seen the piece you've done for tonight. The woman-trafficking stuff.'

'And?'

'And it was very good. Very . . .' Knabbe made a show of struggling for the right word, searching for it somewhere on her office ceiling. 'Very worthy. But you know . . .'

'What?'

'To be honest it was, well, depressing.'

'I'm sorry.' Sylvie's smile had become a rictus grin. 'You're probably right that I underplayed the comedy element of fourteen-year-old East European and Asian girls being sold into sex slavery.'

'Quite.' Sylvie Achtenhagen's irony passed cleanly over Knabbe's expensively barbered head. 'I just think it isn't our kind of thing. I think stories like that have more of a natural home on ARD or ZDF. What we need is something with a bit of zing to it. You know, like this Angel thing in St Pauli. Now that really was—'

'Yes, I know – you've already made it clear you think that was my shining hour. I am following that up, you know. It's just I have to get other stuff out as well.'

'Maybe, Sylvie – and this is just an idea – but maybe we should let someone else have a run with this particular ball . . .'

Sylvie Achtenhagen stood up so suddenly that Knabbe was taken aback. She leaned forward, her face close to his, forcing him off the edge of her desk. 'Don't you dare take that story from me. I told you I've been working on it. And I'm making progress. When that story breaks it'll be me who breaks it. Big time. And if you put anyone else near it I'll quit and take it to another broadcaster. Am I clear on that, Andreas?'

Knabbe stared at her for a moment. Shocked. Alarmed by something he had seen in her face. 'There's no need to get heated,' he said at last. 'I was just thinking what would be best.'

'What's best is for me to finish the job I started.' She was calm again, but something smouldered after the flash fire. 'I guarantee you it will be a killer of a story.'

'Okay,' Knabbe said, some of his composure restored. 'But if this story doesn't break . . .'

'It will. I promise you that.'

There was an awkward silence for a moment.

'Anyway, speaking of the Angel case, there's something you can perhaps help me with,' Sylvie said eventually.

'Oh?' Knabbe's voice was laden with suspicion. 'What?'

'Your business partner. The lovely Frau Brønsted. Or more specifically her corporation, the NeuHansa Group.'

'What about it?'

'Well, the latest victim of the St Pauli killer . . .'

'The Angel?'

'Well, yes, for the moment let's say it is the same killer as before. This latest victim of the Angel worked for a company called Norivon Environmental. Apparently it's a subsidiary of the NeuHansa Group.'

'What do you want me to do?' The suspicion hadn't left Knabbe's tone.

'Fix up an appointment for me with the CEO of Norivon. And maybe even with Gina Brønsted. But don't say it's about Lensch's murder.'

'They'll probably work that out for themselves. I don't know if Frau Brønsted will give you an interview. And I don't know if I like where you're going with this. The NeuHansa Group is my main business partner, Sylvie. And whether you like it or not, we're in the business of television.'

'Trust me, Andreas. I'm not after a scoop on NeuHansa or Gina Brønsted. I just need some background information. And, trust me, when I break this story for you, it will be big. Very big.'

'Okay. I'll see what I can do.'

After Knabbe had left, Sylvie sat and stared out of her office window, not seeing the city that lay dark under a slate sky. The phone ringing interrupted her equally gloomy thoughts. The call was on her direct number and had not come through reception.

'Hello, Frau Achtenhagen.' It was a man's voice and it broke off to cough. 'Excuse me. I believe you are looking into the killings in St Pauli?'

'Yes – who is this?'

'If you don't mind, I'd rather not give my name. Not at the moment, anyway.' More coughing.

'You know something about the killings?' Sylvie Achtenhagen tried to keep the irritation and the boredom out of her voice. There was always someone confessing to the Angel killings, or who knew someone who knew somebody who had said something suspicious; cranks who were receiving messages through their fillings from the spirit world, or who were convinced their husband-slash-boss-slash-pet was the perpetrator.

'Yes. I know a lot about the killings. I know a lot about a lot of things. And what I know is something you will be willing to pay for.'

'Yes, yes – I've heard that all before.'

'No, trust me, Frau Achtenhagen. I have something you have to see. Something really big.'

'Now I definitely have heard that all before and it always ends in disappointment. Can we cut the crap and you tell me exactly what it is that you're trying to sell me?'

'Something that you won't want me to sell to anyone else, that's for sure. You see, I have a pretty good idea who is behind those killings in St Pauli.'

'The Angel?'

'Now, Frau Achtenhagen, we both know it's not the Angel – not the original Angel, anyway. I have a pretty good idea who killed those two men last month and it certainly wasn't the original Angel. But that does bring me to my second point. The most important one and I know you will pay big time to stop me selling it elsewhere. I know the identity of the original Angel. I know her name, where she lives, what she does. I even know why she killed all those men in the nineties.'

'Really? And how do you know that?' Sylvie Achtenhagen scrabbled through the shooting schedules and report notes on her desk until she found a pad and pencil.

'It used to be my job to know things. About people. I worked for the Ministry for State Security in the German Democratic Republic.'

'You're ex-Stasi? Why the hell should I pay some ex-Stasi scum for information about murders in Hamburg?'

'Because I'm a forward-thinking kind of guy. Always have been. I was based in the Ministry's headquarters, in Berlin-Lichtenberg. I was there right up until the fifteenth of January nineteen ninety. There was a mob outside the gates ready to burst in and everyone was busy shredding files. When the shredders couldn't cope, they started to rip them up by hand. It was futile. So many files. Too many.'

'Is there a point to this, Herr . . . ? Listen, what is your name? If you want me to pay you for your story, then I need to know your name.'

'No, you don't. I'm not naive. You people pay anonymous sources all the time. And we both know that you won't be paying me through the usual channels. However, if it makes you feel better about it you can call me Siegfried. It has a nice Wagnerian ring to it, doesn't it?' He started to laugh, but his laughter fractured into a crackling, bubbling bout of coughing. That's more than a cold or flu, thought Sylvie. 'Just listen to what I have to say,' he continued breathlessly when his coughing had subsided. 'Like I said, when everyone else was shredding I was thinking ahead. I took a file. It doesn't look like much: there's not a lot of information in it other than a list of names of people on a training programme. A very special training programme. And the file also named the top three students. The ones who made the grade.'

'Fascinating though this all is,' said Sylvie, 'what the hell has any of it got to do with the Angel killings?'

'Everything. One of these names is the name of the original Angel, and it is my guess that the current St Pauli killer is one of the others. This is a file that I know you must have. And I will sell you the file.' He paused. 'For two hundred and fifty thousand euros.'

Sylvie laughed loudly. 'You have got to be joking. No story is worth that to the station. And certainly not some file on Stasi snoops that I still don't see having any relevance to these murders. This is old news. No one is interested in the Stasi and the HVA any more.'

There was silence on the other end of the line.

'Hello?' said Achtenhagen.

'If you thought I was joking – or if you thought this was all nonsense – then you would have hung up by now. But you didn't because you know that it's the truth. I want two hundred and fifty thousand euros. If I don't get it I will pass this information on to another broadcaster or the press. And the police. You built your career on the Angel killings, Frau Achtenhagen. Are you really going to let someone else take that all away from you? I will call back in a couple of days. In the meantime I'll give you something on account. Check your email.'

The phone went dead.

Sylvie Achtenhagen hung up the phone and stared at it as if it would give up some answers. On her desktop computer she opened up her office email. There were several messages for her but all of them were either internal or work-related. None was from an anonymous source. She waited ten minutes and tried again: still nothing. The idea struck her that perhaps he had sent it to her personal email account, but she dismissed the thought almost immediately: only a few friends and colleagues had her private email address. But there was no harm in checking.

It was there. A message from Siegfried.

There were ways of tracing emails, sourcing ISP addresses, but Sylvie knew that if Siegfried was an ex-Stasi operative then he would have covered his tracks. The free account could have been set up anywhere and the email sent from a cyber-cafe or WiFi hotspot. Achtenhagen opened it. There was no message, just a single name: Georg Drescher. She saw there was an attachment and she opened it. Three colour photographs, scanned in side by side. No names. Each photo was a head-and-shoulders shot of a different girl, aged,

Achtenhagen guessed, between fifteen and twenty. The photographs were formal shots for a state ID card or passport. The hairstyle of one indicated they were of twenty-odd years' vintage. Two of the girls were blonde, the third a brunette, although she had striking blue eyes. There was something disturbing about their faces: a frightening void. It went beyond the usual lack of personality projected from an official-pass portrait. The eyes were dead. Emotionless. Particularly the girl in the middle. As Sylvie stared at her image, something twisted at her gut.

'Siegfried' had told her that one of these girls was the Angel of St Pauli. And as her eyes passed from one blank face to the next, she knew that he had told her the truth.

11.

Emily would be here soon. Then everything in his life would start to make sense again. Peter Claasens had never understood women. He had never really tried, simply because it seemed like too much work.

He had been married for fifteen years and had three children, two of them daughters, but the female world remained a dark continent for Claasens. His wife, in particular, was still a mystery to him. She had turned from the pretty, quiet, unassuming girl he had unintentionally got pregnant to a shrew who nagged him about every evening he spent away from the family home, whether it was business or otherwise. Claasens had to admit, if grudgingly, that his wife had some grounds for her behaviour. Throughout his fifteen years of marriage he had been consistently unfaithful. He had taken great pride, however, in being discreet. Tactful. If his wife had suspicions, then that was what they had remained. He had never been careless enough to furnish her with substantiating evidence. But, there again, his looks were grounds enough for suspicion.

The concept of looks had always puzzled Claasens: why were some people more appealing to look at than others? More desirable? Claasens was a bright man. A very bright man. He had a sharp intellect and was a natural businessman. A commercial predator. Yet people found it difficult to see past his appearance. In the workplace men either resented him or wanted to be seen with him, female colleagues were either awkward around him or flirtatious. And when he didn't respond to the flirting, they became resentful too. But he *had* responded. Often.

It was true, of course, that his appearance had been helpful: he had supplemented his income while an accountancy student by working as a photographic model. He had been offered every job he'd ever been interviewed for. And, of course, even if he hadn't made a lot of money he had become involved with a trendy set from Blankenese. And Blankenese girls usually had money to burn. Peter Claasens had learned that fortune truly favours the fair.

But his looks had also insulated him from real emotion. Isolated him.

And now he stood on the top floor of the nearly complete ScanMedia building and contemplated a career of seduction and adultery. He looked out over Hamburg's darkening skyline and thought about all of the women he had been with when he should have been with his wife. And, at that moment, he felt genuinely, completely remorseful. The reason he stood and contemplated all of the women he had known and felt sympathy for his wife was that all of that was now behind him. Something unexpected had happened to Peter Claasens: he had, at forty-two, fallen in love. From the start it had not been like his other affairs: Emily had not responded to his usual set of manoeuvres and tricks; she had not fallen into bed with him. She had talked to him. She had listened to him. It was as if Emily was blind to how he looked and this gift allowed her to truly see him. And now Claasens found the periods in between seeing her were like being forced to hold your breath until your lungs screamed for air.

Emily was English, with fire-red hair and green eyes. She spoke German fluently but with the sweetest accent and she had clearly never recognised the importance of gender or grammatical case in the language. Emily was also delightfully uncoordinated and clumsy: he had literally bumped into her outside his offices. She had fallen badly and he had helped her to her feet, insisting that she come into his office for a seat. Emily had smiled sweetly and said it was her fault and she was fine, had gathered up her stuff and hurried on. Claasens had just been about to go back into his office when an impulse had prompted him to run after her. He had insisted that the least he could do was buy her a coffee. She had accepted. It had begun.

That had been two months ago. In that short time, this dizzy English redhead had turned his world upside down. She had resisted becoming involved with a married man but he had insisted his marriage had been in terminal decline for some years. When she had announced that she was going back to England, Claasens had told her he couldn't live without her, that he would leave his wife and they could set up home together here in Hamburg. Yet Emily had insisted that no one should be hurt more than necessary: he should tell his wife that he had to leave, that their marriage had run its course, but not mention that he was involved with anyone else. It would be better for his wife, for the kids. It would be better for Emily and Claasens. She had even asked to see the letter he intended to send his wife and had made changes, just so that no one was hurt more than they had to be. Emily was a good person. She was much, much better than he was and when she was around him he became someone better. Someone he could like.

Now he stood at the top of one of the biggest building

projects in Hamburg outside the HafenCity and contemplated the past he was putting behind him.

'Hello, Peter.'

He turned to see her there. The dark woollen overcoat and the beret she wore emphasised the red in her hair and the green in her eyes.

'Hello, Emily.' He smiled and leaned forward to kiss her but she put her gloved fingertips to his mouth.

'Have you brought it?' she asked.

'Yes, I've brought it. And I changed it just as you asked. It's so like you to worry about other people. I've made no mention that I'm involved with anybody. I made the other changes you suggested too. I still think it would have been better if I told her face to face. A letter . . . I just don't know . . .'

'May I see?'

He handed her the letter and she read through it. As Emily had suggested, Claasens told his wife that he could not go on with the way things were, that work had added to the stress, that he was so sorry for the hurt he knew his actions would cause her and the children.

'Perfect,' said Emily, folding the letter with her gloved fingers. She leaned against the metal railing that had temporarily been put up for safety reasons while the top floor of the building was completed. Claasens grabbed her elbow and pulled her back.

'You have to be careful, Emily,' he said paternally.

'This really is a beautiful building,' she said, looking down ten floors into the central atrium.

'It's meant to be a modern interpretation of an old Hamburg Kontorhaus – you know, the red-brick jobs with a huge atrium or courtyard in the middle.'

'Such a strange name,' she said in her accented German. 'What does it mean – Kontorhaus?'

'It goes back to the days of the Hanseatic League. There

would be a Kontorhaus in almost every Hanseatic city in Europe: Hamburg, Bremen, Rostock, Danzig, St Petersburg. There was even a Kontor in London. Bremen and Hamburg are the only cities that are still officially Hanseatic cities.'

'And this building is meant to be like those old Hanseatic Kontor buildings?' Emily leaned and looked over the railing again.

'Yes,' said Claasens, distracted. 'Emily, stand back from the railing. This safety railing is just temporary . . .' He smiled at her, pushing back a strand of red hair and tucking it behind her ear. 'And you know you can be a little accident-prone. We're not even supposed to be here.'

'How high are we?' she asked, leaning further over the railing. Claasens eased her back gently.

'I don't know – four hundred metres, I'd say.'

'That's a lot of forensic distance,' she said absently.

'What did you say, Emily?'

She stood up and turned to him. 'I said it's a lot of forensic distance. It was one of the first things I learned: to place as much forensic distance between myself and the point and moment of death.'

Claasens frowned in confusion. He didn't understand what Emily was saying. And he couldn't understand why her German grammar and accent were now perfect. Her gloved hand sliced up like a blade and smashed into the side of his neck, just below his jawline and behind his ear. The blow somehow made the world dimmer and he felt his legs weaken beneath him. Claasens could not work out what was happening but moved to grab her. She dodged him, moving with a speed and precision he thought her incapable of. The edge of her hand hit him again, on exactly the same spot, and this time his legs folded. Emily stepped to one side and expertly used Claasens's own momentum to propel him over the safety railing.

He didn't even scream on the way down.

She leaned over the railing and looked into the vast well of the atrium. Claasens lay broken on the flagstones nine storeys below, a crimson halo around his head. It looked to Emily as if he had landed on his handsome face.

Emily took the letter he had handed her – the letter she had guided him to write – and threw it over the edge, allowing it to flutter down onto the atrium floor.

Chapter Four

I.

He had only had a brief telephone conversation with her, but Fabel could tell that Sarah Westland's grief had started to bite. She had been very businesslike and composed, but there had been an edginess, like a tight cord, pulled through her voice.

Grief, however, had not seemed to diminish her need for luxury. Fabel had arranged to meet her in her hotel: one of Hamburg's most exclusive, with a view out over the Inner Alster. Sarah Westland had a suite on the top floor and when he knocked on the door, he was surprised it was Martina Schilmann who answered.

'Hello, handsome,' she said, with a wicked smile. She stepped out into the hotel corridor and drew the door closed behind her. 'You can't keep away, can you?'

'You're minding Sarah Westland?'

'Yes. There's always the risk of the press pestering her.'

'Yes, but . . .'

'But we screwed up with her husband. Yes, I know. But it was she who arranged for us to provide security for his German tour. I got in touch with her and told her how sorry I was. She was great about it. She told me that the Polizei Hamburg had explained that Westland had deliberately given us the slip and she seems to have accepted that there was nothing we could do. Thanks for that. Obviously I'm providing her security for free. I also told her that we wouldn't be submitting a bill for her husband's cover. To be honest, it's a bit of damage limitation.'

'How is she?'

'She's tough. But it has got to her, obviously. I don't think she and Westland were soulmates or anything like that, and I get the impression she has no illusions about his fidelity, but they obviously had some kind of closeness, in their own way. Maybe that's what having kids together does.'

'Thanks, Martina. If you don't mind I'd like to talk to her alone.'

'Not a problem. I'll tell her you're here.'

It was more like a grand Venetian apartment than a Hamburg hotel room and Fabel's first impression was of Vivaldi colliding with Bang and Olufsen: a mix of lavish baroque decoration and grand, luxurious furniture with hi-tech electronics. It was the international vernacular of five-star luxury. There was something about it that Fabel found appealing and repellent at the same time: a gut reaction against ostentation. A Northern European Lutheran gut reaction.

Jake Westland's widow was a woman of careworn beauty: Fabel could see that at one time she must have been astounding, but time had frayed the edges of her looks and he guessed her recent bereavement had unravelled them a little more. She was sitting on the sofa under the huge windows that looked out across the water of the Inner Alster to Ballindamm on the far side. Sarah Westland was dressed very expensively but with what Fabel perceived as a vague lack of style. When she spoke to acknowledge his greeting he detected some kind of British regional accent, but he couldn't work out quite where from. English was the only language in Europe that had 'social' accents as well as regional ones and, at one time, Fabel had had a knack of pinning down an Englishman's origin and social class from his accent. But he had been away from the country and the culture for so long that he had lost much of his skill. Sarah Westland, however, seemed confused when Fabel introduced himself.

'You're English?' she asked, frowning.

'No, I'm German. But half-Scottish. I was brought up bilingual and spent a lot of time in Britain when I was a kid. I really am so sorry for your loss, Mrs Westland.'

'Are you?' The question seemed genuine. 'I mean, in your line of work I would imagine that you are used to death. And to talking to the people left behind.'

'You never get used to it,' said Fabel. 'And I am genuinely sorry.'

'When can I take Jake – I mean his body – home?'

'We've arranged the release papers. Sorry it took so long. I'm afraid we can be a little bureaucratic. I take it you've arranged carriage?'

'Day after tomorrow. From Hamburg Airport.'

'Mrs Westland, can I ask you a few questions about your husband?'

'I imagined you would want to.' She eased back in her chair, as if settling down for a longer conversation than she had anticipated. 'If it helps find who killed Jake, then of course I want to help.'

'Has there been any trouble with persistent fans, stalkers – that kind of thing?'

'Just the usual. Nothing sinister. A few oddballs, but that's it. If you're asking if some mad stalker did this to Jake, then I'd have to say it's not anyone we know about. Presumably it was a German who killed him. There's nobody I know of from here who's been pestering Jake or anything.'

'No other disputes or grudges that you know of?'

'Nothing that would lead someone to do that to Jake.' Sarah Westland paused. Her eyes glazed a little.

'You spoke to him on the phone the night of the concert.

Did he say anything unusual? Anything that had happened or anyone he had met that caused him concern?'

'No – we just talked about the concert. The kids. A few of the things we had to get organised after he got back.' Sarah Westland's answer was straightforward, but there was a hint of something in her expression. Fabel decided to come back to the call later.

'What do you know about the charity Mr Westland was supporting?' The Sabine Charity?'

'Jake was involved in a lot of charities, Mr Fabel. I helped him with the management of his donations, et cetera. They covered a wide range of problems, but there were three that were especially close to his heart: a charity in the UK for the victims of sexual assault, one that provided counselling to the children of raped women in Bosnia. And, of course, he worked very closely with the Sabine organisers here in Hamburg.'

'Petra Meissner?' asked Fabel.

Sarah Westland looked at him with a weary expression. 'Yes, Petra Meissner. They worked together very closely. So closely that the press back home started to speculate about the relationship, which, I guess, is why you threw her name in. I am not naive, Mr Fabel – I am only too aware that there were other women, that Jake had affairs. But they were . . .' she sought the right word '. . . insignificant. For all of his reputation as a ladies' man, Jake never really understood women. He never really understood me. That meant that his relationships with women were pretty uncomplicated. He categorised women and Petra Meissner fell into the business-only category. Jake would never muck about with someone who was involved in something so important to him. And it *was* important: he was here for the Sabine Charity and nothing else – his whole German tour was organised to fund that one event in Hamburg.'

'Why was that? I mean, why was it so important to Mr Westland?'

'Do you have laws here about adopted children having the right to know their biological origin?'

'Yes.' Fabel frowned, confused by the sudden change of tack. 'Yes, we do. Adopted children have that right in law.'

'In Britain it's different. You only get that right when you reach adulthood: when you're sixteen. Did you know that Jake was adopted?'

'Yes, I did.'

'He had a very close relationship with his adoptive parents, particularly with his mother. Jake felt that it would somehow be an insult to them to go looking for his biological parents, so he didn't. Not until they were dead. His mother died three years ago and Jake suddenly devoted three months of his life to finding his biological mother. But when he did, he was told that she didn't want to see him. She was a woman in her seventies, living in Manchester. Welsh background.' Sarah Westland gave a small laugh. 'Jake was amazed to find out that he was half-Welsh. He had always considered himself a hundred per cent English. Anyway, despite her making it clear she wanted nothing to do with him, Jake persisted. She wouldn't speak to him on the telephone and she never replied to any of his letters. Jake told me that he understood: that he knew in the early nineteen-fifties illegitimacy carried a great stigma. But he was desperate to meet her, so he just walked up to her house and knocked on the door.'

'What happened?'

'She spat on him. This middle-class, smartly dressed seventy-year-old widow spat on him. Then she slammed the door in his face. I remember he told me how he stood there, in this meticulously neat suburban front garden with spit on his face. It really upset him. He hired a private investigator. When the detective got back to him, Jake was devastated. You see, he had built up this little scenario in his head: that he had been conceived through an act of forbidden love in a cruel and unforgiving time. He was right about the time being cruel and unforgiving. It turned out that he had been conceived by an act of rape. His biological mother had been attacked in a park by a stranger. She had been a teenager at the time. The police never got the man and, let's face it, at that time the rape victim was as much a suspect as the rapist. And because abortion was not an option back then, she had had to go through with the pregnancy and give Jake up as soon as he was born.'

'He never got to speak to his biological mother?'

'Never.'

'And that's why he was so supportive of anti-rape charities?'

'Jake never got over it. To start with, the idea that he had been totally and irreconcilably rejected by his mother burned him up. Then, the more he thought about it, the more he became obsessed with the idea that at least half of his DNA was that of some pervert rapist. He realised that she had spat on him because she hadn't seen her son standing there, but the son of the pervert who raped her. Jake started to identify with all of these unwanted kids in Bosnia who were the products of rape. And with rape victims. Jake seemed to feel connected to them. I always felt he identified each victim with his biological mother.'

'I see.'

'It was something the press never managed to get hold of. Not that there was as much press interest as there used to be.'

They were interrupted by a knock on the door. Martina Schilmann opened the door from outside and admitted a uniformed waitress who placed a tray with a coffee pot and cups on the low table.

'What about your husband's investments?' asked Fabel when the waitress had left. He poured a cup of coffee for

Sarah Westland and one for himself. 'He seemed to do well out of them and he had some here, I believe.'

'Yes, he had quite a few. Particularly here in Hamburg. Jake was funny that way, he could see things in people or places that others couldn't. I guess that's why his investments were all so successful.'

'So why particularly Hamburg?'

Sarah Westland gave a half-laugh. 'Being in the music business, Hamburg was kind of like Mecca to Jake. The Beatles and all that. But I remember he'd been over here on business. A sort of reconnaissance trip, I suppose. He said that Hamburg was the place to put your money. He said that Hamburgers – do you call them "Hamburgers"? – he said that you were all natural entre-preneurs and business people. He kept going on about the something league . . .'

'The Hanseatic League?'

'Yeah – he said that you still had all that trading nous in you. It was all about the Far East, he said. China and India. He said that Hamburg was going to be the big European trading partner with the East. Is it true what he said about Hamburg people?'

'Pretty much.' Fabel smiled. 'There's a joke that the average German businessman would sell his mother, but a Hamburg politician would throw in free delivery.'

'Mmm . . .' Sarah Westland did not seem to get the joke. There again, it wasn't really a time for humour.

'Would it be possible for you to get details of your husband's business dealings?' asked Fabel. 'Could you send them over to me at the Police Presidium? Or I can arrange to have them picked up.'

'I can get someone to do that. But a lot of the information will have to be sent from England. It will probably take a day or two.'

'Thank you for your time, Mrs Westland.' Fabel stood up. She walked him to the door and shook his hand.

'Is there something else?' she asked, reading his expression.

'It's just something about the night Mr Westland died. When I asked you if there was anything unusual about the phone conversation you had with him, you said there wasn't. But you didn't look too sure.'

'There wasn't anything unusual,' she replied. 'Or at least not in what he said . . . what we talked about. It's just that he seemed . . . distracted. Distant. I asked him what was wrong and he said he was tired.'

'That would fit with him turning down the after-concert party.'

'Jake may not have understood me, but I understood him. He was never too tired for a bash. I knew Jake's moods, but this one I couldn't place. It bothered me.

'There's one more thing,' said Sarah Westland as Fabel made for the door. 'I know what people think, what the newspapers are saying about why Jake was in the Reeperbahn and how he met his death. Jake was no angel and, like I told you, I had no illusions about his fidelity. But there's one thing I'm certain about: Jake did not go to that place for sex. He went there for a reason. To meet someone. I'm convinced of it.'

2.

'Am I being deported?' asked Vestergaard with a cold smile when Fabel pulled up at the taxi rank outside the main terminal building of Hamburg-Fuhlsbüttel Airport. A uniformed Federal Police officer walked purposefully over to the car but Fabel stopped him in his tracks by holding his bronze oval Criminal Police disc up to the glass of his window.

'No . . . this is all about arrival, Karin, not departure,' said Fabel. 'I want us to retrace Jespersen's steps, as much as we can with the information we've got. You're a Dane, like Jespersen, and you're new to Hamburg. I've brought you along to point out the things I might miss. Okay, Jespersen arrives. As he's walking through the arrivals hall he makes two calls, one to his deputy . . .' Fabel snapped his fingers, impatient at his own forgetfulness.

'Harald Tolstrup.' Vestergaard helped him out.

'Harald Tolstrup . . . who tells him that his hotel is booked.'

'Harald also told Jens that I wanted to speak to him as soon as possible.'

'Why was that?'

'Simple. I wanted to know what the hell he was up to and to make sure he kept me up to date on his movements. I knew he wouldn't, but I had to try to keep him on some kind of leash.'

'Okay, so then he phones me at the Presidium, but I'm in a meeting so he leaves his number. He comes out of the terminal and takes a taxi into the city. We've not been able to trace the driver who took him, but given the flight arrival time and the time he checked into the hotel it's pretty safe to say he travelled directly to the hotel without stops.' Fabel started the engine again and pulled out. He drove back down towards the city.

'Imagine you're in a taxi. You're Jespersen. You have the scrap of a rumour about a hit woman based in Hamburg that Vujačić let slip six years ago. You have the name of a German detective in your notebook: me. You also have other bits of information at hand, like the name "Olaf", but at the moment we can only guess about their relevance. There's bits and pieces about the East German Stasi and in particular one officer . . . What was his name?'

'Drescher. And Jens had been looking into Gennady Frolov, the Russian.'

'Okay. So you've arrived in Hamburg. What do you do now?'

'Well, I know where I'm going. I'm checked into the hotel and I've given the address to the taxi driver.'

'Yes,' said Fabel emphatically. 'You do know where you're going. But you've only just confirmed it with Tolstrup on the phone.'

'So whoever kills me later that night doesn't know yet where I am staying.'

'Exactly. He was followed. Someone followed him from the airport.' Fabel hit the button on his hands-free phone. It was Werner Meyer who answered. 'Werner, I want you to get someone to contact the chief of security at Fuhlsbüttel. See if you can get the CCTV footage of the taxi rank outside arrivals from about half an hour before until half an hour after Jens Jespersen arrived. Use the phone log to check when he tried to get me at the Murder Commission. That'll pinpoint when he left the airport building.'

'Okay, *Chef*,' said Werner. 'What are we looking for?'

'Jespersen getting into the taxi and leaving. I want the number of the taxi so we can trace the driver, but more specifically I want any trace of someone taking off after him.'

'I'm on it, *Chef*. What do I tell the Nordic ice maiden if she turns up looking for you?'

'She's sitting right next to me, idiot,' said Fabel. 'And you're on speakerphone. Just count yourself lucky that she can't speak German.'

At the other end of the connection, Werner laughed. 'It doesn't matter what language I talk, women never understand me. I'll get the footage organised. When will you be back?'

'Give me a couple of hours or so. Sometime after lunch.' Fabel turned to Vestergaard to see if there was any hint that she had picked up on Werner's jibe. There wasn't.

'Okay, back to Jespersen. Where are you going now?'

Vestergaard frowned. 'Somewhere I could get information on the Stasi.'

'Wrong city. Berlin would have been his best bet for that – the Federal Commission that deals with Stasi files and information is based there. It has offices elsewhere, but all of them are in East Germany. Did he have any plans to travel further?'

'Not that I know of.'

'That doesn't mean he didn't intend to take time to go to Berlin. There's a high-speed rail link from Hamburg. He could have got there and back in a day.'

Fabel drove on into the city and pulled up outside Vestergaard's hotel on Alter Wall.

'Okay,' he said. 'Jespersen stayed here too. He checks into the hotel and goes out. Why?'

'To kill time. To see the city, maybe.'

'Or to meet someone we don't know about.'

'It's possible. Or he may have simply been looking for somewhere to get lunch. He was very regular in his eating habits.'

'So let's say he goes for lunch. Places to eat within walking distance from here . . .' Fabel thought it over, then shook his head. 'Central Hamburg . . . could be any of a hundred places. If there were only some way of narrowing it down.'

'Is it that important to know where he ate?'

'I think it might be. We've established that he was probably followed from the airport. He's tried to speak to me but failed. My guess is that whoever was after him wanted him shut up before he could contact me. Whatever he was putting together, as soon as he started to frame it up and discuss it with others then too many people know about it for them to control it. They follow him here and tail him to where he was eating. It's there that they make contact. Somehow they get someone to gain his trust. A woman. Maybe our so-called "Valkyrie".'

'But surely if he's investigating a female professional killer . . .'

'Remember he doesn't know that they know about him.

Some attractive woman bumps into him and starts a conversation and he doesn't suspect a thing.'

'Jens wasn't really the chatty type.' Vestergaard gave a bitter laugh. 'Particularly in Germany.'

'But remember we're talking about real experts. Prepared, briefed. There will have been something to hook him. And perhaps she appeared to be non-German. Danish, even. Just to get him off his guard.'

'But we don't know where he went for lunch.'

Fabel looked as if he had just got a small static shock. 'The toy!'

'What toy?'

'We found a toy, one of these Hamburg souvenir teddy bears. It was in his hotel room with the rest of his stuff.' Fabel shook his head impatiently. 'Hold on a minute.' He hit the button on his car phone and again got through to the Murder Commission. He asked to speak to Anna Wolff.

'Anna, I'm going to ask you to do something and it's going to sound trivial. Believe me, it's not. Do you remember that teddy bear found at the Jespersen scene? It should be in the evidence locker.'

'It should,' said Anna, 'but it's not. It's on my desk. I've named him Captain Cutie.'

'For God's sake, Anna, that's evidence. You can't just . . .' Fabel drew a breath. 'Forget it. Just read the manufacturer's label and get in touch with them. I want to know who they distribute to in Hamburg. Make it within a three-kilometre radius of Jespersen's hotel. Like I say, Anna, this is urgent. And important.'

'I think I can manage it,' said Anna flatly.

Fabel hung up and turned to Vestergaard. 'If we locate the outlet, then they might have security cameras. Or they might be in a mall with CCTV. And that means we may be able to get a look at Jespersen's killer.'

3.

Sylvie Achtenhagen decided not to drive to Berlin. Instead, she caught the S-Bahn from Altona into Hamburg's main railway station and then took advantage of the gleaming new high-speed train that connected Germany's two biggest cities.

It took just over an hour and a half to get to Berlin. The weather had stayed bright and cold and Sylvie watched the flat North German landscape slide by, occasionally going through the notes she had made.

Much like the train she had just travelled on, Berlin's Main Railway Station was a statement: a promise about the future. Only two years old, the station was now a major Berlin landmark: a weaving of metal and glass on a monumental scale. It said very clearly to the world that this was, after all, the very heart of a new Europe. Sylvie made her way through the main concourse and out to the taxi stand.

'Where to, love?' asked the driver in a thick Berlin accent.

'The Birthler Office.'

'Off to see your file, are you, love?'

The Birthler Office, or BStU, was shorthand for the headquarters of an organisation whose name needed to be abbreviated: the Federal Commission for Preserving the Records of the Ministry for State Security of the German Democratic Republic. Its abbreviated form took its name from the serving Federal Commissioner, Marianne Birthler.

It took only fifteen minutes to get to the Birthler Office and after waiting a further ten Sylvie was greeted by a gaunt-looking man in his early fifties who introduced himself as Max Wengert. Wengert explained that he worked for the department that dealt with media requests for access to files. Sylvie, as a familiar face from television, was used to people reacting differently towards her than perhaps they would normally. There was something about Wengert's broad smile as he greeted her that suggested smiling was not something he did often. In that greeting, she recognised someone she could probably manipulate to divulge more information than he should.

'It's so kind of you to take the time to help me with this, Herr Wengert.' Sylvie smiled sweetly as he guided her into an interview room. 'Personally, as it were.'

'I have to admit to being something of a fan of yours.' He smiled again and exposed tobacco-stained teeth. Sylvie imagined him sitting alone in some tiny Berlin flat watching her on TV. She embellished the image a little too much and felt a shudder of revulsion. But she hid it well.

'Were you able to find out anything about the name I gave you . . . Georg Drescher?' she asked.

Wengert pulled the chair out from the table in the interview room, inviting Sylvie to sit. His long grey face took on a conspiratorial expression.

'Actually, Frau Achtenhagen, it's quite a coincidence – you are the second person to enquire about that name this week.'

'Really? Who was the other enquiry from? Was it another broadcaster, or a newspaper?'

'Neither.' Wengert looked unsure for a moment. 'Well, I suppose it does no harm to tell you. No, it wasn't actually a media enquiry. It came from the police. The Polizei Hamburg.'

'I see . . .' said Sylvie. 'Did they say why they were interested in Drescher?'

'No, they didn't. I couldn't help them. And I'm afraid I can't help you. We do know from other files referring to him that he did exist, but Major Georg Drescher does not have a personal file that we can trace. Nor can we find any other file of a significant nature with reference to him or his activities. All the mentions we have of him are in minor files where he is, sometimes literally, merely a footnote.'

'Isn't that – well – odd?'

'Far from it, Frau Achtenhagen. The Stasi had masses of

files, millions. Every report from an unofficial collaborator was written up, indexed and filed. Take the personal files on individuals: there are six million of them. Out of a total population of, what? Sixteen million? That means there's a lot of inconsequential stuff in there. But the important stuff – the big secrets – a lot of that was shredded or removed. Towards the end of eighty-nine, beginning of ninety, the Stasi saw the writing on the Wall, if you'll pardon the pun – added to which there were thousands of civil-rights protesters outside waiting to get in to tear the place apart and get their hands on the files, which they did on the fifteenth of January. I would imagine it must have been mayhem in Stasi Headquarters in the days and hours before the protesters got in. When they did they stopped the destruction of the files, but a lot of the more incriminating material had already been shredded. We recovered nearly seventeen thousand sacks containing nearly fifty million shredded pages. And we're still trying to put them together. But that's not the whole story. In amongst those civil-rights protesters who broke in were members of the American CIA, who helped themselves to some of the most sensitive information. They wanted to get their hands on lists of agents working in the West. And I would also guess that in amongst the protesters there were more than a few Stasi agents and informers trying to get to their files before anyone else.'

'And you think that's what happened to Drescher's files?' asked Sylvie. 'That he's managed to wipe his existence from the records?'

'Maybe, but not necessarily. We are still trying to put the shredded and hand-torn files back together. It was only last year that we developed a computer-software system that can reassemble the pages digitally and speed the whole process up. Even with that, it's going to take us until 2013. But you can be very sure that there will be some nasty surprises along the way – a lot of former Stasi agents and informers won't be sleeping too easily in their beds, I'll tell you that. Maybe Drescher's files are somewhere in there, waiting to be put together.'

'If they're here at all.' Sylvie let out a long breath in disappointment

'There is something else . . .' Wengert leaned forward, lowering his voice. 'You know that the BStU is going to be absorbed into the State Records Office? It's because of the Hans Hugo Klein investigation. It showed the level to which the BStU has been infiltrated by ex-Stasi – people who could be working inside here to hide or destroy the files we're supposed to be protecting and reconstructing.'

'So maybe Drescher has a friend in here?'

Wengert shrugged. 'Who knows? Sorry I can't be of more help.'

'What about the other names I gave you?'

'Well, unless it is related to your personal file, if you have one here, or unless it is demonstrably in the public interest, I'm not supposed to release that kind of information.'

'Herr Wengert . . .' Sylvie smiled at the official and watched him melt. Men were so easy to manipulate. 'Would I be right in saying that you were one of the civil-rights activists who stormed the Lichtenberg Bastille?'

Wengert beamed with pride. 'Yes. I was.'

'Then you are clearly a man who stands up for what is right. Who cares about the truth. And you've said yourself, this place is probably lousy with ex-Stasi scum. How can we get to the truth if we play by the rules and they don't? I promise you that the people on the list I sent you are not the ones I want to expose. I just want to talk to them, that's all. But they may lead me to Drescher. And he is someone we should care about. I am not asking for you to compromise your ethics, Herr Wengert. I'm asking you to stand by them.'

Wengert stared at Sylvie, an inner struggle obviously going on behind his dull eyes. He stood up, decisively.

'Wait here a moment, please,' he said, and left the room.

4.

Fabel had left Vestergaard at her hotel to freshen up. He had promised her that he would let her know as soon as they ascertained where Jespersen had eaten lunch or if they had uncovered any sightings of a tail from the airport. He felt he was making progress, but the idea that it could all be a wild-goose chase continued to haunt him.

He was on his way back into the office when Anna phoned.

'I've had a call,' she said, 'from a bright-as-a-button, all-eager-as-hell Commissar based down at Commissariat Twelve in Klingberg. She's keen to speak to you. I said you would ring her back, but seeing as you're in the area . . .'

'What's it about?'

'A suicide. It looks straightforward and he left a note. Took a dive and landed on his face. From what she said this guy really does have eyes in the back of his head—'

'Anna . . .' Fabel injected a warning tone into his voice.

'Anyway, she's got in touch because she thinks something's a bit off about the whole thing. She admits her feeling is groundless but she wanted to talk to you about it.'

'She asked for me particularly?'

'I think she's after my job. Her timing's impeccable.'

Fabel let the jibe pass. 'Is she on duty now?'

'Yep. I thought I'd let you know because of this Valkyrie thing. You know, any death that there could be any doubt about.'

'What's her name?'

'Iris Schmale. I'm guessing all that schoolgirl exuberance will make her easy to recognise.'

* * *

Police Commissariat 12, Klingberg, was less well known than Davidwache but architecturally it was probably even more impressive. One of Hamburg's most famous landmarks was the Chilehaus, in the city's Kontorhaus Quarter. The Chilehaus, as almost every Hamburg tour guide would tell visitors, was designed to resemble the sharp-edged prow of a ship. The Klingberg police station had been built in 1906 into the flank of the Chilehaus complex. It was, in itself, a magnificent piece of brickwork.

Fabel suppressed a grin when Criminal Commissar Iris Schmale greeted him in the main office. She was exactly as Anna had imagined her: young, fresh-faced and bubbling with enthusiasm. She had rebellious, vibrant red hair tied back into a long ponytail and her pale complexion was clustered with freckles. It gave her a girlish look.

'I believe you have a suicide that smells fishy,' said Fabel.

'I do, Herr Principal Chief Commissar. The dead man's name was Peter Claasens. He owned and ran a shipping agency on the edge of the Kontorhaus Quarter. From what I can see he had everything going for him. Wife, kids, highly successful business.'

'Lots of people with families and successful businesses commit suicide every day,' said Fabel. 'And I believe the deceased left a note.'

'Exactly!' said Schmale. Fabel failed to suppress a grin at her vehemence. 'That's exactly it. There's something about the suicide note that's . . .' She frowned as she sought the right word. 'Ambiguous.'

'Do you have it here?'

She handed him a sheet of paper. 'This is a photocopy. The note was found several metres from the body. No blood on it. The only fingerprints were those of the deceased.'

Fabel began reading the note out loud. '"Dear Marianne . . ."' He raised an eyebrow at Schmale.

'Wife.'

'"Dear Marianne, I am sorry I have to do this, and I know that, right at this moment, you are angry with me, but I need you to understand that there is no other way forward for me to go. It is tough to leave you and the kids behind, but it is better for me to go. I have made sure you will all be provided for and I don't want you to think ill of me for making the only decision I could make. This is my decision and I want you to know that no one else played a part in it. I'm sorry I won't be around every day to see the kids grow up, but I just couldn't go on the way things were. I know you understand. Goodbye . . . Peter."' Fabel handed the sheet back to Schmale. 'Have you spoken to the wife?'

'Of course. I know that bereaved families often find the idea of suicide difficult to accept, but Marianne Claasens just simply refuses to believe that he committed suicide. And she doesn't strike me as a woman overwhelmed by the shock of it all. She's not in denial – she really is certain that her husband did not kill himself. And that note . . .'

'What about it?'

'Well, it could mean anything. I tried to imagine it out of context – that it hadn't been found at the scene of a suicide. And to me it reads more like someone who's *leaving* his wife, not killing himself: *"I want you to know that no one else played a part in it."* How could anyone else play a part in his suicide? That sounds to me like he was about to clear off with someone else and wanted to keep her name out of it.'

Fabel thought about what Schmale had said and as he did so she watched him urgently, like the accused waiting for the judge's verdict.

'That was good thinking,' he said and smiled. 'About viewing the note in a neutral context. But if this isn't suicide, then it's murder. And if, as you suspect, he was about to leave his wife, that makes her the prime suspect. Have you checked her out?'

'Yes, Herr Principal Chief Commissar. She was nowhere

near Claasens's office. And she has a dozen witnesses to prove it. She was at some function at the St Georg Hospital. She's a consultant there. Oncologist.'

'And Claasens?'

'As I said, he was a shipping agent. He had his own business arranging export/import traffic for major Hamburg-based concerns. He specialised in the Far East.'

'Any suspicious involvements?'

'Not in his business dealings. He seems to have been one of Hamburg's most respected businessmen. And he had political ambitions too, apparently. Was thinking about running for the Hamburg Senate. That's the other thing: suicides don't tend to plan their futures.'

'You said there was nothing suspicious in his business dealings. Was there something in his private life?'

'From what I can gather, Claasens was a bit of a ladies' man. Another reason why I would read a different interpretation into that note.'

'Let me see it again . . .' Fabel read through it once more. 'Okay, I think you may have something. I'll put a team on the case to work with you.'

Fabel left the Klingberg Commissariat and Iris Schmale standing grinning as if she'd won the lottery. She was a smart kid, that was for sure, but, on the face of it, there was nothing to suggest that there was any more to Claasens's death than what it seemed to be: a burnt-out exec taking a dive from his office building. But, walking back to his car as the winter sky glowered down on the Kontorhaus Quarter, Fabel knew the feeling in his gut was the same nagging that Iris Schmale had felt. A policeman's instinct. It was getting dark already. He checked his watch and, knowing she would be home from school, he decided to phone Gabi.

'What's up, Dad?' Fabel's daughter habitually used the

English term. It wouldn't have sounded right for her to call him anything else.

'You free for a coffee?'

'What, now?'

'I could meet you at about six. We could get something to eat. That's if your mother doesn't mind.'

'She's working late. I'll leave a note. Usual place in the Arkaden?'

'Usual place. See you then.'

5.

Fabel sat in the café, looking out towards the Alster. It was too dark now to see the swans gliding across its winter shield of dark water; instead his own reflection stared back at him. He thought he looked tired. And older. The grey had started to insinuate itself into the blond of his hair and the wrinkles were deepening around his eyes.

He sat and sipped the tea he had ordered and waited for Gabi to arrive.

A huddle of young women, barely more than girls, sat two tables away. Students, from the look of them. There were five of them and they laughed and joked in the careless way that only the young seem able to. Fabel found himself envious of an as yet unjaded, unmuted enthusiasm for life that he had felt himself. Once.

His phone rang. It was Anna Wolff.

'The teddy bear that Jespersen bought,' she said. 'It was bought from a shop in the Hanseviertel. I've spoken to them, but the name Jespersen doesn't ring any bells. But that doesn't really mean anything – they have so many customers passing through, a lot of them tourists and foreigners. One thing we do know, though, is that he paid cash. There's no record of him using his credit card.'

'Maybe he got it somewhere else,' said Fabel.

'Nope – the store had them on special order. Picked the jumper design themselves. This is the only place that sells them.'

'The Hanseviertel . . .' Fabel muttered.

'What?'

'Jespersen probably had lunch in the Hanseviertel. Check which restaurants and cafés have CCTV and get the tapes for lunchtime that day.'

'Yes, *Chef*,' sighed Anna. Fabel let it go.

'Anything on the tapes from the Reeperbahn? Have we got a picture of the fake taxi yet?'

'Not yet.'

'Well, chase them up, for God's sake. It's the only lead we've got.'

After he hung up, Fabel turned back to the window to watch for Gabi arriving and only looked in the girls' direction when they started to leave. It was the last girl he noticed. Their eyes met and recognition registered in hers. She was wearing a grungy black jacket and was hatless, her fair hair gathered roughly into a ponytail. Fabel smiled faintly at her, knowing he should know her but unable to place her. She looked away in that swift but casual manner, as if she hadn't seen him, that every policeman recognises as an effort not to be noticed.

It was only after the girls had disappeared around the corner into Poststrasse that Fabel realised the girl was Christa Eisel, the young prostitute who had found Jake Westland dying behind Herbertstrasse. There was something about the realisation that depressed Fabel. It was as if he had been unable to recognise her because he had seen her in an appropriate context. She had been where she should be: with friends of her own age, talking and laughing about life. He wondered how many of her friends knew about her other life. Maybe that was it. Maybe everybody has a double life: another face for another context.

'*What's up, Pops?*'

Fabel was taken aback as Gabi, who had spoken in English, dropped into the seat opposite him. He leaned over and kissed his daughter and then, smiling, let his hand rest for a moment on her cheek.

'You okay, Dad?' There was concern in Gabi's voice.

'I'm fine, sweetheart,' he said. 'It's just that it's good to see you. It's always good to see you . . . Have I ever told you how proud I am of the way you're turning out?'

'All the time, Dad. Is this you softening me up for the big lecture?'

The waitress came over and they placed their order.

'Your mother told you what I wanted to talk to you about?' he asked after the waitress had gone.

'Kind of. Or what she wants you to talk to me about.' Gabi pushed at a small deposit of spilt salt, pushing it into a pile. 'She wants you to talk me out of a police career.'

'Well, I thought you knew me better than that,' Fabel said indignantly. 'And your mother should, too. And one thing I know for sure is that I could never talk you into or out of anything.'

'Sorry, Dad.'

'But I do want to discuss it with you. If it's what you really want, then I'm with you all the way. But I do want you to know what you're getting into.'

'The truth is – but don't tell Mum this – that I've not made up my mind. I'm just thinking about it, that's all. What I want to do is study law and jurisprudence first. Maybe criminology. Then see.'

'That's a good plan, Gabi. Keep your options open.'

'How would you feel if I joined the police?' Gabi looked at Fabel earnestly and for a moment he remembered the serious little face she had always put on when she had been little if concentrating.

'Like I said, Gabi, it's your decision.'

'That's not what I'm asking. I'm asking what you would think.'

For a moment Fabel sat and stared past Gabi and in the direction that Christa Eisel had taken. A girl just a few years older than his daughter.

'I think there are worse paths to take. Much worse. But I won't pretend I wouldn't worry about you.'

'The danger?'

'There is physical danger, that's true. But there's psychological danger too. Some of the things you see. Some of the people you deal with. It's a whole new dimension of life that you wouldn't come across normally.'

'*You* deal with it.'

'Not as well as I should, if I'm totally honest. That's why I nearly chucked it all in last year.'

'But you see, Dad, I didn't know that. You have *never* spoken to me about your work.'

'I'm sorry. Maybe I should have. But the truth is most of police work is boring or depressing. Take my job. It's one of the top jobs you can have in the police and because of all of the stuff you read and see on the TV, you'd think it was exciting and glamorous. Believe me, it's not. Ninety-nine per cent . . . *more* than ninety-nine per cent of the murders I deal with are committed by people of low IQ, fuelled by drink or drugs, in seedy or squalid surroundings. The truth is that murder is vulgar. The vast majority of crime is. There are very few criminal masterminds or genius serial killers out there. Most of the time you end up with someone sitting across the table from you who is, in many ways, just another victim of their own crime. They sit there, probably only just sobered up, confused and wondering how the hell they ended up in the position they're in.'

'But not always, surely?'

'No . . . not always. Then you get the sociopaths, the rapists, the drug dealers, the career criminals who have killed or maimed purely for personal gratification or gain. But again, Gabi, it's not the way you see it on the TV. These are the dregs of society.'

'I think I have a more sophisticated perspective than you seem to think, Dad. I live in the real world. I don't get my ideas from the TV.'

'Fair enough.' Fabel smiled at his daughter. 'I know you're a bright kid, but it's important that you know just what it is you're getting yourself into. It's a job that gets to you. No matter how hard or tough you think you are, something, somewhere along the way, will get to you.'

'Are you talking about me or are you talking about Maria Klee? I know what happened to her. Is that what you're worried about? Tell me, Dad, and I want you to be totally honest: would you be having this talk with me if I were your son and not your daughter?'

'Yes. Absolutely. That has nothing to do with it. This is all to do with who you are, not what gender you are. Some people are cut out for the job, others aren't.'

'Do you think I am?' Gabi asked, with more than a touch of defiance. At that moment, Fabel saw a hint of Renate's fieriness in his daughter's eyes.

'I don't know,' said Fabel. 'I really mean that. Even after all these years, I sometimes doubt that *I* am. I just want you to keep as open a mind as you can about your future.' He paused for a moment, unsure whether to commit his next thought to words. 'I've never said anything bad about your mother, you know that, don't you?'

'I know. I also know that you had good reason to but never did,' Gabi said, her expression sad.

'I'm not going to start now, Gabi, but I do want you not to let her sway you from whatever course you pick for yourself. Me neither. It's up to you, and I know that your mother can be a little . . .'

'Bitter?' Gabi finished the thought for him. 'The truth is

it didn't take her long to realise the mistake she had made. Ludiger never did match up to you for her. Despite all of his charm, he turned out to be a creep.'

'I never did get the story about why they broke up. I'm guessing it was another woman?'

Gabi didn't answer right away. 'Didn't you know, Dad? He knocked her about.'

'Hit her?'

'Not often. And not so badly that it would show. But once is too often.'

Fabel gazed at Gabi. 'I had no idea . . .' His expression suddenly darkened. 'He never laid a hand on you, did he? If he did . . .'

Gabi held her hand up. 'Take it easy, Dad. No, he didn't. Trust me. He would only have got to try it once.'

'The bastard.' Fabel shook his head in disbelief. 'I mean, Renate . . . I would never have imagined her as a battered wife . . .'

'Now, given everything you've just been telling me about police work, I think that's a pretty naive thing for a policeman to say. You should know that you can never tell a victim of domestic violence by their appearance.'

'You say it didn't happen that often?'

'I think it followed the usual pattern. He started to get violent more, for less provocation. I think Mum took the attitude that she had made her own bed so she'd have to lie in it. But eventually she decided to throw him out.'

'Did you ever see him hit her?'

'Oh, no – he was very careful about that. I didn't know about it until Mum told me, after it was all over. She told me then that she wished she'd never split up with you; that when you and she were married it would never have crossed her mind that you could hit her.'

'Shit,' said Fabel. 'I had no idea . . .'

'Well, maybe you can understand a little better now why she's always on your case.'

The waitress returned with their meal. As they ate, they fell into a more general conversation about school, friends, how things were going at home. Fabel always enjoyed his daughter's company and he was glad to move on to lighter topics. But all the time he thought about his ex-wife Renate. How strong-willed and independent-spirited she had always been and how degrading it must have been for her to have been assaulted by Behrens in her own house.

The thought darkened his mood and he found himself also thinking about the brief look that he had exchanged with strong-willed, independent-spirited Christa Eisel. And every time he thought of her, it gave him a bad feeling.

6.

Ute Cranz looked at her watch before casting one final glance over the carefully arranged table. Robert Gerdes would arrive in the next few minutes. Everything was ready: the table set, each course of the meal scheduled for readiness at exactly the right time. And the kitchen. Everything in the kitchen was prepared.

She walked across to the full-length mirror in the hall, by the door. Her deep auburn hair was gathered up, her lipstick and make-up were perfectly done. She was wearing a simple but expensive deep green dress that had a sharkskin lustre to it. For a moment she worried that it made her look reptilian, then laughed at her own insecurity: the dress's colour and sheen simply complemented and highlighted the rich copper tones in her hair. She smoothed the dress over her hips and thighs. She looked great.

If Ute needed confirmation, she got it when Gerdes arrived, exactly on time.

'Frau Cranz,' he said when she opened the door to admit him, 'you look . . . radiant.' His eyes scanned her figure before settling on her face. His eyes were smiling. Knowing. 'I brought these . . .' He held up a large manila envelope. 'These are the details of the lease. I'm sure yours are the same.'

Taking the envelope and placing it on the hall table, she picked up the glass she had left waiting there for his arrival. She smiled and handed it to him.

'A little Prosecco . . . I thought it would be nice.'

'Are you not joining me?'

'I will in a minute,' she said, parting her red lips to expose perfect teeth. 'Would you mind making yourself at home? I've just a few things to finish in the kitchen.'

'Not at all,' he said, with a gracious bow. Ute thought Gerdes had an almost aristocratic look. He was wearing a blazer, a crisp white collar and a blue tie with fine red stripes through it. There was something about him that made him look as though he belonged in a different era. A past time.

She extended her arm in the direction of the dining table, indicating he should sit, excused herself once more and walked through to the kitchen. She closed the door behind her. From where he was sitting, Gerdes would not have been able to see into the kitchen when she opened the door. She had planned it that way. She stood and took a moment to think through all she had to do. Then she cast an eye around the kitchen, just to make sure.

Yes, everything was ready.

Ute stood listening to the soup simmering on the hob and the low whirr of the oven's fan, while all around her the floor, the work surfaces, even the walls to shoulder height, were covered in thick blue plastic sheeting.

To catch any splashes of his blood.

7.

Fabel could tell there was something on Susanne's mind as soon as he came through the door of their apartment. He had become attuned to her moods since they had been together: he knew when something was troubling her, but, like most men, he was capable only of reading the big signs and not the small print.

'How did your talk with Gabi go?' Susanne smiled but still looked preoccupied.

'Fine. You know Gabi, she's a smart kid. Smart enough to make up her own mind about things.' Fabel kissed Susanne. 'What's up?' he asked.

'I've been through the files you gave me on the Westland and Lensch murders.' There was an impatient energy in the way Susanne spoke.

'Okay . . .' Fabel followed Susanne through to the lounge and they sat on the sofa, the files spread out in front of them on the coffee table. 'What about your rule of not talking shop at home?'

'I thought it was *our* rule . . . anyway, I'll let it go this once. There's something not right here. There is no pattern. In terms of victim profile or chronology.'

'But we haven't had enough victims for any true pattern to emerge.'

'You did with the original murders in the nineties. But this time . . . I don't know.' She frowned as she flicked through the notes. 'You're putting your money on a copycat, right?'

'Yes. At least for the moment.'

'Okay, let's say it is a copycat,' said Susanne. 'What kind of killer or killers are we looking at? God knows you're almost as much an expert in the psychology of multiple murderers as I am, so you know that there are four broad groups that female serial killers fall into.'

'Yep,' Fabel said, leaning back in the sofa and placing his hands behind his head. 'Angels of Death, Black Widows, Revenge Killers and Insanity Killers.'

'Right, said Susanne. She got up, went through to the kitchen and came back with a chilled bottle of wine and two glasses. She poured them both a glass.

'Very nice,' he said, sipping the wine. 'You can't beat a nice crisp Chardonnay and a chat about dismembered bodies.'

'Do you want to hear this or not?' Susanne said impatiently.

'Okay. The four groups. And you're trying to pick where our girl belongs?'

'Trying is right. Take the Angels of Death – women who are usually nurses or other medical professionals, who kill the vulnerable, and usually for profit or because they feel they are doing the victim a favour, when all the time they're really getting off on the power trip of having life or death in their hands. She's not one of them.'

'Agreed.' Fabel took another sip of his wine.

'Then there are Black Widows. Black Widows in turn fall into two categories: the profit-motivated and the sexual predator or psychosexually motivated. Their victims tend to be known to them. Intimate. They kill their sexual partners or men they pick up.'

'I'm sleeping on the couch tonight.' Fabel grinned, then wiped the grin from his face in response to Susanne's frown. 'Okay, maybe our girl falls into that category. She does make sexual overtures and plays the part of a prostitute.'

'But she doesn't gain from the killings financially.'

'She did take Westland's phone, diary and wallet.'

Susanne shook her head. 'That's not the kind of score a Black Widow kills for. And I don't see her deriving a sexual benefit from the killings – unless she orgasms because of the act of killing, the violence itself.'

'But that would be extremely rare in a female killer, wouldn't it?' asked Fabel.

'Yep . . .' said Susanne. 'It's very common in male serial-killing behaviour, but extremely rare in female killers.'

'But not totally unknown?'

'You've heard of Irma Grese?'

'The Bitch of Belsen?' said Fabel, frowning. 'Yes, of course I've heard of her.'

'Grese had only turned twenty-three when she was hanged for crimes against humanity, meaning that she began committing those crimes from the age of about nineteen or twenty. She was a small, plain, not too bright and totally unexceptional girl who came from a basically anti-Nazi family; yet she developed a taste – a hunger – for exceptional cruelty. Both psychological and physical. She had a whip woven out of cellophane which would cut prisoners as she whipped them. She shot and beat prisoners to death, and it was clear she derived gratification from it. Everything points to her being a sexual sadist. As a psychological case, she serves as a warning about how female sexual drive can be channelled into political or religious hysteria. The thing about Grese was that she was an absolutely fanatical member of the League of German Girls. She was obsessed with it. These girls were indoctrinated with Nazi ideology at their most impressionable age, and at a key stage in their sexual development. Almost all of the female guards in concentration camps were recruited from the ranks of the League and Grese's sexual maturation coincided with her being in a position of power where she could physically abuse prisoners. It was an exceptional context and an exceptional point in history.'

'And Grese's sexual sadism was exceptional . . .' Fabel concluded the thought.

'With both sets of murders I find the violence – the expert violence – totally atypical of what I would expect. This is behaviour that would normally take a long, long time to mature.'

'So you think it could be the same killer?' Fabel was confused.

8.

She was younger than many of the women he had been with of late. Younger and more attractive.

He had a naturally suspicious nature and found himself

wondering why she had made the running. It was not unusual, though, he told himself. Younger women were known to go for more mature men. Particularly those they felt were intellectually or economically superior. Hypergamy, they called it. He laughed at the thought.

'Do you have family, Herr Gerdes?' Ute Cranz asked as she came in to serve the soup.

'Not of my own.' He smiled. 'I have three nieces, of whom I am very fond. What about you, Frau Cranz? Do you have family?'

'No.' She smiled sadly. 'Just my late husband. I do have a sister, but she became very ill. She's in hospital. Permanently.'

'Oh . . . I am sorry to hear that,' said Gerdes.

'Please, call me Ute. May I offer you more wine?'

'Then you must call me Robert. Yes, please. Aren't you going to join me yet?'

'Perhaps later. I very seldom drink, Robert. I find it muddles me, even a little. But please, I want you to enjoy some.'

Gerdes took a long sip. 'It really is very good.'

Gerdes sat and ate and drank and listened to Ute Cranz. She had that strange ability that women seemed to have: to talk a lot but say nothing. But he smiled and nodded and said the right things at the right time. She certainly was an attractive woman: she had large, dark eyes and her chestnut hair was cut short. She had an appealing figure, too: slim, but with a hint of voluptuousness through the sheen of her dress. Yet there was something about her that troubled him: he was certain they had met somewhere before.

'Have you lived in Hamburg all your life?' she asked.

'Long enough for me to consider myself a native Hamburger,' he said, taking another sip of his wine. 'What about you, Ute?'

'Oh no. I moved here from the East. Mecklenburg. A town called Zarrentin. It's small, but very pretty. It's on a lake. The

Schaalsee. Before the Wall came down it was right on the border with the West. We had an ugly border checkpoint and fences and stuff. But that's long gone now.'

'If you don't mind my asking, how long has it been since Herr Cranz passed on?' asked Gerdes. He was annoyed that his voice sounded, at least to him, a little slurry; yet the wine seemed to have had no other effect on him. 'If you don't mind me saying, you seem tragically young to be a widow.'

'Three years. Nearly four.' She refilled his glass.

She served a typical Hamburg eel soup, followed by duck breasts in a spicy orange sauce and a strawberry-mousse dessert. It was, he had to admit, a well-cooked meal. Afterwards she served coffee and Asbach brandy and asked him to sit on the sofa.

When he stood up, his legs felt wobbly and he had to steady himself on the edge of the table. What was wrong with him? He hadn't had that much to drink. Ute Cranz noticed his stumble but passed no comment. It was embarrassing none the less. He sat on the sofa and sipped his Asbach.

She came back from the kitchen and sat next to him on the sofa. Gerdes smiled weakly.

'I'm afraid I don't feel very well . . .' The words came to his lips with difficulty. He felt numb. And, for some reason, afraid. He decided to stop drinking the Asbach and tried to set the glass down on the arm of the sofa, but it slipped and smashed on the floor.

'I'm sorry,' he tried to say, but the words came out as a low, incoherent moan.

'It's all right,' Ute said, clearly interpreting his meaning but remaining totally unperturbed by his condition. 'It's not your fault. It's because of the metaxalone.'

Gerdes tried to articulate a question but, this time, he couldn't even manage a moan.

'I had to think it through very carefully. I wanted to

immobilise you without there being too much of a sedative or analgesic effect. The great thing about metaxalone is that its effectiveness is vastly increased when it's digested.'

Gerdes tried to move, but he felt as if his arms and legs were made of lead.

'Oh . . . and there's some succinylcholine in there as well,' she said, as if suddenly recalling an ingredient for a cake recipe. 'You know, suxamethonium chloride. I'll be injecting you with some more of that later.'

Gerdes felt a scream rise from deep within, but it failed to break the surface. He felt his head begin to flop backwards. She eased it onto the cushioned back of the sofa.

'Of course, you are very familiar with suxamethonium chloride,' she continued. 'It is a highly effective deep-muscle relaxant and is an excellent assassin's tool: you can make it look like someone has died from natural causes. Heart failure. Unless, of course, some diligent pathologist picks up on hyperkalaemia. But don't worry, the dosage you've absorbed won't stop your heart. It's much more effective intravenously, but the great thing about suxamethonium chloride is that it's colourless, odourless and soluble in water and alcohol. You've ingested quite an amount of it along with the metaxalone over the evening, Robert. Oh, do you mind if I stop this silly nonsense and call you by your real name: Georg? Oh yes, I know who you are, Major Drescher. I know all about you.'

Ute disappeared for a moment into the kitchen and returned with a metal tray that had a disposable hypodermic on it. He wanted to scream, to fight, to grab her and squeeze the life out of her, but he couldn't. He was completely immobilised. He found that he could still blink, but that was all. A great terror surged through him. It was claustrophobia: a panic caused by the realisation that he was trapped within his own body. Ute jabbed the hypodermic carelessly and roughly into his forearm. He felt the needle jab painfully into his skin. He felt it, but he didn't even flinch.

'Yes, I know, Major Drescher . . . that was a little taste of what's to come. The succinylcholine isn't anaesthetic and is only analgesic in muscle tissue. I promise that you will feel absolutely everything I do to you. They use it in many states in the US as part of lethal-injection execution. Highly controversial . . . there's a theory that God knows how many condemned prisoners have died in absolute agony because the anaesthetic part of the injection hasn't worked. But because they have been completely immobilised by the succinylcholine, there is no outward sign that they are in the most terrible pain. Like being burned at the stake, but from the inside out. But, like I say, you know all about it, don't you? That's what you taught your girls, isn't it? Is that what you meant when you told me that you had three nieces?'

How did she know his real name was Drescher? He had painstakingly covered up his traces. Only a professional – a top professional – could have uncovered them. Who was she? Where had he met her before?

Drescher's mind raced and his heart pounded. The thing that frightened him most was that Ute kept disappearing from his field of view. Incapable of moving his head, he could not follow her movements with his eyes. His head was tilted back and he could only see what was immediately before him. Ute reappeared for an instant. He saw a flash of something that looked like a thick roll of heavy-duty blue plastic. She bent down and was lost from view, but he guessed that she was unrolling the plastic on the floor in front of the sofa.

She moved around behind him, tucked her arms under his armpits and pulled him off the sofa. He rolled off the edge and his face slammed painfully onto the plastic-covered hardwood floor. His nose was pressed hard against the floor and he heard his breath hiss and bubble through his bleeding nose. She turned his head sideways, his cheek against the plastic. He was facing the sofa and could see an earring that Ute Cranz obviously had dropped and it had rolled out of sight. He thought how surreal it would be that that would be one of the last things he would see: a forgotten earring under a sofa. He guessed she would find it soon: when she was cleaning up after killing him.

She rolled him onto his back and slid him across the living room and through into the kitchen. Drescher might not have been able to see the whole room, but he now had a pretty good idea of what was about to happen to him. Almost everything in the kitchen that he could see had been covered in the same blue plastic. To protect it from the splashes of blood and other body fluids. There would be no mess afterwards. And while it was happening to him there would be no screams. No cries of agony to alert the neighbours. All Drescher's screaming would echo only in the confines of his own skull.

Ute leaned over him and pushed her face into his. 'I wouldn't have been a good student for you, would I, Major Drescher? There is no forensic distance here, is there? But, you see, I don't care. I don't care about being caught. You will be all over me, Drescher. Your blood, your sweat, your fear . . . I am going to let it cover me. But first, Comrade Major, we're going to have a little slide show . . .'

9.

'Okay,' said Fabel, pouring Susanne another glass of wine. 'We've ruled out that we're dealing with an Angel of Death/Mercy or a Black Widow. So that leaves us with her being a Revenge Killer or simply insane.'

'Insanity is out. Serial killers tend to have identity disorders but only a tiny percentage are clinically insane. And within serial killing there are the two personality types: higher IQ and organised or lower IQ and disorganised. This killer is highly organised. That suggests to me that she's smart and she's not mad.'

Fabel set his glass back on the table. 'Revenge?'

'The original Angel killings in the nineties had revenge all over them. In its most abstract form, I mean. The castration thing was a rather unsubtle way of declaring that she was emasculating abusers. Revenge Killers are most often women who kill a series of individuals because they perceive those individuals to have victimised them in the past. This could be real victimisation – revenge for earlier abuse – or it can be that revenge is exacted on a *type* of person who is targeted by association.'

'But there was no connection between any of the victims. Their paths never crossed and they were picked at random.'

'No, they weren't. They were targeted, Jan, because they were users of prostitutes. Just like the victims of Aileen Wuornos in the USA around the same time. Wuornos had been abused as a child and then as a prostitute. She projected her experience on every man who used prostitutes and saw them as potential abusers. She killed them in revenge for what she had gone through at the hands of men like them.'

'But that only fits with the first series of murders in the nineties. There's no symbolic castration this time round.'

'Exactly,' Susanne said emphatically. 'Castration was the signature for each murder. A fundamental element. If you're dealing with a copycat, why has she dropped this central motif?'

'I know what you mean,' said Fabel. 'That's been bothering me. The answer I've come up with is that it's too messy. And takes up too much time.'

'But if she is the original Angel, or if she's a true copycat, she would feel – I don't know – unfulfilled if she didn't emulate the ritual of the original killings.'

'Okay,' said Fabel. 'So what you're saying is that we had a revenge killer the first time round and now we've got someone pretending to be a copycat?'

'There's something else that bothers me. Women are in the main less violent than men, agreed?'

'Agreed.'

'That is reflected across all aspects of behaviour, including, ironically, serial killers. Less than fifteen per cent of all violent crime is committed by women. And only one in six serial killers is a woman. Of those, the vast majority use non-violent means – poisoning, more than anything else. And if they do use violence, then it tends to be smothering or strangulation. Wuornos, of course, used a gun. But the point is they don't tend to slash, stab or bludgeon victims to death, which male serial killers do. Both the murders in the late nineties and the recent killings are extremely violent and bloody.'

'And also highly efficient,' said Fabel.

'The efficiency fits the pattern. The violence doesn't.'

'I had a call from Ulrich Wagner, the guy at the BKA who's helping me coordinate the setting-up of the Super Murder Commission thing. He told me that a woman has escaped from the secure state mental hospital in Mecklenburg. I've listed her officially as a possible for these murders. Her escape and her activities before being committed were those of a highly organised killer. On top of which she belongs to the fourth group of female serials. She's insane. And that means all bets are off. Oh, by the way, she castrated three victims.'

'That makes her a fit for the first series of murders. Not this.'

'Exactly. And she was confined to the hospital for the whole duration of the first series.'

'I can see why she may be a front runner. But there's still something about the violence of these attacks that doesn't fit with a female serial.'

'So what are you saying? That we're looking for a man dressed as a woman?'

'No, Jan,' said Susanne. 'I'm not saying this isn't a woman.

But has it never occurred to you that we might not be dealing with a serial killer at all?'

'As a matter of fact it has,' said Fabel. He contemplated his wine, swirling it in the glass. 'This doesn't make any sense, I know, but bear with me . . . You know Jens Jespersen's death?'

'Of course – that's the whole reason why Karin Vestergaard is here, isn't it?'

'Quite. Well, I have this feeling that his death is in some way connected with all this.'

'But there's no similarity, surely . . .'

'I've been a policeman for a long time, Susanne, and one thing that I've learned to be suspicious about is coincidences. Wherever I see a coincidence, there tends to be a connection. And I find it one hell of a huge coincidence that Jespersen was down here looking for a female killer and we just happen to have one running around St Pauli.'

'But we're talking about two completely different types of killer.'

'Are we?' said Fabel. 'Karin Vestergaard said that before she and Jespersen busted Goran Vujačić six years ago he talked about this contract killer called the Valkyrie. He said she had been very effective at taking out her targets. She made some look like accidents, others like suicides or natural causes. What if Jake Westland and Armin Lensch weren't victims of the Angel of St Pauli or the Angel Part Two . . .'

'What? They were victims of a contract killer? Then why all the symbolism? Why did she tell Westland she was the Angel?'

'Think about it. That's exactly what she did – she told him to tell us. She injured him to exactly the right degree for him to deliver his message before he died. It doesn't sound like an amateur, does it?'

'So you think we've got someone hiding in plain sight?'

'I think it's a possibility. The *Angel* is maybe really the *Valkyrie*. She wants us to believe she is killing at random.'

Susanne was lost in thought for a moment. 'There is something else that's been bothering me . . .' she said eventually. 'And it confuses things even more. As you know, one other thing that differentiates male and female serial killers is the duration of their activities. Male serials, on average, are active for less than five years. Sometimes for only a matter of months. Female serial killers are active over a much longer period. Ten, fifteen years. Longer, maybe. It doesn't fit with the first spate of killings.'

'You're saying those killings are suspect, too?'

'Yes. But I'm not suggesting it's the same killer. Yet another massive difference between male and female serial killers is the motive. Of the four kinds we discussed, the profit motive is by far the most common. So, if you're right and these recent killings are the work of a professional contract killer, whether she's a serial killer or not is simply a matter of semantics.'

10.

Turning the shower-tap selector to cold, she let the chill water run over skin that protested by bristling into goose bumps. Sylvie Achtenhagen stood in the shower, arms braced against the wall, palms flat against the wet porcelain tiles. Her body was firm and youthful, and she knew it would remain so for some time to come, but, at thirty-nine, she was also aware that time was slowly and insidiously turning up the pressure on her. Where would she be in ten years' time? By then, she would be competing with younger women. She would always be looking over her shoulder. Watching for someone taking away everything that she had worked so hard to build. Someone like her.

Someone who would make the news to find it.

When she could no longer bear the cold and she felt fully alert, Sylvie switched off the shower, wrapped the hotel bathrobe around her, went through to her hotel bedroom and twisted the top off a gin from the minibar. She was staying in one of the older Berlin hotels. It had a worn and weary grandness and the rooms had the old double doors: the inner door opening into the room, the outer opening into the hall. The windows too were the old, robust type. It all gave the hotel a feeling of belonging to an earlier age. And of being more than a little institutional.

After adding tonic to the gin Sylvie flopped down onto the vast bed and started to go through the information she had got from Wengert, the star-struck clerk at the BStU commission for Stasi files. Once she had eliminated the people who had died in the intervening period, she was left with a list of a dozen names, all connected in some way to Drescher. But, as Wengert had said, the connections could be coincidental. Drescher, or someone else with an interest, had made sure the main files were not to be found. Yet Sylvie knew that, somewhere among these dozen names, was the lead she was looking for. And, just maybe, one of them was Siegfried, the ex-Stasi scum who had sent her the photographs and Drescher's name. She took out her notebook and transferred the four most likely names to it. She had addresses for two, a partial address for another and just a town for the fourth. She would see how easy it would be to track them down. The easier they were to find, the less likely it would be that they were Siegfried.

She had just taken out her Baedeker to check some of the addresses when her cellphone rang.

'Hi, it's Ivonne. I've got more information on Norivon, the company the latest St Pauli victim worked for.'

'Anything interesting?'

'Not really. It couldn't be more boring, in fact. Norivon is an environmental waste-management company. They help companies comply with federal and EU regulations regarding waste. They make it go away, basically. But I got some new info through the contact I have in NeuHansa. She said that Armin Lensch, the guy who got wasted, was a grade-one arsehole and universally despised. Ambitious bastard, apparently, and didn't mind treading on toes to get ahead. He was responsible for dealing with companies within the NeuHansa Group and had a reputation as an ass-kisser when it came to management.'

'Anything else?'

'Oh yes – this is the good bit. His little excursion into the Reeperbahn was a regular occurrence. He would go in with a bunch of others from work – none of whom could stand him, by the way – and get completely pissed and even more obnoxious than usual. Anyway, the night he was killed, he had a run-in with the law. Two plain-clothes cops were arresting a woman in Silbersacktwiete and Lensch started to get lippy. So one of the cops kneed him in the balls. A woman cop.'

'Who were they arresting?'

'That I don't know, but they were Murder Commission.'

'What did the female cop look like? Shortish, pretty, dark hair?'

'That I don't know, either.'

'Anna Wolff . . .' said Sylvie, more to herself than to Ivonne.

'Sorry?'

'It doesn't matter. Good work, Ivonne. I've got some names and partial addresses for you. Can you see if you can locate them and get as much info as possible?'

'Sure,' said Ivonne. Sylvie ran through the information Wengert had given her.

'We're looking for a male Stasi officer, probably administrative staff stationed at the Lichtenberg headquarters.'

'Okay,' said Ivonne. 'There was something else I meant to tell you . . . nope, it's gone.'

'Phone back if you remember.'

Sylvie hung up and was tidying the file on the bed when her cellphone rang again.

'That was quick,' said Sylvie. 'You remembered what it was?'

'I hope you're settled into your hotel, Sylvie.' As soon as she heard the breathless voice she knew it was Siegfried.

'What makes you think I'm in a hotel?' she asked.

'Now you're just being stupid. And you're not a stupid woman. Still on the trail of the big story? I suppose you think that you have my name now . . . that you can track me down and get what you want without paying? Oh yes, I know all about your chat with Herr Wengert.'

'You Stasi scum really still have your tentacles everywhere, don't you?'

'There is no Stasi any more, Sylvie. And I resent being called scum. We did what we did because we believed in it. We believed in equality and freedom from poverty and exploitation. And because of that we're now compared with the Nazis. So yes, some of us work together for self-protection.' He had a sudden fit of coughing. 'Anyway, I'm not interested in justifying myself to you. Especially to you. Have you got my money?'

'Do you think I can just conjure up quarter of a million euros based on three photographs and the name of somebody who doesn't exist?'

'Who doesn't seem to exist . . . Drescher and these girls were involved in an operation so secret and so ambitious that every effort was made to keep it hidden even from some of the command structure inside the MfS. Anyway, I thought I'd give you a little more, on account. Simply to prove that I really do have the information I say I have. Take a look under your pillow.'

Sylvie reached under the pillows, sliding her arm along until her hand found something. It was a large brown envelope.

'How did you . . . ?'

'Now, Sylvie,' the husky voice interrupted her. 'Don't be so naive. We were trained to get in and out of private spaces without detection. I'll be in touch.'

The line went dead. Sylvie checked her phone to try to retrieve the number, but it had been withheld.

She opened the envelope. Inside was a magazine and four sheets of copy paper. Examining the magazine first, Sylvie saw it was called *Muliebritas*, and from what she could see was some kind of feminist title. She flicked through it quickly to see if there was anything stuffed into it, or if Siegfried had made any markings on the pages. Nothing. She would have to take time later to study it carefully. In the meantime, the only thing that was of interest to her was that *Muliebritas* was published by Brønsted Publishing, part of the NeuHansa Group.

She turned her attention to the four sheets of paper. Three of them each had one of the images that Siegfried had sent her in the email. Except, this time, there was a name beneath each face: Margarethe Paulus, Liane Kayser, Anke Wollner. The fourth sheet again had the name Georg Drescher, but this time it too was accompanied by an image: a man of about forty to forty-five. He had a strong, handsome face, with deep furrows in his cheeks and creases at his eyes, as if his had been a face accustomed to smiling. His amiable countenance was at odds with the uniform lapel flashes that indicated he was an officer of the MfS. Unlike the other photographs, his picture was in black and white and it was difficult to tell whether his hair was blond or greying. Given that twenty years had elapsed since anyone had worn a Stasi uniform, Sylvie tried to age him in her mind.

She looked at the pictures of the young women again. They were all pretty but gazed blankly and emotionlessly at the camera. Sylvie was again drawn to the girl with the so terribly empty eyes.

Liane Kayser. Her name was Liane Kayser.

11.

Ute Cranz dragged Drescher further into the kitchen. He saw her hover over him, a scalpel in her hand. He felt sick and suddenly thought what a relief it would be to throw up. He guessed the muscle relaxant had eliminated his gag reflex and he would die choking on his own vomit. Without coughing. Without a struggle. At least it would be better than whatever Ute Cranz had planned for him. She pulled at his clothes and he saw the scalpel slice downwards. But he didn't feel its contact: she was cutting through his clothes, tugging the remnants clear of his body. He was naked now and felt cold, probably more from fear than from the temperature of her apartment.

She lifted up the plastic sheeting and slid something behind his head and shoulders so that he was in a semi-sitting position. She sat a bed table across his leaden legs and placed a large laptop computer on it, the screen facing him and almost completely filling his field of vision. She hit a key and the screen filled with a photograph: lurid colours. Blood everywhere. A woman's body lay naked, the head and face hidden from view, jammed between a gore-sodden bed and a blood-streaked wall.

'This is what men do to women. Look at this. Do you see?' Ute pressed the key again. Another scene: this time a dead woman lay semi-clothed in some bushes, a ligature around her neck. 'Do you see?' Another scene-of-crime photograph. 'Do you see?'

She clicked on a command and the screen automatically switched from one scene to the next. Sickening images of murder. Rape. Violent pornographic images of women being abused. Female faces twisted in fear.

'This is what men do to women. What men have always done to women. Men like you.' Ute let the images run for a few more seconds, then she closed the lid and lifted the computer and tray away. Then she squatted beside Drescher and whispered into his ear. 'Women are forced to live in fear. All over the world. Every day. Real fear. Real fear like the fear you're feeling right now. I know you are afraid, Drescher. I know you're very afraid. But still you're asking yourself "Why? Why is she doing this?"' She held a photograph up for him to see. 'Do you know who that is? It's my sister. Margarethe. She's dead. She killed herself. When you had finished with her she went mad and they locked her up. Then she killed herself. The staff at the hospital she was in thought they had taken every precaution to prevent her committing suicide, but when you've been trained to kill others, to kill in so many ways, then it's easy for you to kill yourself. You don't need much in the way of means or opportunity.'

Drescher stared at the photograph and listened, because there was nothing else he could do except stare and listen. The face in the photograph. He knew it. He remembered it. And what terrified him was that Ute Cranz didn't seem to realise whose face, without the make-up, without the change of hair colour, it really was. And all the time his heart pounded within the cage of his locked body.

'I've hunted you for fourteen years. Fourteen years of preparing for this moment. I promised my sister, promised Margarethe, that I would make it right. Well, I will. And I will take my time. Enjoy every moment. Do you remember when you taught your girls about blood supply? How you could use it to quicken or delay death? Remember how you told them about execution by saw in the Middle Ages? The victim was hung upside down and sawn in half, from the groin to the neck. Because they were hanging upside down, the brain stayed supplied with blood and the victim was conscious through the whole thing.' She stood up and kicked away whatever had been supporting his head and neck. His head thudded against the floor and pain stabbed through it. She stood astride his body now and looked down at him. 'You drove my sister insane. You drove her to her death. I am going to drive you mad. You are going to die, but before you die you will be in so much pain that you will lose your mind.'

He looked up at her and thought how beautiful she was. How terribly beautiful.

Chapter Five

It had been a long time since Fabel had had a dream like it. He had been plagued by nightmares throughout his life as a murder detective: the dead would visit him in the night. The victims whose murders he had not been able to solve would glare accusingly at him, holding their wounds out for him to see. The dreams had been one of the reasons he had seriously, a year and a half before, considered leaving the police for good. Then, after he'd made his decision to stay on in the Murder Commission, the dreams had stopped.

But this dream was different from the others.

He stood at the centre of a vast yard enclosed by barbed-wire fences and with a row of low wooden huts at one distant end. He didn't need a sign or a motto above the gates to know where he was. He was German: the symbolism was burned deep into his consciousness. There was no one else in the yard. There were no sounds from the huts. Some dust was stirred from the brushed earth by a soundless wind. He turned slowly: a full 360 degrees.

She was there, standing in front of him.

'You are looking for me?' asked Irma Grese. She was young – only nineteen or twenty – short and stocky, dressed in a shapeless grey dress. She wore the jackboots he had read she habitually wore when tormenting prisoners. She had hard, broad, almost masculine features and a thin-lipped mouth turned down at the corners. Her blonde hair was brushed back from a face that seemed to be half forehead.

'No,' said Fabel, distracted by the rope burn on her throat and neck. 'I'm not looking for you. I'm looking for someone like you.'

'If she is like me,' said Grese, 'then someone made her like me. Do you understand that?' The broad brow furrowed. It was clearly important to her that he understood. 'Someone made her like me.'

'I understand,' he said.

Grese looked Fabel up and down. 'Are you frightened of me?'

'No, I'm not frightened of you. I despise you,' he said. 'I hate everything about you and everything you did. I loathe you most of all because you make me glad they hanged you.'

'No, you are frightened of me. Deep down, all men are frightened of women. You fear me because you fear all women. You are afraid that something like me burns deep inside every woman.'

'That's not true,' said Fabel. 'Your gender has nothing to do with it. You and all the others like you were freaks. Ordinary, dull, nobodies. But freaks. You were waiting for someone to open your cages and let your freakishness escape.'

'We come out of our cages for you, Jan. Don't we?' For a moment Fabel thought he was looking at Christa Eisel, then Viola Dahlke, the housewife they had arrested in St Pauli, but she became Irma Grese again. 'We've been your life for twenty years.'

Suddenly, without moving, without taking a step, Grese was nearer. Her face close to his, looking up at him. She screamed, shrill and inhuman, her eyes wild and her dark eyebrows arching on the too big forehead under the blonde hair. She was, at the one time, terrifying and comical. Her right arm shot up above them and Fabel saw the cellophane whip flash in the pale sunlight.

He woke up.

Fabel turned to make sure Susanne was still asleep. He didn't want her to know he had had another bad dream. It had been so long since the last. Susanne was his lover and as such she had begged him to leave the police to make the dreams stop; but she was also a psychologist, and her concern had always been professionally informed. It wasn't the dreams themselves that worried her, she had explained, it was the hidden turmoil that had caused them. Renate had never worried about the dreams. Renate had never really worried about him.

He got up, went through to the kitchen and made himself a cup of tea. It still took him a while to find things in the new apartment: in his head, especially in the small hours of the morning, he was still living in his Pöseldorf flat.

The phone rang. Looking at his watch, Fabel saw it was five-forty in the morning.

'This had better be good,' he said into the phone.

'It is . . .' It was Glasmacher, one of the Murder Commission team. 'I'm just around the corner from you in Altona. We've got her, *Chef* – we've got the Angel.'

2.

The apartment block had been sealed off and barriers set up in the street fifty metres on either side of the entrance, but the media throng had yet to materialise. There hadn't been time for word to get out. It only took Fabel ten minutes to get to the scene from his own flat and he parked at the barrier, showing his ID to the uniformed officers guarding the location.

A tall pale-complexioned blond man of about thirty, wearing a brown leather jacket and a muffler at his throat, stood waiting for Fabel at the entrance to the apartment block. He sniffed as Fabel approached and Fabel noticed his nose was tinted red-pink.

'You should be in bed, Thomas,' Fabel said.

'I wish I had called in sick. If I hadn't been on call I wouldn't have seen this.' Glasmacher indicated the apartment building with a nod of his head.'

'Bad?'

'Oh yeah . . . One of the worst I've seen. The victim's been tortured for hours. By the way, I've called in a few extra bodies. Dirk Hechtner's on his way over, too.'

'You said we've got the Angel?'

'The m.o. has similarities to both the recent killings and the older ones. Whatever this woman's mission was, it's clearly over. When she was finished, she dialled 110 and said she'd killed this guy and she wanted to "come in".'

'Who's the vic?'

Glasmacher pulled his notebook out of the pocket of his leather jacket, and with it a bundle of used paper tissues. 'Sorry, *Chef* . . . Robert Gerdes, sixty-three, a retired teacher from Flensburg, in Schleswig-Holstein. He's been living in Hamburg for fifteen years. His apartment is the penthouse and he was murdered in the flat below, rented by the woman who claims to have done it.'

Fabel looked up at the apartment building. 'The penthouse, you say? His schoolteacher's pension went a long way. What's the woman's name?'

'Ute Cranz. She's just moved in, apparently. I've got a uniformed unit to take her into the Presidium.'

There was the sound of approaching sirens and two unmarked cars pulled up at the barrier, behind Fabel's BMW. Fabel made a frantic gesture with his hand across his throat and the sirens were killed. Anna Wolff and Werner Meyer emerged from one car while Dirk Hechtner and Henk Hermann got out of the other.

'For God's sake,' said Fabel as they approached. 'We've got no press here yet. Let's keep this as low-key as blocking a street off in the middle of the night can be.'

'Sorry, *Chef*,' said Anna. 'To be honest, it was one of the main attractions of the job for me. If I don't get to toot my siren I'd just as well be a taxi driver.'

'No one would take your cab with all that farting,' muttered Werner.

'Listen, Dick *und* Doof,' said Fabel, unsmiling. 'When you've quite finished the comedy act, I'd like to go in and view the locus.'

'Sorry, *Chef*,' said Anna as unrepentantly as she could manage.

'There's something else you should know,' said Glasmacher. 'The perpetrator was making wild claims about the victim. She's clearly as mad as a hatter. She said he was living under a false name and an invented backstory and that he was really one of the Stasi's top people. She claims he ruined her sister's life.'

'Stasi?' Fabel felt as if someone had passed a faint electric current through his spine. 'She said he was ex-Stasi? Did she say what his real name was?'

Again Glasmacher checked his notebook. 'Yeah . . . she said he was an HVA major called Georg Drescher.'

Someone turned up the current in Fabel's spine.

'Anna, Werner – you come with me,' he said determinedly. 'Thomas, you get back to the Presidium and write up your report. Then get off home and rest up. I'm going to need you fit over the next few days. Dirk, Henk – I want you to phone *Politidirektør* Karin Vestergaard and tell her you're on your way to her hotel to pick her up and bring her into the Presidium. No, wait – bring her here.'

As Fabel moved towards the door, Glasmacher placed his gloved hand on Fabel's arm to check him.

'Brace yourself, *Chef* – I mean it about this one. When you see what she's done to this guy . . .'

Holger Brauner asked Fabel and his team to wait a few minutes before entering the scene. He also insisted that instead of just

the usual overshoes and latex gloves, they should all don full
forensic suits and masks.

'There's a lot of body fluids in there,' he explained. 'We've
got a lot of processing to do. I know you are all experienced
murder detectives and so on, but I have to request that if
you think you're going to throw up you get out of the flat
as soon as possible.'

'That bad?' asked Fabel.

'It's that bad, Jan,' said Brauner.

Fabel couldn't help noticing how stylish and spacious
the apartment was. The lounge and dining room were open-
plan, with a large sliding window that opened out onto a
small terrace. The furniture was expensive-looking and
Fabel guessed this had been a furnished let. One of Brauner's
bunny-suited team was taking photographs of the dining
table: it had been set for two and there were still used
plates and wine glasses on it. A numbered tent card sat
on the floor beside the sofa, next to where a brandy
glass had shattered, spilling its contents on the polished
beechwood.

Fabel took Glasmacher's advice and braced himself
emotionally as he and the others entered the kitchen.

He found that he could not tear his eyes away from it.
It was as if his brain was trying to make sense of what it
was he was looking at; or more as if his brain was trying
to deny what he was looking at had been human. It lay
on heavy-duty blue plastic sheeting over the kitchen
worktop. The head had been propped up and the round
white orbs of the lidless eyes stared at Fabel. The sheeting
extended across the floor and sheets of it had been duct-
taped to the wall. There were splashes of blood everywhere,
but around the body and on the floor immediately next to
the worktop the blood was mop-smeared. She had cleaned
up as she had worked.

Behind him, Fabel could hear Anna breathing heavily

through her forensic mask. Werner muttered something obscene. Holger Brauner eased past the statues of Anna and Werner and stood next to Fabel.

'I've never seen anything like it, Jan,' he said. 'She has an amazing knowledge of human anatomy. See the tourniquets around the upper thighs? She used those to restrict blood flow while she worked on the legs. And as you can see from the exposed bone, she has cut through muscle tissue while avoiding the femoral artery. Similarly she used a surgical clamp on his groin to stop him bleeding out from the castration.'

Fabel heard Anna's heavy breathing turn to gasps and she rushed out of the kitchen.

'There is absolutely no doubt whatsoever about premeditation, Jan,' said Brauner. 'She laid everything out in advance, sheeted up the room, immobilised the victim somehow . . . She even had a saline solution for his eyes, once she had removed his eyelids. It's obvious it was important to her that he saw her working on him. Poor bastard.'

'How long do you think it would have taken him to die?'

'The truth? I honestly don't know. Herr Doctor Möller will be able to give you an indication after the autopsy. But my guess is that he was maybe alive for up to an hour of this abuse. How much of that he was conscious for is anyone's guess . . .' Brauner pointed to a metal tray next to the body. 'That's full of broken phials. From the smell I'd say they were capsules of ammonia carbonate. She obviously broke them under his nose to rouse him when he passed out from the pain.'

Anna came back into the kitchen, keeping her head down and not looking up from the floor. 'Dirk and Henk are back, Chef. They've got the Dane with them.'

'Okay.' Fabel placed an arm around her shoulder and turned her away from the body. He looked into her face: above the surgical mask and framed by the elasticated hood of the forensics suit, she was very pale, her eyes red-rimmed. 'Are you all right, Anna?'

'As you know, not my strong point. But hey, never mind – you'll have me issuing parking tickets soon.'

'That's enough, Anna,' said Fabel, but without anger. He could see she was in a state. 'You head back to the Commission and go through what Thomas has got before he heads home. Werner – you go with her. I'm going to have a look upstairs at the victim's apartment.'

On the way out of the apartment Fabel dumped his forensic suit and mask at the door, but he retained the gloves and overshoes. He had just gone out onto the landing when he saw Karin Vestergaard coming up the stairwell with Dirk Hechtner and Henk Hermann.

'Your colleagues told me this might have something to do with Jens's death,' she said without preliminaries. Fabel saw the grim determination on her face and was reminded that Jespersen had been more than a colleague to her.

'Truth is I don't know yet, Karin. The killer called it in herself and we've got her down at the Presidium. She definitely could be our St Pauli killer. But the thing that is most interesting is the tale she's been spinning. We've got a male victim, sixty-three years old, a retired teacher from Flensburg called Robert Gerdes. But – and wait for this – the woman who tortured and killed him says that he is really a former high-ranking Stasi officer and that his name is Georg Drescher.'

For a moment, Vestergaard looked stunned. 'Can I see this victim?'

'Trust me, it's best not to. She really did a number on him and anyway you'd have to get all suited up. I sent for you because I'm going to have a look through the victim's apartment. He lived upstairs. I thought you might like to help. Maybe you'll pick up on something relevant to Jespersen.' Fabel turned to Hechtner and Hermann. 'I want you two to go through the killer's apartment – everything except the murder scene in the kitchen. Bag everything.' He turned back to Vestergaard. 'After we're through upstairs, I'd like you to listen in on my questioning of the suspect.'

'Lead on . . .' said Vestergaard grimly.

3.

The penthouse had been finished to the same quality and in the same style as the apartment below. It was slightly larger and better use had been made of the space available, but the main difference was the furnishings. Like its downstairs neighbour, the flat was ultra-modern and bright, but much of the furniture was traditional. Some looked like genuine antiques. Fabel thought of the man who had occupied this space and somehow couldn't connect it with the mass of bloody tissue lying on the kitchen counter downstairs.

'He's got some nice furniture,' said Vestergaard in an unusually conversational tone. 'Walnut, most of it. Some maple. I've seen this kind of stuff before. It's Hungarian art deco, a lot of it. Made in the nineteen-thirties. Some of the other pieces are French.'

Fabel looked at her questioningly.

'Hobby . . .' she said and he nodded. They walked slowly through the apartment. There was a lounge, a study, a bedroom and an open-plan kitchen and dining room. They stopped for a moment in the study.

'No sign of a struggle,' said Fabel. 'It doesn't look like he even had company recently. The whole party must have taken place downstairs. But I'll have Holger's forensics boys give the place a thorough going-over.'

Vestergaard picked up a sketch pad that had been lying on the desk. Fabel noticed that it was the same brand and size as the ones he used for laying out his thoughts during an investigation. Vestergaard flipped through it and gave a couple of small laughs. In response to Fabel's questioning look, she turned the open pad towards him.

'Whatever else he did,' said Vestergaard, 'he had a talent for caricatures. That's meant to be your illustrious Chancellor, Angela Merkel, isn't it?'

'Yes – you're right, he wasn't half bad.' Fabel grinned. 'I know Frau Merkel is keen to promote good international relationships, but I really don't think she would do *that* with Monsieur Sarkozy. And I don't think he's really quite that small.'

'I have to say he had expensive tastes . . .' Vestergaard put the drawing pad back down and examined a deco bronze on the desk: a stylised eagle perched on a walnut base. 'For a retired school teacher from Flensburg.'

'Exactly what I was thinking,' said Fabel. 'I think we should start here in the study. You take the desk, I'll go through the filing cabinets and the bookshelves.'

Three-quarters of an hour later they had examined every piece of correspondence, every bill, the victim's notebook and his desk diary.

'Either he had a very limited social life or a very secret one,' said Vestergaard. 'Even with official and household correspondence – there's nothing here other than the barest minimum of paperwork. No personal computer. This is either a life only half lived, or a cover. And from the look of the furniture and the quality of the selection in his wine rack, he was not a man of an ascetic disposition.'

Fabel wandered through to the lounge and looked around. 'So, Major Drescher, this is where you hid yourself.' He turned back to Vestergaard. 'I got on to the Federal Commissioner's office in Berlin to dig up his files. Nothing. Only the odd mention here and there. He did a good job of hiding himself and I thought we'd never find him. Now he's dropped right into our laps.'

'He's still hiding from us, Jan,' said Vestergaard, looking around the study.

Before heading back to the Presidium, Fabel asked Holger Brauner if his team could seal off the penthouse apartment and give it a good going-over once they were finished with the primary locus.

As he and Karin Vestergaard headed out of the apartment building and towards his BMW, Fabel noticed that the street had a completely different look to it in the daylight, even the winter daylight. He took a few deep breaths of the cold air. Over the years Fabel had found that after visiting a murder scene there was one aspect, one image, that haunted you for weeks afterwards. This time, every time he closed his eyes, it was the lidless stare of Drescher's corpse.

'You okay?' asked Vestergaard.

'Yeah . . . I'm fine.' Fabel sighed. 'Just another day in the meat factory.'

When they arrived at the Presidium, Fabel fetched coffee for them both and they sat in his office drinking it.

'We should take a break before questioning Cranz,' said Fabel. 'It's going to be a long haul.'

There was a knock on the door and Werner came in. Something about his face told Fabel that relaxation time was over.

'This is all seriously messed up, Jan,' he said, not bothering to switch to English for Vestergaard's sake.

'What is?'

'The woman we've got in custody rented the apartment under the name of Ute Cranz. But she claims her real name is Ute Paulus, and that she is the sister of Margarethe Paulus—'

'Hold on,' said Fabel, the weariness swept from his expression. 'The woman who escaped from the secure hospital in Mecklenburg?'

'The very same.'

'So Ute Paulus has taken up her sister's trade of knack-
ering male victims? It would certainly explain why Margarethe
has been able to stay out of sight, if she has had outside
help.'

'Ah, well . . . that's where it all gets very complicated.'
Werner gave a wry smile and rubbed the stubble on his scalp.
'I've been in touch with the state hospital in Mecklenburg
and I spoke to the chief psychiatrist there who's responsible
for Margarethe Paulus's case. It's a Dr Köpke. According to
Köpke, there is no Ute Paulus. No sister. Just Margarethe.'

Werner placed a printout of a file photograph on Fabel's
desk. 'That is Margarethe Paulus, taken a year before her
escape. I've had a look at the woman in custody. The hair
colour is different, but apart from that, if she's a sister she
would have to be a twin.'

'*Shit.*' Fabel turned to Vestergaard and explained everything that Werner had just said. 'What else did Köpke say?'
he asked, turning back to Werner.

'Two things. First, he needs to talk to you urgently. He
needs to know the identity of the victim and how he died.
Dr Köpke says that he might have information that will be
indispensable to us. He would also like to talk to any criminal psychiatrist or psychologist who sits in on or monitors
the interview – which he strongly recommends we do.'

'And the second?'

'That we use maximum security when dealing with
Margarethe Paulus. He said that she is probably the most
dangerous individual that he has ever dealt with.'

On the way down to the interview room, Karin Vestergaard
took a call on her cellphone. After a brief exchange in Danish
she paused to make a few notes in her notebook. Fabel waited
for her.

'That was my office in Copenhagen,' she said as they

continued along the corridor. 'The NCID in Norway have been doing some more digging into Jørgen Halvorsen's affairs. They have found a contact he had here in Hamburg. We can talk about it after you've interviewed this woman. Do you think she's the one who killed Jens?'

'I don't know. There seems to be a hell of a lot of coincidences going on and she fits perfectly as someone we should be looking at for all these killings, if it weren't for the simple fact that we know absolutely for certain that she was locked up in an asylum. There's no way she can be either our *Angel* or our *Valkyrie*.'

'But she was out when Jens was killed,' said Vestergaard.

'True. She's well worth a look for it. I'll establish her whereabouts at the time – if I can.' Fabel stopped their progress along the corridor by turning to her. 'Listen, Karin, this will just be our initial interview to establish basics. It won't take long. I'd like us to talk the whole thing through afterwards. There's another couple of deaths that have cropped up that are not, strictly speaking, being treated as murder. I just think there's so much going on that there's a chance we'll miss something.'

The woman who waited for them in the interview room looked nothing like a killer. Professional or serial. The forensics department had taken all her clothes for examination and she was now dressed in a shapeless disposable white overall. She was of slim build and was, Fabel couldn't help noticing, very attractive. She looked up at him with empty disinterest as he entered, as if she had no stake in what was happening and his presence had nothing to do with her. Fabel recognised her from the photograph sent from the Mecklenburg hospital. He went into the interview without Vestergaard, leaving her to join Werner and Anna in the adjoining room from where they could watch the interview on the monitor.

Fabel nodded to the uniformed officer who had been

watching over the prisoner, sat down opposite Paulus, laid his papers out on the metal desk and informed her of her rights.

'I want you to understand something, Margarethe,' he said. 'I will be interviewing you again later, with another officer, and we will have a psychologist in the room as well as a lawyer to represent your interests. We can talk about things in more detail then. In the meantime, I want you to simply confirm your name for me.'

'I am Ute Paulus. You called me Margarethe; I am not Margarethe Paulus. She is my sister.'

'But that's simply not true, Margarethe. There is no Ute Paulus. You have no sister. It's a matter of record.'

She laughed coldly. 'Records are falsified all the time. In the East people's records were changed or falsified all of the time. I am not Margarethe. I am Ute.'

'Who is this?' Fabel asked and slid a copy of the hospital photograph across the table to her.

'That is Margarethe.'

'That is you. Listen, there's no point in denying it. We have samples of your fingerprints and they match those of this patient.' He jabbed a forefinger at the picture on the table. 'Margarethe Paulus, thirty-eight years old, born in Zarrentin, north-west Mecklenburg. You have no sister, no brother and both your parents are dead. This is you. And you were committed to the Mecklenburg state secure hospital in May nineteen ninety-four.'

Paulus said nothing. Fabel drew a long breath.

'Why did you do what you did to Robert Gerdes?'

'His name wasn't Gerdes.' There was no anger in her voice. There was nothing in her voice. Or in her eyes as she spoke. 'His name was Georg Drescher and he was a major in the Stasi.'

'Why did you do what you did to him?'

'I thought you said we would only talk about this later,'

she said. She placed her hands on the metal surface. Her fingers were long and slim. He noticed how clean her fingernails were, and then remembered that Brauner's forensics team would have scraped beneath them for trace evidence. Fabel found it difficult to imagine those fingers committing the horrors he had witnessed in her flat.

'I want to go back,' she said.

'Go back where? To the apartment?'

'To the hospital.'

'How can you go back to the hospital if you're not a patient there?' asked Fabel. He pointed again to the photograph. 'This is the patient. Margarethe is the patient. You say you're not Margarethe.'

'That's where I see my sister. Where I talk to her. I visit her. Now I can visit her all the time.'

Fabel sighed and gathered up the papers. 'I think we really should wait until later.'

'I want to go back now,' she repeated, but there was no insistence in her voice. 'To the hospital.'

'I'm afraid you won't be going back for some time. You're going to have to stay with us for a while.' Fabel stood up.

'I want to go back. To the hospital.' Margarethe stood up too. Fabel held his hand out to stop her. 'You have to remain sitting, Margarethe. Stay here. The officer will take you back to your cell.'

Margarethe's hand seized Fabel's wrist and he was amazed at the strength in the slender fingers. He moved his other hand to free himself but was stunned by the blow she delivered to his forehead with the heel of her free hand. He heard the uniformed officer rush forward. Margarethe grabbed Fabel by the hair and rammed his face into the metal table as she used him for leverage and swung a high kick at the other policeman's head. Fabel heard the uniformed cop slam into the interview-room wall and gasp for breath. He felt her fingers probe under his arm to find his service SIG-Sauer automatic but the anti-snatch holster resisted her tugging. He thrust his weight against her and she fell onto the floor. Despite the adrenalin surging through his system, he noticed how gracefully she fell, rolled and sprang back to her feet. The other cop was pulling himself to his feet and he launched himself from the wall at her. It was a clumsy move and she dodged him easily, slashing him across the throat with the flat of her hand. Fabel made to draw his weapon and she leaped across the table at him, hitting him at chest height with her knee. His head slammed painfully against the wall and he heard his automatic clatter on the floor. The door next to him suddenly burst open and Werner, Anna and two uniformed officers rushed into the room.

'Get my gun!' yelled Fabel.

He pulled himself to his feet in time to see Margarethe slam a fist into Werner's face. Anna Wolff got behind her and wrapped an arm around her throat in a tight grip. Margarethe slammed her elbow into Anna's ribs but Anna didn't let go. Instead, she let herself drop, her weight pulling Margarethe to the floor. Werner and the other officers threw themselves onto her and, after a few seconds of desperate struggling, Margarethe was handcuffed.

'Yours, I believe . . .' Fabel looked up to see Karin Vestergaard staring down on him, his service automatic in her extended hand.

'Thanks,' said Fabel and allowed her to help him up. 'That went well, I thought . . .' He felt something trickle down his forehead and when he gingerly reached up to touch it, his fingertips were wet with blood.

Werner, Anna and the others hoisted Margarethe to her feet. She looked directly at Fabel and the look chilled him. There was no rage, no hatred, just the same emptiness in the eyes that he had noticed when he'd first entered the inter-view room. It was as if the intense violence that had just exploded there had simply never happened.

'Get her back to her cell,' said Fabel. 'And keep her restrained.' The uniforms ushered Margarethe, who didn't even seem to be breathing hard, from the room. Anna and Werner stayed behind. There was a trickle of blood from Werner's nostril.

'You should get that looked at,' said Vestergaard, nodding towards Fabel's head.

'I think I should . . .' said Fabel, taking the folded handkerchief that Vestergaard handed him and holding it to his head. 'You did well, Anna. She took some taking down.'

'A woman's touch. I thought it looked like you and Grandad here needed help.' Anna grinned knowingly at Werner. 'What with you having your asses kicked by a girl.'

'How's the uniform?' asked Fabel.

'He'll be fine,' said Werner, dabbing the bleeding nostril with the back of his hand. 'He's going to have one hell of a sore throat, that's for sure.'

'Get him to the hospital,' said Fabel. 'Any blow to the airway can be very dangerous and she knew what she was doing.' He leaned against the interview-room wall and drew a deep breath. 'Shit . . . she knew what she was doing.'

'I gather that's what Dr Köpke, the Chief Doctor from the Mecklenburg state hospital, wanted to tell you. He was on the phone again . . . when you were in there with psycho-girl.'

'I'll phone him,' said Fabel. 'But first, could someone get me some codeine and a plaster for my head . . .'

4.

'Where have you got her now?' The voice on the other end of the connection sounded genuinely anxious.

'Safely back in her cell, Herr Doctor,' said Fabel. 'Where she can do no harm.'

'I wouldn't count on it,' said Köpke. He had a deep voice.

A little scratchy. Fabel heard a metallic click and a crackle over the connection. A cigarette being lit. A medical man should know better, thought Fabel. 'I really did want to warn you before you tried to interview her.'

'I didn't get the message—' Fabel started to say, but Köpke cut him off.

'She's killed again?'

'Yes. A male victim. And she castrated him.'

'What was his name?' Köpke's tone was more demand than question.

'I can't—'

'Was the victim called Georg Drescher? Or did Margarethe claim he was Georg Drescher?'

'I can't confirm or deny the identity of the victim, you should know that.'

'Look, Herr Principal Commissar, you and I can play games and more people can die, or we can be straight with each other and maybe save a few lives. What will it be?'

'What is it you have to tell me, Dr Köpke?'

'First of all, you need to make sure that Margarethe is confined with maximum security.' There was the sound of a blown-out breath and Fabel imagined the cigarette smoke billowing around the unseen psychiatrist. 'You should have her watched by no fewer than two, ideally three, guards. Secondly, do what you can to make your demands sound like requests. She will respond with maximum hostility to any suggestion that you are commanding her to follow your will. And, trust me, Herr Chief Commissar, that hostility will be very professionally directed.'

'I've already got the picture,' said Fabel, involuntarily touching the gauze taped to his forehead.

'Ah . . .' Again there was the sound of a cigarette being drawn upon, followed by a hasty exhalation. 'I thought you might. I also need you to get a court order over to me as soon as possible so that I can legally transfer the records of

Margarethe Paulus's treatment to you. I have tapes and video of my sessions with her and, trust me, you will want to hear all of them.'

'In the meantime,' said Fabel, 'how about a little unofficial summary?'

'Margarethe Paulus was a child of the GDR,' said Köpke. 'Her parents, from what I could gather, were bohemian, free-thinker types who fell foul of the authorities. They ended up in prison and both died of cancer before reunification. Margarethe was taken into care by the state. It's what she says happened to her afterwards that should interest you. Before I go any further, I have to tell you a little about her medical history. When she was still in the care of the state orphanage she started to have severe headaches. She would have been about eight at the time. Margarethe was admitted to hospital and it was suspected that she was suffering from a brain tumour. The operation revealed a growth in her brain which was subsequently declared benign, but the nature of the tumour is in some doubt – it was a reasonably large teratoma that could have been interpreted as *fetus in fetu*.'

'I'm sorry . . .' Fabel sounded more irritated than apologetic. 'You're going to have to explain.'

'A teratoma is a tumour that is composed of all kinds of tissue. There can be hair, teeth, eye tissue in it. Sometimes it can have limbs – a hand or a foot, for example. In rare examples, a child is born with what appears to be a twin inside it. *Fetus in fetu*. Medical opinion is divided on whether these are actual foetuses that have formed within their twin, instead of alongside it, or if they are simply a more complex form of teratoma. Whatever they are, they are incapable of independent life. What was removed from Margarethe's brain had the appearance of a rudimentary foetus. Somehow, maybe later after reading up on the subject, she decided that she had had a sister living inside her.'

'And she still believes that?'

'We learned to handle Margarethe and – with appropriate medication and management – she was able to live amongst the general hospital population. I'll come back to why the medication and handling were so important, although I think you've experienced the reason first-hand. Anyway, Margarethe would sit over by the window for hours on end, talking to no one except her own reflection.'

'Her sister,' Fabel sighed.

'That's what we established in therapy, yes. But this is where I get to the most important bit. The tumour that was removed was benign, but it was large. When you take something like that out of someone's brain things change. The chemistry changes; intracranial pressure alters and parts of the brain that have been constricted are relieved and have room to expand, particularly if the patient is a child. In Margarethe's case, her personality changed. She had been a normal, emotional child of average ability. After the operation, she became distant, remote. But her academic and sporting ability improved radically. And that brings me back to the claims she has made.'

'Which were?'

'You have to remember that here in the East our post-war experience was very different. There are things that went on here that you couldn't imagine. That we still have problems accepting. But what Margarethe told us was so incredible, so fantastic, that we put it down to schizoid paranoia. But then, as time went on, I began to have doubts. I mean, some patients have the most detailed and elaborate paranoias, but this was just *too* elaborate. Part of my job is to try to expose the falsehood of a paranoid delusion, to find a crack and use logic to lever it open so that the patient themselves, with the aid of the right medication, can see their fantasy for what it is.'

'But there were no cracks in Margarethe's story.'

'None. I did a little research, too. At the Federal Commission for Stasi files. I discovered that many of the names she had given me were indeed real former Stasi people. But she had first given me this information at a time when the files were still being collated and reassembled.'

'So if she was telling the truth . . .'

'It still didn't change the fact that she was very seriously disturbed. Or that she had murdered someone. The other thing was that there was this massive rage and hunger for revenge burning deep inside her. And most of it was directed at Georg Drescher. You see, Herr Fabel, Margarethe claims she was one of three young women selected by the Stasi and trained by Major Georg Drescher.'

'Trained as what?'

'Assassins. She claimed that she and her friends were trained to use a whole variety of methods to take human life, as well as concealment, espionage techniques – even how to seduce their victims. She said they were given code names. They were called the Valkyries.'

Walking into the Murder Commission incident room, Fabel felt like he was an unprepared act walking into the spotlight, centre stage. There were always times like this during an investigation – a development, a breakthrough, or another murder – when suddenly there was an electric tension in the air and the entire team looked on him expectantly. The truth was his head hurt, he was tired and felt sick, and he was struggling to deal with the enormity of what he had just heard from Margarethe's psychiatrist.

Anna handed him a coffee and a couple of codeine. 'You realise the mistake you made,' she said in a low voice.

'I'm sure you're about to tell me.' Fabel flipped the tablets from his palm into his mouth and washed them down with too-hot coffee.

'You made a sexist judgement,' said Anna. 'And don't go off on one – I'm not saying you're a sexist. But what happened in there happened because you treated her differently because she was a female. You saw what she did to that guy in her apartment. If she had been a male suspect she would have been handcuffed to the restraint on the table.'

'I'll bear it in mind in the future,' Fabel said and turned his attention to the rest of the room. 'You've all heard that we have had a breakthrough. Well, I don't know how much of a breakthrough we've had. Another man is dead. Tortured and killed as an act of revenge. It may well be that Margarethe Paulus is also responsible for the murders in the St Pauli district, as well as that of the Danish detective, Jens Jespersen.' Fabel took another sip of coffee and sat on the corner of the desk nearest the front. 'We retrieved a single blonde hair from the Westland murder scene, which we had good reason to believe belonged to the killer. I have to tell you before we go any further that we don't have a DNA match with the woman we have in custody.'

'That doesn't mean it wasn't her,' said Werner. 'It could equally prove that the hair didn't belong to the killer.'

'Could be,' said Fabel. He was distracted by the arrival of Dirk Hechtner and Henk Hermann 'I didn't expect to see you back so quickly,' said Fabel. 'I told you to bag all the suspect's stuff.'

'We did,' said Hechtner. 'There wasn't much to bag. She had three changes of clothes, one dressy, one businessy, one casual. We've handed what looks like a surgical kit over to forensics. From what we could see she had taken the tools she needed from the kit through to the kitchen.'

'What else did you find?' asked Fabel.

'Four thousand euros in cash,' said Henk Hermann. 'A gun—'

'What kind of gun?' asked Fabel.

'Nothing that I've seen before,' said Henk Hermann. 'It looked a bit like an old PPK, but it was clearly not that old and it had "Made in Croatia" stamped on the side. So we

ran it through the computer. Apparently it's . . .' Henk referred
to his notebook '. . . a PHP MV-9. It was developed by the
Croatians in the early nineties, during the Independence War.
Apparently, amongst gun freaks it's a bit of a collector's item.
A rarity. There was also this really weird glove-knife thing . . .
really odd. It was a leather strap that fastened around your
hand and wrist, with a hidden metal plate that fitted in your
palm and a short curved blade that stuck out of the bottom.
We're guessing it was some kind of weapon rather than a
tool.'

'Where is it now?' asked Fabel.

'We gave it to forensics for testing,' said Dirk Hechtner. 'If
that blade has been used as a weapon, then I'll bet a week's
pay we'll get blood out of the leather bit.'

'Good,' said Fabel. 'Anything else?'

'A make-up kit,' said Dirk. 'It had several shades of hair
dye, different types of make-up – not ordinary women's
cosmetics, it was stuff you could use to alter your appearance. Other stuff too . . . it took us a while to work out what
some of it was for. Cheek prosthetics to change the shape of
her face, that kind of thing. We also found a folder with
paperwork to support her identity as Ute Cranz.'

'Wait a minute,' Anna said. 'Margarethe Paulus was an
escaped loony on the run from a mental hospital where she'd
spent the last fifteen years. Where the hell did she get all
these resources?'

'Now that,' said Fabel, 'is a very good point. It's pretty
obvious that she had outside help. Very professional outside
help. Let's go back to what we've found out. The victim is
a Robert Gerdes, except he probably isn't. It looks pretty
certain that he was Major Georg Drescher, a former major
in the HVA wing of the East German Stasi. What we know
so far is that Drescher was the control for three highly trained
female agents, specifically trained as assassins. It kind of looks
like Drescher embraced the free-market economy with relish

and set up his own little Murder Incorporated, right here in the Free and Hanseatic City. It is perfectly safe to assume that Margarethe Paulus, while she may be a former protégée of Drescher, was not one of his active hit women. Mainly because, as Anna pointed out, she was locked up in a Mecklenburg secure hospital.' He took a deep breath. 'What we have here is the suggestion that there is a female contract killer – one of the world's most successful – operating out of Hamburg. And she's called, supposedly, the Valkyrie. Now we have an ex-Stasi officer killed by one of the three women he was supposed to have trained. And these female political assassins also went by the name Valkyrie. Maybe Drescher was the outside help. For argument's sake, let's accept he has one or both of the other Valkyries operating under his command, but let's say business is too good and he's turning work away. Maybe he wanted to expand the business and add another of his former protégées to his staff.'

'Isn't that unlikely?' asked Werner. 'Think about it: what you're talking about is a highly skilled and disciplined operation. You wouldn't take on a nutcase.'

'Maybe he thought she wasn't a nutcase when she was under his command. That he could control her. That he provided a context for her to function in.'

'Oh yeah,' snorted Anna, 'that'll be it. Every woman needs a man to complete her, after all.' Then, before Fabel could respond: 'I think you're way off, *Chef*. He couldn't have misjudged her that much – look what she did to him.'

'But look at the resources she had at her disposal within weeks of escaping from the hospital. If Drescher didn't do it, who set her up with everything she needed?' asked Fabel. When no one responded he moved on. 'What else have we got?'

'I chased up Theo Wangler,' said Anna, 'and I've got a still from the Reeperbahn CCTV of the fake taxi,' said Anna. 'I'm afraid it doesn't help much. They've done everything they could to enhance it, but it's worth nothing. The Merc had false plates and you can't see the face of the driver clearly enough for identification. You couldn't even really say whether it was a man or a woman at the wheel. But we've had more luck with the Hanseviertel. You were right – Jens Jespersen had lunch there. There are no cameras in the basement restaurant itself, but we picked up this . . .'

Anna handed Fabel a print of an image taken from the CCTV. Jespersen was standing next to the glass elevator in the central atrium, near the restaurant. Next to him was a woman with a mass of chaotic blonde hair. Her face was partly turned from the camera and detail in the enlarged image was fuzzy. But it was clear enough to establish that Jespersen and the woman were engaging each other in conversation.

'You get more than this?' he asked Anna.

'Nope. A few shots of her back, that's all. They went their separate ways: he went out onto Neuer Wall and she headed out onto Poststrasse. But that doesn't mean they didn't arrange to meet later. We've been able to work out a height for her, though, from the security-camera shots – roughly one seventy-three or -four centimetres tall, give or take heels.'

'Get someone down to the restaurant to—'

'Done it,' interrupted Anna. 'I've got someone to take a photograph of Jespersen and a copy of that.' She nodded towards the CCTV image. 'And talk to all of the staff who were on duty at the time. So far, nothing.'

'Okay,' said Fabel. 'We're going back to Drescher's apartment. This time we're going to take it apart. If these Valkyries are real, and we remove Margarethe Paulus from the equation, that leaves two more out there. And one of them, or maybe both, were working for Drescher. Now they are rudderless. It would appear we've had as many as two highly trained professional killers under our noses for years. Now they are out there on their own and maybe desperate. It's not an idea

I'm too comfortable with. What is it, Werner?' Fabel had noticed his deputy's thoughtful expression.

'What are we putting out to the press about the murder?' he asked. 'There weren't any outside the place when I left.'

'What's your point?' asked Fabel.

'If Gerdes is this Major Drescher, then he was a spy by training and by inclination.'

'So?'

'So I'm betting that if he was running a contract-killer business, then he would have run his assassins as a spy cell. Strictly need-to-know basis. They will have had a close bond, but I'll bet that they *never* came anywhere near his apartment.'

'I get it,' said Anna, suddenly animated. 'So a murder in that apartment block or street won't really mean anything to the Valkyrie unless the name Gerdes or Drescher is associated with it.'

'Exactly,' said Werner. 'I'll bet she doesn't even know the name Gerdes.' He turned to Fabel. 'What if we "lose" the story, or disguise it as something else for a while? That means the Valkyrie won't know he's dead. Then, if we can work out the mechanism for contacting her – or them, if there are two – we can nail them.'

Fabel rubbed his chin thoughtfully and was reminded by the stubble rasping under his fingertips that he hadn't had a chance to shave before rushing out to the Drescher murder scene. And that was how he saw it now: the *Drescher* murder scene.

'It's an idea . . .' he said. 'Sylvie Achtenhagen wasn't outside the flat, so that would suggest that no one is making the connection yet. I'll talk to the press department, see if they can fudge for a while . . . Okay, Werner – let's run with the idea. The first thing we have to do is find out how Drescher contacted the Valkyrie. Let's take his place apart.'

'I've never seen you on the telly,' said the old woman as she set the tray with coffee and baked biscuits on the table.

'It's a satellite station.' Sylvie smiled as she took the cup handed to her. The coffee had a caramelly aftertaste. *Rondo Melange*. 'I see you don't have satellite. Our station covers most of the North. You really should have satellite. Don't you watch a lot of TV?'

'Oh yes – I have the TV on all day. Company, you see. And I would love to have satellite, but I can't afford it.' The old woman sat down. 'Who is it you said you were looking for?'

Sylvie estimated that the woman wasn't really that old. Maybe seventy. But, like many women of that age, she had given up: she was slightly overweight and saggy, and her pale skin looked rough, with a reddened eczematous disc to the right of her chin.

'You worked for the MfS? Back then, in the old days, Frau Schneeg?' Sylvie asked.

'Oh yes . . .' Frau Schneeg raised her hands and emptied her expression of anything that could be interpreted as guile. 'But I wasn't anything to do with all that kind of thing. You know, the snooping and stuff. I was just a filing clerk.'

'I understand that, Frau Schneeg.' Sylvie smiled. 'Naturally. But you *were* involved in the personnel records department.'

'Yes – pensions, staff allowances . . .'

'Exactly. I was wondering if you could tell me if you knew any of these people.' Sylvie laid the sheet out on the table, next to the embroidered doilies and the coffee and biscuits.

'I really don't want to get involved. You know what I mean: people here don't know I worked in the ministry. I moved here to Halberstadt after the Wall came down. I have a niece here.'

'I understand, Frau Schneeg.' Sylvie replaced her smile with a concerned frown. 'But I promise no one will know. I just want to find some of these people and no one need ever know where I got the information. That's if you can help me at all. I'm looking for people who worked with either Colonel Adebach or Major Drescher.'

'I don't know . . .'

'My station would be most grateful if you could help,' said Sylvie. 'I'm sure we could fix you up with a satellite box and dish – and a few subscriptions.'

For a moment Frau Schneeg looked at Sylvie intently, then said: 'Let me have a look at your list . . .'

6.

They sat in the living room of Drescher's apartment, each of them wearing the same empty expression of dull frustration.

'We've been here before,' Karin Vestergaard said to Fabel.

'There must be *something* here.' Fabel sighed.

'We're not looking in the right places,' said Werner. 'We're not devious enough. That's what comes of growing up in a democracy.'

Fabel snapped his fingers. 'Werner, you're brilliant. You are absolutely right – we don't know where to look. Or how to look.' Taking out his wallet, he retrieved the business card Martina Schilmann had given him. He flipped it over to where she had handwritten her mobile number and keyed it into his cellphone.

'Martina . . . It's Jan Fabel.'

'Hi, Jan. What can I do for you?'

'Lorenz, your Saxon chum. You said he was ex-Volkspolizei.'

'Yes, what of it?'

'Did he serve after the Wall came down? In one of the new forces?'

'No.' Martina sounded suspicious. 'What is this all about?'

'Why didn't he continue his police career?'

'Jan,' she said, with a sigh, 'I can see where you're going with this. Let me save time. The answer is yes, he was linked with the Stasi. That's why he couldn't get into one of the new forces. Why do you want to know?'

'I have an apartment here that's refusing to give up its secrets. The occupier was ex-Stasi. I need to know where to look.'

There was a silence at the other end of the connection.

'Give me the address,' Martina said at last. 'I'll bring him over myself . . .'

It took Martina Schilmann half an hour to arrive. Fabel had cleared the uniforms from the street, to attract as little attention as possible. In the digital age of cellphones that could take photographs and video, it never took long before someone was on to the television or newspapers. The city was no longer asleep and a heavy police presence in the street would be fully exposed to view.

Fabel had instructed the uniformed cops downstairs to conduct Schilmann and Lorenz Dühring directly up to the penthouse apartment.

Fabel guessed that Martina had been taking a day off: she was dressed in jeans, a heavy sweater and a thigh-length leather coat. Her blonde hair had been tied back in a ponytail and her face was naked of make-up. It made her look younger, more natural, and Fabel couldn't help remembering why he had been attracted to Martina in the first place. It was as if she had read his thoughts and she smiled shyly.

Lorenz lumbered into the background: tall, thickset and dark.

'This is *Politidirektør* Karin Vestergaard of the Danish National Police,' explained Fabel in English. 'We are cooperating on this case.'

The two women shook hands. A little coldly, thought Fabel.

The dynamics of female relationships remained a mystery to him.

'I'm afraid Lorenz doesn't speak English,' said Martina. 'Poor chump got stuck with Russian at school.'

Fabel turned to Vestergaard. 'Lorenz was a policeman in the former GDR. In the Volkspolizei. He wasn't allowed to become a member of the new, post-change police forces because only members of the Volkspolizei who were free of any connection to the Stasi were allowed to continue as policemen.'

'He's ex-Stasi?'

'He was one of their little helpers, let's say,' said Martina. 'And he received training from them, which is what Jan was counting on. By the way, Jan, for your information, I didn't know what Lorenz had been involved in. I guessed he'd been a Stasi unofficial, but, let's face it, it's a skills set that's very useful in my line of work. I asked him on the way over here if he had taken part in house searches and he told me he had.'

'Frau Schilmann told me that an ex-Stasi officer lived here,' Lorenz piped up in German.

'That's right,' said Fabel. 'A major in the HVA.'

'HVA?' Lorenz rubbed his heavy chin with forefinger and thumb. 'Those boys knew what they were doing when it came to hiding stuff. You're sure he has something here? I think it's more likely that he would keep anything sensitive in a different location.'

'Could be,' said Fabel. 'But my money's on him operating from here.'

'He would feel reasonably safe here, I suppose,' said Lorenz. 'I mean, it's not like in the GDR. He probably thought this flat would never be searched.' He cast his eye across the books on shelves. 'It makes things quicker if I don't tidy up behind me. Is that a problem?'

'Do what you have to do,' said Fabel.

* * *

It took Lorenz less than half an hour.

'Like I thought,' he said in his Saxon baritone when he came back through to the living room. 'He felt secure here. You were right about him using this as an operational base, so I reckoned there was no point in shifting heavy furniture, bookcases, et cetera. He would want to conceal his stuff but have reasonably easy access to it.'

'You learned that from the Stasi?' asked Martina.

'Journalists and writers – we were taught that they had to keep manuscripts, typewriters, that kind of thing handy. Serious dissidents and foreign agents – they were a different kettle of fish. That's why I thought this guy might be difficult. If he was HVA. But this couldn't have been more straightforward.'

Lorenz led them through to the study. He lifted up the deco-style bronze bird and gave the wooden base a twist. A compartment was exposed in which sat a small steel tool, almost like a nail twisted into a flattened hook. Lorenz took the hook and leant down beneath the desk. What looked to Fabel like a small chip in a floorboard was actually a perfect fit for the hook. Lorenz inserted the hook, gave it a half-twist and lifted a square of floorboard. The whole operation took less than fifteen seconds.

'It's nothing more than having a secret drawer,' said Lorenz. 'It was secure enough but easy and quick to get to. I haven't touched anything in there.'

Fabel snapped on a pair of latex gloves and knelt down to examine the contents.

'There's a black laptop computer in here, along with its power supply. Also a bunch of data sticks. Nothing else – no notebooks or files. Just this . . .' He eased out a copy of a magazine that had been folded lengthwise.

'Don't tell me he hid porn in there,' snorted Werner.

'Werner, go down to the flat below and ask Holger Brauner or Astrid Bremer to come up with a few large evidence bags.'

Fabel unfolded the magazine. He showed Vestergaard and Martina Schilmann the title. 'Now I could be wrong,' he said, 'but I don't really see Drescher as your typical feminist.'

'*Muliebritas*,' Vestergaard said aloud.

'It's a feminist title,' explained Fabel. 'The title is Latin. It's where the English word "muliebrity" comes from. The female equivalent of virility. There's a subtle difference from femininity. We would translate it as *Fraulichkeit* in German. I suppose you have a Danish word for it.

'*Kvindelighed*,' said Vestergaard.

Fabel stared at the magazine. 'I tell you what else this is: a prime example of synchronicity. The night Jake Westland was murdered, there was a massive feminist protest in Herbertstrasse that contributed to the confusion. And it was organised by *Muliebritas*.'

Werner reappeared with some evidence bags. Fabel slipped the magazine into one and handed it to Vestergaard. Easing the computer and its power connector out of the recess in the floor, he placed them in a tagged evidence bag, putting the data sticks in a separate one.

He turned to Vestergaard and Martina. 'We'll get this stuff down to Tech Division and see if they can get into the computer. I'm guessing it's encrypted, but the tech guys will be able to get through it. God knows how many paedophiles we've nicked because they thought they'd locked up their porn safe and sound.'

'A paedophile is one thing,' said Astrid Bremer, who had appeared behind them. 'A professional spy is another. That is what we've got here, isn't it?'

'I think so, Astrid,' said Fabel. 'But from a pre-digital age. This was maybe one area he wasn't too hot on. How are you getting on downstairs?'

'It'll take a while. Days, maybe. But Holger said he could spare me if you need something special up here.'

'Anything,' said Fabel. 'We've got one killer in custody but there's another one, maybe even two, on the loose. And she's connected to the victim, Drescher. I need anything that can point us in the right direction.'

'Do you think she's been in this apartment?'

'No. Probably not. But if there's a trace of anybody other than the vic having been in here I want to know about it. Also, if you come across anything unusual let me know. But can you start with this.' Fabel handed Astrid the copy of *Muliebritas*. 'This doesn't belong here. It could have been handled by the person we're looking for. Either that or it's the mechanism he used to contact her. I need it checked before we start going through it with a cryptologist.'

'I'll get right onto it,' said Astrid, and she smiled broadly at Fabel.

The first thing Fabel did when he got back to the Presidium was to phone Criminal Director van Heiden to approve the overtime for his team and the extra officers he would need to draft in. Van Heiden gave him the authority immediately and without question, which surprised Fabel a little: he had become used to his superior being grudging about any extra expenses on an investigation, as if he personally had to finance them. But, there again, this case had started off as three: Jespersen's death, the Angel killings in St Pauli and Drescher's torture and murder. It was all getting too messy, too political and the media were focusing on it. Complication was something van Heiden had difficulty dealing with. Fabel guessed that his superior was under pressure to clear it all up as quickly as possible.

'Are you convinced all of these crimes are connected?' asked van Heiden.

'Pretty convinced,' said Fabel. He gestured to Karin Vestergaard, who had just come into his office, to sit down. 'It's safe to assume that this GDR hit squad called the Valkyries has been operating for profit from here in Hamburg. Drescher ran it and he's been killed by one of his former trainees.'

'He didn't recognise her?' asked van Heiden.

'I get the impression she was a reject, probably because of her mental-health problems. And it was a long time ago. She probably just dropped off his radar and out of his memory.'

'Okay,' said van Heiden. 'Keep me informed. So I can keep others informed.'

'Of course.' Fabel hung up and turned his attention to Vestergaard. Again he noticed that she had done something with her make-up that had subtly changed her look and once more Fabel was struck by how attractive her face was, yet how forgettable. Maybe it was something that Margarethe Paulus shared with her. Maybe the appearance of the Valkyries had been a criterion: attractive but forgettable. Maybe that was why Drescher had not recognised his killer.

'You said you've been given new information from the Norwegian investigators of Halvorsen's murder?' Fabel asked her.

'The Norwegian National Police have been in touch with me through my office.' Vestergaard leaned forward and placed a note on Fabel's desk. 'This man – Ralf Sparwald – is someone Jørgen Halvorsen seems to have had contact with. It's believed that Halvorsen visited Hamburg to talk to him.'

'Who is he?' Fabel examined the name and address written on the note.

'He's a doctor of some kind. His name was flagged up when the Norwegian police got a warrant to access Halvorsen's email account. They could only get what is still in his in-box, uncollected. There was an out-of-office reply from this guy's email address. The Norwegians knew I was in Hamburg and that there was a possible connection here, so they sent this on to me.'

Fabel checked his watch. Most of the day had been spent at the Drescher crime scene or in briefings. It was now six-thirty p.m. 'Okay – so you think I should speak to Sparwald? It'll have to be tomorrow now.'

'No, I think *we* should speak to Sparwald, if that's okay with you.'

Fabel shrugged. 'I don't mind you coming along to observe. But please don't forget whose inquiry this is.'

'Somehow I don't think you'll let me forget,' said Vestergaard, and smiled.

The address Vestergaard had given Fabel for Sparwald was to the north of the city, in Poppenbüttel, in the Wandsbeck district. Wandsbeck had once been part of Schleswig-Holstein and had only been incorporated into Hamburg at the same time as Altona and even now, sitting on the shores of the Alster River, Poppenbüttel still felt more like a country village than a suburb.

As soon as Fabel and Vestergaard arrived, it was clear that the address they had been given was Sparwald's place of work rather than residence. SkK BioTech was located in an unobtrusive, low-level building set in an expanse of well-laid-out garden and fringed with winter-bare trees. Five smallish flags flew from poles set next to each other, UN-style, in the garden: the SkK BioTech logo fluttered in the cold breeze next to the flags of the EU, Germany and, Fabel noticed, the white-on-red Nordic cross of Denmark. There was another flag beside it.

'They must have known you were coming,' Fabel said to Vestergaard, with a nod to the Danish flag. He looked at the flag next to it. It was a non-national pennant: a white field with a small flared red cross on it.

The small, dumpy receptionist took a while to come to the desk from an office behind. From her reaction, SkK BioTech was not accustomed to visitors, particularly ones without an appointment. Fabel held up his police identity card.

'We need to speak to Herr Sparwald, if he's available.'

'Herr *Doctor* Sparwald,' corrected the receptionist. She looked from Fabel to Vestergaard and back. She had the nervousness and vague expression of groundless guilt of someone unaccustomed to dealing with the police. 'I'm afraid he's not here. He's on leave. Another two weeks.'

'I see . . .' Fabel considered his options for a moment. 'What is it you do here?'

'I work in the admin department. Deal with correspondence and answer the phones.'

Fabel laughed. 'I'm sorry. That's not what I meant. I meant what does SkK BioTech do, exactly?'

'Oh . . .' The fleshy cheeks of the small receptionist coloured. 'We work for medical research companies. Herr Doctor Lüttig could tell you more. Shall I fetch him?'

'If that's not too much trouble,' said Fabel.

Fabel and Vestergaard exchanged a smile when the receptionist left. She returned with a tall, thin and lugubriously sombre man in his late forties. He was dressed in a white lab coat but, to Fabel's mind, he had the look of a Lutheran preacher from some remote Frisian island.

'I'm Thomas Lüttig. I believe you are looking for my colleague Ralf Sparwald. Is there a problem?'

Again Fabel held up his ID. 'I'm Principal Chief Commissar Jan Fabel of the Polizei Hamburg Murder Commission. This is *Politidirektør* Karin Vestergaard of the Danish National Police.'

'Murder?' Lüttig's grave expression became, somehow, graver. 'What's this got to do—'

Fabel held up his hand. 'Please, don't concern yourself. Nothing at all directly. We're just helping out our Norwegian colleagues with a few inquiries. I believe Dr Sparwald is on leave?'

'Yes. He won't be back for . . . let me see, he's been away a week, so he won't be back for another two and a half weeks,' said Lüttig.

'That's a long holiday,' said Fabel.

'Yes. It is. I suppose it had to be . . . China you see. I suppose if you travel that far you've got to make it worth your while. Although I really could do with him here . . . Dr Sparwald is my deputy, you see, as well as being the most senior analyst.'

Fabel began to translate into English for Vestergaard what Lüttig had said.

'I studied at Cambridge, amongst other places,' Lüttig interrupted him. 'It's quite in order for me to speak in English if that makes things easier.'

'Thank you,' said Vestergaard, and smiled. 'You couldn't arrange cover for him? A trip to China takes a lot of arranging – you must have had a fair bit of advance warning.'

'That's the thing. I didn't. Ralf sort of sprung this on me out of the blue. He's like that – he is a very committed environmentalist. That's why he works here: the group we do work for is heavily involved in environmental clean-up. But even with warning, it would be practically impossible to find someone to fill in for him. Or at least anyone with a remotely similar set of skills.'

'Can you explain what it is you do here?'

'Basically we're an analysis laboratory,' said Lüttig. 'We're a wholly owned subsidiary of an environmental and biotechnical group. We do all of their analytical work. Toxicology. Everything from soil samples to human tissue. We specialise in evaluating environmental impacts and identifying pollution-related health risks.'

'I see,' said Fabel. 'Do you know what part of China Dr Sparwald is visiting?'

'I'm sorry, I don't.'

'Is he travelling alone, do you know?' asked Vestergaard.

'Again, I'm not really sure. He said something about a Norwegian friend.'

Fabel and Vestergaard exchanged a look.

'Didn't you say you were helping the Norwegian police?' Lüttig frowned. 'Is Ralf in some danger?'

'No, no,' said Fabel. 'Not at all. It's just that he may have information that could be useful to us. This Norwegian, do you know his name?'

'No. Ralf just mentioned he might be travelling with a Norwegian friend. Are you sure Ralf's not in danger? The Chinese authorities don't always take kindly to foreign environmentalists.'

'Do you have Dr Sparwald's cellphone number?' asked Vestergaard. 'We could perhaps reach him on that.'

'Certainly,' said Lüttig. 'I'll get it for you.'

'You said you are a wholly owned subsidiary of a group,' said Fabel. 'Would that be the NeuHansa Group?'

'That's right.'

Fabel handed Lüttig one of his Polizei Hamburg visiting cards. 'If you hear from Dr Sparwald, I'd be grateful if you could tell him I would like to speak to him as a matter of urgency. And if you come across anything that you think would be of interest to us, please give me a call.'

'Of course.' Lüttig turned back to Vestergaard. 'I'll get you Ralf's number and home address.'

'How did you know that SkK Biotech was owned by the NeuHansa Group?' Vestergaard asked Fabel as they walked back to the car.

'That.' He thrust his chin in the direction of the pennant flying beside the other flags. 'The small red cross. In German we call that a *Tatzenkreuz*. You know, the flared cross you see on German military vehicles. Well, the one on that flag is less flared and it's red on a white background. It's a Hanseatic cross. I'm guessing it's some kind of corporate logo. That and the Danish flag made me think of Gina Brønsted, the owner of the NeuHansa Group.'

'Is it significant?'

'Not significant. Coincidental. The most recent victim of the St Pauli Angel also worked for a NeuHansa Group company. But that's not unusual – so do a lot of people.'

'Funny things, coincidences,' said Vestergaard. 'I tend not to believe in them.' As they were about to get back into his car, she handed Fabel the note Lüttig had given her with Sparwald's home address on it.

'Nor do I,' said Fabel.

When they got back from SkK Biotech, Fabel found a thick legal envelope on his desk. He had just picked it up when Werner came in. Karin Vestergaard diplomatically excused herself and left the two men alone.

'She's becoming your shadow,' said Werner. 'Doesn't it get on your nerves?'

'As a matter of fact it doesn't. I would be every bit as hands-on if you got yourself killed in Copenhagen and I went up to find out what happened.'

'What can I say?' Werner grinned. 'I'm touched.' He nodded towards the envelope. 'That arrived half an hour ago and I just left it on your desk. It's the details of Westland's investments, correspondence, that sort of thing. Westland's widow sent them over like you asked.'

'Thanks. I'll look at it later. Anything else new?'

'Yes, there is, as a matter of fact.' Werner swung open the door and called through to Dirk Hechtner, who came in carrying an evidence bag, which he placed on Fabel's desk. The bag contained a curved blade attached to a leather device that looked halfway between a wrist-strap and a glove.

'Things have just got even more interesting,' said Dirk Hechtner. 'This is one of the things we found in Margarethe Paulus's apartment. We did get positive traces of blood from the leather . . . unfortunately they were too small and too degraded to get a match. However, we did manage to get a sample of dried blood from around the base of the blade.

Or at least Astrid Bremer did. But we still weren't able to get a match.'

'A match with whom?' asked Fabel. 'There's no sign that this was used in Drescher's murder.'

'No, not Drescher. I did some digging . . . tried to find out what the hell this thing is. I got a name for it. It's called a *srbosjek*. I thought this might be the weapon used to kill Goran Vujačić in Copenhagen. You know, the Serbian gangster.'

'Vujačić?' Fabel frowned. 'What made you make the connection to Vujačić?'

Hechtner nodded towards the object in the evidence bag. 'This is a particularly horrible device with only one purpose: to murder. It was designed for the *Ustaše*, the fascists who ran Croatia during the Second World War. The *Ustaše* believed in an ethnically cleansed Croatia, free of Serbs, Gypsies, Jews . . . They set up their own concentration camp, Jasenovac, where they murdered a million or more. They were very hands-on about it all: they clubbed, stabbed or hacked their victims to death, all of which was very labour-intensive. So they came up with the *srbosjek*. It was used to cut throats with maximum speed and minimum effort. That's why I made the connection with Vujačić – *srbosjek* is Croat for "Serb Cutter". It struck me that maybe someone was being poetic.'

'More like they're trying to tell us something.' Fabel picked up the evidence bag. The *srbosjek* was an ugly, vicious-looking thing, even if you didn't know its history. 'But this definitely wasn't the weapon used to kill Vujačić. His throat wasn't cut: the blade used to kill him was more like a thin stiletto or a needle file, pushed into the heart from under the sternum. But good work, Dirk. You may be on to something.'

Fabel met Susanne in the Presidium canteen for lunch. She had spent an hour on the phone with Köpke, the Mecklenburg

State Hospital Chief Psychiatrist. Karin Vestergaard had phoned Fabel and explained that she needed to catch up on a few things with her office. There had been something about her manner on the phone that made him feel that she was not being entirely straightforward with him. But he dismissed the thought: Vestergaard knew that if she withheld anything from Fabel he would shut her out of the investigation into Jespersen's death.

'You look tired,' said Fabel as they picked up their trays and inched along in a queue of blue uniforms. Susanne had a large thick leather-bound notebook tucked under her arm. Fabel could see Post-it notes sprouting like foliage from its edges and he noticed that she had jammed various other folded sheets between its pages.

'I've had a lot to take in,' she said wearily. 'You say you've spoken with Köpke?'

'I've had that pleasure,' said Fabel, with a wry smile.

'I don't think I've been talked at like that since I was a first-year student,' said Susanne. She broke off to place her order with the canteen assistant. 'He's not the most patient of people, is he? In fact, for a psychiatrist, he doesn't seem much of a people person.'

'If you mean he's an arsehole,' said Fabel, 'then I would agree with your professional assessment. I thought you southerners were direct and outspoken.'

'I'm acclimatising. Another year or two up here and I'll be locking up all that emotion deep inside till it rots away at me, just like the rest of you. Anyway, arsehole or not, I had to take a hell of a lot of notes while I spoke to him. He was well prepared. And he thinks we should be too, before we talk to Margarethe Paulus again.'

'He has a point,' said Fabel.

'How is the head?' asked Susanne.

'It's fine – it really wasn't too bad. It's my pride that's taken the bruising.'

'What, because you were beaten up by a woman?' They found a place over by the window and reasonably distant from the majority of occupied tables.

'Because I mishandled the whole situation. What have you got?'

Susanne dropped her notebook with a thud onto the canteen table. She looped a stray lock of raven hair behind her ear, slipped on her glasses and started to flick through her notes.

'She's a psychopath. That's for sure. But, whatever else has been going on, she's not a serial killer. Köpke insists that she could not be responsible for any of the other killings.'

'That's not right – she had escaped from the hospital before Jake Westland and Armin Lensch were killed. And Jespersen, too. She could well have committed those murders. The only thing she's in the clear for is the original Angel killings.'

'No, no – that's not what Köpke means. Margarethe may well have been available to commit those other murders, but Köpke is certain that she was focused exclusively on killing Drescher. She would have no compunction about killing others, but she saw herself as being on a mission. The only other people she would have murdered would have been anyone who stood in the way of her killing Drescher.'

'Maybe she found out that Jespersen was on Drescher's trail,' said Fabel between mouthfuls.

'Isn't that pretty unlikely? Anyway, let me summarise what Köpke told me: Margarethe Paulus is a psychopath, but it's difficult to decide whether she's a primary or a secondary psychopath. Primaries tend to be born that way or are genetically predisposed to psychopathy, whereas secondaries are made that way by experience, environment or as the result of drug abuse, et cetera. Margarethe clearly went through a neurological trauma as part of her childhood brain surgery. Maybe her psychopathy is iatrogenic, the adverse side effect of medical intervention. But it's hard to tell – psychopathy only really begins to manifest itself in adolescence. We're all egocentric as kids: it goes with the territory. But whereas we mature and get an idea of ourselves as social beings, psychopaths don't. The scary thing is that there's a good chance that one in every hundred of the population are psychopaths.'

'You're kidding . . .'

'No joke. And a lot more are borderline. We've all known someone who is totally egomaniacal. The husband who dumps his wife of twenty years along with his kids without a second thought. Or the business boss who sacks loyal workers without a twinge of conscience . . . A lot of people we consider self-centred arseholes are often psychopathic. They have a piece of their make-up missing. The majority of psychopaths in society manage to fit in and never become involved in criminal or overtly antisocial behaviour.' Susanne took a sip of her coffee. 'You know we were talking about Irma Grese, the Bitch of Belsen? Well, maybe that's a perfect example of someone who could have gone through life and had a perfectly normal existence. That's the danger, Jan, that when someone like Hitler comes along he can tap into that one per cent of the population. When you have a core of people who are incapable of feeling guilt or remorse, and who possess absolutely no capacity for pity or compassion or empathy for other human beings, you can persuade them to do almost anything.'

'And Margarethe is one of those people?'

'Not quite. There's nothing borderline with Margarethe. Köpke says she's a true sociopath and, quite unusually, she's suffering from a dissocial personality disorder, rather than an antisocial personality disorder.'

'What's the difference?' asked Fabel.

'Mainly that she can function, or seem to function, more normally. Dissocial sociopaths don't get into trouble to the same degree – delinquency, criminal behaviour, that kind of thing – as the antisocial type. And they're better at disguising their behaviour. She won't have sought out opportunities to act antisocially, but she will act without pity to get or do whatever she wants. The main thing is she has absolutely zero empathy for other human beings. She is simply incapable of simulation . . . imagining that other people have feelings or even the same kind of consciousness as she does.'

'Ideal for a professional assassin,' said Fabel.

'Not really. As you've experienced yourself, the typical individual with full dissocial personality disorder has an extremely low violence threshold. So does an antisocial, for that matter. If everything she has claimed about the Stasi training is true – and bear in mind all sociopaths are inventive, compulsive liars – then her trainers would no doubt have identified her instability and dropped her from the programme. Another trait of the disorder, unfortunately for Drescher, is the tendency to pin the blame or responsibility for their failures on others. Combine that with a tendency towards obsession, and you've got the ultimate stalker from hell. Köpke believes that in Margarethe's case there's co-morbidity with another personality or even a schizoaffective disorder . . . or maybe it's to do with the neurological damage done in childhood. Something that makes her even more focused and obsessive. Her belief that her sister exists, and the way she allows the sister to speak and act through her, isn't psychopathic, it's psychotic. Delusional. In Margarethe we have something extra going on in the mix: sociopathy with a twist.'

Fabel looked through the window, out across the treetops. The sky was heavy and grey. 'Do you think the other so-called Valkyries will be similar? Sociopaths, I mean?'

Susanne shrugged. 'To take human life for money doesn't show a lot of empathy for others. But sociopaths are ego-maniacal, narcissistic and extremely impulsive. I'm guessing that these women who were trained as professional assassins had a high degree of self-discipline and were willing to subordinate their will to that of others. But that doesn't make them any less dangerous. The opposite, in fact.'

'I don't want you sitting in on the interview, Susanne,' said Fabel. 'You can watch from the other room through the CCTV.'

'That's no good, Jan. I need to be able to observe her closely. And I want to be able to ask her questions. Surely you will have her restrained this time?'

'Okay . . . but if she kicks off again, you leave right away. I'll have extra bodies in there with us.'

Susanne's perfect porcelain smile had a hint of wickedness about it. 'I don't know, Jan . . . you're going to have to learn to deal with your fear of women or I'm going to end up a permanent chaperone.'

Fabel, Susanne and Anna Wolff were seated in the interview room before Margarethe Paulus was brought in. Karin Vestergaard, Werner and others from the Murder Commission team were in the connecting room, watching on closed-circuit TV.

When Margarethe was brought in by two uniformed officers, her wrists braceleted in Speedcuffs, her strong, attractive face was as impassive as it had been before.

'Sit down, Margarethe.' Fabel indicated the floor-fixed chair. One of the officers unfastened her Speedcuffs, only to use them again to fix her right hand to the metal securing loop on the table. A tall woman of about forty took the seat next to Margarethe. She was Lina Mueller, the state-appointed attorney.

'This is Frau Doctor Eckhardt,' said Fabel, gesturing towards Susanne, 'from the Institute for Judicial Medicine. She is a criminal psychologist and she has spoken to Dr Köpke, who of course you know. Frau Doctor Eckhardt will have some questions for you. You will have already spoken to Frau Mueller, who is here to represent your interests.'

'I don't need a lawyer,' said Margarethe. Again it was a simple statement of fact, made without resentment or anger.

'We feel you should have one present,' said Anna. 'It's your right.'

Margarethe didn't respond, in voice or expression.

'What is your name?' asked Fabel.

'I am Margarethe Paulus.'

'But you told Herr Fabel earlier that you were Ute Paulus,' said Anna.

'You are confusing me with my sister,' said Margarethe. 'Ute is my sister's name.'

'Where is your sister right now?' asked Susanne.

Margarethe gazed at the small, reinforced-glass window. 'My sister is resting. She is waiting for me.'

'Where is she waiting?' asked Susanne. Margarethe remained silent. Inanimate.

'Margarethe,' said Fabel, changing tack. 'There are a number of killings that have taken place in Hamburg since you escaped from the hospital. I would like to ask you what you know about them. Do you understand?'

'I have an IQ of one hundred and forty,' said Margarethe. 'Dr Köpke has probably already told you that. There is not a question you are capable of asking that I would be incapable of understanding.'

'Okay, Margarethe. I'm impressed, if it's important to you that I am impressed. Let's start with the most recent murder. Robert Gerdes.'

'You know by now that Robert Gerdes was not his real name. It was Georg Drescher. And it wasn't murder, it was an execution. I told your colleagues when I phoned that I had executed Drescher.'

'So it was you who tortured and killed him? It wasn't your sister?' asked Susanne.

'We both did. Ute tracked him down and found him. She kept her promise. She promised me she would make it all right for me, and she did. But when we killed him we acted together. We were one.'

'Why the torture?' asked Susanne. 'All that terrible pain. What did he do to you to have deserved that?'

Margarethe sat mute. Fabel repeated Susanne's question, but it was as if Margarethe could not hear him. Fabel had years of experience of silences in interviews: he had learned to read them, interpret them. Sometimes a suspect's refusal to speak said more than their answers. This was different. It wasn't a silence, it was a complete shutting down of all responses. He knew then with absolute certainty that Margarethe would answer only those questions that suited her. He just hoped that he would get enough from her to start putting what had happened into some kind of under-standable context.

'A week ago,' Fabel broke the silence. 'A young man called Armin Lensch was murdered in the Kiez district of Hamburg. His belly was sliced open with a blade. What can you tell me about that?'

'I can tell you nothing about it. It had nothing to do with me. I didn't kill him.' Margarethe's frighteningly blank expression suggested a complete lack of guile. Of emotion. Of anything.

Fabel placed the *srbosjek*, still cased in a clear plastic evidence bag, on the table. He kept a firm hold on the bag, just outside her reach.

'Did you use this on Armin Lensch? Is this what you sliced open his belly with?'

'I've never seen that before,' Margarethe said, looking at the weapon without interest. 'And I wouldn't use that for slicing open a gut. That's for cutting throats.'

'If you haven't seen that before,' said Fabel, leaning forward, 'then how do you know how it's used?'

'I've never seen your car, but if I did I would know how to drive it. And I know that that is called a graviso knife.

Or a *srbosjek*. It was used by Croat *Ustaše*. It's very simple but highly effective. But it's not an assassin's weapon, particularly. This is for killing large numbers of people. Although I have to say that used expertly, it would silence and kill a single meeting efficiently.'

'Meeting?' asked Susanne.

'That's what we call them,' said Margarethe. 'A meeting is when the agent and the target encounter each other and the mission is executed. We call them meetings because there should be no engagement with the target prior to execution, making the meeting the first and final encounter. We also call the target a meeting.'

Fabel placed a second evidence bag on the table. It contained the automatic that Dirk and Henk had found.

'Is this yours?' he asked.

'I've never seen it before,' she said.

'It was retrieved from your apartment. Again, there is a Croatian connection.'

'I know. It's a Croatian PHP MV-9 automatic. It's about eighteen years old. It was a model developed in a rush for use in the Independence War.'

'Okay,' said Fabel. 'Once again I'm impressed by your encyclopaedic knowledge of weapons and assassination techniques. But your knowledge of this weapon could come simply from the fact that it is yours. That you had it ready to use if your drugging of Drescher didn't work out as planned.'

Again an empty stare. Margarethe was attractive. Her features perfectly proportioned. But there was still something about the way she looked at him that reminded Fabel of the photographs he had seen of Irma Grese. The same void in the eyes and expression. He had no way of knowing if Margarethe was lying to him. After nearly twenty years as an investigator of murders, of conducting interviews like this, he found himself lost in a strange country, completely without any recognisable landmarks.

'Who are "we"?' asked Susanne, filling the silence. 'You said "We call the target a meeting."'

'My sisters and I. The Valkyries.'

'How many Valkyries were there?' asked Anna Wolff. Margarethe stared at her for a moment, still expressionless, before answering.

'Only three of us were selected for final training.'

'But you didn't finish your final training,' said Fabel, 'did you?'

'I was selected along with the other two. Out of dozens of girls who in turn were the best of the best. Only three of us were chosen to be Valkyries. It was Drescher who dropped me from the programme.'

'Is that why you killed him? Is that why you kept him alive to suffer first?'

Margarethe gave a small smile. It was the first time Fabel had seen her smile and it did not reach her cold, empty eyes. She shook her head. 'I didn't kill him because he dropped me. I killed him because he chose me . . . because he selected me for this kind of life in the first place. My head . . .' She winced as if some terrible migraine was cutting through her. 'The things in my head. He put them there. And I can't get them out.'

'What things?' asked Susanne.

'I've already shown you. They were all there for you to see. In the flat. I didn't think I was being ambiguous.' There was a flicker of impatience in Margarethe's expression. On anyone else it would have gone unnoticed, but it flashed across the empty canvas of her face. 'He taught me how to kill. That more than anything. Him and the others, all the different ways to kill. How to shatter someone's nose and drive the bone fragments into their brain. Or cut off the blood to the brain with an embrace and kill without the meeting knowing what was happening. How to seduce a man, or a woman, and fuck them in a way that they become completely obsessed with you. How to cut yourself off from your own body so that you can do anything, with anyone. How to follow someone without them knowing, to hunt and trap them and kill them in an instant. They told us we could learn from everything. No matter how bad it was, we could benefit from it. Every war, every crime, had a lesson to be learned.' She nodded to where Fabel had shown her the forensic-bagged knife. 'That's where I learned about the *srbosjek*. And more. So much more. And the thing was . . . the totally mad thing was that they tried to teach you that you could switch off from it all and have a normal life in between the meetings.'

Fabel paused for a moment, leaning back in his chair, as if creating a punctuation mark in the interview.

'I have to say, I am most impressed with your organisational abilities. Planning, arranging the apartment below Drescher's. Very impressive. But there's no way – absolutely no way – you could have organised that yourself in the time available since your escape from Mecklenburg. Who is helping you, Margarethe?'

Another hollow stare and silence.

'Okay,' sighed Fabel. 'Jens Jespersen. *Politiinspektør* Jens Jespersen of the Danish National Police. Someone picked him up in a restaurant in the Hanseviertel and persuaded him to meet with her later. Then, when they were in bed together, she killed him with an injection of suxamethonium chloride. Exactly the means you used to immobilise Georg Drescher. You've just described to us the way Major Drescher and his Stasi colleagues trained you in concealment, disguise and seduction techniques. Those sound to me exactly the kind of skills used to get Drescher into a vulnerable position and kill him. I suppose you are going to tell me that you don't know anything about that?'

'I don't.'

'I don't believe you.' Fabel fixed Margarethe with a penetrating stare that failed to penetrate.

'I don't care whether you believe me or not.'

'I have a colleague of Jespersen's in the other room, watching this interview. His superior officer. She is here because *Politiinspektør* Jespersen was here to try to find Georg Drescher. He was also following up rumours that a female contract killer, going by the name the Valkyrie, was operating out of Hamburg. That is a hell of a lot of coincidences, Margarethe.'

No comment, no shrug, no expression.

'He was here to find the man you were hunting. In turn he was hunting a killer called the Valkyrie, and he was killed with the same drug you used on Drescher. You killed Jens Jespersen, didn't you? He got in the way of your mission. A secondary target. Or what would you call it: *an unplanned meeting*?'

Margarethe ignored Fabel and turned to Susanne. 'You are a criminal psychologist?'

'I've already told you that.'

'And you have spoken with Dr Köpke?'

'Yes.'

'So you think I am a psychopath.'

'I believe you have dissocial personality disorder, yes. But I think you have something else going on as well. You're not just psychopathic, you're psychotic. Delusional.'

'Really?' said Margarethe. 'Then you know that I will be kept in an institution, probably for the rest of my life.'

'I don't think you can ever be reintegrated into society, no. Or cured of your problems. Maybe the psychosis, with drug therapy. But no, you will be confined for the rest of your life.'

'Although I disagree with your diagnosis, Frau Doctor Eckhardt, I agree with your vision of my future. I will never be at liberty. And if I am a psychopath, then I have absolutely no sense of accountability or responsibility. And punishment is meaningless to me. So could you explain to Herr Fabel that there is absolutely no point in me lying to him about which murders I did or did not commit?'

'There are other reasons for lying,' said Fabel. 'To protect others. Maybe you weren't working alone. Perhaps you decided to have a class reunion with your fellow ex-Valkyries. That would explain all the money and resources you have at your disposal. Maybe it was one of your sisters who killed Jespersen.'

'Maybe it was,' said Margarethe. 'But I know nothing about it. And even if I did, I owe them no loyalty. They left me behind. Only my sister stayed by me. Promised to make it right.'

There, thought Fabel. There I saw something. For the first time in the interview he saw an opening. Hardly a crack, but something that could be worked at. Pried open.

'Yes, Margarethe,' he said sympathetically. 'They did leave you behind. Betrayed you. They went on to become true Valkyries while you were thrown aside and rejected. After all that horror, all that pain, all those horrible, horrible things they put into your head. Is that the real reason you tortured and killed Drescher? To achieve some kind of fulfilment? Do you have *any* idea of the kind of money they will have made out of their meetings? Oh yes, when the Wall came down, Drescher and his girls embraced capitalism with real enthusiasm. They have been killing for private enterprise as a private enterprise.'

'She . . .' said Margarethe.

'What?'

'She. Not they. Georg Drescher had a favourite. He works with only one woman. The other Valkyrie has no part of it. She has another life.'

There was a short, electric pause. Fabel felt his pulse pick up a beat. He was aware that Anna and Susanne were staying very still and quiet.

'Names, Margarethe,' he said. 'What are their names? The

woman Drescher worked with, the professional killer. What is she called?'

'We were friends,' said Margarethe. Now there was emotion. Not much, just a hint of wistfulness. 'As much as we could be friends. All three of us were loners – part of what they needed from us. But, in our own way, we were friends.'

'They left you behind, Margarethe. You owe them nothing.'

'You don't have to tell me that. You don't need to manage me. I will tell you what I want to tell you. Not what you think you can make me tell you.' She paused. 'It was a rule that we didn't know each other's names. They were very strict about that. We knew each other as One, Two and Three. I was Two.'

Fabel felt the hope slip from him. He sighed.

'We got on well,' said Margarethe. 'We were supervised most of the time. Watched and monitored. Our sleeping quarters were kept separate. But we were trained together for most things.'

'Did the other girls tell you anything that gave a clue to their true identities?' asked Fabel.

'They thought they could control us completely. Make us like machines. But they couldn't.' Margarethe smiled. Not a fake smile. Not something she had been trained to use at appropriate moments. *Her* smile. And it terrified Fabel. 'Liane Kayser. Anke Wollner. It was our rebellion. Our way of keeping a little of ourselves outside their control. We told each other our real names.'

Fabel kept his gaze on Margarethe, but to his left he heard Anna Wolff scribbling the names into her notebook before rushing out of the interview room.

'There was something else. We knew that we would be sent to different places. That we maybe wouldn't see each other again. So we worked out a plan. A place we would meet.'

'Where?' Fabel tried to keep his tone dispassionate.

'You have to remember, we were all living in the East. We didn't know then that the Wall would come down. We didn't know that one or more of us might be sent into the West, into deep cover. So we picked somewhere we all knew. Halberstadt.'

'In Saxony-Anhalt?'

Margarethe nodded. 'One of the girls, Liane, came from Halberstadt. She said that if we needed each other we would meet at the cathedral in Halberstadt.'

'How would you know to come?'

'Two newspapers, one in the GDR, one in West Germany. We would run an announcement. It would be a quote from *Njál's Saga*: "The heavens are stained with the blood of men, as the Valkyries sing their song." If we saw the announcement we would know to meet up in Halberstadt at eight a.m. on the first Monday of the month following the announcement.'

Fabel leaned forward. 'So, if we ran this announcement in the appropriate newspapers, we could bring the other two Valkyries to Halberstadt?'

Margarethe shook her head. 'It was compromised. They caught us talking about it. We were stupid: we were being trained by the Stasi and didn't think that they would have bugged us.'

'So you don't think the others would respond to the announcement?' asked Fabel.

'No. And we didn't arrange another code. After that we were separated. We didn't see each other again.'

'And you've had no contact since then? With any of the other Valkyries?'

'None.'

'You said Drescher had a favourite. This is the woman you think he's been operating with. Which one, Margarethe? Who was his favourite – Liane Kayser or Anke Wollner?'

'Anke Wollner. Liane . . . well, Liane was different. She

didn't respond as well to discipline. She wanted things her own way. It was Anke who was Drescher's little protégée.'

Anna Wolff came back into the room and retook her place. She responded to Fabel's inquiring look with a sharp shake of her head.

'I'll ask you again . . .' Fabel turned back to Margarethe. 'If it wasn't one of the other Valkyries, who set you up with everything you needed to kill Drescher?'

The blank mask fell again.

'Was it someone else from the Stasi? Maybe someone who worked with Drescher and saw him as a threat.'

Nothing.

'Does the name Thomas Maas mean anything to you? Ulrich Adebach?' Fabel ran through the other names he had obtained from the BStU Federal Commissioner's office. It was clear that they had come to a dead end. It was almost as if Margarethe had realised that she had opened up too much and was now shutting down. No, thought Fabel, she was too much in control for that. Any information she had given had been released in a controlled manner.

Fabel terminated the interview and Margarethe was taken back to her cell under heavy guard. Fabel ordered that she be placed in a video-surveillance cell.

'So nothing on these names?' Fabel asked Anna as soon as they were in the corridor.

'Nothing. But that's hardly surprising, *Chef*. If these girls were chosen by the Stasi, especially if they were orphans or from broken homes, then I would guess that the first thing the Stasi would do would be to wipe all trace of their real identities from the public record. An easy thing to do if you're in charge of that selfsame public record.'

'I want you to get back on to the BStU Federal Commissioner's office in Berlin.' Fabel leaned against the wall. 'Give them these names and see what comes up. The Stasi thought they were invulnerable – maybe they thought any mention of the girls' real identities within the context of a Stasi HQ file was relatively safe.'

'It's a very, very long shot, *Chef*,' said Anna.

'At the moment it's the best we've got.'

They were joined by Karin Vestergaard and Werner Meyer, who had been watching the interview from the next room.

'Well?' Fabel asked Vestergaard.

'I don't know,' she sighed. 'It's difficult to read expression and body language over a CCTV link.'

'There was none to read, believe me. There's a very big chunk of humanity missing from Margarethe Paulus. But you heard what she said about Jespersen's death. She claims she had nothing to do with it and she has a point when she says she has nothing to gain by lying about it.'

'That's the thing,' said Vestergaard. 'I tend to believe her.'

'So do I,' said Fabel. 'So where does that leave us?'

'Well,' said Anna, 'we've got a professional assassination in Norway, Jørgen Halvorsen, and the death of Jens Jespersen in Hamburg. It's pretty safe to assume that they are directly linked.'

'Then we've got the murders in the Kiez – the Brit Westland and Armin Lensch,' said Werner. 'The so-called return of the Angel of St Pauli. They must be connected.'

'And the murder of Georg Drescher,' said Anna. 'Whether Margarethe was involved in the Jespersen and Halvorsen killings or not, there is a connection. So effectively we have three sets of murders that have a common link, and that link is this Stasi conspiracy to place Valkyrie assassins in the West.'

'There's maybe one more,' said Fabel. 'Peter Claasens – the suicide that maybe isn't a suicide in the Kontorhaus Quarter. Maybe the link lies there.' He turned to Karin Vestergaard. 'And I think maybe you and I should take another look at this environmental analyst Sparwald, who has had some kind of contact with Halvorsen.'

'I've been thinking about that,' said Vestergaard. 'If they were both supposed to be travelling to China, and Halvorsen didn't make it, then who's to say that Sparwald did?'

Fabel straightened up from leaning on the wall. 'Do you still have the address?'

Karin Vestergaard held out the note that Sparwald's boss had given her.

'Let's go,' said Fabel.

7.

Fabel rang Sparwald's cellphone number from his car.

'Number unavailable,' he said to Vestergaard as he snapped his phone shut.

'That's not surprising, if he's in a remote part of China.'

'Like you say, if that's where he is,' said Fabel. He looked at the note Lüttig, Sparwald's boss, had given them. 'But I hope to God he is. If Sparwald really was due to make this trip with a Norwegian travelling companion, and that travelling companion was Halvorsen . . .'

Sparwald didn't live far from his work. But if you were someone who appreciated the environment, Poppenbüttel was not a bad choice of place to live. Even in winter, with its branches bare and its tones muted, Nature still made her presence felt here. Sparwald lived in a small house near the banks of the Alster, set tight into a mass of trees. The house was constructed out of wood, but most of the south-facing side of the house was made up of windows, over which shutters had been pulled.

'It reminds me of a lot of the houses we have in Denmark,' said Vestergaard. She pointed to a large area of the garden that had been dug up. There were spiralled coils of pipe lying on the muddy exposed undersoil. 'Look – he's been installing a geothermal energy converter. It's not finished. Now that's a very odd project to leave half-done when you're about to go off to China for a month or so.' She nodded up towards the roof. 'And these solar panels are new. It doesn't look to me like they're connected. Sparwald was obviously in the middle of a pretty major home-improvement project.'

Fabel rang the front doorbell and knocked on the door for good measure. As he expected there was no answer. He turned to Vestergaard.

'I'm going to have a look around the back. See if you can find a window where the blinds haven't been drawn.'

Fabel made his way around the side of the building. Again there were signs of work in progress: building materials propped against the side of the house; tools left out. Fabel tried the back door. It was locked.

'Jan!' He heard Vestergaard call from the other side of the house. He ran around, slipping on the mud churned up by Sparwald's excavation for the heat pump.

'Take a look at this,' said Vestergaard. 'There's a space between the blind and the edge of the window.'

He peered through but could see nothing. He took a small torch from his pocket and shone the beam through.

'You see it?' said Vestergaard.

'I see it,' said Fabel. For a moment he tried to convince himself it was just a shoe. But he knew that what he saw, just visible from behind the sofa, was a foot.

He called the Presidium from his cellphone and told them to send a blue-and-silver from Police Commissariat 35 at Poppenbüttel.

'And could you alert the Forensics Department. It would appear we have a murder scene here.'

'This is different,' said Vestergaard without a hint of irony. It had taken less than two minutes for the first uniformed unit to arrive and for the door of Sparwald's home to be shattered with a ram. The first thing that had struck them on entering the house was the smell. The real stench of death. They found Sparwald's body in the lounge, his foot projecting beyond the edge of the sofa, as they had seen through the window. This was horror of a different kind from that they had experienced at the Drescher scene, and Fabel understood exactly what Vestergaard had meant by her comment. The smell was because Sparwald had lain undiscovered for days, maybe weeks, but the method of his death had been much cleaner than Drescher's. Without symbolism or ritual. Without passion.

Fabel and Vestergaard had put on forensic overshoes and latex gloves before entering the house and instructed the uniformed officers to do the same. Clutching a handkerchief to his mouth and nose, Fabel bent down and examined Sparwald, who lay staring up at the ceiling, the skin on his face pale and blotchy. There was a bullet hole in the middle of his forehead and another under his jawline. This had been the professional, efficient extermination of a life.

'You realise this is exactly the same m.o. as the Halvorsen killing?' Vestergaard too held the back of her hand to her nose to diminish the smell of death, but Fabel noticed that otherwise she seemed untouched by the scene. Her brow was slightly furrowed, but it was the concentration of a professional analysing the facts she was presented with.

'Yes,' said Fabel. 'I'm guessing he's been killed with a low-velocity hollow-point.'

'The Valkyrie,' said Vestergaard, but quietly, as if to herself.

Poppenbüttel police station was part of Polizei Hamburg Division East and could not have been more different from Davidwache or Klingberg. Police Commissariat 35 was situated on Wentzelplatz, next to the S-Bahn station. The Commissariat was an imposing, brand-new construction composed of solid modernist blocks, angles, curves and sweeps. There was, Fabel thought, something almost intimidating about the severity of the building and he found himself thinking just how much more approachable Davidwache must seem to the public.

Fabel had assembled the resources he needed there, bringing in Holger Brauner and his forensics team, plus Anna, Werner, Henk and Dirk. The Poppenbüttel uniformed branch had kept on the on-duty shift after its replacement came on, doubling the number of officers available. Fabel had also made a call to van Heiden, whose disapproving tone all but suggested that he held Fabel personally responsible for another murder being discovered. But, again, there had been no reluctance to comply with Fabel's request for more officers.

The first people Fabel spoke to were the forensics team. Brauner had rolled up in a convoy of vans carrying twelve specialists and all the technical support they needed to carry out a thorough processing of the scene.

'If you don't mind,' Brauner said to Fabel, 'I'd like Astrid to go in alone to start with. She has a knack of getting trace from older scenes.'

'It's up to you, Holger,' said Fabel. 'It's your thing, not mine. But she must be good – normally you would be all over a scene like this like a rash.'

'Trust me, Jan, she is. One of the best I've worked with.'

Fabel held a cramped briefing in the Commissariat's main conference room. His strategy was simple: to get every door knocked on, every memory jogged, every detail noted. At the same time, he hoped against hope that the forensic survey of the murder scene would reveal something that would point them in the direction of the Valkyrie. He and Vestergaard plotted out when the assassin had been in Oslo, and an estimate, from Astrid Bremer's initial observations, of when Sparwald had died. From that Fabel worked out a rough schedule for the killer, and put a team on to looking at flights, trains, ferries. It was a long shot, particularly as they were dealing with someone who clearly did not leave traces. Or make mistakes. Ever.

Fabel got home about ten and told Susanne what his day had yielded.

'You look bushed,' she said. 'Have you eaten?'

'I grabbed something at Poppenbüttel.' He sighed. 'We spent hours trying to trace her steps. I don't know, Susanne . . . this killer, the thing with Margarethe Paulus, sometimes I think it's all beyond me. For the first time in years I feel totally lost with a case.'

Susanne smiled and pushed back a lock of hair that had fallen over Fabel's brow. 'Do you want me to tell you what I think?'

'Of course I do. I always want your opinion. You know that.'

'I'm not talking about my professional opinion. I mean my personal opinion.'

'Okay.'

'Men are always trying to work out the secret of being a success with women. You're always asking each other that. The answer is that the man who is most successful with women is the man who has no secret. The man who doesn't treat them as if they're from another planet.'

'Are you trying to improve my courting skills?'

'No, Jan. You did all right in that department. But this case . . . because you're dealing with women, with a female serial killer and/or a professional female assassin, you think you have no frame of reference. The truth is there *are* differences in the offending behaviours of each gender. But you are basically thinking about this all the wrong way because you're thinking about it in a different way. Just do what you do, Jan. Forget the gender and focus on the crimes.'

Fabel thought about what Susanne had said. 'You might be right,' he said.

'Come on,' she said. 'Let's go to bed. You need a good night's sleep. Things will look different in the morning.'

It took a while for Fabel to drift off and when he did fragments of dreams punctuated his sleep. Vague fragments. Irma Grese. Margarethe Paulus. And another woman whose face he could not make out.

8.

'You're looking for me.' He broke off. Another coughing fit and muffled sounds indicating he had covered the mouthpiece with his hand. When he came back on the line his voice sounded harder, more determined, as if annoyed at his own weakness. 'I know you've been looking for me.'

'Of course I've been looking for you,' said Sylvie Achtenhagen. 'What did you expect? Have you got more information for me?'

'You've seen all you need to see. You don't need to look for me. You don't need to find me,' said Siegfried. 'I want us to meet.'

'Face to face?' asked Sylvie. As she spoke, she looked out of the hotel window. It was a transit hotel, one of the ones just off the autobahn, and she watched the rain-fudged dark shapes of cars and lorries drift silently along the ribbon of motorway in the near distance.

'Face to face,' he said. 'Have you got my money?'

'You know the answer to that already. You know it's not that simple.'

'Everything in life is as simple as you choose to make it. Decisions about life and death are the most straightforward. A decision about whether you want someone else to get this scoop is a simple one.'

'Listen,' said Sylvie, 'we can sort something out.'

'Of course we can. I want something from you and I know you will give it to me. Like I said, it's simple.'

After Siegfried hung up, Sylvie remained at the window for a moment, still watching silent cars in the distance. She was closing in on him. She knew that. He knew she was looking for him because she had obviously been looking in the right places. Sylvie went across to the bed and laid out the sheets with the names she had narrowed it down to. They were all over the East of Germany and one was back in Hamburg. One of these was Siegfried, she was sure of it.

Sylvie rose early the next morning and drove the fifty kilometres to Dresden. There she met with a retired accounts clerk called Berger. Berger, like Frau Schneeg, had sought to hide his past as a Stasi officer by moving from his home town to Dresden. Nonetheless, word, Berger explained, had a habit of getting around.

'You were on Ulrich Adebach's staff, is that right, Herr Berger?' Sylvie looked around his apartment. Clean but small and cheaply furnished. Depressing.

'You say there's something in this for me?' Berger asked. He was a small man in his sixties, his hair still dark, his face narrow and pinched.

'I can pay you something,' said Sylvie. 'If the information is useful.'

'And no one will know about my involvement? My helping you?'

'No one knows I'm here, Herr Berger, and no one will find out, I promise you. Anything you tell me will stay between us.'

'Yes. I was on Adebach's staff. He was an old bastard.'

'How long?'

'Six and a half years. From nineteen seventy-seven until eighty-four. Then I was transferred.'

'Voluntarily?'

'No. I ended up in another department, going through tapes of bugged conversations, that kind of thing.'

'Why were you transferred?'

'Adebach got a new adjutant. A mean bastard called Helmut Kittel. He had it in for me.'

'While you were on Adebach's staff, did you ever come across a Major Georg Drescher? He was HVA or special operations. I think he might even have been Section A. I have reason to believe he worked on a project called Operation Valkyrie.'

Berger thought hard. Sylvie could see he was making a big effort to earn his money. 'No . . . I can't say I ever came across him at the department. Never heard of any Operation Valkyrie, either.'

'It involved the training of young women for special operations.'

Again Berger looked gloomily thoughtful, then his expression lightened. 'Wait a minute, there *was* something . . . I remember Adebach requested some files that had been couriered in to be brought through to him. The courier had asked for Kittel – he'd obviously been told to deliver them into his hands so that he could in turn take them in to Adebach. But Kittel was on a meal break so I took the files through. Adebach was on the phone and he told me to wait. He checked through the files and then waved me away. But I do remember the files had photographs of young women in them. Teenagers, really. They also had an HVA stamp on them. When Kittel came back from his meal break he went crazy. Not long after that I was transferred.'

'What did Kittel look like?'

'A miserable streak of piss. He was about one metre ninety tall and as skinny as a rake. Probably because of all of the cigarettes he smoked. A real chain-smoker.'

'How old was he?'

'Thirty, maybe,' said Berger with an expression of distaste. 'Looked younger. He was the real boy wonder of the department.'

'So he was involved with whatever project was in the files?'

'I don't know if "involved" is the right word. He was a gofer. A filer and paper-shuffler. But he would have had sight of a lot of the files that crossed Adebach's desk.'

Sylvie sat quietly for a moment, looking around without taking in the meagre, dull apartment.

'Was that useful for you?' asked Berger expectantly.

'Oh yes,' said Sylvie. 'I think Herr Kittel and I have already crossed paths.'

'I'd watch him, if I were you. I heard he went on to bigger things. Investigations. Rooting out undesirable elements. He developed a nasty reputation.'

'It's all right – Siegfried and I understand each other only too well . . .' said Sylvie, ignoring Berger's confused expression.

9.

It was a bright morning. Again there was a welcome freshness in the air and Fabel woke to find himself in a more optimistic mood. Karin Vestergaard was already at the Presidium when he arrived and he waited patiently while she made various phone calls in Danish.

'Sorry about that,' she said. 'I got my office to see if they could find out anything about Gina Brønsted and NeuHansa from a Danish perspective. It would appear that Brønsted has almost as many business interests in Copenhagen as she does here in Hamburg. Added to which she has companies across all the Scandinavian countries.'

'Nothing dodgy?' asked Fabel.

'Not that we know about. She seems to be very active in environmental management and technologies. She helps other corporations become greener. It's a big business now.'

'I've arranged a meeting with her this afternoon,' said Fabel. 'Believe me, it wasn't easy. But this morning we don't have far to travel . . .'

Fabel was as good as his word: the Hamburg State Police Academy on Braamkamp was less than a kilometre distant from the Police Presidium. It was here that officers were shaped for command and developments in policing analysed, developed and passed on to the city's officers. It was a building Fabel was only too familiar with. When he arrived the main hallway was filled with between-classes students. He found himself thinking about his daughter Gabi and how her recently announced decision could lead her here too.

Principal Commissar Michael Lange was not an officer whom Fabel had encountered before. From what Fabel had been able to find out, Lange had started off in the Polizei Schleswig-Holstein and had transferred to the Polizei Hamburg early in his career. He was now a lecturer in the Hamburg State Police Academy; but it was Lange's experience early in his career that brought Fabel to his door.

The older uniformed officer at reception directed Fabel and Vestergaard up to the first floor of the Academy. A tall, lean man in a blue Hamburg Schutzpolizei uniform was leaning into the corridor from his office, clearly watching out for Fabel after having been told of his arrival by reception.

'Principal Chief Commissar Fabel?' Lange smiled and extended his hand as Fabel approached. Lange was about forty but Fabel felt he had the eyes of an older man. But that was maybe just because he knew of Lange's experience.

'Call me Jan,' said Fabel. 'This is *Politidirektør* Karin Vestergaard of the Danish National Police. Could we speak in English? It would save me a lot of translating.'

'Sure,' said Lange. 'I just hope my English is good enough.'

'Thanks for arranging to see me so soon,' said Fabel. 'It's just that the case I'm working on has a Balkan connection and Anna Wolff, whom I believe you know, suggested I should talk to you.'

'I'll help if I can,' said Lange. 'You said on the phone you were looking into Goran Vujačić's death. And his background.

Of course his death wasn't in our jurisdiction but in yours, Frau Vestergaard.'

'Vujačić's death may not have been in our jurisdiction, but the murder of the Danish detective who was investigating it is,' said Fabel. 'He was one of Frau Vestergaard's officers. We suspect that the Danish officer was murdered by the same professional assassin who took out Vujačić. I take it you understand that this must stay between us, Michael?'

'Of course.'

'We suspect that this person is a contract killer, based here in Hamburg. And that makes everything our jurisdiction.'

Lange pursed his lips meditatively. 'You're right. We do have jurisdiction under Section Seven of the Criminal Code if the perpetrator is a German national. And you say no one outside the Commission is aware of this? What about top brass – shouldn't they be told?'

'The Police President has been briefed,' said Fabel. 'But at the moment we're keeping it tight. There's been another murder, committed by someone else, but it is related to the investigation and we're trying to keep it quiet until we flush out this killer.'

'And you think there may be something in Vujačić's background that could point you in the direction of more solid evidence?'

'Truth is, I don't know. But if this Valkyrie – that's what this contract assassin is supposed to be code-named – if this Valkyrie is based here, then he or she would have a pretty good motive for taking Jespersen out of the equation. And Vujačić is the connection.'

'Okay, I'm glad to help if I can. The jurisdiction issue may not be an issue at all. But I only know about three years of Vujačić's life. The three years he was active in the Bosnian War. And even then Vujačić was not a leading figure. More a footnote in the diary of atrocity, so to speak. We never got enough to indict him, mainly because he successfully argued a special defence of alibi. He had gall, I'll say that. He never tried to hide, like most of the others. But there again, that actually worked in his favour. Flight is a judicially acceptable indicator of possible guilt.'

'So you think he was innocent?'

'Like hell. Goran Vujačić was clever and more than a little lucky. I wasn't personally involved in his case, but I was able to access the files through OSCE.' Lange referred to the Organisation for Security and Cooperation in Europe. 'Vujačić had already assembled a gang around him. The writing was on the wall as soon as NATO got involved in the conflict and I think that Vujačić started to look at the bigger picture. But Vujačić was there. In the rape camps. In the forests by the mass graves. He was up to his elbows in it all, except that he had half a dozen affidavits swearing he was lying wounded in a hospital bed in Banja Luka.'

'This unit or gang of his . . . Petra Meissner of the Sabine Charity told me they called themselves the Dogheads or something.'

'Yep. *Psoglav*. It's Serbian for "doghead", but it's also a mythical creature that Serbs – Bosnian Serbs in particular – used to believe in. A pagan demon or werewolf-type thing. The *Psoglav* unit was little more than an organised-crime gang and that's exactly what it became after the conflict. There was talk – little more than a rumour, mind – that Vujačić and his *Psoglav* chums got heavily involved in people trafficking after the Bosnian War. All kinds of bad stuff: organ farming, selling women into the sex trade, slave-labour sweatshops, that kind of thing. But you'd have to talk to the Europol organised-crime division about that. As far as I'm aware, Vujačić was not directly active in Northern Europe. Sorry, that's not that helpful, is it?'

'I appreciate it anyway,' said Fabel.

'One thing I would say,' said Lange, 'is that Vujačić was

one of the most evil sons of bitches to walk the earth. The stories about what he did to Bosniaks, Croats and ethnic Albanians . . . particularly what he did to women. I tell you, I saw more than my fair share of beasts out there, and Vujačić was right up there with the worst of them. Unfortunately it's not always about who deserves justice most, but about who you can get the evidence on. Vujačić was such a cunning little bastard that we never had anything more than rumour on him. It's not a very policeman-like thing to say, but when he got topped my first reaction was that he got what he deserved. The only pity is that he didn't suffer the same way the people who fell into his hands did.'

Fabel nodded, watching Lange. There are some things, he thought, even in this job, that it's better not to see. To know. At that moment he knew he was talking to someone whose dreams were even darker, even more terrifying, than his own.

'Thanks, Michael,' said Fabel. 'If anything else comes to mind, please let me know.'

Fabel and Karin Vestergaard had just stepped through the revolving doors and into the bright double-storey reception atrium of the Police Presidium in Alsterdorf when they were stopped in their tracks by a determined-looking Anna Wolff.

'Don't take your coats off,' she said, with a grin. 'We'll take your car, *Chef*. I'll give you directions. There's someone I want you to meet . . .'

The café Anna took them to was in the Sachsentor pedestrian zone in Hamburg-Bergedorf. When they arrived, a young woman with a pretty but rather severe face and long dark hair was waiting for them. Sandra Kraus sat with a huge canvas bag at her side, the strap still over her shoulder, and tapped the café table with the tips of her fingers as Fabel, Vestergaard and Anna approached, almost as if she was announcing their arrival with a drum roll. She didn't stand up but smiled at them. Fabel noticed that it was like when Karin Vestergaard smiled: nothing of it seemed to reach the eyes.

'I've known Sandra since we were kids,' said Anna after she had done the introductions. 'She was the smartest student in the whole school. And she is an absolutely brilliant cryptologist.'

'Really?' said Fabel with genuine interest but looking questioningly at Anna. He was slightly distracted as Kraus drummed her fingers again on the tabletop. He turned to her and found the intensity of her gaze disturbing, as if she was looking at him as an object rather than a person.

'Yes – really,' said Anna, with more than a hint of defiance. 'And trust me, bringing you here to meet Sandra isn't a waste of time. I gave her a copy of *Muliebritas*. The same issue we found in Drescher's flat.'

'Does she know . . . ?'

Anna shook her head. 'You told us to keep a lid on the Drescher thing and that's exactly what I've done. Sandra only knows that we may have a coded message in this magazine. To be honest, that's all she's interested in.'

'And did she find anything?' asked Vestergaard.

'It took her five minutes to find the message and crack the code. No more.'

'Are you trying to tell me that an amateur cryptologist can break a code created by one of the world's most successful secret police and espionage agencies?' Fabel smiled patronisingly.

Kraus drummed her fingers on the table again, took a sip of her coffee and then spoke briskly. 'I have advantages that they didn't have. I have an inbuilt ability to recognise patterns in things. What you see as complexity, I see as structure and ultimately simplicity.'

'There's more,' said Anna. 'I got all of the issues of *Muliebritas* for the last three years. Drescher was using it regularly to communicate with the Valkyrie. Sandra has decoded dozens of messages.'

'It really wasn't that difficult. The person who called himself "Uncle Georg" in the announcements used a combination of polyalphabetic cyphers. Basically he used a Vigenère Square with a staggered shift of Caesar cyphers. Basic stuff. For example . . .'

She took a pad and pencil out of the huge shoulder bag and wrote ALTONABALKONSFOURTHIRTYPMTHURSDAY on the pad. Fabel noticed that Kraus's handwriting was perfect, the capital letters corresponded exactly with the lines on the pad.

'That becomes VLEYLRJEGKZXQWWYMTSSPKGTHT-SEPJLET,' she continued. 'Of course, a long jumble of letters like that would be very easily noticed by anyone looking at the magazine, and would attract the attention of any cryptologist, so he buried them in several personal ads throughout the announcements section. He put in thanks notices that listed names. The initials would give several of the encrypted letters in each announcement.'

'And you're absolutely positive that you have interpreted the codes correctly?' asked Fabel.

'Like I said, it was a simple enough encryption. In principle. But for three hundred years the Vigenère cypher was considered unbreakable simply because to decode the encryption you have to know which word was used as the keyword. In other words, what the vertical letters are on the axis of the Vigenère Square.'

'And you worked it out?' asked Fabel. 'How?'

'I just saw it. I have this knack for frequency analysis of letters and recognition of common pairings. I read all the messages and I could see the patterns. You're only supposed to be able to do frequency analysis with monoalphabetic cyphers; not with a polyalphabetic cypher like this one where an encrypted letter can be decoded as more than one original.'

'But Sandra can do it,' said Anna with clear pride in her friend's abilities. 'Tell him the keyword, Sandra.'

'Valkyrie,' said Kraus, again drumming out the same tattoo with her fingertips on the tabletop. 'The word used as the keyword was Valkyrie.'

As Anna drove back to the Presidium, Fabel sat in the passenger seat and went through the messages Sandra Kraus had decoded.

'These are all times and places,' said Fabel over his shoulder to Vestergaard, who sat in the back. 'Obviously he passed anything sensitive on in person. This was just used to set up a meeting.'

'So that means we can now do exactly the same,' said Vestergaard. 'We can lure this Valkyrie out into the open. Assuming she really doesn't know about Drescher's death.'

'We've still got the lid tight on that, but for how much longer I don't know.' Fabel turned to Anna. 'That's an interesting friend you've got there.'

'Sandra? She's great. She has a genius IQ.'

'I guessed that much,' Fabel said, with a small laugh.

'And she's an Aspie.'

'A what?'

'Did you notice her drumming her fingers all the time? Same rhythm, same number of beats. Or how she's got an unnerving way of seeking eye contact with you?'

'As a matter of fact I did,' said Fabel.

'Sandra has Asperger's syndrome. But she calls herself an Aspie. She doesn't see herself as a sufferer from a disability. Just different, and she's cool with that. She campaigns for a group that promotes neurodiversity . . . the idea that there is more than one type of mind. She calls us NTs – Neurologically Typical.'

'I thought people with Asperger's have difficulty with interpersonal relationships. You said she's your friend . . .' said Vestergaard from the back seat.

'A good friend,' said Anna. 'Sandra has problems in some areas, but, as you could see, there are compensations in others. And she has taught herself coping strategies and stuff. I've learned not to judge. It's funny: Sandra said that one of the stereotypes people have of Aspies is that they have little or no empathy for the feelings of others. That's why it's often difficult to recognise a male Aspie: who can tell the difference from a normal man?'

Vestergaard gave a loud laugh. Fabel shrugged.

'Well, one thing's for sure,' he said. 'Your friend Sandra has probably given us our biggest break in this case so far.'

The preliminary forensics survey of Sparwald's house had, as expected, surrendered nothing much. Fabel was surprised, however, at just how much Astrid Bremer had been able to read from such meagre trace evidence. She was still at Poppenbüttel when she phoned him at his office in the Presidium.

'I've had the body removed and we'll get the autopsy report, obviously. But my guess is that the victim was dead before he hit the floor. The killer put another bullet in him, firing along the victim's already supine body and causing an entry wound under his chin. Very professional job. The last shot was probably insurance. Professional meticulousness.'

'There was a similar murder outside Oslo,' said Fabel. 'Exactly the same modus.'

'My guess is that the victim didn't let the killer into the house. There was a book beside him on the floor. No prints other than his own and it's obvious he dropped it when he was shot. And I found powder traces on the wall by the lounge door and on the edge of the door itself. Again no prints on the door handle or anywhere else that I could see. I'm guessing that the killer opened the lounge door, stepped in and fired before the victim had time to respond. The killer didn't need to go any further into the room, so she retraced her steps back along the hall to the front door. It was a hunch, but I was right: there is no evidence of the door having been forced, but there is some fresh scratching around the lock. She picked it.'

'But nothing we can get DNA from? Or any trace of any kind?' Fabel failed to conceal his frustration.

'A faint partial bootprint in the hall, bearing traces of soil from the garden, but that could have been anyone's and made at any time. And, anyway, it's not big enough to give us a match.'

'Great,' said Fabel.

'Sorry. I did my best,' said Astrid and, even over the phone, Fabel could tell that she meant it. 'I went over everything three times. Tried all the tricks. There just wasn't anything to find.'

'It's not your fault. Holger told me that if anyone could get something, you could. He also said you're the best he's worked with for cold scenes.'

'Thanks,' Astrid said. 'But whoever killed Sparwald is better.'

After he'd hung up Fabel made his way into the main Murder Commission meeting room. Werner, Anna, Henk and Dirk were waiting for him. He had also invited Karin Vestergaard to join them, but she had phoned in to say she'd be a few minutes late.

'You know,' said Werner, 'if we're looking for a Valkyrie, we couldn't go far wrong looking at the Danish ice maiden. She's a cold one all right.'

'She's a good cop, from what I can see,' said Fabel.

'Listen,' said Anna, 'while we're on the subject of people we should be thinking about . . . I'm not being funny, but there are two women we should maybe take a long hard look at. Martina Schilmann and Petra Meissner.'

'Why Martina?' Fabel searched Anna's face for meaning. 'She's ex-Polizei Hamburg, for God's sake.'

'She was also involved with Westland and was there at the

scene. Let's face it, we've only got her word that she was at the opposite end of Herbertstrasse all the time she said she was. And she was brought up in the GDR, as was Petra Meissner. Both fall within the age range we have for the Valkyrie.'

'What?' said Fabel dismissively. 'So now we're going to suspect all women from East Germany? We'd better bring in Chancellor Merkel, then. She was brought up in Brandenburg, after all.' Fabel sarcastically put on an expression of enlightenment. 'And she was in the Free German Youth!'

'Seriously, *Chef*,' pressed Anna. 'We can't ignore the fact that two women involved with Jake Westland spent their youth in the GDR.'

'But Martina's background will have been thoroughly checked out before she was allowed to join the Polizei Hamburg. And I would say that Petra Meissner's public profile is far too visible for her to operate as a professional killer.'

'Maybe so,' said Anna. 'But if Martina Schilmann is the Valkyrie, then her backstory in the GDR would be as solid as it could be . . .'

'Okay, check it out.' Fabel turned to Hechtner. 'Dirk, were you able to get any more on who "Olaf" might be – the name in Jespersen's notebook?'

'Nope, sorry, *Chef*. From the little we've been able to piece together, there's nothing to suggest Drescher ever used "Olaf" as a pseudonym. No Olafs that we can see connected to Goran Vujačić, Jake Westland or Armin Lensch either. We're still looking into any Olaf that Ralf Sparwald might have known.'

'It could be incidental,' said Fabel. 'Maybe nothing to it all.'

Fabel waited until Vestergaard arrived and the rest of the team had assembled in the Incident Room.

'Okay. We've got a break,' he said addressing the whole team. 'Thanks to Anna, we've cracked the code behind

Drescher's messages to the Valkyrie. All the messages have been simple time-and-place set-ups for meetings. It's an example of institutional thinking. They formed their working system in a time before reunification, using the methods of the Cold War. I'm guessing that Drescher was uncomfortable with new technology, otherwise they could have used the Internet or anonymous email accounts. Having said that, there's no evidence that they didn't use these means in addition to the magazine announcements.'

'Why do it at all?' asked Werner. 'After all, they could have simply phoned each other. No one knew who Drescher was and she could have had an untraceable cellphone.'

'Like I said, institutional thinking. Drescher was in the same city as the Valkyrie, but their entire relationship had been created to operate at long distances, with the Valkyrie working on her own most of the time. When they set up in Hamburg, post-Reunification, they kept their old way of working. Inflexibility, I suppose.'

As he spoke, Fabel noticed that Astrid Bremer, the deputy head of the forensics team, had come into the Incident Room and was standing at the back.

'Anyway,' continued Fabel, 'we've managed to get the cooperation of *Muliebritas* magazine. They're going to hold us a space in the next issue. It's due out next week, so we've had to work fast to get our wording right. There doesn't seem to be any regular meeting place. The only common element is that it seems to always be in an open space, presumably so she can check it out as she approaches him, but with enough people around for them to be inconspicuous. As far as we can see, all meetings have been in Altona or Hamburg city centre.'

'What about the Rathausplatz in front of the City Chambers?' asked Anna. 'We could put someone on each corner and on the U-Bahn entrance.'

'I suspect that would be a little too public for the Valkyrie.

Drescher always picked quieter venues. People milling about but not crowds. The other thing is we want to limit the risk to the public if things go pear-shaped.'

'What if we used the Altona Balkon?' asked Werner.

'Drescher used it once before, as far as we can see. The last meeting, in fact.'

'What about the Alsterpark next to where you used to live, *Chef*?' said Anna. 'On the shores of the Outer Alster? It would be reasonably easy to secure but quite difficult for the Valkyrie to spot us.'

Fabel thought for a moment. 'That sounds good. Anybody have any objections?'

There were none.

'Okay,' said Fabel to Werner. 'Let's get this encrypted and spread across three announcements, the way Drescher did: "Alsterpark at Fährdamm. Eleven-thirty, Wednesday". That gives us a week to get it all set up. In the meantime, I'm going to do a bit of digging into Goran Vujačić's history. It was his untimely demise that brought Jens Jespersen to Hamburg.' He turned to Vestergaard and spoke in English. 'I'd like you to come along with me, if that's okay. I'd also like us both to go and visit Gina Brønsted. The NeuHansa Group keeps cropping up in all of this.'

'Of course,' she said and smiled in a way so cool that it reminded him of Margarethe Paulus. 'It would be my pleasure.'

After Fabel had set the team about their various tasks, Astrid Bremer came over to him. She looked young and girlish and, for a moment, Fabel found it difficult to imagine her being an expert on death.

'I think I have something,' she said.

'From Sparwald's house?' asked Fabel hopefully.

'No, from the Drescher apartment. We have a fingerprint specialist who can extrapolate prints from very faint or old traces. I found a packet of *Rondo Melange*, the popular East

German coffee. I just thought it was odd that a man trying so hard to conceal his Stasi past and living with a phoney West German history would have something like that in his cupboard. Well, I've just heard back from my fingerprint guy. We've got a print that doesn't belong.'

'The coffee was a gift?'

'That's what I thought,' said Astrid. 'And a gift from someone who knew of Drescher's GDR background. And that could only be one person . . .'

Fabel had just walked into his office to fetch his coat when his phone rang.

'Hello, Principal Chief Commissar Fabel? This is Dr Lüttig – Thomas Lüttig at SkK Biotech. I heard about Ralf . . . one of your people came round. A young woman.'

'Commissar Wolff, yes. I'm sorry about Dr Sparwald, I know you valued him as a colleague.'

'He was my friend as well, Chief Commissar. Anyway, you asked me to tell you if anything out of the ordinary came up. Well, after I heard about Ralf I spent the afternoon going through all his stuff. There is something . . . It would appear Ralf was doing some work for which there's no company authorisation. Some kind of private project.'

'Oh?' Fabel reached into his drawer and took a notebook out. 'What kind of private project?'

'From what I can see, he has been having blood samples tested. Not many – it looks like just three samples, each from a different donor. I found the samples and some paperwork. It seems very strange indeed.'

'How so?'

'The tests were very specific. Ralf seems to have been looking for PBDEs. Also, he was doing the tests himself and wasn't keeping proper records. But I did find a note relating to each of the samples. The first said: female, twenty-two, Hunan Province.'

'China . . .' Fabel spoke as much to himself as to Lüttig.

'Yes. But the second one isn't. It says: female, twenty-two, Bitola.'

'Bitola?'

'I checked it out on the Internet. It's a city in Macedonia. Very industrial.'

'What are these PBDEs?' asked Fabel.

'Polybrominated diphenyl ethers. They're used a lot in flame-retardants. And in a thousand other things. There's a great deal of concern about their toxicity.'

'You said there was a third sample. What was that labelled?'

'Well, yes . . . it's this third sample that's causing me the most concern. It was labelled Hunan Province, same as the first blood sample. But it's human tissue. And, from the tests Ralf was doing, I'm guessing it's a sample of human thyroid. Which means it has been taken post-mortem. And there's something else.'

'What?'

'From what I can see of his results, the level of PBDEs in these samples is astronomical.'

'What does that mean?' asked Fabel. 'Could it be fatal?'

'Potentially, yes. Like I said, they're incredibly toxic and you need a special licence to dispose of them. The jury is still out on what damage they actually do, but they are suspected of causing problems with the thyroid gland, the endocrine system generally and even neurological damage.'

'Thanks – that could be useful, Dr Lüttig.' Fabel paused. 'By the way, does the name "Olaf" mean anything to you? Someone whom Ralf Sparwald may have known?'

'No, I can't think of anyone. Is it important?'

'Probably not,' said Fabel.

He didn't like business types.

It didn't matter how exalted or lowly they were in their arcane corporate hierarchies, they all, to Fabel, seemed to have had some kind of personality-ectomy. He had recently flown to Frankfurt for a meeting with the city's Murder Commission. On the flight, Fabel had sat in his British tailored sports jacket surrounded by Boss-suited clones and feeling like an extra in the film *Gattaca*. He had promised himself he would blow his brains out with his SIG-Sauer before owning a BlackBerry.

Fabel even found it difficult at times to hide his disdain for the type of police officers who seemed to be in 'the business of policing' and who dressed in the same corporate-clone style as their commercial counterparts.

But it was the business leaders at the top of the tree who wound Fabel up most of all. Sometimes, it was as if they thought themselves medieval barons. In a way, Fabel supposed, they had a point: Hamburg was a city, and a state, that had built its history and independence on a foundation of trade. Instead of having total control over the lives of serfs and bondsmen, the Hanseatic city's tycoons and magnates held employees, subsidiaries, suppliers and not a few of Hamburg's politicians in their thrall. And most of Hamburg's politicians were businessmen themselves.

It had been Fabel's experience that Hamburg's business leaders often felt themselves above and beyond the reach of common mortals like policemen.

So it didn't surprise Fabel that it took his personal intervention to arrange an appointment with Gina Brønsted. He had asked one of the Presidium's administrative assistants to set up a meeting but she had got nowhere, constantly being fobbed off by someone comparatively low down in the NeuHansa food chain.

'That's not a problem,' Fabel had said when Brønsted's secretary's secretary's assistant had said it was 'quite impossible' for an appointment to be made within the next week or so. 'I quite understand that Frau Brønsted is very busy. I'll send a marked police car to her home tonight and bring her into the Presidium. And don't worry, I'll be sure to tell her that you were so protective of her office time.'

Fabel was informed that Gina Brønsted would see him later that afternoon. As soon as the appointment was confirmed he phoned Hans Gessler of the corporate crime division and asked him if he would mind coming along at such short notice.

'Will you be bringing along the Little Mermaid?' asked Gessler.

'What are you talking about?' Fabel was genuinely confused.

'That little Danish beauty I've heard you've grown attached to.'

'If you mean *Politidirektør* Karin Vestergaard, then yes, as a matter of fact she will be there. Gina Brønsted is a Flensburg Dane and I thought it might be useful. And anyway, *Politidirektør* Vestergaard has a direct interest in this case.'

'Count me in,' said Gessler.

Given the trouble that he had had in securing an appointment with Gina Brønsted, Fabel was surprised when, as he was leaving the Presidium, he was handed a note at reception telling him that Gennady Frolov's office had been looking for him, asking if it would be possible for Fabel to talk with the Russian. Frolov was on Fabel's *to do* list and he made a mental note to follow up the call when he got back.

The NeuHansa Group had its offices in a brand-new building in the HafenCity. Fabel had picked up Gessler and Vestergaard and drove through the city from the Presidium down to the shores of the Elbe. They crossed over the short cantilevered bridge into the Speicherstadt.

'This is amazing,' said Vestergaard as they entered the maze of narrow cobbled streets, cathedral-sized red-brick warehouses and interconnecting canals.

'The Speicherstadt was a toll-free zone right up until a few years ago,' said Gessler eagerly, leaning over from the back seat. 'I think it was two thousand and four . . . up until then the Speicherstadt was an independent free port and the world's biggest bonded area.'

Gessler was a shortish but good-looking man in his forties with a reputation for being a bit of a ladykiller. Fabel had noticed when he picked him up at the Presidium that Gessler was wearing a Hugo Boss suit. And tapping something into his BlackBerry.

Fabel had also noticed that Gessler's eyes had lit up as soon as he had introduced him to Karin Vestergaard. The light had failed to catch in hers.

'There's been a lot of new building,' explained Fabel. 'The Hanseatic Trade Centre in the Speicherstadt itself as well as the HafenCity, which is all new. Gina Brønsted has head-quartered her NeuHansa Group in one of the biggest and newest buildings. Rumour has it she has a thirteen-million-euro penthouse apartment *above the shop*, as it were.'

They passed through the Speicherstadt and into the HafenCity. Glass and steel were everywhere, but it was obvious an effort had been made to extend something of the spirit of the old Speicherstadt into the architecture of the twenty-first century.

'Very impressive,' said Vestergaard.

'It's not finished,' said Gessler. 'There's going to be an opera house to compete with Sydney – the Elbphilharmonie Concert Hall.'

'How do you want to handle this, Jan?' asked Vestergaard as if she hadn't heard Gessler.

'I'll ask her about Lensch, her employee, and Claasens, the export agent. She also met Westland the night he died. This is all quite . . . *involved*. She's a Flensburg Dane – I think I told you that already – meaning she's German by nationality but Danish by ethnicity and first language. If I'm struggling, maybe you can jump in. Also, I'll leave the questioning about

Jespersen to you.' Fabel turned and spoke to Gessler. 'Hans, I smell a rat here. I'm not saying Brønsted herself is directly involved with any of these killings, but NeuHansa is always there in the background.'

'I don't interrogate people, Jan – I interrogate paperwork and computer data. If there's a link between NeuHansa and these murders, then there will be something on file, some-where, something that might look innocuous but which will point us in the right direction. I need to get access to their files. When you introduce me, it would be best not to disclose my department, unless she asks specifically.'

'Okay.' Fabel swung his door open and got out, followed by Gessler and Vestergaard. He heard Gessler give a low appreciative whistle and when he turned he half expected the corporate cop to be staring at Karin Vestergaard's legs. Instead Fabel followed his eyes to a massive, sleek luxury motor yacht anchored further down the quay. The yacht had the look of something equally suited for space travel as sailing: a long, elegant white needle with a superstructure of black glass and elongated arches. A helicopter sat on the aft deck.

'I know what that is,' said Gessler. 'That's the *Snow Queen*. Ninety metres and it came in at about a million euros a metre.'

'Gennady Frolov's yacht?' asked Fabel, his eyes still following the lines of the mega-yacht. Fabel was not a sailor, and he had no real interest in boats, but it struck him that the *Snow Queen* was one of the most graceful objects he had ever seen.

'Yep,' said Gessler. 'Take a good look . . . this is as close as you or I will ever get to that kind of wealth.'

They headed into the NeuHansa Group building. A recep-tionist who looked as if she'd been recruited from a model agency rather than a business school asked them to wait in the vast pillared atrium. They sat on one of the dozen white leather sofas, each of which looked several times more expensive than the one that Fabel and Susanne had at home. Like the mega-yacht docked half a kilometre along the quay, this was intimidation by wealth.

'Do you want to get a drink afterwards?' asked Gessler while they waited. 'We could *deconstruct* the interview.'

'Sorry,' said Fabel, although he knew the true direction of Gessler's invitation. 'I'm meeting a friend in town.'

'And I have work to do for my office in Copenhagen,' said Vestergaard without a smile.

After waiting ten minutes, they were conducted up to the eighth floor of the NeuHansa building.

The office suite was populated only by a few workstations and a handful of male and female staff who looked as if they'd come from the same model agency as the downstairs receptionist. Another point in the making: a lavish underuse of some of the most expensive floor space in Hamburg. Fabel, Gessler and Vestergaard were led into an inner office. It was huge and plush and looked more like a trendy hotel suite than a working environment. A tall, slim woman in her early to mid forties stepped out from behind an impossibly huge desk, indicating that they should all take a seat on the sofas arranged around a coffee table. Gina Brønsted was what Fabel would have described as a handsome woman. Attractive, but with a jaw so strong that it hinted at the masculine. Her blonde hair was cut shortish, but in a manner that softened the severity of her features. Everything about her – her hair, her cream jacket and skirt suit, the matching shoes, her simple sky-blue blouse – was understated and tasteful. It also screamed wealth. Fabel realised he was looking at the flesh and blood equivalent of the luxury yacht anchored outside.

'Frau Brønsted?' asked Fabel, remaining standing.

'Herr Fabel.' She smiled and extended her hand. 'Please . . . sit. Excuse me a moment.' She walked over to the door and said something to the woman who had shown them in.

'I've asked Svend Langstrup to join us. Herr Langstrup is

in charge of all security matters as well as being one of my team of legal advisers.'

Fabel responded by introducing Karin Vestergaard and Hans Gessler. As Gessler had suggested, Fabel didn't mention that he was from the Polizei Hamburg's corporate crime division.

On hearing Vestergaard's name, Gina Brønsted smiled broadly and began speaking in Danish. After a short exchange she turned back to Fabel.

'I'm sorry, I don't often get a chance to speak my native language.'

'If you don't mind, for Frau Vestergaard's sake we'll speak in English.'

'That's not necessary,' said Vestergaard in lightly accented German. 'I'll be able to follow what's said.'

Fabel stared at Vestergaard blankly for a moment. 'Good . . .' he said. He gave a small laugh and shook his head. 'That will save a lot of time . . .'

'I must say, Herr Fabel, that I have a pretty good idea what it is you want to talk to me about. I've already been through it all with that annoyingly persistent lady from HansSat TV.'

'Sylvie Achtenhagen?' Fabel shook his head. 'She's been here?'

'Pushing her luck. I reminded her that I had a controlling stake in the station she worked for. She's a very arrogant individual, you know.'

'You don't say,' said Fabel without a hint of irony. At that moment a tall dark-haired man of about forty walked into the room and smiled at everybody. He was slim, but broad across the shoulders. At some point his nose had been broken and there was a faint scar on his forehead, just above the eye. He didn't look to Fabel like a legal adviser, unless lawsuits in Denmark were settled in a boxing ring. The man introduced himself as Langstrup and sat down.

'You take care of security for Frau Brønsted?' asked Fabel.

'Amongst other things, yes,' answered Langstrup, without the Danish accent that Fabel had expected. Fabel guessed he was a German Dane like Brønsted herself. 'With Frau Brønsted's rising political profile, as well as her success in business, there are sometimes threats to her safety.'

'There have been threats?' asked Vestergaard.

'Potential threats.'

'We're here to discuss a number of recent deaths. All of these deaths have some connection to the NeuHansa Group. Not always directly, but there always seems to be a tie-in.'

Gina Brønsted frowned. 'Naturally if we can help we will do all we can.'

'You are standing for Principal Mayor, Frau Brønsted?'

'That's public knowledge. I don't see—'

'Could you tell me something about your political platform?' asked Fabel.

'I really don't see the relevance,' said Langstrup.

'Indulge me,' said Fabel to Brønsted, ignoring Langstrup. 'Let's say I'm a floating voter.'

'My political platform is pretty much the same as the one my business is built on. Europe is unifying: some day soon there will be a Federal Europe and its economic power will dwarf that of the United States and even emerging superpowers like China and India. Already Europe is an economic and mercantile singularity. That means that old national borders are meaningless and there is an opportunity for new transnational alliances to be built. I am not a *German* politician. I am a *Hamburg* politician. As far as business is concerned, my vision is to build alliances with other Northern European cities and create and share the kind of prosperity that national governments are incapable of delivering.'

'Like the old Hanseatic League,' said Fabel. 'Hence the NeuHansa name.'

'The Hanseatic League is long dead and gone. Hamburg

adopted the title "Free and Hanseatic City of Hamburg" a century and a half *after* the League had ceased to be an active economic or political force. But the *idea* lived on. You still see it today – all around you. Here. If the Hanseatic ideal hadn't lived on in the Hamburg psyche, then the Speicherstadt would not have been built here. And this, the HafenCity – it's another example of Hamburg's independence and entrepreneurial spirit.' Brønsted talked with force but, Fabel thought, without genuine passion. He realised he was listening to a party political broadcast. Well, he thought, he had asked for it, after all.

'Ten, fifteen years ago,' continued Brønsted, 'when the rest of Europe was navel-gazing about the future of the world economy, Hamburg saw that China and the Far East, as well as Eastern Europe, offered a massive trading opportunity. So we acted and built dedicated facilities to make the most of that opportunity. Look at what's happening just a few hundred metres from here in Sandtorhafen. A vast area of the HafenCity devoted exclusively to trade with China. Do you realise that of the ten point eight million container units Hamburg is expected to handle this year, one out of every five of those containers will be traffic to or from China? My politics are simple. Hamburg needs the freedom and independence to build on her successes, to build alliances with other cities in Scandinavia and the Baltic and together to outclass every other trading location in the world.'

'All good in theory,' said Fabel. 'But, like you said, ultimately the Hanseatic League failed.'

'It lasted in one form or another for nearly three hundred years, Herr Fabel. It was a superpower within Europe. A mercantile rather than a military superpower. It had military might, but it hardly ever used it. War is bad for business. I think that's a pretty good model for the future of Europe.'

'But you're a Dane,' said Karin Vestergaard. 'A German Dane, admittedly, but you know that unbridled capitalism just doesn't fit with the Danish character. Yet you include Copenhagen in your plans.'

'This isn't unbridled capitalism,' said Brønsted. 'It's about generating great wealth and sharing it. Capitalism with social democracy. And nothing could be more Danish as a concept.'

'I'm sure you didn't come here just to discuss the politics of the NeuHansa Party,' Langstrup said. Fabel noticed Langstrup had small, hard eyes.

'Could you tell me what you know about Armin Lensch?' Fabel asked Brønsted. 'The young man who worked in your export department.'

'Nothing.' Brønsted shrugged. 'I have over a thousand employees. Obviously I was distressed to hear about his death. And the manner of his death. But I wasn't even aware of his name until I was informed that the latest victim of the Angel of St Pauli was an employee.'

'Would you mind if we had a look at Lensch's recent work-load?' asked Gessler. He smiled his ladykiller's charming smile. 'It might help us.'

'Help you how?' asked Langstrup. 'His death was clearly not connected to his work.'

'Oh,' said Fabel. 'And how can you be so sure of that?'

'He was the victim of a random serial killer, for God's sake.'

'Not so random, as far as I can see,' said Fabel without diverting his attention from Gina Brønsted. 'It is by no means certain that the so-called Angel of St Pauli was responsible for Lensch's death. And, if you prefer, we can obtain a court order to see his files.'

'That won't be necessary,' said Brønsted and Fabel thought he caught her fire a warning look at Langstrup. As if she was saying: *Be seen to cooperate.* 'Just let us know what you need to see.'

'We won't know until we see it,' said Gessler. 'So we'll have to look at everything, really.'

'I saw Gennady Frolov's yacht, the *Snow Queen*, moored along the quay. Do you have business dealings with him?' asked Fabel.

'The yacht is there because that is the regular mooring for private vessels of that size. But yes, I have had dealings with Herr Frolov. In fact, I have an interest in the Flensburg boat-yard that designed and built the *Snow Queen*.'

'Vantage North?' asked Vestergaard.

'Yes – Vantage North.' Brønsted made an insincerely impressed face. 'You've done your homework.'

'And other than your involvement with Vantage North, do you have any other dealings with Frolov?' asked Fabel.

'As a matter of fact, we are in the middle of negotiations over a joint project. An environmental project.'

'Through your company Norivon?'

'Yes. Why the interest in Herr Frolov?'

'Do you know Peter Claasens, the export agent?'

'Of course I do . . . or did. I heard about his suicide. Claasens Exporting did some work with us. Occasionally.'

'Did you ever meet him?'

'Maybe once. Or twice. Official functions, company events or exhibitions, that kind of thing.' Brønsted smiled politely and held Fabel in her earnest Danish-blue gaze. There it was, he thought: impatience. Annoyance. Just a hint of it, but enough.

'And you met Jake Westland the night he died?'

'Before he died, yes. Before his performance. He was supposed to come to a post-event party but didn't turn up.'

'What did you talk about?' asked Vestergaard. Again Fabel noticed how good her newly found German was.

'The event. The charity – the Sabine Charity – that the concert was in aid of. I really can't remember: it was the usual meaningless chit-chat.'

'Did he do or say anything out of the ordinary?' asked Fabel. 'Did he seem preoccupied or distracted?'

'No.' Brønsted frowned and made too big a show of trying to remember. 'No, I can't say that he did.'

'Okay,' said Fabel in a way that suggested he was mentally ticking off names on a list. 'Another employee, another death . . .'

'Ralf Sparwald?' interjected Langstrup who had followed the exchange intently, his small hard eyes on Fabel.

'Ralf Sparwald,' repeated Fabel, still focused on Brønsted.

'I'm afraid I didn't know him either. I heard about his murder. Is it connected to Armin Lensch's?'

'So, to summarise . . .' Fabel ignored the question. 'You didn't really know Jake Westland, who died within a matter of hours of talking to you; you didn't really know Armin Lensch who was the next victim in St Pauli and who happened to work for you; you didn't *really* know Peter Claasens and met him only a couple of times, but he was an export agent who worked under contract to your company and fell to his death; and you really didn't know Ralf Sparwald, another of your employees, who was professionally executed in his own home.'

Langstrup leaned forward on the sofa, his small, hard eyes smaller and harder. 'If you have a specific accusation to make against Frau Brønsted, I suggest you make it. But if you continue with these insinuations, then this interview is at an end. And I think you should bear in mind the fact that Frau Brønsted is standing for Principal Mayor . . .'

Fabel didn't answer for a moment but watched Gina Brønsted, who remained impassive and silent. 'Let me get this absolutely clear,' he said to Langstrup. 'I am investigating a series of murders and this interview only ends when I say it ends. I am quite happy to make it more formal and move it to the Murder Commission. Secondly, you're supposed to be in charge of NeuHansa's security. Did it never strike you as strange that so many people working for or connected to the company are meeting untimely ends? It must be saving your pension fund a fortune.'

'As a matter of fact it did,' said Langstrup. 'We've been looking into it. My people have found no link between the company and the deaths. Coincidence. The NeuHansa Group has thousands of employees, hundreds of contractors and subcontractors – it's not really that much of a stretch.'

Fabel laughed in disbelief. 'A few years ago, I hunted a serial killer who was obsessed with fairy tales. I tell you, Herr Langstrup, he was more anchored in reality than you are if you believe that a NeuHansa connection with every murder we are investigating is a coincidence.'

'Well, not *every* murder has a NeuHansa connection . . .'

'What do you mean?' asked Fabel.

For a moment Langstrup looked caught off guard. 'Oh, wait . . . no, you're right. I thought the Claasens death wasn't connected, but of course it is . . . I forgot he did work for us as an export agent.'

'I see,' said Fabel, exchanging a knowing look with Vestergaard.

'The Chief Commissar has a point,' Brønsted said to Langstrup. 'I think we should be doing all that we can to cooperate.'

'Of course.' Langstrup smiled dryly.

Fabel asked that Hans Gessler be allowed full access to the company's files. Brønsted offered predictable assurances that NeuHansa would do all it could to aid the investigation and instructed Langstrup to give Gessler anything he needed.

'One more thing, Frau Brønsted,' said Fabel. 'Does the name *Valkyrie* mean anything to you?' He watched her face for any reaction or recognition. All he got was a frown.

'I don't understand . . . I mean, of course it does, Germanic mythology, Wagner, that kind of thing . . . and of course the plot to kill Hitler—'

'No, I mean in a business context. Does NeuHansa have anything to do with anything or anyone using that name?'

Brønsted pursed her lips and shook her head. 'I can't say that we do. I'll check it out if you like.'

'Have you ever heard of any of these women: Margarethe Paulus, Liane Kayser or Anke Wollner?'

'Can't say that any of those names ring a bell.'

Fabel could read nothing in Brønsted's expression. He toyed with the idea of throwing in Georg Drescher's name to see what kind of reaction it got, but decided against it. That was a lid he wanted to keep on tight for the meantime.

The rest of the interview was devoted to questions about details. About what Ralf Sparwald had been working on; about who else had talked with Westland at the pre-concert party; about the overlap of function between Norivon Environmental Technologies and SkK Biotech. About anything that Fabel thought he might be able to get some kind of reaction to. After about an hour, he stood up and thanked Brønsted for her time.

Once Fabel, Gessler and Vestergaard were outside on the street, Fabel drew a deep breath.

'Hans,' he said to Gessler without taking his eyes off the yacht. 'Every NeuHansa file, every databank, every transaction – I want you all over that company like a rash. I'll speak to the powers that be and get you all the time and people you need.'

'I thought you might,' said Gessler. 'If there's something there to be found, we'll find it. I take it you now know who hired the Valkyrie? Or at least hired her through Drescher?'

'Langstrup slipped up,' said Fabel. 'Of course there's a murder that is not linked to the NeuHansa Group.'

'Drescher's,' said Vestergaard.

'Exactly. And we've nailed the lid down on that one for the time being. No one knows about it. Which means Langstrup, despite trying to cover it up, was talking about a murder that, as far as he and anyone outside the Murder Commission is concerned, hasn't happened yet.'

'The question remains,' said Vestergaard, 'whether Langstrup is running his own little empire or if Gina Brønsted herself is behind these killings.'

'I don't know,' said Gessler. 'Langstrup looks as if he knows how to handle himself. And he looks like he's had more than one run-in with someone else who can handle themselves. But he just doesn't strike me as the brains of the outfit.'

'Me neither,' said Fabel.

It was nearly the end of the working day. Fabel dropped Gessler off to pick up his car at the Presidium, made a quick call to Gennady Frolov's office and fixed up an appointment in two days' time. After doing a quick check with the Commission that nothing had come up while they had been out, Fabel drove Karin Vestergaard back to her hotel.

'You know what I'm going to ask you, don't you?' he said, reverting to English again as they drove through the city centre.

'I have a pretty good idea.'

'You have a hell of a nerve, do you know that? I have extended you every professional courtesy. Damn it, I've extended personal courtesy and hospitality too. I introduced you to Susanne and you sat through the entire meal allowing us to believe we needed to speak English. I must say, you're one hell of a fast learner. You seem to have progressed from not understanding a word to being totally bloody fluent in a matter of two weeks.'

'*Übung macht den Meister* – isn't that what you say in German? Practice makes perfect?'

Vestergaard was smiling mischievously. It totally disconcerted Fabel: it was the first time, other than brief glimpses during their meal together with Susanne, that he had seen anything like a genuine unguarded expression on her face.

'I'm sorry, Jan,' she continued. 'You're right, it was deceptive of me. But it really is better for me to speak in English.'

'You didn't seem to be struggling back there. Where the hell did you learn to speak German like that?'

'I was brought up in South Jutland, just north of the border. My father was the opposite of Gina Brønsted: where she's a Danish German, he was a German Dane. He spoke Sonderjysk dialect and German at home. German was my third language after English at school.'

'Well, I can see you've retained a lot of it.'

'There's something else I ought to tell you . . .' she said tentatively.

'Okay, let's have it.'

'It wasn't strictly true, what I told you about never having been to Hamburg before. I worked here during my breaks at university.'

'Let me guess – to improve your German?'

'Sorry.'

'It doesn't matter in itself, Karin, but we had a deal – how the hell am I to know what else you've kept to yourself?'

'I've been totally straight with you, Jan. I just wasn't sure that you'd be straight with me. I suppose I thought that if you thought I didn't speak the language . . .'

'And I take it by now your mind's been put at ease?' Fabel pulled into the semicircle of cobbles in front of the hotel.

'Yes, it has. We're on the same side, Jan. I promise you.'

Chapter Six

There was no good reason to travel over to the other side of town for a drink, but Fabel felt the need to visit the bar that had been his local for all the time he had lived in Pöseldorf. He wasn't entirely sure why he missed it so much: he had never really spent a great deal of time there, but it had been somewhere he had been known; where staff and other customers acknowledged his presence with a nod or a wave. It had been an anchor in his life: a point of reference that had helped him keep a bearing on who Jan Fabel was.

Fabel sat at the corner of the bar, sipped at his Jever beer and thought about women. Whether he liked to admit the fact or not, it had been the women in his life who had determined its direction. Right down to the tiniest degree.

It was a woman who had steered him into a career as a policeman.

Fabel had attended the Carl von Ossietzky University in Oldenburg before studying European history at Hamburg University. While he had been there he had never quite managed to get involved in all of the expected student indiscretions. But he had been a good-looking kid and had had his pick of the girls. One of them had been Hanna Dorn, a fellow student and the daughter of one of Fabel's tutors. Hanna had been a pretty, carefree sort of girl and they had both known, Fabel guessed, that they were not in it for the

long term. They were having fun with the arrogant careless-
ness of youth. Now, every time Fabel thought about Hanna's
face, he concentrated hard to remember every detail. It was
a face that, if what happened hadn't happened, would have
faded, along with her name, into the dusty, indistinct archives
of his memory.

One night, after they had been going out for about two
weeks, Hanna had been making her way back alone to her
flat after being with Fabel on a date. He had had an assignment to finish. Hanna never made it home.

Lutger Voss had been a thirty-year-old hospital orderly at
the St George Hospital. The only thing about Voss that had
been exceptional was his psychosis. Voss had intercepted
Hanna on her way home and abducted her.

The autopsy and forensic evidence had later revealed that
Voss had tortured and repeatedly raped Hanna. When her
body had been found, Fabel, as her boyfriend and the last
person to see her alive, had been questioned for hours by the
Polizei Hamburg until they had become convinced of his inno-
cence. But Fabel had never become as convinced of the absence
of his responsibility: having an assignment to complete had
not seemed reason enough not to have walked her home.
Even now, more than twenty years later, he often woke up
in the middle of the night racked with guilt because he hadn't
been there to save her.

Lutger Voss had been committed to a secure hospital three
days before Fabel had graduated. The day after, Fabel had
applied to join the Polizei Hamburg.

The young barman placed a fresh Jever on the bar in front
of Fabel without him having ordered it. When Fabel raised
his eyebrows quizzically, the barman nodded in the direction
of a tall, lanky, balding man who was approaching him.

'You're late,' Fabel said.

'You're obsessive.' Otto Jensen grinned, in exactly the same
gormless way Fabel remembered from their student days

together. 'Or maybe just depressive. I saw you when I came in. I'd offer a penny for your thoughts but I don't think I'd get my money's worth.'

'I was thinking about women,' said Fabel.

'Don't worry,' Otto kept grinning. 'It's your age. It's not so bad – a midlife crisis is like puberty but without the acne.'

'I was thinking about Hanna Dorn.'

Otto's grin faded. 'Hanna? What made you think of her after all of these years?'

'Otto, my friend, there's hardly a week goes by that I don't think of her. Or at least what happened to her.'

They were interrupted by the barman bringing a wheat beer for Otto.

'Every time I interview a sex killer, I think of Voss,' continued Fabel once the barman was gone and he felt the cloak of loud music and other voices close around them. 'Every time I read the forensic report on a rape and murder victim, I think of Hanna. If it hadn't been for what happened to her I would never have become a policeman. I wouldn't have singled out Murder Commission work as a career.'

'And if I hadn't read Heinrich Böll I wouldn't have devoted my life to books,' said Otto. 'That's life, Jan.'

'How is business?' asked Fabel. Otto ran Jensens' Buchhandlung bookstore in Hamburg's elegant Arkaden.

'We're clinging on. I did a book launch for a science-fiction author last week who very graciously announced that his next book would not be appearing on our shelves. He is releasing it exclusively as a downloadable e-book and audio book. We are, he assured me, finally attaining the "post-literate society" that many science-fiction authors, including himself, had long predicted. So move over – I may become a copper myself.' Otto took a large sip of his wheat beer. 'Anyway, why did you suggest meeting up here? It's not your local any more.'

'That's why I was thinking about women,' said Fabel

gloomily. 'Do you remember when I first moved here, to Pöseldorf?'

'When you and Renate split up.'

'Exactly. You know, Otto, I like to think of myself as some kind of freethinker, liberated from dogma or prejudice or preconception; someone who sees the world afresh from my own perspective. It's a pile of crap. The truth is that I'm just as much a product of my background as anyone else – just a simple, parochial, predictable bloody Northern German Lutheran. When I married Renate and then Gabi came along, I thought, this is it. This is my life. For the rest of my life. Then, when Renate pissed off with Behrens, my world came apart at the seams. And I ended up here, in my attic flat around the corner, rebuilding my life. Then, just when I got settled here and had a real idea of where I was with everything, I meet Susanne and all of a sudden I'm living in Altona and part of a couple again.'

'I know,' said Otto, with a mockingly sympathetic frown. 'The bad beautiful woman took away your freedom. How can you live without sitting on your own eating takeaway meals in front of the TV? Are you trying to say you're sorry you got involved with Susanne?'

'No, not at all. What I am saying is that, every step of the way, there's been a woman defining the moment for me. Hanna, Gisela Frohm . . .'

'Jan, I don't know where you're going with all this.'

Fabel smiled and slapped his friend on the shoulder. 'Don't look so worried, Otto. It doesn't suit you. I'm just – I don't know – it's just this case I'm working on. It's all about women.'

'Oh God, yeah – this "Angel of St Pauli".'

'That's only part of it. There's this other thing as well. A female assassin. Probably based here in Hamburg.' Fabel caught the expression on his friend's face. 'What is it?'

'You . . .' Otto made a show of being shocked. 'You have

never talked to me about a case you've been working on. Never.'

'I'm becoming indiscreet in my old age. And if I can't trust you, Otto, I don't know who the hell I *can* trust.' Fabel took another sip of Jever. 'Anyway, at the moment everything I'm involved in seems to involve violent women. Speaking of which, Renate has been busting my balls as well.'

'What about?'

'Gabi has expressed an interest in a police career. It's all my fault, apparently.'

'Probably is. I find it's best just to assume you're always in the wrong. It works for me with Else. Anyway, I'm sure Gabi has been influenced by you. It's not surprising that she's thinking about becoming a police officer.'

A table became free in the corner and they took their beers across to it. As Fabel chatted with his friend, he felt himself relax. Otto was one of the most clumsy and disorganised people he knew, yet Fabel knew that this bumbling two-metre-tall gawky tangle of chaos had one of the sharpest minds he had ever encountered. They had been friends since their first meeting and Otto had the ability to puncture Fabel's occasional bubble of self-indulgence or self-importance. As they talked, Fabel became distracted: there was an older man by the bar whom Fabel knew he had seen before but couldn't place. The man was dressed casually but everything about him reeked of wealth: his white hair was immaculately groomed and he wore an expensive-looking deep blue cashmere sweater. He looked out of place in the bar but Fabel guessed he was here as an indulgence to his companion, an exceptionally pretty woman who stood to his side and three decades behind him.

'I'm guessing she went for his looks and personality.' Otto had followed Fabel's gaze to the couple. 'It's called hypergamy, Jan: the tendency for women to select partners of a higher socio-economic level. We should consider ourselves lucky that Else and Susanne weren't too fussy.'

'They're not a couple,' said Fabel. 'She's a diversion for him. That's not what's bothering me. It's the guy – I'm sure I've seen him somewhere before. Do you know him?'

Otto reached into his jacket pocket, put his glasses on and leaned forward, peering in the couple's direction.

'For God's sake, Otto.' Fabel eased his friend back. 'You know you said you could always become a policeman if the book trade died off? Forget it. I'm guessing you'd find covert surveillance difficult.'

Otto grinned. 'Call it hiding in plain sight. As a matter of fact I do know him. Well, not *know* him, know *of* him. That's Hans-Karl von Birgau. He's some kind of business big shot, from an aristo family. I can't for the life of me remember the kind of business he's in. Does that help?'

'Not really.' Fabel frowned. 'I just can't remember where I've seen him before, but I have. Somewhere.'

'Maybe he double-parked his Rolls-Royce and you gave him a ticket.' Otto laughed heartily at his own joke.

The older man and his young consort faded from Fabel's thoughts when they moved through to a table at the back of the bar. Fabel and Otto stayed in the bar for another hour or so, although Fabel, as usual, switched to Alsterwasser shandies.

Fabel suggested they get a taxi and he would drop Otto off on his way back home. After the warmth of the pub the night air was cold and damp. The breeze had picked up into a wind which maliciously threw chilled pellets of rain in their faces. Fabel had called for a taxi on his cellphone and he was annoyed to see that it hadn't arrived. He spotted von Birgau and his youthful companion as they dashed past them from the pub. Lights flashed on a brand-new Range Rover Vogue that was parked a little way down the street. The man and the girl climbed in and they drove off.

'Maybe it was his daughter,' said Otto, with a wry smile.

A beige Mercedes pulled up and Fabel found himself checking its roof sign and licence number before getting in. Otto did most of the talking until they pulled up outside his house. Fabel was aware that he was tired. And something was nagging away at the back of his head.

'Altona,' he said when the taxi driver asked him where to go after they had dropped Otto off. They had only travelled a few blocks when his cellphone rang.

2.

Fabel knew the restaurant. He and Susanne had eaten there once or twice over the last three years. It was that kind of restaurant: only the seriously rich or seriously careless with their money could afford to be regulars there. It had huge picture windows that looked out across the harbour. Or at least it used to have huge picture windows. Fabel got the taxi to take him as close as it could to the restaurant: the road was blocked by two huge green MOWAG armoured cars, the word POLIZEI emblazoned white on their angled flanks. Three Heckler-and-Koch-armed MEK police officers, in full riot gear, blocked his path.

'Fabel, Murder Commission.' He showed them his ID. 'Bomb?'

'Looks like it, Chief Commissar,' said one of the MEK officers, a woman. 'It was planted in a car, from what we can see.'

'Is the area safe for me to go in?'

'Yes, Chief Commissar. The forensics team are still in there, though, doing their stuff.'

'I'll try and stay out of their way.' Fabel walked down the street towards the restaurant. A few of the street lights had been blown out and temporary lighting had been set up on stands to allow the police and forensic technicians to do their job. The glass-covered road and pavements glittered in the arc lights as if strewn with jewels.

'Thanks for the call, Sepp.' Fabel extended his hand to a tall heavily built man with a nose that looked like it had been broken more than once. Criminal Chief Commissar Stephan Timmermann of the Polizei Hamburg's Anti-Terrorist Branch shook Fabel's hand.

'Hi, Jan. Think nothing of it. We thought it was terrorists to start with, but the target was Gennady Frolov. He has his new yacht moored in the harbour. The *Snow Queen*. He was in the restaurant for some kind of business meeting when his car went up. And boy, did it go up. I remembered that memo you circulated asking for background on Frolov, so I thought you might be interested and gave you a shout.'

'I appreciate it, Sepp. Any fatalities?'

'Unbelievably, no. A few injuries, none too serious. The restaurant had valet parking – you know, like the Americans – and they use walkie-talkies to communicate from the maître d' to the carhops so that the cars or taxis are always waiting as soon as a guest exits the restaurant. We reckon that by sheer chance the frequency they transmit on was the same as the remote trigger for the bomb. The maître d' radios for a car and boom, you've got a two-ton bulletproof Mercedes scattered across Hamburg in bite-size pieces.'

'It must have been a big bomb,' said Fabel. The cold night air was helping him to shake off the fuzziness he still felt from his beers with Otto.

'It was,' said Timmermann. 'I reckon it was placed underneath the chassis. The car was one of those heavy bulletproof jobs, like I said, and its mass actually absorbed a lot of the blast. But I think that was the intention. The Merc was designed to withstand bullets from outside, so the bomber placed the device underneath, knowing that the blast energy would be concentrated in the cabin of the car. It's called confined detonation velocity. However, it still produced enough explosive brisance to shatter every window around. But whoever planted this device knew there would be a limit to the shrapnelisation of the car body – because it was so heavily reinforced. All the injuries to bystanders are from flying glass.'

'What kind of bomb?'

'Early days, Jan, but you know we'll be able to put it together. However, if you're asking for my initial feeling, it would all indicate a blast velocity of somewhere around the eight-thousand-metres-per-second mark. That means it wasn't TNT. My money's on military-grade Composition C or some other RDX-based explosive. Electrical ignition. And remote radio initiation seems obvious. One of the lab rats has picked up a fragment of what looks like a semiconductor. Very professional job – *except* the one thing the bomber forgot to do was to build in a signal shield. That's why the busboy's radio set the bomb off.'

'Is Frolov one of the injured?' asked Fabel.

'No. He was inside the restaurant and away from the windows. One of his bodyguards was outside at the time and has had her eardrum burst. Martina Schilmann. Ex-Polizei Hamburg. Of course, you know her, don't you? Weren't you and she . . . ?'

'Long time ago.' Fabel sighed. 'Is she all right?'

'A percussive injury like that from a blast causing a burst eardrum could be nasty. And it will definitely be painful. But apart from that she's fine. One of the carhops is in a worst state, but nothing life-threatening there either.'

'Is Frolov still here?' asked Fabel.

'Yep. Back inside for the moment. We moved him into a MOWAG armoured unit until we did a full sweep of the restaurant for a second bomb. It's an old terrorist trick: set off one bomb prematurely to send a mass of people running for cover to exactly the place where they've hidden the second, bigger device. But nothing.'

'We're not dealing with a terrorist here.' Fabel frowned. A bomb. 'But it doesn't fit my suspect either.'

'Oh?' said Timmermann. 'Why?'

'The bomber missed his or her target. My girl doesn't miss. Ever. The other thing is I wouldn't put a bomb down as her choice of weapon. A bomb is the weapon of choice of the indiscriminate and the cowardly – the terrorist at the end of the command wire or who has set the timer in advance to keep as much distance as possible between himself and potential harm, without caring how many innocent people get in the way.'

'And that doesn't fit with who you had in mind?'

'No – I'm dealing with a perfectionist. A precision thinker and worker. This is all too . . . too *sloppy*. This doesn't feel right for my girl.'

'I'm not too sure, Jan,' said Timmermann. 'I'd take issue with this not being a precision weapon. The confinement of the blast and the sophistication of the explosive and the device . . . Like I said, the only thing that doesn't fit with me is that the bomber didn't shield the detonator from third-party radio transmissions.'

'Anyway,' said Fabel. 'I think it's time I had a chat with our Russki chum.'

'I'd do that,' agreed Timmermann. 'Frolov's own security people are kicking up. They're all ex-Soviet special-forces types. All they're interested in is putting as much distance as possible between Frolov and the scene.'

'Then I'll try not to detain him. See you later, Sepp.'

There was even more glass inside the restaurant than there was on the street outside. Fabel again had to hold up his ID to an MEK cop wearing a black riot suit and body armour and cradling a Heckler and Koch MP5 machine pistol.

The tables nearest the windows were empty and Fabel noticed the strange mix of the normal and the abnormal that one always found at scenes of sudden, violent crime. One table had the food still in place, untouched on its plates, the restaurant's exclusive cutlery untouched and the expensive table linen still white and crisp, except for a vivid spatter of blood that had begun to spider at the edges, like red ink spilled on a blotter. Dark droplets dotted the knocked-over silver candlestick. Other tables had been upended, either by the blast or by panicked diners rushing to seek refuge at the rear of the restaurant.

A man in his fifties with greying blond hair and a goatee beard sat at one of the tables at the back with a group of other men. Two were standing, watching Fabel as he approached. Fabel could tell from their conformation that these were not the brains of the outfit.

'Herr Frolov?' As Fabel drew near, one of the bodyguards placed a restraining hand on Fabel's shoulder. Fabel looked up at the heavy and smiled.

'I'm going to have you arrested if your hand is still there by the time I finish this sentence. Do you understand, Ivan?'

The man with the goatee said something in Russian to the heavy and the hand was lifted.

'Yes, I'm Herr Frolov.' He stood up. 'And you are?'

Fabel held up his ID. 'Principal Chief Commissar Fabel of the Polizei Hamburg Murder Commission.'

'Murder? But no one was . . .' Frolov made a sweeping gesture with his hands that indicated the chaos in the restaurant.

'I know. More by chance than anything, I have to say. But my main interest in this incident is that it may be connected to some other murders. And you were the target.'

'Undoubtedly.' The Russian spoke with only a slight accent and his German had the near-perfect grammar of someone who had studied the language seriously. 'The device was placed in my car. By the way, you must excuse the zealousness of Ivan and my other *protectors*. As you can imagine, they are rather agitated by what has happened.'

'Who did it?' asked Fabel.

'The bomb?'

'You must have some ideas,' said Fabel.

'Because I have so many enemies?' Frolov smiled bitterly. 'That would be because I'm a Russian *oligarch*, wouldn't it? And that means, of course, that I can't be entirely straight. Scratch a Russian businessman and you'll expose an organised criminal. Isn't that right?'

'Herr Frolov, you're doing all the talking here. I didn't imply anything by my question. And I know that you're not a crook. I've already checked you out.'

Frolov laughed. 'Corporate crime division?'

'And organised crime. Both say you're clean.'

'Ah, but do you believe them, Herr Fabel? Someone with my wealth and influence could bury a lot of embarrassing evidence under a mountain of money.'

'They have no evidence against you – which doesn't mean that you're not involved with anything criminal. But, for what it's worth, I've had years of dealing with crooks and I can smell them a mile away.'

'And do I *smell*, Herr Fabel?' Frolov seemed to be trying to read something in Fabel's face.

'No. You don't.'

'I do not do anything that is illegal. You have my word. I broke the laws of the former Soviet Union, I was a black marketeer. I sold illicitly distilled vodka and dealt in prohibited luxury goods. But that was the only way to do business back then. My crime was to be a businessman in a society that criminalised entrepreneurship. But this is not the Soviet Union. Hamburg is built on entrepreneurship. I don't have to break the law to be what I am. In fact, I am a champion of the rule of law here.'

'Like I said,' said Fabel, 'I believe you.'

'But you don't understand what I'm saying. I'm explaining *why* I was targeted.'

'Because you don't break the law?'

'Because I scrupulously investigate every deal I'm potentially involved in. I have any potential partner examined to the tiniest detail. And if I find *anything* untoward, I report it to the relevant authorities.'

'Were you about to report something?' asked Fabel.

'I don't think whoever planted the bomb was sure what I was or wasn't going to discuss with OLAF next week.'

'Did you say Olaf?' Fabel felt something tingle on his neck. The name in Jespersen's notebook. 'Who exactly is Olaf?'

'Not who – *what*. OLAF is the European Anti-Fraud Office. OLAF is an acronym of its French title, *Office Européen de Lutte Anti-Fraude*.'

'Of course.' Fabel shook his head. 'I just didn't make the connection.'

Frolov looked at Fabel for a moment. 'I take it this information has some significance for you?'

'You could say that,' said Fabel.

'Anyway,' continued Frolov, 'I report anything dodgy to OLAF, Europol, Eurojust or Interpol. I have contacts in each organisation. But I have fewer and fewer opportunities to do so these days: word has got out about how I operate, so it tends to be only those businesses who have nothing to hide who approach me.'

'But you have something you want to talk to OLAF about?'

'I arranged to send them some information and talk to them next week. I'm guessing that this little firework display was intended to dissuade me.'

'So you think this was a warning rather than a serious attempt on your life?' asked Fabel.

'Trust me, I was not meant to die. You see, my death would change nothing: the papers would still go to OLAF with or without my presence. This bomb was intended to scare me off sending the information on to OLAF and from having any more discussions with them.'

'Then you know who's behind it all?'

'Tell me, Herr Fabel, do you have any suggestions? Something tells me that you might.' Frolov smiled. It was a charming smile and Fabel guessed it came from the oligarch's arsenal of business weapons.

'I'd rather it came from you, Herr Frolov.'

'I have interests in every corner of Europe and I was dealing with a Balkan-based company. My investigators came up with a connection to cigarette smuggling into the EU. That in turn led us to a non-governmental organisation which was fraudulently benefiting from EU funding while in turn funding the warehousing and distribution of contraband cigarettes. Small-time stuff.'

'Enough to go to all this trouble?' Fabel indicated the shattered restaurant.

'Not in itself.' The smile had left Frolov's face. 'My staff includes what you would call forensic accountants and, well, private investigators. One of the investigators died recently in a car crash. He was drunk and speeding. Except I knew him personally – a Karelian called Kontinen. His father had died of alcoholism and Kontinen was a sworn teetotaller. He was also a very thorough man. And a careful driver. So we dug deeper. Kontinen had been looking into our Balkan partner but had come across something much, much bigger.'

'What?'

'Kontinen had found out that the company in the Balkans had been using a Serb warlord-cum-gangster as a sub-contractor.'

'Goran Vujačić?'

Frolov stared at Fabel for a moment. 'Do I sense that our paths have just crossed?'

'Tell me more about Vujačić's operation,' said Fabel.

'First of all you need to know that Kontinen had discovered that Vujačić was involved in some dirty business out there that was not connected to the company we were investigating. Vujačić was as scummy as they come: a drug and human trafficker who was selling women into slavery and prostitution. He had been moving and warehousing the contraband cigarettes for the Balkan company, but he had also been subcontracting for somebody out here in the West.'

'What kind of subcontracting?'

'Vujačić ran three warehouses, using women as slave labourers. We tipped off the Serbian authorities and Vujačić disappeared. Unfortunately, so did the women. What happened to them we don't know. Vujačić moved into major drug trafficking and ended up dead. In the meantime, we believe he found a new location for the greenwashing operation.'

'China?' asked Fabel.

'Our paths cross again . . . yes. Western China.'

'What exactly do you mean by *greenwashing*?'

'One thing I've learned as a businessman is that the environment is setting the agenda these days. There are a thousand and one legislative and regulatory bodies out there ready to shut you down if you breach environmental standards. Greenwashing is when you take action on the cheap to make it *appear* that you're complying. Green plus whitewashing equals greenwashing – get it? Anyway, one of the things you do is fake shipment manifests for sensitive waste and send it out of the regulatory zone to somewhere like an impoverished former Soviet republic—'

'Or China or the Balkans.'

'Exactly,' said Frolov. 'But less so the Balkans nowadays. Democratisation and regeneration are the enemies of this kind of enterprise. Anyway, you ship the stuff out of the regulatory zone, in this case the EU, and when you ship it back it's been processed. Or it simply disappears. But the point is that because it's been outside the regulatory zone, there's no health-and-safety or any other control on the conditions or pay of the workers.'

'So what was being *greenwashed*?'

'Electronics, mobile phones, that kind of thing. Our investigator, before he died, had been in touch with a Norwegian journalist who had gathered some evidence. The journalist had obtained some samples from the warehouses and had got conclusive results. What they were I don't know, my people are still trying to trace the journalist.'

'Don't bother,' said Fabel. 'The journalist and the analyst he sent the samples to are both dead. They were getting close to proving something because the killer didn't even take the time to try and fake accidents. They were both shot in the head. Professional executions.'

'I see . . .' Frolov sighed.

'But I know what they were testing for,' continued Fabel. 'Polybrominated diphenyl ethers. And I know where the operation was moved to: Hunan Province in China and Bitola in Macedonia, although I guess Vujačić had to quit Macedonia too.'

A black-uniformed MEK officer came over.

'We can move Herr Frolov out now, Chief Commissar.'

'Just a minute,' said Fabel. Then, to Frolov: 'You're their number-one target now – you realise that, don't you? As soon as Vujačić got himself caught he had enough information to perhaps do a deal with the Danish police. So he was killed in Copenhagen. They killed your investigator, then Halvorsen, the Norwegian journalist, and Sparwald, the analytical chemist. Each of them died for having *part* of the evidence. And you have it all.'

'I guess I'd better keep a low profile . . .' Frolov shrugged. 'Now, Herr Fabel, are you going to tell me the name of who was behind all this? Or shall I tell you?'

'I'm investigating three other murders,' said Fabel. 'Armin Lensch, who worked for Norivon, an environmental waste-management company and part of the NeuHansa Group. Peter Claasens, a shipping agent who managed Norivon traffic – I'm guessing one or both of them tripped up over some irregularity and were killed before they got the chance to tell anyone, or even work out the real significance of what they had found. Then there was the murder of Jake Westland, the British rock star.'

'*He* was involved with this? I thought that was the work of some crazed serial killer.'

'That's what you were supposed to think. The truth is that Westland was as careful with his investments as you are. He obviously smelt a rat. Because of his . . . well, his *ancestry*, I suppose you'd say, he would be particularly sensitive to anything that suggested the abuse of women. Poor bastard, he was probably lured to his death thinking he was meeting someone with information.'

'So you already suspected Gina Brønsted?' asked Frolov.

'Yes. Or at least some element within the NeuHansa Group.'

'Trust me, Herr Fabel. Look no further than Brønsted. You said you've developed a nose for crooks over your years as a policeman. Well, believe me, you develop the same kind of instinct when you're in business. I'm sure you have a lot of experience with sociopaths in your line of work. Well, so do I. A certain ruthlessness, a lack of empathy, even a lack of conscience is positively encouraged amongst the commercially ambitious. The next time you talk to Gina Brønsted, take a long look into her eyes. I promise you, you'll find nothing there.'

Fabel could see that Frolov was sincere about what he was saying. Whether it was Brønsted or not behind the attack, it was clear that Fabel had been wrong: this bombing *was* the work of the Valkyrie. She had deliberately missed with the same precision with which she usually hit her target. A warning. Timed perfectly.

'Where were you when the bomb went off?' he asked the Russian.

'Here – this was our table. With things the way they are, we thought it was a good idea to sit away from the window.'

'We?'

'Frau Schilmann. An ex-colleague of yours. She's been co-ordinating my security here. Much to the annoyance of Ivan.'

'Well,' said Fabel, 'if you don't mind we'll take over now. Consider yourself under the protection of the Polizei Hamburg until you leave.' He frowned. 'Frau Schilmann suggested that you sit here?'

'Yes.'

'But she went outside?'

'Yes. She chose the wrong moment to take a cigarette break.'

'Okay,' said Fabel, with a smile. 'Let's get you somewhere safe.'

3.

'We're in a race against time.' Fabel stood at the front of the inquiry room, the screen lowered behind him. The forty to fifty officers assembled were reduced to shapes edged with the light from the projector. 'We have been keeping a murder under wraps for as long as we can. Drescher – or Gerdes as he was known – lived a solitary enough life, but he had neighbours, knew women, probably socialised with people we haven't traced yet. He's being missed right now, and it's only a matter of time before his death becomes public.'

Fabel clicked the remote. The state hospital photograph of Paulus came up on screen.

'This is Drescher's killer: Margarethe Paulus. Dr Eckhardt suggests that she is probably psychotic rather than psychopathic. She is delusional. But her wildest story of all happens to be true. She is a *Valkyrie*. One of three highly trained and disciplined professional female assassins. The names of the other two Valkyries are Liane Kayser and Anke Wollner – although we can be sure that neither of them have used their real name in years. It looks like one of them, Liane Kayser, was either rejected in the same way Margarethe was or has gone her own way under an assumed identity. That leaves Anke Wollner, who seems to be our best bet to be the Valkyrie. Although, as I say, it's all pretty academic. These names are useless to us because the full machinery of the Stasi was brought to bear on hiding them and creating new identities.' Fabel clicked the remote and another face filled the screen.

'This is Gennady Frolov. He's the other reason we're under pressure. He's had his final warning from the Valkyrie – in the shape of the bomb down by the harbour. Now he's on borrowed time. The Valkyrie never misses.'

'She missed with the bomb,' said someone from near the back.

'No, she didn't. Like I said: a warning.'

Another click.

'These are the personal ads that have come out in this month's issue of *Muliebritas*. We have – or rather Commissar Wolff's friend has – matched the frequency and style of all the previous ads, including the tell-tale three-letter code that identifies each ad as a message carrier: it tells the Valkyrie that Drescher wants to meet with her in the Alsterpark next to the Fährdamm. Eleven-thirty, Wednesday. So if our girl has picked this message up, and believes it's genuinely from Drescher, then we're in business tomorrow.'

Another click.

'This is the Alsterpark. We'll have observers and sharp-shooters on the roofs of the buildings behind the park, but it's a long range from that distance and we can't keep members of the public away. I'm going to have to rely on all of you on the ground. You're going to double as joggers, park workers, business people – and we'll have a couple of you in uniform too. The main thing is that there should be nothing to scare the Valkyrie off. And, trust me, she knows what she's looking for.'

'Surely the main thing she'll be looking for is Drescher,'

said Anna. 'Which might be somewhat problematic. Not to mention smelly.'

'Aha,' said Fabel, with a sense of triumph. 'This is where our double comes in . . .' He walked over to the door, opened it and called out into the corridor. 'We're ready for your close-up.'

Werner stepped into the Inquiry Room to cheers, catcalls and laughter. He was dressed in an expensive English tweed jacket that was straining at the buttons, and a roll-neck cashmere sweater. But the real source of amusement was the grey-blond wig pulled over his bristle-cut scalp.

'Okay, okay . . .' Fabel gestured as if calming traffic. 'Settle down. What you've got to remember is that she'll only see him from a distance. We have got to take her down fast and effectively. This isn't a deranged serial killer or some hairy-arsed drugs dealer settling a score. I have to be honest and say that I've never dealt with a murder case like this before. Killing people is the Valkyrie's trade. God knows how many people she's killed, but she's very, very good at it. Now, I don't expect her to come heavily armed – my guess is that she won't carry a weapon routinely. That way she could be caught out. But remember: this woman does not always need a weapon. She can kill with her bare hands, quickly and efficiently.'

'You could be doing more to make me feel better about this,' said Werner, with a crooked smile.

'And that's why Werner will be wearing Kevlar body armour beneath his coat and jacket. But I've asked that we're supported by some of our special-tactics colleagues from the Polizei Hamburg MEK unit. Maybe even get some help from GSG-9 . . .'

Fabel paused for the collective groan.

'I'm not saying that we can't handle this ourselves, but I'm not going to lose anyone on this operation. I just want us to have people there with similar training to that of our

Valkyrie. We'll have a full joint briefing tomorrow morning, seven a.m.'

Fabel clicked the remote again and Gina Brønsted's face came up on screen.

'This is where it gets all political. Frau Brønsted here is a very powerful woman with a lot of very influential friends. I am also absolutely convinced that she is the person who's been commissioning the hits carried out by the Valkyrie. Hans, are you there?' Fabel shielded his eyes against the glare of the projector and peered into the audience.

'Here, Jan,' said Gessler.

'I have arranged for all the seizure warrants you'll need. As soon as we take the Valkyrie down, you hit NeuHansa with your team. I need the proof that Brønsted is the Valkyrie's client.'

Fabel wound up the meeting and grabbed a coffee and sandwich in the canteen before going up to his office. Martina Schilmann was waiting for him. Her hair was pulled back into a ponytail and he could see that she had a dressing in her ear. She looked tired and pale. And more than a little annoyed.

'Sit down, Martina,' he said, with a smile. 'How are you?'

'Sore. In more ways than one. I got the message that you wanted to see me. That's good, because I wanted to see you. Do you realise that you've really screwed up my business? What do you think you are doing, telling Gennady Frolov that the Polizei Hamburg will handle his protection?'

'Martina, you're not that naive. A serious offence was committed in the harbour last night. A lot of people have been injured, including you. Gennady Frolov is the victim of an attempted murder. That makes it our business, not yours. You should know that. Anyway, I didn't tell him to sack you—'

'No, you didn't tell him to sack me. But you asked him a

lot of questions about me, didn't you? Where I was when the bomb went off, why I was outside . . . You successfully put the idea into his head that I might be involved.' Martina stared at Fabel and her scowl became a frown and then an expression of disbelief. 'My God – you really *do* suspect me of something. I don't believe this.'

Fabel looked at the sandwich on his desk, sighed and dropped it into the wastebasket.

'It's not like that, Martina.'

'No? What *is* it like?'

'I don't suspect you of anything. It's just . . . well, you never really know someone.'

'For Christ's sake, Jan – we *slept* together for six months.'

'This case – it's . . . *complicated*,' Fabel said awkwardly. 'There are three women involved: Margarethe Paulus, Liane Kayser, Anke Wollner. All of them were brought up in the old GDR and they were trained as assassins. And all of them were given new identities. Margarethe Paulus is deranged and was the woman behind Drescher's torture and murder, Liane Kayser has dropped off the radar and is presumably living a normal life under an assumed name and Anke Wollner, we believe, became the Valkyrie. And planted the bomb last night as a warning to Frolov.'

'I do not bloody believe this!' Martina's face flushed red and her eyes glinted hard. 'So which one do you think I am, Jan? Do you think I went outside and shattered my own eardrum by detonating the bomb at close range? Or do you have me down as the reincarnation of the killer who's disappeared from sight?'

'I'm not accusing you of anything. I just wanted you to tell me what happened last night. If you saw anything unusual. You are a witness, for God's sake. I *have* to question you.'

'We were just about to leave,' said Martina in a steely tone. 'When we arrived, I directed Frolov and his entourage away from the windows – I'd phoned the restaurant in advance and told them to reserve a table towards the back. Frolov and his business acquaintances were on to their coffees and brandies. I told Lorenz to stay with Ivan, Frolov's own security guy, and I went outside for a smoke. The Merc was parked just a little further down the street and I was telling the busboy we would need it out front when he got the message from the maître d'. Then boom . . . no more Merc and no more eardrum. I didn't have my hands in my pockets, by the way, Jan. You can ask the busboy. Just in case you were wondering if I had a remote detonator stashed.'

'Did you see anyone other than the busboy outside?' Fabel ignored Martina's gibe.

'No. No one within sight to set the bomb off other than the busboy. Oh yes . . . and, of course, me.'

'Martina, this isn't helping. Frankly I don't give a shit if our protecting a potential murder victim doesn't fit in with your business plan. All I want to do is to put together some kind of picture of this hit woman. I'm asking you to think like a police officer again. Was there anything you saw or heard that might have been connected with the detonation?'

Martina sighed. 'No. Not really. Except I don't think it was the radio transmission between the maître d' and the busboy that set the bomb off. Everything else was too professional for the detonator not to be selectively shielded.'

Fabel raised a questioning eyebrow.

'I did a course,' explained Martina. 'But the other thing is that the blast was at the same time as the radio went off, but not *exactly*. Not simultaneous. So that fits with the bomb being a warning.'

'That's where we are with it,' said Fabel.

'But it still doesn't jell with me . . .' Martina's earlier anger seemed to have dissipated. 'It was all done very professionally, and with great precision, and that fits with this killer. But that's what she is: a killer. Sending out warnings doesn't fit.'

'Mmm . . . you could be right,' said Fabel. 'But like you say, everything else fits.'

'Maybe she's extending her service offer.' Martina smirked. 'Moving with the times to match the needs of the market.'

'Could be . . .' said Fabel. 'But if she is, then that's where we'll nail her. If she doesn't stick to what she knows best.'

Fabel was interrupted by Anna Wolff, who came into the office without knocking. She had a copy of *Muliebritas* in her hand. She tossed it onto Fabel's desk.

'Here's the new edition,' she said, slamming her hand flat on the magazine. 'Our ad's in it.'

'Yes, Anna – I know,' said Fabel as if talking to an importunate child.

'But ours isn't the only one,' said Anna. 'Someone else is trying to communicate with the Valkyrie . . .'

4.

You surround yourself with things, she thought. With *stuff*. You surround yourself with things to fill the gaps. At one time it had all seemed so important. To have nice things. Like the coffee table she had had specially imported from Japan. Or the Danish Hans Jørgen Wegner-designed Ox chair that had cost her over six thousand euros. She sat on the sofa and stared at the magazine.

Maybe it was Uncle Georg who had got to her. He had been so . . . *melancholic* when they last had met. It had disturbed her. They had all called Georg Drescher 'Uncle'. With hindsight, like everything else they had done to Anke, Liane and Margarethe, it had been so very carefully calculated. Not quite a father figure. Definitely not a lover. An uncle. An older male to whom they could turn and on whom they could always rely. Their trainers had tapped into adolescent female psychology to position Drescher perfectly in their minds. Socialism didn't matter. The GDR didn't matter. The only thing that mattered was that they would never, *ever* let their Uncle Georg down.

Then, when the world had shifted on its political axis, socialism disappeared, the GDR was no more. Even Margarethe and Liane, by that time, were no longer there: Margarethe was now so disturbed that she was useless as a potential agent. The only thing they had achieved, Uncle Georg had confided in Anke later, was to turn a seriously disturbed girl into a dangerously disturbed killing machine. And Liane . . . well, Liane had been *too* perfect. Liane had exactly what they had been looking for: a singular ruthlessness and complete disregard for others. But that had also included Uncle Georg, the Stasi, the state. Liane had learned every lesson to perfection and had been deployed in the West before they had realised their mistake. Liane would use the skills they had taught her exclusively to achieve her own ends.

That left only her. Anke. Not that she had called herself that in years. She had been Uncle Georg's favourite. After the Wall had come down, Drescher had set up his own little enterprise, sending Anke out to kill people she didn't know on behalf of people she didn't know. Not for ideology, not for state security, but for cold, hard cash.

And that had suited her fine. Anke had known that Margarethe had been smarter and Liane had been prettier, but Anke had had the sense to recognise a successful partnership. And the partnership with Uncle Georg had worked out just fine. But now there were hints of sentimentality creeping in with the old man. And there was no room in this business for sentimentality.

Uncle Georg had kept the old, Cold War methods of staying in touch. Using the magazine for rendezvous messages. There were five dead-letter drops that he used throughout Hamburg. He had told Anke that he was an old dog who had learned his last trick so long ago. But Anke knew the truth: Uncle

Georg used these methods to keep Anke at arm's length; the snake charmer's fear of being bitten.

But it was an unjustified fear. Uncle Georg was as close to family as Anke had ever known. Or would ever know. That was not to say that she had never considered the possibility of killing him, to protect her identity should he through age or for whatever other reason lose his professionalism. But she knew that when the time came for them to part ways, she would let him live out his retirement in peace. Probably.

She put the magazine down. This made no sense at all.

Two messages. One from Uncle Georg. And the other. The other message was as wrong as it was possible to be. The wrong place and the wrong time. *Muliebritas* was the signal Uncle Georg used to alert her that he needed to see her; that he had another meeting for her to fulfil.

But this shouldn't be here. She read it again: *The heavens are stained with the blood of men, as the Valkyries sing their song.*

It had been their code. The one they had agreed on if they ever wanted to contact each other. But she had never wanted to keep in touch with the other two. She had known, even then, that she was the only true Valkyrie. Margarethe was mad and Liane had her own agenda.

Anke knew it couldn't be one of the other girls. *Muliebritas* had not existed back then. And their plan had been compromised. Whoever had placed the announcement knew she would know it wasn't Liane or Margarethe. Too obvious to be a trap.

She looked again at the decoded message from Uncle Georg. An appointment tomorrow. She would keep it. She would ask Uncle Georg what he made of the other message.

Fabel and Anna were on their way back from talking to Gennady Frolov on his yacht. Frolov's need for luxury equalled his desire for security, so Fabel had agreed to allow him to return to the yacht. The compromise was the two blue-and-silver police cars parked on the quay and the Harbour Police launch moored alongside.

Surrounded by so much opulence, Fabel had found it difficult to focus on his questions. They had met Hans Gessler from the corporate crime unit at the yacht; Gessler must have been more accustomed to dealing with the obscenely wealthy, because he plodded through all the questions he had for the Russian and his accountant, a grumpy and surprisingly scruffy Russian called Krilof. Krilof had given Gessler a CD containing all their files on NeuHansa, Gina Brønsted and Goran Vujačić.

'We're trying to go paperless,' said Krilof without irony or a hint of a smile on his crumpled face. 'This is basically what we're handing over to OLAF. It's enough to bury Gina Brønsted for a long time.'

Fabel was heading back to the Presidium when he got a call from Dirk Hechtner.

'Where are you, *Chef*?'

'I'm just passing through St Georg. I've got Anna with me. Why?'

'We've just had a shout, *Chef*. Henk and I are taking it, but it's on your way. Well, kind of. A woman's been strangled in an apartment in Barmbek-Süd. Sounds like a little afternoon delight that's gone sour.'

'God – we're doing good trade these days. Maybe I'll transfer to New York for a quieter life. I take it this has nothing to do with the Valkyrie case?'

'Doesn't sound like it,' said Hechtner. 'Just a good old-fashioned straightforward, banal, sordid murder – the way they used to make 'em. We don't even have to hunt down the killer. A uniformed unit have nabbed him at the scene. You want to call in?'

'I'll see you there.'

Hechtner gave Fabel the address in Barmbek.

'Have you thought any more about my future?' Anna spoke without turning to Fabel, instead staring straight ahead through the Hamburg drizzle.

'Anna, now's not the time.'

'If you don't mind,' she said, 'I'd like to *make* it the time. Listen, *Chef*, I don't want to beg for my job, but whatever assurances you want from me, I'm ready to make them. I love this job. I don't want to do anything else.'

'Okay.' Fabel drew a deep breath. 'Will you consider going on an anger-management course?'

'You're kidding – right?'

'Anna, you said *anything*. It wouldn't necessarily have to be through the Polizei Hamburg. It doesn't have to go on your permanent record. But if you want to stay, I insist you do it.'

'Do I get a time-of-the-month allowance? I do the anger management but get to go menstrual-mental every four weeks?'

'This isn't a joke,' said Fabel.

'Sorry. I was winding you up. I'll do it. Thanks.'

It was fitting weather for visiting a murder scene. The sky was steel-grey and the air was clingy-damp with a faint chill drizzle. It turned out not to be an apartment after all, but a cheap hotel with 'suites' for rent.

When he pulled up outside, Fabel saw Dirk and Henk come out of the main entrance with a tall man. The man had grey hair and was dressed in a long, expensive-looking blue coat. He was being placed, handcuffed, in a silver and blue police car. As Fabel nodded a greeting to his officers, he realised he had seen the man somewhere before. Somewhere else where his appearance of prosperity and respectability had looked out of place. His eyes met Fabel's briefly before a uniformed officer pressed his head down gently as he guided him into the car.

'Someone you know?' asked Anna.

'No,' said Fabel. 'I've seen him before, that's all. Twice.'

There were two uniformed officers at the scene: an older Obermeister stood at the foot of the bed while a young cop stood outside in the hall, interviewing a hotel cleaner. Holger Brauner, the head of the forensics team, was working with an assistant, both suited up in blue coveralls and surgical gloves.

Fabel knew the older uniformed officer: a man called Hanusch with twenty-five years behind him. It was normal for uniform branch to team up a less experienced officer with a senior man: it eased the passage of the inexperienced into the world of violence and death that was part of everyday police work. Unexpectedly, it was the older policeman whose face had drained of colour. There was a melancholic expression in the eyes that had seen so much over the years. The younger officer in the hall, however, had had the eager electricity about him of someone high on adrenalin.

Fabel followed the older cop's gaze. A pretty girl of about twenty lay on the bed. Her eyes stared back at the uniformed policeman, bloodshot and glazed. Her mouth gaped slightly, her lips bluish and her tongue protruding. The ruptured capillaries in the skin of her neck had created delicate blue spiderweb threads. Fabel looked at her face and felt something lurch deep inside.

'Oh Christ . . .' he said. He looked back at Hanusch: the older uniformed cop smiled sympathetically. Like Fabel, Hanusch wasn't looking at the body, at this sordid scene, with the eyes of a professional policeman. He was looking at the broken remains of a young girl with the eyes of a father.

'I suppose we'd better inform the parents,' said Hanusch. 'I'll get on to locating them. She must have ID somewhere.'

'It's okay,' said Fabel. 'I'll do it. I know where they live. Barmbek, a few blocks away.'

Fabel felt the inquisitive gazes of both Anna and Hanusch on him, but all he said was: 'She was going to be a doctor, you know. Her name was Christa Eisel. She was studying medicine at Hamburg University.'

6.

'What's up?' asked Susanne. 'You sound down.'

'I am. Just the usual. I've just come from a murder scene. Girl of about nineteen. A medical student moonlighting as a hooker. Some old perv strangled her.'

'My God,' said Susanne. 'Not the girl you told me about before: the one who found Jake Westland?'

'Yes. The very same. I tried to tell her, Susanne, but she wouldn't listen.'

'It's not your fault, Jan. Is her death connected to the other killings?'

'No – just a coincidence. Well, not that much of a coincidence in that world. That's what I tried to warn her about. And I know it's not my fault, but I feel, I don't know, *responsible* somehow.'

'It's your age, Jan. You're at that stage in life that you start to see more and more people as sons or daughters.'

'Thanks, Dr Eckhardt, that's cheered me up. Not only is the world going to hell, but I've got one foot in the grave.'

'Just about sums it up. Seriously though, are you okay?'

'Yeah, I'm fine. I just wish you weren't going away tonight.'

'It's only for a few days. I've been promising my mother for ages.'

'Will I see you before you go?'

'Depends on when you get back from work, but I doubt it.

The train leaves at seven. Good luck with this set-up – you know, catching the Valkyrie. Phone me at Mum's and let me know how it goes tomorrow.'

Fabel wished Susanne a good trip and hung up, wishing he had arranged his night out with Otto for that evening instead of the night before. Chances were he'd be working anyway. With an operation like the one they were about to pull in the Alsterpark there was no such thing as too much preparation.

Fabel wandered through to the main open-plan Murder Commission office and spoke to Anna Wolff.

'Has *Muliebritas* been able to give us any more details about that other ad?'

'Nope,' said Anna. 'They've done their best, but their records lead to a dead end. Somehow, someone was able to hack into their database and place the ad without a trace.'

'That's the only answer?'

'It's the only answer we want,' said Anna. 'The only other explanation is that it was someone working within *Muliebritas* itself who placed it.'

'Not impossible,' said Fabel, 'given that *Muliebritas* is a NeuHansa-owned publication.'

'Like I say, we're in trouble if it is an insider. Then they'd know about the set-up tomorrow.'

Fabel made a grim face. 'God, I hope not.'

'Should we call it off?' asked Anna.

He thought for a moment before shaking his head decisively. 'I don't know who placed this ad, but it's not the Valkyrie. It's someone trying to establish contact. We've got a week and a half before the first Monday of the month, which was supposed to be the prearranged meeting time if that notice appeared. I've spoken to the BKA Federal Crime Office and the Halberstadt police and they will help us set up surveillance for that date. Let's just hope we nab her tomorrow instead.'

* * *

Fabel worked late. He went through all the arrangements with the team methodically, then went through them again twice more before letting his officers go. He sat in his office until eight p.m. He again went through the transcriptions of the interviews that he, other officers and Susanne had had with Margarethe Paulus. The overwhelming feeling he got from reading them wasn't horror or anger or revulsion, just a profound sadness.

The Valkyrie Project had been the child of another time, another mindset. Another Germany. In its cold, calculated ruthlessness, the Valkyrie Project had been conceived without any thought for the girls who were selected. Their lives, their dreams and their hopes were to be totally disregarded. They were instruments of the state and nothing more. In many ways, the Valkyrie Project had been typical of every action carried out over forty years by the Stasi.

All the girls' dreams had been stifled. There was something in that. Flicking through the interview transcripts, Fabel found what he was looking for: a scrap of conversation, in between the hard questioning.

Principal Chief Commissar Fabel: Why did they pick you and the other girls?

Margarethe Paulus: We all had something they wanted. Or a mix of things. We were all sporty, we all did well at school, we were all loyal to the Party. Can I have some water?

Interview break while water is brought for interviewee.

Principal Chief Commissar Fabel: You said all the girls were sporty. What was your sport?

Margarethe Paulus: Everything. Especially athletics. But not good enough for serious competition. It was different for Anke, though.

Principal Chief Commissar Fabel: Anke Wollner? Why was that?

Margarethe Paulus: Anke and Liane both had special talents. Liane was great at languages, for example. And debating. But Anke's talent could have got her into the Olympics. She was a world-class junior skier. And an excellent shot, of course. Her speciality was the Nordic biathlon. But that was all stopped when she was inducted into the project.

Fabel snatched up his desk phone. When the hotel reception answered he asked to be put through to Karin Vestergaard's room.

'Karin? It's Jan. Listen, I'm on to something. Of the other two Valkyries, Anke Wollner is our most likely candidate to be the one that Drescher set up as his pension plan, right?'

'Looks that way.'

'Margarethe Paulus said in an interview that Anke had a promising career as a world-class athlete cut short by her induction into the Valkyrie Project.'

'What of it?'

'The Stasi could make all of her records disappear . . . wipe all trace of the name Anke Wollner off the face of the earth, just as they did with the other two girls. But *not* if she is on record outside the GDR. If, at any point, she went with a team into another country, even if it was another Warsaw Pact state, then she'll be on record. Maybe even a photograph . . .'

'It's a long, long shot, Jan,' replied Vestergaard. 'Her name might have been on record somewhere at some time, but it's no use to us. Why do I get the feeling that that's not the only reason you're calling me?'

'The Jørgen Halvorsen murder. It took place in Drøbak, near Oslo?'

'Yes . . .'

'The other thing that Margarethe told me was that Anke's speciality was winter sport. Cross-country skiing, Nordic biathlon, Nordic combined, that kind of thing.'

'I still don't get—'

'Imagine if you were a world-class junior winter sportswoman, growing up in the GDR late seventies, early eighties. What would be the biggest event – the one to make the biggest impact on your consciousness?'

'The eighty-four Winter Olympics in Sarajevo or . . .'

'Exactly, or the eighty-two Nordic Skiing World Championships in Norway. And the venue was the Holmenkollen Ski Centre in Oslo. Like I said, this is just another bit of wild speculation, but what if the Valkyrie *is* Anke? Maybe she got a little nostalgic, wanted to see the place she dreamed as a kid that she might compete in one day. Or simply had to kill a little time before she got down to killing Halvorsen?'

'I'll get on to the Norwegian National Police,' said Vestergaard. 'Holmenkollen is a visitor centre and museum now – maybe they've got CCTV.'

'That's what I thought. Thanks, Karin. Like I said, it's a long shot, but if it gives us a face . . .'

Fabel called Susanne on her cellphone. She was already on the Munich train and they chatted for a while. He told her he was going to pick up something to eat on the way home and get an early night. Tomorrow was going to be a big day.

Fabel ate at a café-restaurant in Altona Altstadt before going home. He felt like taking a shower but decided to leave it until the morning: he was tired and wanted to get to sleep and was worried that a shower would revive him too much and keep him awake. It was about ten-fifteen when he fell into a deep, deep slumber.

He had no idea how long he had been out. The boundary between sleep and wakefulness was blurred. He had become vaguely aware of Susanne warm and next to him. He felt her breasts against his back, then her mouth and tongue on his neck; her hand on his flank, his thigh, his belly. Her hand was now around him: caressing, stroking, bringing him to life. His wakefulness and his arousal stirred together.

Then his confusion.

Susanne was away. He had spoken to her on the phone. He felt her tongue in his ear. No, not her tongue. Not Susanne's. He was now, suddenly, fully awake. He tried to spin around to see who was in the bed with him when something drew tight across his throat. He couldn't breathe and his head felt suddenly light. He reached up and was rewarded with a further tightening of the garrotte around his neck.

'Lie still,' she whispered into his ear. As a lover would. 'Lie still or you'll die.' The pressure around his throat eased, yet she still held him in her other hand, stroking. 'I don't want to kill you,' she whispered. A low, breathless whisper. 'But I will if you don't do as I tell you. Do you understand?'

Fabel tried to speak, but the garrotte had stifled his voice. He nodded his head.

'Do you know who I am?'

He nodded again. He felt the light-headedness ease with the loosening of the ligature. His mind raced and he thought about struggling, fighting for his life. But he knew that she would strangle him as soon as he moved.

'I am a Valkyrie.' Her voice was soft and warm in his ear. Still her hand worked on him. 'But I am not the one you are looking for. Do you understand that?'

Fabel was confused. He moved his hand up to his throat. She gave the garrotte another twist. Fabel felt the throb of his pulse in his neck below the ligature, but not above it. Just pins and needles. The dark world of his bedroom becoming darker. Red-black darker.

'I said: do you understand that?'

He nodded.

'I was – *am* – Liane Kayser. I am not Anke Wollner. Anke is the one you want, not me. I did not work for Georg Drescher. Since the Wall came down I have lived my own life. I have done my own thing. I am not a professional killer.

Or, at least, I am not a professional killer any more. And anything I might have been involved with is not your concern. But I want you to understand that I still have all of the skills they taught me. I could finish you right now – you *do* understand that, don't you, Jan?'

Fabel nodded again.

'I'm going to ease the garrotte so you can talk. If you do anything stupid I will tighten it again, but this time all the way. It has an inertia slide on it. That means I can tighten it fully and walk away: the ligature will be fastened tight and you won't be able to do anything to stop yourself strangling to death. Even I won't be able to release it if I tighten it fully. Do you understand?'

Once more, Fabel nodded. Feeling the ligature ease again, he gasped for breath. She was still touching him below. Stroking him.

'Take your hand off me!' His voice was urgent and raspy.

'Why?' she said. 'You seem to be enjoying it.'

'Take your hand off me *now*.'

She let her hand slip away after one last long, lingering stroke.

'When you tell them . . . when you make your report – will you tell them about that? About how you were hard for me? About me touching you down there?'

Her hand was back on him and Fabel grabbed her wrist. She rewarded him by shutting off his air supply.

'Let me go,' she said. Again the ligature eased when he complied. 'Will you tell them? They'll ask you if you were hard. If you were enjoying it. They'll ask you if you did anything to encourage me doing that. If you invited me into your bed, even if you didn't know who I was. Then there's your partner, Susanne . . . will you tell her? There will always be doubt. People will talk behind your back. There will always be a nagging doubt in the back of Susanne's mind.'

She removed her hand.

'That's what it's like for women. All the time. Every time a woman or a girl is raped or sexually assaulted.'

'That's crap.' The ligature made Fabel's voice high and tight. 'I know the truth. I don't need this half-assed demonstration. I've seen so much violence against women that I know what it's really like.'

'But *did* you enjoy it, Jan?' She kept her voice a whisper. A seductive hiss in his ear. Did she think he'd recognise her voice? wondered Fabel. 'A little hand relief? Did you know that in Victorian England society women would faint all the time. It wasn't considered unusual. It was put down to "female hysteria". It was a genuine phenomenon. And do you know what it was all about?'

Fabel didn't answer. She jerked on the garrotte around his throat. 'I asked you a question.'

'No,' said Fabel, his voice a rasp.

'Sexual repression. Women in Victorian England were not allowed to enjoy sex. They were made to feel dirty if they did. So the phenomenon of "female hysteria" became an accepted medical fact. Do you know how they cured it? A doctor would perform a pelvic massage until the woman underwent what they called a hysterical paroxysm. In other words, the family doctor would offer hand relief. Can you believe that? And all the time Victorian Englishmen were using prostitutes on a scale that dwarfs anything going on today. We weren't much better here in Northern Germany. At least they knew a bit more about sex in the south.'

'You didn't come here to talk about Victorian English or Wilhelmine German sexual kinks. What do you want?'

'Lie on your belly. Do it.' Fabel complied. She forced his head sideways, facing away from her. 'If you see my face,' she explained, 'I'll have to kill you. I came here about the notice in *Muliebritas*.'

'What notice?' said Fabel, his cheek buried in the pillow.

'You know what notice.' She twisted the ligature tight.

Tighter than she had before. When she released it Fabel gasped for breath, his lungs screaming for the oxygen.

'The quote from *Njál's Saga*,' he gasped. 'Is that what you mean?'

'Did you place it?'

'No.'

The ligature tightened again.

'Did you place it?'

Incapable of speaking, Fabel shook his head and again she turned his air supply back on.

'If you didn't place it, then who did?'

'I don't know . . .' Fabel's voice was still small and tight.

'You said something about tomorrow. What is in *Muliebritas* that has to do with tomorrow?'

'I can't tell you. I won't tell you. And anyway, you don't want to know. It's to do with Anke. About catching her. If I tell you, you become part of it all.'

'All right,' she said. 'I won't interfere. I want you to catch her. I want this all to be over so that I can get on with my life again.

'Listen to me, Fabel . . .' She still whispered in his ear, but this time there was nothing seductive in her tone, just a hiss of menace and threat. 'You're a policeman. You've seen so much over the years. You've seen so many women battered, raped, strangled, abused. So many girls and women whose last moments were spent in terror. And unimaginable horror. But you can imagine it, can't you? You have to imagine it. You've looked at what other men can do to women and you've asked yourself that dark, dark question: am *I* capable of that? So much pain, so much fear. And there have been times you've been filled with that dark, dark fear: what if it happened to my daughter, to my partner, to my mother . . . Well, listen to me and remember what I tell you: the Valkyrie you're looking for is Anke. Not me. Leave me alone. Don't come looking for me. Don't even *start* looking for me. If you do, I will target every woman close to you. Your lover, your daughter, your mother – I will make them victims. I will make them suffer before they die. Do you understand?' She tightened the ligature again. 'I can't hurt them if I'm dead or in prison, so I'll make sure I get to them *before* you get to me. If I get the slightest hint that you're on my trail, I'll come after them. Put your hands behind your head.'

Fabel did as he was told. He felt something sting his neck. Something cold in his veins. The darkness of the bedroom deepened. He left the world.

7.

This time wakefulness came on him like an explosion. Sudden, complete, raw.

Fabel threw himself from the bed and slammed painfully onto the floor. He leaned against the wall and pulled himself up until he was standing on shaking, unsteady legs. He looked around the bedroom wildly, seeking out every shadow. Stumbling to the wall switch, he flooded the room with painfully bright light.

She was gone. He found his trousers and scrabbled through the pockets until he found the key for the secure cabinet where he kept his automatic. He took the safety off and snapped back the carriage before leaving the bedroom, going through the whole apartment, room by room, switching on the lights and sweeping each room with his gun. It was only when he was sure he was alone that he went into the bathroom and surrendered to the nausea that had churned in his gut since his first moment awake. Whatever she had injected into him had left him with a thundering headache and a sick feeling that didn't clear even after he had vomited.

Fabel moved over to phone the Presidium but checked

himself. There was something he had to do first. He went back into the bathroom and took a long shower.

Holger Brauner wasn't on call and it was Astrid Bremer who turned up. A uniformed unit had been first to arrive, and they had insisted on knocking up every one of Fabel's neighbours to find out if they had seen or heard anyone coming into the building.

'That's totally unnecessary,' Fabel had complained. 'The woman who broke in here is too professional to allow herself to be seen coming or going.'

The young uniformed Commissar had smiled politely and indulgently and, with total disregard for Fabel's rank, had gone ahead and done what he felt ought to be done. And he was quite right, thought Fabel reluctantly.

'Why on earth did you have a shower?' asked Astrid Bremer. 'You of all people should know better than that. She might have left DNA traces on you.'

'What's that supposed to mean?' snapped Fabel.

Bremer seemed taken aback by Fabel's vehemence. 'Nothing – just that if she had a garrotte around your neck, she was pretty close to you. Forensic distance, I mean. She might have left something behind.'

'I needed to freshen up. That's all.' The door opened and Fabel nodded to Werner as he came into the room. 'I felt groggy after whatever she pumped into me.'

'I see . . .' Bremer searched his expression. 'Are you okay now?'

'I'm fine.'

'You look shaken up, Jan,' said Werner. 'The on-call police doctor is here. He wants to check you out.'

'Like I said, I'm okay.' Raising his voice only turned up the volume of pain in Fabel's head. 'Okay, maybe he should give me a once-over.'

'We need to find out what she injected you with,' said

Bremer. 'The police doctor will want to do that, but I'd like to do my own tests – do you mind if I take a blood sample?'

'Okay,' said Fabel impatiently. 'Take it.' He rolled up his sleeve.

'You'll have to provide the doctor with a second blood sample for an HIV test. Standard practice for any Polizei Hamburg officer who's been stuck with a needle. Obviously it's meant for accidents when searching drug users, but it's regulations . . .'

Bremer took her sample. 'Do you know which other rooms she was in? Apart from the bedroom, I mean?'

'What are you getting at? Do you think I entertained her beforehand?'

'Take it easy, *Chef*,' said Werner. 'Astrid's only doing her job.'

'I wasn't getting at anything, Herr Fabel,' said Bremer with sudden formality.

'I'm sorry, Astrid.' Fabel rubbed his neck. 'It's been a trying night. What's the time?'

'Five-twenty,' said Werner.

'Shit. Once I'm done with the quack you and I will have to get over to the Presidium. We've got to get everything set up for the sting in the Alsterpark.'

'Are we going ahead with that?' asked Werner. 'I mean, I know what she told you, but it would be a pretty safe bet to assume that your lady visitor was the Valkyrie.'

'No, Werner – that was Liane Kayser who came here last night. The whole point of her visit was to let me know in no uncertain terms that she was not Drescher's hit woman.'

'Did she know that Drescher was dead?'

'I don't know,' said Fabel. 'She didn't say anything to suggest she did. But she definitely was sure that I would know who she was talking about when she mentioned the name Drescher. One thing's for certain, she's not *the* Valkyrie. That's Anke Wollner. Liane Kayser came here tonight because she has a life worth protecting. She was giving nothing away. Well, she did give one thing away, if inadvertently.'

'What?'

'I have a funny feeling that she was abused as a child. Or a rape victim. Some trauma that changed her personality and made her a candidate for the Valkyrie project.'

'Why?' Astrid Bremer looked at Fabel with a puzzled frown. 'What gave you that idea?'

'I don't know,' lied Fabel. 'Just a couple of things she said about how men treat women. It's just a feeling I get.'

8.

It was, Fabel imagined, pretty much how it would be preparing a set for a movie scene: everything had the semblance of normality, of reality, but nothing was what it seemed. No one was who they were pretending to be.

It was odd to be there, running a major operation a few hundred metres from where he used to live. He knew this area so well.

Fabel, code name Kaiser One, was on the third floor of one of the grand villas on Harvestehuder Weg which looked out over the trees, across the Alsterpark and over the Outer Alster itself. The Polizei Hamburg had been able to secure the permission of the owner, a prominent Hamburg businessman keen to be seen cooperating with the authorities. It was the best vantage point they could find: from here, with the binoculars, Fabel could see almost everything happening within the immediate area of the Fährdamm. The Fährdamm was a quay for the small red and white ferries that criss-crossed the Alster, Hamburg's inner-city lake. Running past the Fährdamm and along the water's edge all the way around the Alster was the Alsterpromenade. If she came, she would come along the Alsterpromenade or down the tree-lined avenue leading from Pöseldorf to the Fährdamm.

She could park a car there. Fabel saw the official Hamburg City works van sitting to one side of the avenue with a group of park workers standing smoking outside it: the MEK unit he had requested to assist them.

Beside the ferry point was a café-bar, closed at this time of day, and on the other side a row of benches where people could sit and contemplate the views across the lake. Fabel's view of the bench itself was still partly obscured, even in winter, by a tangle of naked tree branches.

A thickset figure with greying hair sat on the bench. Kaiser Two: Werner. Fabel felt a knot in his chest. Werner looked too heavy for Drescher. The Kevlar bulletproof vest was adding to his bulk. What if she didn't go for it? The Valkyrie had been meeting with Drescher like this for nearly twenty years. What if she recognised the sham from a distance? What if she were just to walk away, realising that Drescher must be either dead or in custody, that her relationship with her control was compromised? The thought of the Valkyrie out there on her own, uncontrolled and untraceable, sent a chill through Fabel.

'There's a woman approaching,' one of the undercover officers radioed in. 'I think she came in from Milchstrasse.'

Fabel picked out the woman with his binoculars. She was tall and slim but he couldn't tell her age easily and her hair was hidden by a heavy woollen hat. She was carrying a shoulder bag.

'She's heading down onto the path,' said the officer.

'Follow her,' ordered Fabel. 'Werner, she's going to approach from your right. Remember what we discussed.'

As Fabel expected, and as they had arranged, Werner didn't reply by radio. Instead he opened a copy of the *Hamburger Morgenpost* and turned his back to the approaching woman, resting his arm on the back of the bench as if to prop up the broadsheet newspaper.

'She's closing in,' Fabel said over the radio, using one hand to keep the binoculars trained on her. She wasn't walking quickly, almost strolling. 'Herzog Five . . . close the gap between you and her. I want you ready to assist Kaiser Two if he needs it.'

Fabel could see the officer following her. Further back there was a young woman in jogging gear, using the railings as a bar against which to do stretching exercises. Anna Wolff. Sweeping the binoculars along the path past Werner he could see a man and woman dressed in smart dark coats and business wear, standing having a conversation: both planted police officers. Herzog Five, following the woman, was a young male officer dressed casually in a black-hooded jacket. He had closed the distance between him and the woman. The woman stopped and leaned against the railing at the water's edge. She seemed to be looking out across the Alster to the distant spires that rose above the city.

'*Shit*,' said Fabel in English. 'Don't stop . . . *don't stop* . . .' he said under his breath, willing the officer following the woman to keep walking. He did. He kept his step and pace unbroken and walked straight past her.

'She's one hundred metres from the bench,' the officer said over the radio. 'I'm going to pass Kaiser Two. There's a bench twenty metres past him. I'll sit there and wait.'

'No,' said Fabel decisively. 'Turn up the path towards Milchstrasse and cut back along Harvestehuder Weg. Herzog Four – where are you?'

'I'm still in position,' answered Anna Wolff. 'South-west corner. I have the woman in sight.'

'Get over there as fast as you can without drawing attention to yourself. Herzog Six and Seven, stay where you are but be ready to move in.'

He watched Anna as she started jogging in the woman's direction.

'She's on the move again,' said Anna over the radio.

Fabel swept the binoculars along the path.

'All units, stand by.'

The woman was now less than ten metres from Werner. Five. Two.

She walked past him without so much as a glance in his direction.

'Do I stick with her?' asked Anna.

Fabel was still tracking the woman with his binoculars. She greeted a man coming in the opposite direction, looping her arm through his. Fabel watched as the couple turned off the Alsterpromenade and headed off together up the avenue towards Pöseldorf.

'It's obviously not her. She's meeting someone.' He felt his heart sink. He knew then that she wouldn't be coming. She was probably doing exactly what he was doing at that moment: surveying the scene from a distance, through binoculars, and failing to be convinced by Werner's unconvincing wig and too bulky frame.

'Stay sharp,' Fabel said into his radio. 'She's maybe still going to show.' He scanned the Alsterpromenade, following it from the south, along the water's edge and up to the Fährdamm. Nothing. He saw Werner still sitting on the bench. He followed the couple walking arm in arm up the avenue and past the MEK troops dressed as park workers. He noticed the dark Lycra-clad Anna jogging past them.

'Herzog Four,' he radioed to Anna. 'Loop round and take up your previous location.'

Anna didn't reply.

'Herzog Four, do you read me?'

'Stand by . . .' Over the radio, he heard Anna breathing hard as she ran. He watched her through the binoculars. She stopped jogging and leaned forward, hands on her knees, as if exhausted from a much longer run than her brief jog. The couple, arm in arm, passed her.

Anna straightened up and pressed her hands into the small of her back, stretching her spine. A casual gesture.

'She-wolf! She-wolf! She-wolf!' Anna's voice over the radio was so urgent and excited that Fabel found himself looking at her casual figure again. Then the adrenalin surged into his system, slowing time. 'Herzog Four to Kaiser One, I have a visual on She-wolf.'

'Where? Where is she?' he shouted into the radio.

'The couple,' said Anna. 'It's her. I can't be sure, but I think she's got the guy at gunpoint. I think she made Kaiser Two and sussed it's a set-up and just grabbed the guy as a decoy.'

'Shit.' Fabel cursed to himself, then pressed the send button to call the MEK unit. 'Wolf Five – it looks like we have a potential hostage situation.'

'We heard,' said the MEK commander. 'If it is, we've got to take her before she gets out of the park and into Pöseldorf. Do we go?'

Fabel hesitated. 'Herzog Four, are you sure it's She-wolf?'

'I can't be positive, Kaiser One. She's got a tight grip of his arm and he doesn't look happy. She's pressed against him and could have a gun in his ribs.'

'Wolf Five to Kaiser One. Do we go or not?'

Fabel checked Anna through the binoculars. She was still playing the part of a spent jogger. He could see that half of the MEK troops disguised as park workers had disappeared into the back of the van. He followed the couple with the binoculars as they made their unhurried way out of the park. If it wasn't the Valkyrie, he had nothing to lose. If it was, then she clearly knew they were on to her. She would spot anyone following her into the city. If Fabel let her go unfollowed, she might let her hostage go unharmed. Or not.

The alternative was to try to take her down in the park. The chances of the hostage surviving were not good; nor were the odds against one of the police team being injured or killed.

'Wolf Five to Kaiser One . . .' Fabel could hear the impatience in the MEK commander's voice. 'I repeat: do we go or not?'

Fabel lifted the radio to his mouth.

9.

'I didn't think you'd be back today,' said Ivonne. She brought in a coffee and a pile of papers, which she laid on Sylvie's desk. 'How did you get on in the Far East?'

'Fine. I'm close to finding who it is I've been after. The person with all the answers. I'm only back in Hamburg for a few days. Is this the stuff?'

'Yep – everything you asked for. All the information I could dig up on Gennady Frolov as well as everything I could find on the NeuHansa companies you asked about. And the latest copy as well as a few back numbers of the magazine you asked about – the one behind the protest in the Kiez the night that English pop star was murdered. By the way, Andreas Knabbe is looking for you. You should answer your cellphone messages sometimes. Actually, you should answer your cellphone sometimes.' Ivonne made a pained face. 'When I say Herr Knabbe is looking for you, I mean it in an angry-mob-with-burning-torches way. I don't think he was too happy that you weren't here to cover that bomb blast down by the harbour. The word is that Gennady Frolov was one of the diners in the restaurant.'

'Frolov?' Sylvie frowned. 'Sounds like he was probably the target. What does he want? Knabbe, I mean.'

'Probably your scalp. Oh, another thing. There's been something funny going on in Altona, not far from where you live. Four days ago the street was blocked off and a pile of police were going through a couple of apartments. Then nothing.'

'What's the official line?'

'At the moment there isn't one.'

'They're stalling,' said Sylvie. 'They won't give out mis-information, so they're trying to say nothing for as long as they can. Who's on the story?'

'That creep Brandt is following it up.' Ivonne wrinkled her nose in distaste. 'You know, the one who smells.'

'He couldn't find his ass with both hands, far less uncover a story,' said Sylvie. 'Anything else?'

'Nope . . . should there be?'

'It's just that I was expecting a message. No one called Siegfried has phoned or emailed?'

'Not that I'm aware of.'

After Ivonne had left her office, Sylvie began leafing through the information Ivonne had compiled. She was in the middle of the latest issue of *Muliebritas* when an announcement caught her eye: an extract from *Njál's Saga*.

> *The heavens are stained with the blood of men,*
> *As the Valkyries sing their song.*

Now that, she thought to herself, is one hell of a coinci-dence.

10.

He was hesitating. She could sense it. She knew it would be Fabel, head of the Murder Commission, who would have oversight of the operation. She cursed her stupidity: after all these years, after all the coded messages and rendezvous with Uncle Georg, she had simply not considered that it would be a set-up. She should have thought it through. Especially that other announcement, in the wrong place.

'I have a wife and children,' said the man whom she held tight with her arm looped through his. 'Please don't kill me.'

She pressed the barrel of her Beretta PX4 Storm automatic

harder into his ribs, urging him forward with a tug on his arm. 'If I were going to kill you, you'd be dead already. If anything happens to you it'll be the fault of the police. I know what I'm doing, they don't. If you want to stay alive and see your wife and kids again, then shut up and keep walking. Once we're in the city and I can lose myself in the crowds, I'll let you go.'

She kept their pace even, unhurried. There had been a cop behind her, closing the gap as she had approached the bench. That was what had alerted her first. Then that stupid woman pretending to be a jogger. But, of course, she had realised from twenty metres away that it wasn't Uncle Georg on the bench. It was a stupid, clumsy set-up and she had been stupid and clumsy to walk into it.

He's watching me now, she thought. My money would be somewhere in an upper storey on Harvestehuder Weg.

'Tilt your head close to mine,' she hissed at the man. He was tall, nearly ten centimetres taller than she was. 'Make it look like we're a couple and you're talking to me.'

Maybe, she thought, the manoeuvre had worked: maybe they had crossed her off their list and were seeking some other woman approaching, alone. She thought about the man on her arm. The fake Uncle Georg had probably looked at her as she had passed, but she had turned her face away as if looking out across the water. Only this man had seen her up close. If she got out into Pöseldorf, she would take him up a side street. She didn't have the silencer on her gun, so she would finish him with her knife.

If she got out into Pöseldorf.

They had passed a Hamburg Parks Department van a couple of seconds ago, with a group of workmen standing beside it. She felt like laughing: they could have thrown in at least one older or overweight cop, just for appearances. The workmen had special weapons and training written all over them. Polizei Hamburg MEK unit. Six of them. Body armour under overalls, probably. She knew that these men could move fast and could keep pace with her on a long foot-pursuit. To become a member of the Polizei Hamburg's MEK squad you had to be able to run three thousand metres in less than thirteen minutes thirty seconds. But the body armour would slow them. Legs and heads. If it came to it, she would go for legs and heads. They had a massive advantage in numbers and equipment, but she had a big advantage in knowing that they would do it all by the book. By numbers.

Fabel was watching her and hesitating, she knew he was. Every second he hesitated brought her closer to the city, to streets and people. Once she was there she could get away. And if they came after her she would create so much havoc. She would lose them in a tidal wave of dead civilians.

The polycarbide knife. The Beretta. Three spare clips, fourteen rounds each, in her shoulder bag.

She could see straight up Alsterchausee. The trick was not to start rushing. She kept calm. Kept her grip on the hostage constant and firm. She was nearly there. He wasn't going to call it. Fabel wasn't going to call it.

Uncle Georg.

They had Uncle Georg. Then the realisation hit her. They *didn't* have Uncle Georg: he was dead. She dug deep into herself to feel something. And she had to dig deep. So little feeling.

She thought about the talks they had had together. She thought about when she had been fifteen and he had taught her everything she knew. She remembered sitting on the grass outside the training school on a summer's day. She had felt the sun prickle on her neck. She remembered the cool orange juice they had drunk together and the few moments they had chatted – Uncle Georg, Liane, Margarethe and her – about silly, inconsequential things.

'This is a golden moment,' Uncle Georg had explained.

'Between meetings, you should enjoy these moments. Savour them.'

And in that golden moment she had truly felt that the other girls were her sisters; that Uncle Georg really was her uncle. She had glimpsed a life that she had never known. It had been a perfect golden lie for a perfect golden moment. But even in that lie she had discovered what it must have been like to have been part of a family.

And now Uncle Georg was dead.

For a moment, in the middle of the chill Hamburg winter, she felt the warmth of that long-gone summer afternoon. She found the pain, the grief that she had dug for.

It was then that she heard them running towards her from behind, shouting for her to let her hostage go and to stand still.

Fabel had called it, after all.

Chapter Seven

1.

Anke Wollner spun around, pulling the man she held captive in front of her as a shield. She knew, of course, that there would be other MEK and Criminal Police closing in behind her, but the main threat would come from the front. The six MEK men had broken into three teams of two. Standard formation, by the book.

She saw the other cop, the woman dressed as a jogger. She was yelling at Anke to stand still. Anke fired twice at the woman cop, hitting her in both legs. She went down and started to scream. Anke aimed for her head but was aware of the MEK officers advancing towards her, three moving, three covering. She fired into the face of the first. The others opened fire, but their shots went wide: they were clearly afraid of hitting her hostage. She fired twice more. One miss, the second took off the side of an MEK man's head. Two dead cops. One heavily wounded. They would pull back to avoid any civilian injury. Anke backed up towards Harvestehuder Weg, keeping the hostage in front of her. He was shaking violently and she was having trouble steering him. Checking behind, she saw two cops duck down behind a parked car. She fired into the windows, shattering them and sending glass flying. She fired three shots into the petrol tank, then a round onto the asphalt where the petrol had already started pooling. The sparks from the round hitting the road ignited the petrol and the rear of the car lifted into the air as the tank exploded. She heard screams from behind the car and other officers came running up. She could see a car screech to a halt further up Harvestehuder Weg, stopped by a uniformed officer.

Anke released her grip on the hostage and sprinted in the direction of the car. As she did so, she turned and shot the hostage once, in the stomach. He fell down onto the road, vomiting blood onto the wet street. Then he started screaming. They would have to deal with him. As Anke ran towards the car she heard automatic fire. Something slapped the back of her calf and she was surrounded by the angry hornet zipping of bullets around her, but she kept running. They had to control their fire. There were houses to the left of her and a stray bullet could take out a civilian. That was their number-one disadvantage. She didn't care who died or was injured: they had to.

A uniformed officer to her left turned and reached for his side arm. She kept running, her Beretta stretched out in her rod-steady arm. She fired twice and hit the uniformed cop – who she knew would not be body-armoured – twice in the chest. The driver of the car sat gawp-mouthed. Anke ripped open the driver door and pulled the driver, a young woman, from the VW Polo. Anke then shot her in the legs: another casualty to slow things up. She slammed the Polo into gear and reversed at high speed up Harvestehuder Weg. There were more shots and the windscreen shattered, but Anke didn't turn. If they were going to hit her, they would. Her only chance was to get away as fast as possible. She spun the car into a 180-degree skid on the wet street and floored the accelerator again. She could see blue lights in her rear-view mirror.

They were chasing her.

'The one thing about a police chase,' Uncle Georg had told her, 'is that the police will almost always win. Make them think they're in a vehicle pursuit and then get out of the vehicle as quickly as possible.'

She took the corner at Pöseldorfer Weg at high speed, tyres screeching. Turning sharp right into a side street, a cul-de-sac, she pulled into the kerb, reversing to park normally behind another car. She saw the blue lights flash past the road end. A second police car slowed down almost to a halt at the end of the cul-de-sac, obviously checking it out, before taking off after the first car.

Anke got out of the car as quickly as she could, but found her leg was stiffening up. She could feel the wet in her shoe and inside her trouser leg. She couldn't look now. She needed to get away. Put as much distance as possible, as quickly as possible, between herself and the car.

She still had her shoulder bag strapped across her chest. She released the empty magazine from the Beretta's grip and slammed in a full one. She walked without limping along the quiet street and took a sudden left turn through the gate of one of the houses. She could see it was a substantial villa that had been converted into apartments. She walked up to the main door as if she had done so every day in her life and checked the names on the buzzer board. There was an apartment with two different surnames. It was by no means guaranteed, but she guessed it was lived in by an unmarried couple without kids, probably a younger couple. They would probably be out at work. She pressed the buzzer. No answer, which was what she wanted. She then proceeded to press every buzzer until she got an answer. An older woman's voice.

'Delivery,' said Anke.

The door lock was buzzed open. Anke pushed open the door and shoved the toe of her boot in to stop it closing completely. She pressed the old woman's buzzer again.

'Sorry,' she said. 'Wrong address. I thought this was Pöseldorfer Weg.' After listening to the old woman's complaints, Anke let herself in and eased the door quietly shut behind her. She stood for a moment and caught her breath, listening out for the sounds of a suspicious old woman on the stairwell. When she was convinced she was alone, she climbed the stairs to the first floor. She found the flat she was looking for and picked the lock.

Once inside, she checked every room to make sure that the flat was really empty. She looked down at the wooden floor. She had left bloody footprints all along the hall. That meant there was a trail all the way up the stairs and probably from the car. Even if it wasn't visible, it would be very easy for a police sniffer dog to follow. She would have to be quick. Going through to the bedroom, she checked out the woman's wardrobe. She was a size bigger than Anke, but that didn't matter: a size smaller would have been useless. Anke laid out a range of trousers, jumpers and jackets on the bed and made a quick selection from them. She also found a shoulder bag to replace her own: smaller, but it would do.

The bathroom was small, and Anke had to lean against the wall as she eased out of her shoes, trousers and tights, leaving a pool of blood on the tiled floor. She turned her calf to examine the wound: the bullet had not lodged in her leg but had carved its passage by gouging out a chunk of flesh. There was no bath, but Anke was able to take down the shower head and run hot water over the wound before wrapping a towel tight around her calf. She found the bathroom cabinet and tipped everything out into the basin. She took a second towel and doused it with antiseptic. There was a bandage still in its wrapper but no other dressings. She went into the bedroom again and went through the drawers until she found a packet of sanitary pads which she took back through to the bathroom.

Anke removed the towel from her leg and pushed the antiseptic-soaked pad into the wound. The pain exploded hot and sharp and she suppressed a scream into an inhuman sound caged behind her tightly clenched teeth. Applying two sanitary pads to the wound, she bound them in place with the bandage. When she was finished, she washed her hands and the sweat from her face. There was a photograph on the dresser, presumably of the couple who lived in the flat. The woman was tall and slim like Anke and didn't look a full size bigger, but she had dark hair and an olive tone to her skin. Anke reckoned her make-up would be heavier and darker than that which Anke normally used, and she spent five minutes in front of the mirror completely changing her face with a few strokes of the woman's make-up brush. She then changed into the clothes she'd laid out, putting on a pair of knee-length boots under her trousers. It was a struggle to get the left boot zipped up over the wound, but Anke reckoned the boot would help keep the dressing tight and in place.

Once she had put on the change of clothes, including an ankle-length coat and a beret-style hat, Anke looked at herself in the mirror. A different woman with a different style, a different history, a different life.

Before leaving the flat, Anke tried to work out what to do with her discarded clothes. Her DNA would be all over them. But there again, she thought, her DNA was now all over half of Hamburg. There was no forensic distance this time.

It was over. She knew that. Uncle Georg was dead. Or captured. She had to get out of Hamburg. She had identities she could use, she had enough money to live on for the rest of her life. Maybe this could be a new beginning. The next twenty-four hours would tell.

She put the Beretta, the magazines, her polycarbide knife and the box of sanitary pads into her shoulder bag. She went over to the window and checked out the street below. It seemed quiet, but she could hear the sound of sirens in the streets all around. She was going to have to walk through it all and out of Pöseldorf.

And then she would be free.

2.

Fabel had watched it all. He had stood and watched as Anna had been gunned down. He had seen the flashes, then Anna crumple to the ground. He should have stayed where he was, but, without thinking, he found himself running down the stairs and out onto the street, screaming into the radio for an ambulance.

By the time he got to Anna there were already two MEK officers tending to her, applying first-aid-kit pressure pads to the wounds in her legs. Werner was there too, brushing the hair away from her face. Fabel felt sick as he saw the crimson bloom on the white gauze of the pressure pads.

'Anna . . .' He dropped to his knees beside her. 'Anna . . . I'm so sorry.'

Her face was pale, almost grey. Her breathing was shallow and short, but she shook her head and smiled weakly. 'Not your fault. Mine. I'm ready for that anger-management course now . . .'

The ambulance arrived and the paramedics set to work on her, ordering Werner and Fabel to stand back. Dietz, the MEK commander, approached them.

'What the hell were you doing?' Fabel screamed in his face. 'How the fuck did you allow this to happen? I brought you into this because this is *exactly* what I didn't want to happen.' He pointed in the direction of the paramedics working on Anna.

'Before you start shooting your mouth off, Fabel, I'd remind you that two of my men are dead, two more critical from burns. This isn't my fuck-up – it's yours. Why the hell didn't you give us the say-so to take her down before she got to the road? She knew that we would have to choose our shots if she got between us and occupied buildings. There . . .' He jabbed a gloved finger in the direction of the park. 'That's where our chances were best.'

Werner, now without his wig, placed his considerable bulk between them. 'Pack it in, for God's sake. This isn't helping. Jan, we've got three more down – the hostage is critical, shot in the gut. We've got a dead uniform and another wounded civilian. It's a mess, all right.'

'Have we found the car yet?'

'No. It can't be that hard – the windscreen's shot out.'

'This bitch isn't going to be scared into a panicked flight,' said Fabel. 'My guess is she's dumped the car very close and stolen another. I want the control room at the Presidium to alert us to any stolen cars in a five-kilometre radius. Or a damaged Polo being abandoned. In the meantime, get every mobile unit to check alleyways, side streets, disused sites – anywhere she might have dumped it. But I'm pretty sure we'll find it close by. And have every woman walking alone stopped and questioned. Minimum two officers. And extreme caution.'

'There's something else,' said Dietz. 'I'm pretty sure I hit her. There's some blood on the road further up where she ran. I think I got her in the leg.'

'She'll have tried to find somewhere to get fixed up. She's still here, Werner. We've got to find her.'

3.

Pöseldorf was one of Hamburg's trendiest addresses. The property was expensive and the shops and restaurants exclusive. But Pöseldorf had started off as Hamburg's poor quarter and the layout was a tangle of cobbled streets.

Anke used as many alleys and access lanes as possible,

even clambering over walls to avoid using the main streets. She found herself on Hallerstrasse, near the TV studio and the Rotherbaum tennis stadium. The street was lined with cars, but most were expensive newer models with complicated immobiliser and alarm systems. She walked on. She would have to walk back to where she had left her own car. She needed to get it out of the area before it was treated as an abandoned vehicle, giving the police a positive ID and address for her. But she had parked far enough away from the Alsterpark to feel relatively secure. It was a decision that she regretted now with every step she took. Her calf throbbed and her entire leg began to ache, a result of the sudden and severe muscular contraction after the bullet had hit. It would not have been too long a walk if she had been able to continue straight along Mittelweg, but she knew that the police would, by now, be stopping almost every woman walking alone, so she was forced to take the most circuitous route, more than tripling the distance she had to cover.

Anke felt an enormous relief when she turned the corner and saw her Lexus saloon parked where she had left it. She sank into the leather seat and stretched her injured leg out straight, allowing herself a moment to rest. She eased her hand up the back of her boot and felt the wet leather. When she got back to the apartment she was going to have to stitch the wound, which, given its position, would not be easy.

Leaning her head back against the seat, Anke closed her eyes for a moment. She turned suddenly when she heard someone knocking on the side window.

Anke smiled and slid the window open. She assessed the situation: young policewoman – very young – alone, foot patrol, inexperienced. Every one else hunting the killer from the Alsterpark.

'Is this your vehicle?'

'Yes, it is. Is there a problem?'

'You've been parked here too long. I'll have to give you a ticket. What's your name, please?'

You're checking my name against the database, thought Anke. You've already radioed in the index number. It'll be flagged up later. Her identity, her address, all compromised.

'Jana Eigen.' She gave the name she'd been living under for the last ten years. A name that had become as real to her as Anke Wollner. Now it was lost.

'May I see your ID card and driver's licence?' The young policewoman was trying hard to project authority. Anke estimated she was no older than twenty-three; pretty, with dark hair under the police cap. Her blue police jacket was a size too big for her, giving her an almost childlike appearance.

'Sure,' said Anke, reaching into the shoulder bag sitting next to her on the passenger seat. 'Here it is.'

Anke's first shot hit the policewoman in the throat. She dropped beside the car. Anke swung the door open but it jammed against the policewoman's body and she had to squeeze out, hurting her leg as she did so. The young policewoman was face down, the oversized blue waterproof jacket bunched up like a turtle's carapace with the word POLIZEI emblazoned on it in white. A sickeningly wet gurgling sound issued from her and she was trying to crawl away. Anke fired a second round into the back of the policewoman's head and she lay still. There were screams from onlookers and Anke knew that she'd have to move fast. The policewoman's body obstructed the car so Anke had to drag it out into the road. Then she jumped back in the car and sped off.

She would have to dump the car. She would have to find a safe place.

4.

It was pretty much what Fabel had expected. Van Heiden had not been angry, nor had he lectured Fabel, but he had communicated, more by silences than words, that things could not be worse and, if the axe fell, then it would fall squarely on Fabel's neck.

What hadn't helped had been the media attention. Accounts of the shootings on Harvestehuder Weg were repeated on every news bulletin, on every channel, and not just in Hamburg. The Presidium was like a medieval castle under siege, with satellite-dish-topped vans parked outside and TV crews pointing their cameras at the building. Fabel even got a message that Sylvie Achtenhagen had been trying to get in touch with him.

'She said it's very urgent,' the cop at reception had told him.

'I bet she did,' said Fabel, scrunching up the note, leaning over the reception desk and dropping it into the wastebasket.

After leaving van Heiden, Fabel phoned Werner at the hospital.

'How's Anna?'

'Still in theatre,' said Werner. 'I'll phone as soon as she comes out and I hear anything. Try not to worry, Jan. She's tougher than either of us.'

After Fabel hung up, there was a knock on the door and Dirk Hechtner came in.

'You okay, *Chef*? I mean—'

'I know what you mean. I'm okay. Thanks for asking. What have you got?'

'The gun recovered from Margarethe Paulus's apartment – we've traced it. It used to be owned by a Zlatko Ljubičić, a Croatian. And listen to this: Ljubičić was arrested during the same sting as Goran Vujačić. He was Vujačić's bodyguard.'

'Where is he now?'

'I'm chasing that up,' said Hechtner. 'The Danish police had to let him go: it's not illegal to be a gangster's bodyguard unless you can be nailed for doing something illegal yourself. He worked in Copenhagen as a security guard for a while. After that, I don't know yet. But it's a hell of a coincidence that there's a Vujačić connection after all.'

'Anything else?'

'Yeah – I checked out Svend Langstrup, Gina Brønsted's head of security; no form. But he's a former officer in the *Jægerkorpset*, that's the Danish special forces. He has dual nationality: Danish and German. Langstrup ran his own security company for a while – and yes, I'm way ahead of you, I'm checking with the Danish police to see if it was his company that Zlatko Ljubičić worked with. From what I can see he's on a huge salary. He lives out in Blankenese.'

'Okay, keep on it. I'm heading down to the Ops Room.'

The Operations Room was more crowded than usual and Fabel's heart sank when he saw both van Heiden and Police President Steinbach amongst the other officers. For Fabel, having his superiors present when he was trying to run an inquiry was like having a teacher peer over your shoulder while you did your homework.

But he could tell by van Heiden's face that his bad-news day had just got worse.

'We've lost another one,' said van Heiden. 'The bitch has killed another police officer.'

'Who?'

'A young female officer called Annika Büsing. She was twenty-four, Jan.'

'Where?'

'Rotherbaum.' Henk Hermann joined them. His long, thin, freckled face pale and grim beneath a mop of red hair. He checked his notebook. 'The car was a black Lexus GS450h saloon. Six months old. The owner is a Jana Eigen. She lives in Blankenese.'

'Wealthy.'

'Looks like it. And not at home.'

'Okay, Henk, you and Dirk take the Rotherbaum murder. I'll head over to the address we've got for Frau Eigen.' He turned to van Heiden. 'I've got all of my team committed. I could do with someone to come to Blankenese with me.'

'I'll do it,' said van Heiden.

'Do you have a service weapon?'

'Of course I do . . .' said van Heiden. Then, less indignantly: 'But it's in my locker. I'll go get it.'

'If you don't mind, I'd like to take Karin Vestergaard along with us. I've sent a car to pick her up. She has a vested interest in seeing this concluded. We're not the only ones to have lost colleagues.'

Fabel was aware of another figure at his shoulder. He turned to see Hans Gessler of the corporate crime division.

'I heard about Anna, Jan,' he said. 'I'm really sorry. How is she?'

'I'm waiting for word.'

'I just wanted to let you know that I've been through Frolov's information on Gina Brønsted and NeuHansa. We've got enough there to nail her – but not for these murders. There's no direct evidential link. But she's toast as far as tax evasion, falsification of permits and fraud are concerned.'

'I want her. There's got to be something that ties her in with ordering these Valkyrie hits.'

'Not from her end. Maybe if we could find Drescher's bank accounts . . . I'll look into it, but it could be a numbered account in Switzerland.'

'See what you can do, Hans. Give me something. Anything.'

5.

It wasn't the ideal day for a walk by the beach.

The water of the Elbe frothed and snapped at the bitter wind that whipped at it and the dull steel-grey fog that smothered it. He had his fists rammed deep into his coat pockets and a woollen hat pulled tight over his ears, but he walked unbowed, his wet and chilled face full into the wind. He had walked here two summers ago with his wife. They had talked then about the future. About how maybe the time was right to have kids.

He stopped and watched the fog-fudged outline of a freighter slide by, further out in the Elbe, in the deep channel just beyond Ness-sand, the nature-reserve island. The freighter was dark and massive in the gloom and as it passed it sounded its horn, a low, plaintive dinosaur cry in the fog.

He had just turned back into the wind to continue his walk when he saw a figure ahead of him. Another shadow in the grey gloom. The figure was standing still, staring out at the ship. Or at nothing. He drew close. He saw the profile now and the wisps of blonde hair from under the woollen hat. A woman.

'Hello.'

The woman gave a start and turned to face him. Her hands snapped out of her pockets and she held them at her side. For a moment he thought she was going to attack him.

'I'm sorry,' he said. 'I didn't mean to startle you.'

'Walking,' she said. 'I was just walking.'

'Are you all right?'

She gazed at him blankly and, for a moment, he was struck by how terribly empty her expression was. Then she smiled.

'I'm sorry,' she said. 'Yes, you did startle me. Not your fault. The fog.'

'Are you sure you're all right?' The concern in his voice was genuine.

She shrugged self-deprecatingly. 'Truth is, I've got a bit lost. I parked the car somewhere . . .' She waved her gloved hand vaguely along Strandweg in the direction of the ferry pier. 'I needed some fresh air. A walk. I didn't account for the fog being so thick.'

'It's not a night for walking on the beach,' he said.

'Then what are *you* doing?' She smiled at him again. He noticed for the first time how pretty she was. Totally different from Silke, his wife, but very pretty.

'I live near here. I know where I'm walking.'

She looked up to where Blankenese loomed in the fog, a dark mass punctuated by yellow lights. 'You live here?'

'Yes . . . just over there.' He pointed.

'Could you walk me back to the path then, please?' she asked. 'I've actually lost where I came through the wall onto the beach.'

'Certainly,' he said. He held out his hand. 'My name's Svend Langstrup.'

'I'm Birta. Birta Henningsen.'

6.

They had just parked outside the villa in Blankenese when they got the message that Jana Eigen's car had been discovered in woods south of Sülldorf.

'My God,' said Fabel. 'That's just north of here. Walking distance.'

'Jana Eigen is Anke Wollner?' asked Vestergaard.

'And Anke Wollner is the Valkyrie.' He pulled his automatic from its holster and checked the magazine. '*Shit* – she's come back. There's something in the house that she needs.' He turned to van Heiden. 'Horst, we've got to make sure she's not in here. We could wait until reinforcements arrive.'

'They didn't do much good in the Alsterpark. Let's go.'

Fabel gestured for van Heiden to wait and reached into

the glove compartment. He took out a SIG-Sauer automatic, in a holster and wrapped in a shoulder harness. He held the weapon out to Karin Vestergaard but did not release it when she took it. Instead he turned again to van Heiden.

'What the hell,' said van Heiden, with a shrug.

Vestergaard took the gun, took off her coat and slipped on the holster before snapping back the carriage on the automatic and reholstering it.

By Blankenese standards, it was quite a modest property. Three bedrooms, two bathrooms, a dining room, kitchen and lounge. All of which were unoccupied. Their sweep of the house was made even more stressful by the urgent shrieking of the alarm that Fabel had set off when he had forced the door. Once they were satisfied that Anke Wollner was not at home, Fabel phoned the Presidium and asked that a forensic team be sent out to check out the house.

'And for God's sake get on to Commissariat twenty-six in Osdorf and let them know that it's a false alarm,' Fabel said. 'And get them to send someone out to switch the damned thing off.'

They searched the house. Every drawer, every wardrobe, every cupboard. Fabel pulled down the extendable ladder and checked out the attic. At first sight there was nothing: no arms cache, no briefcase full of currency and passports, none of the accoutrements of a professional killer. Like Georg Drescher's flat, this house felt unlived-in. Everything in the house was expensive and tasteful, yet there was no sense of permanent habitation about the place: as if it were an extended hotel room rather than a home.

'That's a Hans Jørgen Wegner Ox chair,' said Vestergaard.

'Danish?'

'Very Danish. Even more expensive.'

'It's not here.' Fabel spoke loudly to be heard over the din of the house alarm. 'Whatever it is she came back for, it's not here, not in this house. I don't get it at all.'

'A change of car, maybe?' suggested Vestergaard. The alarm shut off and they reholstered their guns.

'Could be, I suppose,' said Fabel. 'In which case she's moved on already. But she knows this address is compromised. I don't think she would risk coming back here for a car that would also be registered to this place.'

He heard the sound of vehicles pulling up outside. Three uniformed officers arrived with a man in overalls. Fabel told them to make sure nothing was disturbed more than it had already been by their search, and informed them that the forensics team was on its way.

'So you think she's still in Blankenese?' asked van Heiden.

'If she dumped the car and came here on foot, then she has a purpose.' Fabel went over to the uniformed Commissar who had arrived with the alarm engineer. 'You're from PK26 in Osdorf?'

'Yes, Herr Principal Chief Commissar.'

'Can you get on to the Commissariat and tell them we need as many bodies as possible down here right now? We're searching for a woman called Anke Wollner who lived in this house under the name Jana Eigen.'

Something akin to shock crossed the young Commissar's face. 'My God – you mean the person who killed those cops in the city centre? You think she's here?'

'Just get on to Osdorf and get people out here.'

Fabel turned back to Vestergaard and van Heiden. 'Why would she come back? I know I'm repeating myself but it doesn't make sense. We can assume that she has several alternative identities up her sleeve and we failed to contain her at the crime scene. She could, presumably, disappear into thin air. She must have worked out by now that something's happened to Georg Drescher.'

Fabel froze.

'They gave him up . . .'

'What?' asked van Heiden.

'Hold on.' Fabel used his cellphone to call the Presidium and asked to speak to Hans Gessler.

'He's left for the evening,' said the duty officer on the other end.

'Then patch me through to his cellphone.'

There was a pause. Fabel covered the mouthpiece and spoke to van Heiden and Vestergaard. 'They gave Drescher up. It was Gina Brønsted who hired the Valkyrie all these years. Drescher had enough on Brønsted to send her away for life. It would be his pension policy. When Brønsted was tidying up the loose ends of Westland, Claasens and Lensch, she had already planned to tidy up Frolov and Drescher too. She used the other Valkyrie, mad Margarethe Paulus, to do her dirty work. It was Brønsted who provided Margarethe with all of the cash and resources she needed. But she never did anything directly . . .' He held up his hand and turned his attention back to his cellphone.

'Hi, Hans? It's Fabel – where did you say Svend Langstrup lived?'

'What? Oh . . . Blankenese.'

'Do you have the address?'

'I think it's somewhere just behind Strandweg. Hold on . . .' After a few moments, Gessler came back with the address.

'She's here to kill Svend Langstrup,' said Fabel once he'd hung up. 'And then, if I'm right, she'll go after Gina Brønsted.'

7.

Langstrup brought the wine through to the lounge. Anke sat on the rug in front of the fire and watched the flames. The fire's glow accentuated the perfect sweep of her cheek and jawline, and added gold to her pale blonde hair.

'Warmer?'

'Mmm, I am now,' she murmured contentedly, despite the persistent nagging of her leg wound. Anke looked around the room. She took a full mouthful of wine. Her eyes fell on a silver-framed photograph on a side table. In it Langstrup and an attractive woman with strawberry-blonde hair stood together in a garden. They both faced the camera and Langstrup embraced her, his arms wrapped around her shoulders. They both wore smiles: his one of complete contentment. Joy. The woman's was different. As if she wasn't really there behind the smile. It was something that Anke recognised.

'Your wife?'

He nodded, but did not look at the photograph. 'Yes. That's Silke.'

'She's very pretty.'

'Yes.'

'Where is she tonight? I don't think she'd approve of you bringing strange women in from the beach and plying them with drink . . .'

'Silke had problems. Mental-health issues.' He stared into his wine glass. 'Depression. She committed suicide.'

'Oh God – I'm so sorry. I shouldn't have asked . . .'

'You weren't to know. It was a natural enough question,' Langstrup said and took a long sip of white wine. 'It was two years ago. The police said it was unclear whether it was accidental death or suicide. She didn't leave a note, you see.'

'Is that why you were down by the water?'

'I don't know. Yes, maybe.'

Anke looked at the photograph again; at the mask of a smile pulled over a void.

'I really am so sorry,' said Anke and she stood up. 'I know what it's like to lose someone like that.'

'Do you? I'm sorry to hear that.'

'My uncle.' She took another sip of wine and gazed at the fire. 'I know it doesn't sound much, but he was more than my uncle. More like a father. My parents . . . well, my parents weren't around and he brought me up. Taught me everything I know. All that I am I owe to him.'

'He died recently?'

'Yes.' She placed the wine glass down on the coffee table and turned to face him square on. Langstrup looked up at her quizzically. 'Is everything all right?'

The doorbell rang.

'Excuse me,' he said. He stood up and shrugged apologetically. 'I don't get many visitors, but tonight . . .'

The ringing of the doorbell became insistent. Then banging on the door. Langstrup frowned and made towards the hall.

As soon as Langstrup turned his back to her, Anke leapt forward. The black polycarbide knife arced round and caught him in the side of the neck. She locked his head with the other arm and used her weight to drag him down onto the floor, but he was strong and skilled. His elbow slammed into her ribs and they crashed into the coffee table. The knife was still in his neck but she had misjudged it and obviously had missed the carotid. She could hear the front door being kicked in. She let go of Langstrup and leapt to her feet, slightly off balance because of the wound in her calf.

The front door flew open and banged against the hall wall. She snapped the Beretta from the waistband of her skirt. Langstrup rolled over, clutching the hilt of the knife rammed into his neck, his small, hard eyes now wild and full of terror. The way she had wanted it.

The three police officers burst into the living room and aimed their weapons at her. Screaming at her to drop the gun. She recognised one of them as Jan Fabel, who had headed the operation in the Alsterpark. She knew the woman was Karin Vestergaard, the boss and former lover of Jens Jespersen, whom Anke had killed in his hotel room. Anke had a choice, she knew that: take them on or finish Langstrup. She looked at the two men and a woman at the door. Their faces were tight and anxious. She smiled at them. It's not so bad, she wanted to tell them. Don't be scared, killing really isn't so bad.

The adrenalin in her system slowed everything down. She felt, for a moment, outside time. She thought about Liane and Margarethe. She thought again about Uncle Georg. She thought about all the meetings she had had, all the last moments she had shared.

Anke Wollner made her decision. She fired four shots into Langstrup, all of them into his head, before the police opened fire.

8.

Outside, afterwards, Fabel, Vestergaard and van Heiden sat together in the back of a police bus with blacked-out windows. It was an oasis of quiet while outside a maelstrom of police, forensics and press swirled around them.

'Are you okay?' Fabel asked them both, but his question was aimed more at van Heiden who sat grim-faced, his elbows resting on his knees and his gaze fixed at some spot on the floor of the bus.

'Why do I get the feeling that we've just participated in an assisted suicide?' asked van Heiden.

'We did what we had to do,' said Vestergaard. 'We would have been next.'

'I guess that ties up the Valkyrie case,' said van Heiden to Fabel.

'Yes, I suppose it does,' said Fabel. 'Other than nailing the person who instigated and paid for all of this mayhem. Gina Brønsted.'

'But . . . ?' Vestergaard read the doubt in Fabel's face.

'Anke Wollner killed Halvorsen in Norway, probably Vujačić in Copenhagen, Westland, Lensch, Claasens and Sparwald here in Hamburg. I know why and for whom she killed.' Fabel frowned. 'But we still don't know who the original Angel of

St Pauli was. It doesn't make sense that it was Wollner. And, as I know only too well from the house call she made on me, there's a third Valkyrie out there. Liane Kayser.'

'Who is clearly leading a normal life and has nothing to do with all this,' said van Heiden.

'Maybe so . . . but she made it very clear to me that she is more than willing to kill to protect that life.' Fabel shrugged and stood up. 'Anyway, I have a hospital visit to make.'

'Anna Wolff?' asked van Heiden.

'Anna Wolff,' said Fabel. 'I need to talk to her about her future.'

Epilogue

Epilogue

i.

It stung. It stung like hell, but Fabel knew that he had to
let it go. But one day, he swore, he would get enough on her
to put her away for good. He glared at the television monitor
in the Murder Commission's main office. He glared at two
faces he knew.

'Isn't this an embarrassment for the NeuHansa Group?'
asked Sylvie Achtenhagen. 'And an indictment of you personally that you employed and trusted a man who turned out
to be a criminal? Someone who ordered and paid for the
murders of so many people?'

'The first thing I want to make clear is this,' said Gina
Brønsted, with a smile that suggested she was talking to children. 'The corporate crime division of the Polizei Hamburg
has placed me and all of my business dealings under the very
closest scrutiny and there is absolutely *no* evidence to suggest
that I knew anything about Svend Langstrup's criminal activities. He was obviously running his own covert empire within
the NeuHansa Group. It is true that he got away with this
for some time, but there was no way . . .'

Werner switched off the TV with the remote.

'Don't eat yourself up over that bitch, Jan,' he said. 'You've
got to let it go. She'll be caught out sooner or later. I believe
the guys at corporate crime are as determined to nail her as
you are.'

'And OLAF,' said Fabel grimly. 'And Økokrim in Norway. And the Danish National Police. Gina Brønsted is going to have to tread very carefully from now on.'

'What about this first-Monday-of-the-month deal? You know, the message in *Muliebritas*? That's Monday coming: are we going to stake it out?'

'No point,' said Fabel. 'Three Valkyries: one dead, one back in a mental institution, and the third will do anything other than attract attention to herself.'

'True . . .' Werner chuckled maliciously. 'Anyway, she comes round to yours if she wants a chat.'

Fabel shot him a look and Werner gathered up some papers from his desk and left the office. Once Werner was gone, Fabel picked up the phone and punched in a number.

'Hello, Frau Meissner? Jan Fabel here. I got your invitation to talk to the Sabine Charity about the Polizei Hamburg's initiative on violence against women. I'd be delighted to . . .'

ii.

The last meeting of the day had gone on late. They had arranged for caterers to bring food in and, eventually, they had been able to crack open a bottle of champagne to seal the deal. After all the negative publicity, Gina Brønsted had had to do some tough negotiating and make some firm assurances. But things were back on track.

Because the meeting had gone on so late, Brønsted had decided to stay over in her penthouse above the offices. Truth was, she loved it here, with the huge windows looking over the harbour and out towards where they were building the new opera house. She poured herself a glass and drank in the view and the champagne at the same time. She was going to own this city one day. And Copenhagen.

Something caught her eye, reflected in the window glass. She spun around.

'What are you doing here?' Brønsted's tone was more puzzled than angry. 'How did you get in?'

'Do you know who I am?' asked the blonde woman standing in the middle of Brønsted's living room.

'What the hell do you mean?' Real anger now. 'Of course I know who you are. Now will you tell me what the hell you are doing here? I have nothing more to say to you.'

'Do you know my name?' asked the woman.

'Of course I know your name. Have you lost . . .' Bronsted's voice trailed off. Her focus was now fixed on the gun that the woman had lifted out from the folds of her black coat.

'My name isn't what you think it is. My name – my *real* name – is Liane Kayser. I am a Valkyrie. You know all about the Valkyries, don't you, Gina?'

'I . . .' Brønsted's expression turned from realisation to fear. 'Listen, I can give you work . . .'

'You mean you can use me. The way you used Margarethe and Anke? Do you know, the funny thing is that I didn't know I cared. I thought I was incapable of feeling anything for anybody. But I do care. They were the closest thing I had to family. But I *am* going to do something for you, Gina. I know you like making the news. I'm going to make you news. Tomorrow you will be big news. I promise you.'

'I can make this right for you . . .' Brønsted's eyes darted around the room. The panic button. The phone. Both a universe away.

'You know Gina, you're right. You can make it right for me.' Liane Kayser pulled the trigger twice, the shots muffled by the suppressor attached to the Makarov PM automatic. Brønsted fell to the ground. She was breathing in short, rapid gasps. The blonde woman took a few steps closer.

'Do you know what the word Valkyrie actually means? It comes from the Old Norse *Valkyrja*. It means *chooser of the slain*.' She pulled the trigger twice more. Head shots. 'Goodbye, Gina.'

iii.

It had changed so much since she had last been here.

Halberstadt was somewhere Sylvie Achtenhagen had visited as a young girl. That had been back then, of course; before the Wall came down. The city hadn't made much of an impact on the young Sylvie: it had looked pretty much like every other GDR town or small city she had visited. Halberstadt had been bombed flat at the very end of the Second World War, four weeks before the German surrender had been signed. Many suspected that the bombing had been a final vindictive act of vengeance.

Whatever the motive, the British had, with full moral vigour and righteous zeal, all but wiped the pretty little city off the face of the earth and had completely destroyed the medieval heart of Halberstadt. Then, with equally full moral vigour and righteous zeal, the communist government of the GDR had rebuilt it as a workers' city. Ugly Plattenbau concrete housing blocks had crowded around the city's cathedral and all that was old or traditional had been replaced with the modern and functional. And then the Wall had come down and Halberstadt had been reclaimed by its people.

Halberstadt is a city without suburbs. It sits self-contained on a grassy plain before the Harz mountains. As she drove towards it, Sylvie had the impression of a fairy-tale picture-book town, its red roofs, half-timbered buildings and the spires of the cathedral and the Martinikirche sitting prettily and perfectly in its landscape setting. But it was as she navigated the town itself that she saw the real differences that had been made since she had last been there. The monolithic Plattenbau apartment blocks were mostly gone and the medieval Altstadt had been faithfully restored and the square in front of the cathedral had again been opened out, allowing the majesty of the building to breathe and be appreciated. It was as if this small city had been given its soul back.

The hotel was a converted eighteenth-century mansion in the heart of the city and Sylvie's room was high-ceilinged and wood-panelled, furnished with what looked like genuine antiques. Sylvie found it disconcerting to sit in baroque luxury in the heart of a city that she had only ever known as part of the communist past she had put so far behind her.

From her cellphone she called the number she had been given.

'Frau Achtenhagen?'

'Yes.'

'Meet me in the Cathedral Treasury in fifteen minutes. I'll find you.'

Helmut Kittel was a wreck of a man. He was tall, but his shoulders had become rounded and his chest hollowed. His skin tone was a jaundiced grey and his hair thin and dull. He had followed Sylvie out of the Cathedral Treasury and had sat next to her on the bench in the gardens by the cathedral.

'I got your message,' said Sylvie.

'I knew you would.' He smiled.

'Did you see the news? About Gina Brønsted?'

'I did.' His breathing was wet and rattling.

'You realise that it was the work of the third so-called Valkyrie – the one whose name you say you know. I admit that the information is now very valuable. You have proof of the identity of the third Valkyrie?'

Kittel broke into a spasm of coughing: deep, racking coughs that made his eyes water. After it had passed he leaned back against the bench, breathing hard and deep as if at some extreme, oxygen-deprived altitude.

'Cancer?' Sylvie asked without malice.

He shook his head. 'Emphysema. Too many cigarettes. The cold seems to make it worse.'

'Well, the information you've got is newsworthy. Very

newsworthy. And the more newsworthy, the more we'll pay for it.'

He smiled bitterly. 'And you make the news, don't you?'

'Do you have the file or not?' Sylvie failed to keep the impatience from her voice.

'There were twelve girls to begin with,' Kittel said. 'They narrowed it down to three. But then, in the final stages of training, they had to reject one of the final three. Liane Kayser. They realised they couldn't rely on her. She had sociopathic tendencies, they said. You couldn't tell to look at her, to talk to her, apparently; but they realised that she was incapable of serving anyone but herself. That she would do anything, kill anyone, just so that she would achieve what she wanted to achieve.' He turned to her and smiled. 'No, Frau Achtenhagen, I don't have the file. There is no file other than the photographs I sent you. I'm the only person who knows who Liane Kayser is.'

'I see,' she said, still smiling and letting her eyes range over his face as if she were trying to read it.

'I saw you interviewed once, on TV,' he continued breathily. 'You were talking about being a television journalist today. How it's not enough to be passive, waiting for events or for a story to land in your lap. I remember you said that you have to make the news yourself, almost. The Angel of St Pauli case really did make your name, didn't it? No one had the inside angle on it that you seemed to have; always one step ahead of the others. You really did make the news, didn't you . . . Liane? I know you're the Angel of St Pauli. And I know you did it to boost your TV career. I'm also pretty sure it was Anke who carried out the last series of killings. I'm guessing that Drescher told her to make it look like it was your work. That you were back again.'

'So where is the file?'

'I told you. There is no file.' Kittel laughed and his laughing caused him to cough violently again, clasping his handkerchief to his mouth. When the coughing subsided and he took the handkerchief away, she noticed it was speckled bright red. 'We both knew it would come to this, Liane. The fact that you're here. The fact that you knew where to come when you saw the announcement in *Muliebritas*.'

'Does it hurt terribly?' she asked, looking at the blood-flecked handkerchief.

'Sometimes.' He nodded and the promise and the fear of the pain burned in his eyes. 'They destroyed all the files. The only one who knows about your real identity is me.' He smiled. No arrogance, just a sad, almost childish smile. 'I knew you'd come. I knew you'd find me. I don't want to die fighting for breath. I want the pain and the fear to go away. I don't want to be afraid any more.'

Sylvie smiled and gently pushed back a strand of hair from his damp brow. She leaned close and whispered into his ear. 'I know, Helmut. I know . . . It was nice to hear you call me Liane. No one has called me that in years. Now, no one ever will. Thank you for that, Helmut.'

As she spoke to him soothingly and without menace, Kittel felt something push upwards into his chest. He felt suddenly breathless in a way that he had not before. But there was little pain. He stared into her eyes, first in surprise but without fear, then with something that looked like gratitude.

'It's better this way, Helmut,' she said, easing the long needle out from under his ribcage and allowing his heart to rupture. 'No more pain. No more sweaty, frightened nights racked with coughing. I've taken away your pain for ever.'

Sylvie Achtenhagen checked that there was no one around and stood up swiftly, walking off towards the park exit. Behind her a thin middle-aged man sat on the bench, staring, unblinking, past the leafless trees, across to the double braced spires of the Martinikirche.

Acknowledgements

Thanks to my wife, Wendy, for her support and advice; to my editor Paul Sidey and my agent Carole Blake; to Tess Callaway, Joanna Taylor and James Nightingale; to my copyeditor Nick Austin; also to my friend and translator, Bernd Rullkötter.

The Hamburg police remains one of the most open and transparent forces in Europe and I again owe special thanks to the leadership and officers of the Polizei Hamburg, particularly Erste Polizeihauptkommissarin Ulrike Sweden and Polizeipräsident Werner Jantosch for their help, support and enthusiasm for my work.

I want to express my gratitude to and affection for one of the greatest cities in the world: Hamburg.

The Rosary Girls

Richard Montanari

Only a killer hears their prayers . . .

In the most brutal killing crusade Philadelphia has seen in years, a series of young Catholic women are found dead, their bodies mutilated and their hands bolted together. Each clutches a rosary in her lifeless grasp.

Veteran cop Kevin Byrne and his rookie partner Jessica Balzano set out to hunt down the elusive killer, who leads them deeper and deeper into the abyss of a madman's depravity. Suspects appear before them like bad dreams – and vanish just as quickly. While the body count rises, Easter is fast approaching: the day of resurrection and of the last rosary to be counted . . .

'Be prepared to stay up all night' James Ellroy

'A specialist in serial killer tales . . . a wonderfully evocative writer' *Publishers Weekly*

arrow books

THE POWER OF READING

Visit the Random House website and get connected with
information on all our books and authors

EXTRACTS from our recently
published books and selected
backlist titles

**COMPETITIONS AND PRIZE
DRAWS** Win signed books,
audiobooks and more

AUTHOR EVENTS Find out which
of our authors are on tour and
where you can meet them

LATEST NEWS on bestsellers,
awards and new publications

MINISITES with exclusive
special features dedicated to our
authors and their titles

READING GROUPS Reading
guides, special features and all
the information you need for
your reading group

LISTEN to extracts from the
latest audiobook publications

WATCH video clips of
interviews and readings with
our authors

RANDOM HOUSE INFORMATION
including advice for writers,
job vacancies and all your
general queries answered

Come home to Random House

www.rbooks.co.uk